WORLD OF WRECKAGE

WORLD OF WRECKAGE

TORTH BOOK THREE

ABBY GOLDSMITH

Published in 2024 by Podium Publishing, ULC
www.podiumaudio.com

WORLD OF WRECKAGE

PART ONE

*"No one can cross the border into the realm of Torth.
Any attempt means death."*

—Alashani warning

VIGILANT FOR BETRAYAL

Weeks had passed without any sign of the Empire's monstrous enemies. Rain poured down. The dead city remained black, sticky, and silent.

The Giant is dead, many Torth assured each other.

> *There is no way he could have survived*
>> with his chest punctured (a deadly wound)
>>> *and his powers deactivated.*

Servants of All claimed that they had a reliable way to detect active Yeresunsa. It involved global electromagnetic activity, wind patterns, and some secret mojo that no one dared quiz the highest ranks about. However, the Servants also claimed that the Torth Homeworld threw off false positive signals. The entire planet strobed with Yeresunsa indicators, so they could not determine whether the Giant was alive or dead.

They were just guessing.

The Upward Governess did not trust guesswork.

What if the Betrayer and the Giant stumbled upon a secret cache of medical supplies or whatever had sustained Jonathan Stead when he'd hidden in the dead city?

The Betrayer is surely dead, her audience crooned to her.

> *You are safe on a sunny planet,*
>> *probably making yet another error in judgment.*

The Upward Governess could not deny that she had made a blunder. Yes, fine. The enemies had escaped her home planet thanks to her own lapse in good judgment about Yellow Thomas, who had become the Betrayer. At the very least, she probably should have installed spy cameras in his suite in order to guard against a potential betrayal.

She had trusted her mentee.

So, yes, every calamity that followed was technically her fault. The Megacosm was rife with replays of brave Torth military ranks dying in battle against the Giant.

Those death scenes were finally losing popularity in favor of fresher news stories, such as the upcoming invasion of Earth.

But still.

We are vigilant, her inner audience harmonized.

We have this handled.

Enjoy your frosted fruitcakes.

The Torth Majority figured they had indulged the Upward Governess a little bit too much. Very few Torth owned as much as she did: an indoor lake, a three-story aquarium, a menagerie, a biological museum, as well as hundreds of gardens and immersion holograph decks.

What most of them failed to take into account were tranquility meshes. The Upward Governess never impeded her own processing speed, so she soothed away her problematic *(illegal)* emotions through unconventional methods. She used environment and food as therapy.

She tapped her data tablet to release a stream of alien brine shrimp into her aquarium. As she watched her bony plated eels feed, her inner critics seemed a little less relevant.

If the Betrayer was dead, then how had he managed to visit the Upward Governess in the Megacosm for a few fleeting milliseconds? That had occurred days after his disappearance in the dead city.

There was no way she had misidentified his gargantuan mind, with its primitive oddnesses.

He had been imprisoned. She was sure of it. But he wasn't in the Isolatorium.

So much time had passed since then, one might reasonably assume that he had died. Why else had he quit trying to ascend? Even though the Majority rejected him, he would not have given up. Anyone sane would have kept at it.

But it was best to filter out normal proclivities when trying to assess the Betrayer. She had misjudged him before.

Another supergenius rolled into the Upward Governess's audience. *Even if the Betrayer lives, so what? He must have run out of medicine. He is surely dying by now.*

The Death Architect was a dying child, too, of course. She wore her curly hair in pigtails tied with ribbons. Smart Torth filtered out that detail, as well as her frail, underdeveloped body and young age. In the ecosystem of minds, the Death Architect was a ripe supergenius. She was more than eleven years old *(in human years)*, which, given her memory and processing speed, made her a whale in comparison to nearly everyone else—essentially small fish and plankton.

The Upward Governess thought of her young competitor as more of a shark. A megalodon of unknown size and strength. Like any bottom feeder, the Death Architect preferred the murky depths of esoteric scientific discussions—except when she was spying on her fellow supergeniuses.

I calculate less than a 0.0000001 percent chance that the Betrayer will ever pose a threat to Torth, the Death Architect thought, utterly devoid of emotion.

The Upward Governess disagreed. *I estimate a 77.45 percent likelihood that the Betrayer is still dangerous, even taking a margin of error into account.* Her estimate ought to alarm any self-respecting Torth. *If the Betrayer found a way to survive in the dead city, that implies that the Giant found a way to recover from his wounds. If both of those outlaws work together . . . ?* The dangers seemed painfully obvious to her. *Then a lot of innocent Torth will die.*

If only she could explore the dead city in person. If she were able-bodied, she would travel to the Torth Homeworld, and she would probably find clues that everyone else in the universe had missed.

Pathetic, her inner audience thought.

Perhaps they were right.

But what else did the Upward Governess have to live for? The Betrayer had stolen the last dregs of NAI-12 medicine. He might as well have triggered a blaster glove at her heart and exploded her chest.

She just wanted to live long enough to crush his future and destroy everything he had ever valued.

Hm. The Death Architect was capable of sending the Majority into a froth, but she never made waves. She was always agreeable. *I suppose the Betrayer might still live*, she conceded. *But it is unlikely, and in any case, he is beyond Our ken, at least for the time being. Let Us (the Torth Empire) use Our collective resources wisely.*

She directed her own massive audience to the upcoming conquest of Earth. A fleet of warships approached the backwater solar system of humankind. The ships were cloaked, and agents on Earth had made sure they would avoid detection by the primitive natives.

We should have colonized Earth a long time ago, the Death Architect thought. *The natives will likely wreck the biodiversity of their own homeworld if they are left unchecked for just a few more generations.*

Billions of Torth chorused in agreement. Many disparaged the flimsy, age-old arguments about keeping Earth in pristine condition.

Various high ranks chimed in, trying to claim scientific fiefdoms for Earth's colonization. A top Indigo-Blue biologist wanted to study monotremes. A top geologist wanted to hike through the Tsingy needle rocks of Madagascar.

Humans ought to be shipped off to other worlds and bred as slave stock, the Death Architect proposed.

That was met with less enthusiasm. A minority of Torth did want to own and collar their inferior genetic cousins. But most Torth still felt uneasy about putting human slaves in situations where they might befriend other sapients—or where sexually deviant Torth might be tempted to exploit their inferior cousins.

There were risks.

Nobody wanted to deal with Torth hybrid babies.

The Upward Governess hardly cared about the debate on human slaves. She wove in and out of the minds of Red Ranks on the Torth Homeworld, scanning the dark vista of the dead city. Many ambitious military ranks elected to get enhanced night vision surgery. They patrolled the perimeter wall. They peered into the ever-present black downpour.

Nothing moved out there.

You (Upward Governess) are very paranoid, the Death Architect thought with lazy certitude. *Even if the Betrayer does show up, even if he becomes a nuisance once more, his love for primitive slave species can easily be exploited. I have done experiments.*

She replayed some of her more gruesome experiments. Slaves would mutilate themselves, or others, for the sake of a beloved parent or child.

Bring Me his defenseless foster family, the Death Architect requested from her orbiters. *I will make a torture chamber perfectly designed to destroy the Betrayer.*

Military ranks thrummed with approval. They liked everything the Death Architect imagined.

The Upward Governess wiggled her fingers at a nearby slave, demanding snacks. She needed something to soothe away her mysterious feelings of disquiet and unease. She focused extra hard on the motions of the bony plated eels and glowfish in her aquarium.

Perhaps the Death Architect was right?

Perhaps the Betrayer was already defeated or easily defeated?

The Upward Governess was uncertain that anyone could predict the actions of the boy formerly known as Thomas. She used to be certain that he wanted a long life. She had trusted him to team up with her and do whatever it took to thrive.

How had he misled her?

Whenever she drifted off to sleep, she reexamined her unwise faith in her former mentee. Every time she awoke in her massive bed, a momentary panic seized her until she became fully conscious and aware that the Betrayer was not currently stealing from her.

Her hair was falling out, she wheezed on every breath, and she had a long list of ailments related to obesity and lifelong muscular atrophy.

That galled her.

It should gall everyone. She was the eldest living supergenius. She was so old, in fact, that she had actually menstruated for the first time, a few days ago, like a common slave or an animal. She had delayed the onset of puberty with hormone therapy, but that could not last. Now puberty was just another ailment she had to endure.

If she could live just a few more weeks, she would become the eldest supergenius in Torth history.

Yet no one valued that incredible achievement! No one cared about the wealth of knowledge she had amassed over fourteen—nearly fifteen—years. The plasmic polymers she had invented, and her parking structure designs, were going to be her legacy.

It wasn't enough. Not nearly enough.

The Upward Governess was certain of one thing: she had to stop the Betrayer before he could do anything that worsened her reputation.

She was not going to let him catch her asleep. Not ever again.

CHAPTER 2

INFINITE STRENGTH

Many hundreds of followers straggled behind Ariock Dovanack—a line of bobbing lanterns vanishing into the darkness of the river cavern. The hollow boom of rushing water drowned out the creaking of wagons and the complaints of people who were exhausted from walking nonstop.

"*Aonswa.*" Jinishta had an edge to her tone, despite the messiah title she used for him. "Your army is having trouble keeping this pace." She peered up at him, her albino face pallid in the darkness.

"They're not my army," Ariock pointed out.

He had not asked people to abandon their families and march with him toward danger. Just the opposite. Ariock had begged everyone to turn around and go home. Why should he worry about protecting fools? He had enough to worry about, with keeping Thomas alive.

The boy lay in his arms, fighting for every shallow breath. Ariock could sense Thomas's heartbeat with his powers, and it was a sluggish arrhythmia. Vy had said that Thomas needed life support machinery. He ought to be in a hospital.

Instead, he was stuck with a steam power level of technology, along with the rest of them.

The Alashani healers refused to help. Orla, their most skilled healer, refused to get close enough to Thomas to heal him.

So Ariock marched toward other worlds.

The River of Tears connected all cities and settlements of the Alashani underworld. If the hidden civilization was a leaf, then the mighty river was its central artery. As Ariock passed aqueducts that fed mushroom farms, fisheries, and riverside villages, the messianic army swelled in size.

A holy prophet had proclaimed Ariock to be "the One" before her dramatic death. Now zealots believed that his heroic future was inevitable, and Ariock was losing the energy to argue with them. He had marched nonstop for more than two days. Healing Thomas left him exhausted, and the intervals were becoming more frequent.

"Ariock? Listen to me." Jinishta sounded kinder than usual.

Ariock did not slow. Every second mattered for Thomas's life.

The riverside was lined with crumbling blocks, the most ancient of which were etched with script writing and mold. The last exit had to show up soon. Ariock was looking for the skyward path, which would take him to the rainy surface—to the Stratower.

"No one has infinite strength," Jinishta said.

That was easy for her to say. No one's life depended on her strength.

Ariock sent another wave of healing energy through Thomas's frail body. It affected the boy like a drop of water to someone dying from pneumonia. Passageways temporarily opened up, but the underlying failures remained.

Jinishta jogged to keep pace with him. "Ariock, I will be proud to help you fight Torth. I will be glad to fight by your side. But in your current condition?" Concern weighted her words. "You are guaranteed to lose."

Ariock felt as if he was already fighting a savage battle. And losing.

For the first time in days, he slowed a little bit, his feet screaming for a rest.

Just the sight of Thomas, looking so deathly ill, stoked his helpless rage. It wasn't fair. Hadn't Thomas gone against his own best interests in order to save Ariock? Repeatedly. Thomas had risked his life to keep his friends alive and safe.

And Ariock had repaid his telepathic friend by letting him rot, uncared for, ignoring his frail condition.

"*Aonswa!*" The shout came from Gav, the albino who served as Ariock's guide. "The exit is here." Gav pointed to a decrepit causeway bridge that spanned the river, leading to an unlit tunnel.

Judging by the fallen rocks and general look of dilapidation, this exit had not been used for many centuries.

Everyone was afraid of Torth realms. Nevertheless, Ariock approached the bridge with a surge of hope. He was done with caves. He would obtain help for Thomas, and medicine, even if he had to battle a space armada on the way.

Only a few people looked the least bit eager to follow him beyond this point. Yuey wore a huge grin on her rubbery nussian face. Next to her, Weptolyso, the former hall guard, looked formidable and ready to kill Torth. He had already killed quite a few, and he had also fought kamikaze members of his own tanklike species, killing them in self-defense. He had said that he wanted to try to persuade nussians to turn against their Torth masters.

Kessa looked more cautious than enthused.

Vy sat next to her in the wagon bed, and she looked just as cautious.

Everyone else looked terrified. Cherise and Flen. Orla. Shevrael. Haz. Nulshta. So many others.

Ariock hoped they would listen to their own misgivings and turn around. He didn't think he could protect a thousand followers while fending off bombs and climbing the Stratower and keeping Thomas alive. He might be strong enough, but his multitasking had limits.

Gav offered an apologetic smile. "This is as far as I will go. Sorry." He dipped his knees, the common gesture of respect.

"Thank you, Gav," Ariock said with sincerity.

"Good luck and fare well." The guide was already hurrying away in the opposite direction of the army. At least that albino was wise enough to head home instead of having faith in prophecy.

The crumbling bridge might fall into the river if Ariock marched across without firming it up first. He wanted to sit and rest, but instead, he probed outward with his powers, binding stones together. He interlocked rocks in order to strengthen submerged pillars.

A worry, deep inside his mind, tried to negate his urgency. Didn't he need a plan?

Kessa had said as much, several times. So had Thomas.

But they offered no suggestions. All Kessa did was click her beak and shoot worried looks at Thomas. Perhaps Thomas could lay out a plan, but he hardly woke up anymore. All he did was take tiny sips of water, give dire warnings, and sleep.

We'll be fine, Ariock assured himself.

All he had to do was get to the spaceport atop the Stratower. That was the only spaceport he knew was functional, after the Torth had sabotaged their own more accessible spaceport. He would find the launchpads. Steal a streamship. Maybe steal some medical supplies along the way. What could go wrong?

"Ariock. Can we rest for a minute?"

If that voice had come from anyone other than Vy, he would have ignored it. But Vy understood exactly what he was trying to do, and why.

She slid off the wagon bed.

Wagons would be useless once they entered Stratower City, Ariock realized. Wheels of bent iron could not compete with the speed and instant maneuverability of frictionless hoverbikes and hovercarts. He needed to figure out a comfortable way to carry both Vy and Thomas.

"I don't see how we can get home," Vy said. Her gaze slid to Thomas, then back up to Ariock. "Without a pilot."

"He's still alive," Ariock pointed out.

Thomas was the only person among them who could read Torth glyphs and operate Torth machinery. Slaves were forbidden from learning how to use advanced technology. Ariock and his friends had watched the boy operate a Torth spacecraft, and it was all holographs and incomprehensible menus floating in the air. Thomas must contain knowledge from a million Torth pilots.

"And if he has trouble," Ariock went on, "you can figure it out."

Vy looked extremely doubtful.

Well, hadn't she gone to school? She had even graduated from a university. She must know things about computers.

"With help from Cherise," Ariock amended. "And Kessa." She was smart. "And maybe that ummin who was interested in learning about Torth technology?" He ought to remember the gawky adolescent, but more than one hundred and fifty refugees had come with him from Duin. "What was his name?"

"Varktezo?" Vy still looked skeptical.

"Right," Ariock said. "Varktezo." The adolescent ummin had mimicked Thomas's every motion.

"I'm not even sure he's here," Vy said. "Most of the refugee ummins stayed back in Hufti, with Pung."

An adolescent ummin hurried toward them, shoving past adventurers. Ariock's deep voice tended to carry. Varktezo must have heard his name mentioned. "Does the Teacher need me?"

When Varktezo saw the sickly figure of Thomas, he lost some of his enthusiasm. "Teacher?" He looked toward Vy. "Will he be okay?"

"Varktezo," Ariock said. "Can you fly a spaceship?"

The adolescent blinked. As he processed the question, he looked taken aback, then terrified, then self-assured, all in quick succession. Those fast-shifting facial expressions evoked Thomas, who sometimes ran through a range of reactions in the space of a second. There was a lot going on behind Varktezo's gray eyes.

In the end, the adolescent ummin stood straighter, his beak screwed tight in a determined way. "I'll figure it out."

Ariock wanted to clap Varktezo on the back for being so willing to brave danger, despite his obvious fears. But ummins were too small for back-clapping, so Ariock settled for a grateful nod. "Thanks."

Vy bit at her lower lip. "I'm not sure anything can revive Thomas." The anguish in her voice revealed her guilt. "I'm just not sure, Ariock. He's really sick."

Ariock shared the same guilt, the same despair. From what little he understood about Thomas's NAI-12 medicine, it stabilized the neuromuscular disease, but it did not reverse any damage done. Just as Ariock could not undo scars or amputations by using his Yeresunsa powers, injections of NAI-12 could not undo muscular deterioration that had already happened.

Every second Thomas lived without his medicine, chain reactions of failures happened at a cellular level inside his body.

Even if Ariock managed to sneak inside the spaceport atop the Stratower... even if Vy and Varktezo proved to be capable pilots, and even if they landed safely on Earth . . . by the time they got there, a refresher supply of NAI-12 might not be enough to save Thomas.

Their quest might be futile.

"I have to try." That was all Ariock could say. "Thomas deserves a chance. I owe him this."

Beyond Vy, hundreds of albino people unpacked wagons, illuminated by lanterns. Some relaxed or chatted. The messianic army was making camp for the first time in nearly three wake cycles. They assumed Ariock was stopping to rest.

He turned to the bridge, eager to leave the worshippers behind.

"Wait." Jinishta sounded frustrated and pleading. "Ariock, it is madness to rush up there when you are exhausted."

Ariock used to respect her opinions.

Jinishta had taught him better methods for controlling his powers. She was his cousin, and he had assumed she was kind. But now? She hindered him. She would not even force Orla, the teenage healer, to help him.

Jinishta loved her people. And her people hated Thomas as nothing but an evil, worthless burden.

"Don't come with me," Ariock told her. "Stay underground."

A formidable look entered Jinishta's lavender eyes. Ariock recognized that stubbornness. She wasn't planning to yield in this sparring match.

But he just didn't have time to fight.

So he straightened to his full height, his hair brushing the stalactites, and he amplified his voice by manipulating the airflow acoustics. The last thing he wanted to do was pretend to be their messiah. But he was running out of time, and choices.

"Stay underground." Ariock's words filled the cavern, overpowering the rush of the river. "I refuse to lead this army to death. All of you must stay behind." He felt like a fraud, but he forced himself to sound like a demigod. "I . . . I command it."

CHAPTER 3

SUICIDE PELLETS

"You're the messiah now?" Jinishta gave him a critical look. "When it pleases you?"

Ariock avoided her withering glare. It did feel wrong to take advantage of her people's beliefs. But what else could he do?

Thomas's life spark guttered like a candle in a gale. That one tiny spark was all Thomas had left. Ariock was doing the mental equivalent of cupping his hands around an ember, willing it to stay alight.

"Turn the army around," he said in a more normal tone of voice. "Or you'll be marching to your deaths. I've warned you multiple times. I can't protect every one of you. It's too much to ask."

"Don't you think I know what's up there?" Jinishta demanded. "I've slain Torth before." She saw that Ariock was losing interest in her arguments, and she quoted, "'An army follows at his heels.'"

Ariock hated that prophecy. *He will lead you into light and restore you to your former glory. Follow him or perish.* Yeah, right.

"None of you should follow me." His deep voice boomed off the walls. "No army. I command it."

Albinos glanced at each other, torn. At least a few looked ready to pack their belongings and head home.

"You are forgetting something." Jinishta whipped out a spear and banged it against the rocky ground. "No one goes into the Torth realm unless they have sworn the Warrior's Pact. That includes you."

Ariock began to argue. He wasn't going to waste time on a pointless ritual.

"Your cargo people will have no choice but to protect the Alashani," Jinishta cut in. "Up there, they are at our mercy. They must obey us." She glared at Weptolyso and Yuey, then Kessa, making sure they understood that they were the equivalent of backpacks and gear.

Lastly, she aimed her disgusted glare toward Thomas. Quite a few Alashani wrongly held Thomas responsible for the death of their holy prophet. Jinishta was probably one of those. At least no one had tried to outright assassinate the boy.

"But you are not cargo." Jinishta shifted her glare to Ariock.

"I don't care about your—" Ariock began to say, but she interrupted again.

"You need weapons." She held up one black-gloved hand in a signal.

Several Yeresunsa warriors used their powers to peel back a wagon cover, revealing giant-size black spears. A leatherwork quiver and folded black woolens completed the gift.

Ariock forgot his protests for a moment. The power to shoot lightning bolts gave him a certain satisfaction. However, when he'd gotten hit with the inhibitor serum—when he'd had to combat Servants of All up close—he had needed something solid. He'd ended up swinging Torth bodies at other Torth.

Blaster gloves were too small for him to use. When the Torth had forced him to fight mad beasts in the prison arena, he had ripped apart jaws or eyes with his bare hands, and that savagery had made him feel like a beast himself. All that time, he had yearned for a weapon. A spear, or anything.

These extra-large spears might come in handy.

"Thank you," he said. "Tell Byureal I'm grateful." The Yeresunsa ironworker must have crafted them especially for the messiah. They would be well weighted.

A few spears would not fend off armies and nuclear bombs, but Ariock was eager to test them, to see if he could hurl them bullet-fast.

"You have earned your spears." Jinishta presented Ariock with a ridiculously small black pouch, like something a lady would use to store jewelry. "You must carry this, as well."

Ariock cautiously took the pouch.

"Be careful with it," Jinishta said, watching his big fingers. "I put twenty suicide pellets in there for you. One is enough to kill a warrior like me." She patted the loose scarf around her neck, which she would use to veil her face whenever she was aboveground. "We all store them inside our scarves. I think you should put at least five inside yours." She indicated the gift of woolens.

Suicide pellets.

"I will distribute pellets to your cargo people, as well." Jinishta indicated the nussians, ummins, and humans. "They must sacrifice themselves if captured by Torth. And if they refuse?" Her distrustful glare slid toward Thomas. "Then we must do the honors. We will kill them before killing ourselves."

Ariock threw the pouch back at Jinishta.

She caught it with well-trained reflexes, but Ariock must have committed a blasphemy. Warriors gasped.

He didn't care. Let them see who he was, not the idealized messiah they wanted him to be.

"I've contemplated suicide before," Ariock admitted. He had, in fact, tried to kill himself, but he wasn't going to share something so personal in public. "I never want to think that way again." Too many people, such as Thomas, were relying on him to survive and to stay strong.

"You must swear to die if captured." Power boosted Jinishta's voice, making her louder than the river and impossible to ignore. "That is the Pact. It is the law."

She offered him the suicide pouch again.

"No." Ariock used his powers to float Thomas to an alcove, around a corner of the dilapidated tunnel. His friend should be out of harm's way, at least for a few minutes. "I'm not an Alashani. I don't obey your laws."

Jinishta's eyes grew fierce with outrage.

"Your people have pressured me into enough unreasonable promises." Ariock used power to boost his own voice. Vy looked like she wanted to intervene, but he was never going to be a prisoner again. "Before I ever met you," he told Jinishta, "I promised to protect my friends with my life, no matter what. I am their shield. I don't get an easy death." He glared down at her. "Thomas is my friend, and I will not allow him to die while I still live."

Jinishta's voice grew ugly with rage. "Then you do not have permission to leave this realm!"

Ariock adjusted his stance, resigned to a fight. "I'm going. And you do not have permission to follow me."

The air between them crackled with ionization.

Jinishta twirled a spear in the air above her head. All chatting ceased as warriors raised their veils and seized spears.

Ariock spread his awareness into a bubble shield. Everyone knew that he would win a sparring match against Jinishta, but he had never fought an entire Yeresunsa army.

Did it really have to be this way?

"Wait." Vy limped between them. "Jinishta. Ariock. Will you listen for a minute?"

Jinishta solidified her stance. "I can make many allowances for the messiah," she said. "But there is a limit." She gripped a spear in each hand. "The Alashani must matter to him. The messiah is supposed to save us. Not doom us."

"That's fair. Makes sense." Vy held her arms apart, as if separating the combatants. Her ivory-carved leg threw off her balance. She wouldn't be able to hold that pose for long.

The tension in her limbs, more than anything else, got Ariock's attention.

"How about if we each make a concession?" Vy said, peering from Ariock to Jinishta. "Jinishta, you'll leave the army behind." She hurriedly went on, seeing Jinishta's defiance. "But you'll come with us, okay? That way, you can kill Ariock or Thomas if they get captured." She turned to Ariock. "Is that all right?"

While Jinishta mulled it over, Ariock nodded. It was a good concession. Alone, Jinishta would have a lot of trouble killing him, or anyone under his protection.

Vy saw them listening and lowered her arms. Ariock gave her a look of gratitude.

"The prophecy states that an army will follow at his heels," Jinishta said stubbornly.

"Then he will return," Kessa said. "He will come back to lead the army."

Vy seemed to recognize a good idea when she heard it. "Right," she told Jinishta. "Ariock has to fulfill the prophecies, so he'll come back."

Ariock couldn't imagine ever returning to the cave cities, but he offered a somber nod.

Jinishta scrutinized him for a long time. Judging by her face, she was waging an internal battle, and Ariock dared not interrupt that process. He waited patiently.

"The prophet Migyatel proclaimed your cousin to be the messiah," Kessa reminded Jinishta. "If you trusted her, then you have to trust Ariock."

Jinishta looked ill at ease. No doubt she had expected the messiah to obey Alashani laws and be a righteous individual. She seemed flummoxed that Ariock kept defying her.

Now, judging by her face, she felt backed into a corner. Everyone watched her. She dared not say anything that cast doubts on Ariock's holiness in front of her peers and supporters. Otherwise they would find a new premier Yeresunsa, one who was a true believer.

"All right." Jinishta tucked her spears away.

Ariock nearly collapsed with relief. He hadn't known how massive a burden the messianic army had seemed. Without a thousand worshippers tagging along, he and his friends might actually have a chance to get off this planet and survive.

Jinishta seemed to make an internal decision. "I will bring one warrior for every person you bring."

Ariock hoped she was joking.

"Your *rekveh* is one." Jinishta pointed out others. "Vy. Weptolyso. Yuey. Kessa. And Cherise, I assume?"

"Don't forget me!" Varktezo piped up.

Ariock clenched his fists. He faced Jinishta like an immovable wall, blocking her path. "They're not cargo. And I can't be bothered with looking after your extra warriors. The Torth city is a lot more dangerous than anywhere your warriors have ever been. There's no way—"

"I understand that." Jinishta gave him her fiercest glare. "You need to understand that we avoid the Torth realms because one mental scan will entail death and enslavement for all the Alashani. If any one of us makes a mistake up there . . . ?" She held Ariock's gaze, making sure that he understood her entire world was at stake. "If you or any of your cargo friends get caught by Torth, then it will be up to me and my warriors to protect the Alashani people. You clearly do not have a care for us."

She wasn't wrong, exactly.

Ariock let go of his arguments. The compromise felt like poison to him, but he could not fault Jinishta for caring about her civilization.

"Ariock shouldn't have to babysit your people," Vy said heatedly. "He doesn't need a bunch of extra distractions."

Jinishta shot her a glare. "We will be responsible for ourselves. Unlike you, cargo girl. Aboveground, you and Ariock both will be grateful to have warriors who are willing to help you along."

She might be right, but Ariock had no intention of putting up with abusive sarcasm while he was busy sneaking through a Torth city.

"Aboveground," Ariock said firmly, "all of you will follow my commands." He folded his huge arms to show that he meant it.

Jinishta assessed him, taken aback. She was the premier Yeresunsa. Every warrior, including Ariock, was supposed to obey her commands.

"This is not negotiable," Ariock warned her. "Down here, this is your world. But up there"—he pointed—"that's where I come from. I know Torth cities and storm-filled skies better than you do."

A soft breeze rippled through the river cavern. Ariock hadn't realized how much air he was inhabiting until it moved with his angry mood. He forced himself to let it go.

"Fine." Jinishta made the concession in a biting tone. "Aboveground is your realm. But down here? I am the leader."

Her grab to reclaim authority seemed petty, but Ariock figured there was no harm in being a gracious winner. He gave a nod.

"You promise that I lead the army as long as we are below the filthy surface lands?" Jinishta said.

"Yes," Ariock said impatiently.

Jinishta lifted her delicate chin. "Good. Give me one pendulum swing before we leave."

That was equivalent to an hour. Ariock opened his mouth to refuse.

"You agreed to obey me. Thank you for waiting." Jinishta whirled away, shouting commands to her warriors as if Ariock had ceased to exist. "Aral! Shassatel! Tavish! You will come with me, so prepare yourselves for danger. Compose farewells to your families and friends."

Ariock realized that he had, stupidly, given Jinishta authority over him for an undefined, open-ended period of time.

"You should be grateful," Thomas said weakly. "She could have demanded a week."

That was true.

And, Ariock supposed, an hour was fair enough. His friends could use the time to finalize their armor and gear. He could . . . well, he supposed a short rest, to freshen up and think a bit, wouldn't hurt.

He needed to be in top shape as a protector.

If he failed, it wasn't just Thomas's life at stake. It was the Alashani civilization. It was everyone he cared about.

"Will you set a timer?" he asked Vy. She wore the wristwatch. Ariock was glad when she tapped it, rather than judging him for caving in.

Vy understood. She knew everything that was at stake, and she trusted him to make the right choices.

CHAPTER 4

STARLIGHT OR CANDLELIGHT

Albinos marched past Cherise, their nymphlike faces grim and uncertain. The air held the electric charge of unsettled Yeresunsa. The messianic army had marched nonstop, prepared for just about any challenge—except for the challenge of turning around and going home.

But Flen was in a happy mood.

He hummed as he adjusted Cherise's daypack straps. "You'll want to say goodbye to Vy, won't you, my love?" he asked.

"Um, yes."

Cherise wished she could be totally authentic with her boyfriend. Instead, she stalled, relacing her boots, pretending to be indecisive about how to arrange her belongings.

Flen was still a stranger to her in some ways. They were still getting to know each other. The last thing she wanted to do was wreck his good mood.

But she wanted to speak to her own personal savior before he exited the underground.

She still carried the origami lion that Thomas had folded for her when they'd first met. She didn't want to let him slip away forever with this painful rift between them. She wanted to let him know that she forgave him.

She even loved him, still. Despite everything.

Cherise had tried to trick herself into believing otherwise. She had tried to make a clean break, to give her heart to someone else. And Flen was nice. He tried so hard to be likable—it was endearing. He frequently gave Cherise gifts.

Every activity she used to do with Thomas had been his idea, on his terms. Like chess. Flen, in contrast, was uncomplicated.

Flen brushed Cherise's black hair with his fingers. He liked to touch her copper skin, and to bury his face in her hair, so otherworldly. "We'll be all right," he whispered. "I promise."

He kissed her ear.

Cherise was growing used to being kissed. She no longer flinched.

She turned to snuggle against her boyfriend, reveling in intimacy. She loved Flen's woolly scent. He would look downright alien on Earth, but she had gotten used to his round head and long neck. His arms fit around her perfectly.

A young woman argued off to one side. "You have no right to stop me from following the messiah!"

"You have never been aboveground, Orla." That firm voice belonged to Jinishta. "The messiah will only allow eight warriors for this journey, and I am sorry, but you have not even sworn the Pact. You refuse to help him heal his *rekveh*. You must stay behind."

Orla made a savagely bitter sound. "But you're going to take *Flen*?"

Flen broke off his kisses. He stood and gently tugged at Cherise, trying to get her to follow him away from the argument.

"Flen has earned his spears," Jinishta replied in a pedantic tone. "He has slain cannibals. But mostly," she admitted, "I chose Flen because I would not part him from Cherise."

"That's not fair!" Orla sparkled with static electricity, proving that she had not truly mastered control of her powers. "I'm the most powerful warrior in Hufti besides you!" She glared at Jinishta. "The messiah needs me!"

Her red-faced tirade reminded Cherise of girls in middle school. Orla was the equivalent of a neurosurgeon among the Yeresunsa, but she was actually younger than Cherise's seventeen years.

"Just give me a chance to slay Torth!" Orla demanded. "I will earn my spears!"

Vy limped into the gathering crowd. "Orla, if you're really determined to help the messiah, I have an idea."

Orla looked wary.

"Heal Thomas," Vy suggested. "Or show Ariock a better way to do it."

Orla recoiled in horror, as if Vy had told her to eat sludge.

Jinishta gave Vy a considering look. After a moment, she turned to Orla. "Yes," she said. "If you're brave enough to heal the *rekveh*, then I will bring you aboveground as one of the lucky eight."

Orla looked visibly sickened.

"I went within the *rekveh*'s range," Jinishta pointed out. "And I am still here."

Orla looked furious, but she had no further arguments. Perhaps she realized how desperate and drained Ariock was. Warriors whispered that his strength must be infinite. Anyone else would have collapsed from a warning headache.

"Orla can have my place among the lucky eight." Flen clasped Cherise's hand. "We're going to stay behind."

Jinishta stared hard enough to make Cherise shrink back.

"What?" Vy looked wounded. "Cherise? Are you . . . are you thinking about staying behind?"

A wrenching sensation tore through Cherise. During their months in the Alashani cave city, Vy had begun to treat Cherise more like an actual sister rather than the mute orphan who lived in her mother's house.

How could she say goodbye?

Did she really want to spend the rest of her life as a cave woman in the land of albinos? If she stayed with Flen, she would become the only human on this dark world. She would lose Vy. And Ariock, and Kessa, and Weptolyso. She would be forced to say a silent goodbye to Thomas as well.

"Wait." A frantic drum beat inside Cherise's heart. "I need more time to decide."

Flen gave her a hurt, questioning look. He had expected Cherise to follow him anywhere.

"You're out of time." Jinishta's tone was heavy, like iron. "Are you saying you want to remain here, Cherise, as an Alashani? You don't want to return to paradise?"

Earth had never been a paradise for Cherise.

But her foster sister looked beseeching.

Cherise supposed that Vy could afford to confront deadly risks, secure with her overpowered and overprotective boyfriend. Ariock might carry Vy and Thomas both.

But not the warriors. Ariock was likely to leave Flen behind or abandon him in a dangerous situation.

Anyhow, it was unfair to expect Flen to sacrifice everything just for Cherise. He wanted to make Cherise part of his world, not the other way around. There were plenty of good reasons for that. If Flen left this planet, he would become nothing but a weird alien.

Like her.

"I need your decision," Jinishta said. "Are you staying behind or coming with us?"

Cherise searched Flen's gaze for a hint that he might care about what she was contemplating giving up for him. Sunlight. Starry night skies. Meadows and lakes. Trees. Butterflies. The ocean. Flocks of birds. All the things that were missing from his world of caves. It was so much.

"I know this is hard for you, love," Flen said. "But it's death up there." His gaze begged her to understand. "Stay with me. You'll have chambermaids. We'll go on walks together, every pendulum orbit."

That did sound nice.

When Cherise had rushed to join the messianic army and her foster siblings, she had left behind unfinished pieces of artwork. She wanted to complete her latest masterpiece of songbirds amid elm branches.

Besides that, Cherise loved snuggling with Flen in his palatial bedchamber. She wanted to check out street performances or explore craft bazaars with Flen's sister. There were so many artisans underground! Cherise could reinvent herself as one of them.

Surely that lifestyle was worth never seeing sunlight again?

Flen let go of Cherise's hand. "Why are you so hesitant?" He threw a dark look up the tunnel, and lanterns flickered along his path of sight. "You still care about that *rekveh*. Don't you?"

Flen's bitter tone threw Cherise out of her own thoughts.

"No," she said. "I'm with you. Not him."

"Then why are you spending such a long time deciding?" Flen asked.

Cherise didn't understand why her boyfriend needed so much reassurance so often. She curled her hand around his thin arm, trying to show how much she cared.

"Is it Ariock you're in love with?" Flen demanded.

Ariock? Cherise stared at Flen. How could he even consider that as a possibility? Ariock was in love with Vy, and Vy had to be partially insane to go for someone whose propensity for violence matched his gigantic strength. Ariock was more than a little scary. He might kill a lover by accident if he just woke up on the wrong side of the bed.

"Every woman is in love with the messiah," Flen muttered darkly.

"That's not true," Cherise said.

Flen looked unconvinced, every line of his lean body standing out with tension.

Vy backed away, looking embarrassed to be caught up in a relationship argument.

"This isn't about love," Cherise tried to explain. But she felt stung. Did Flen honestly see her as some kind of superficial fool who just wanted bigger and stronger men?

If that was what Flen believed, then maybe he was projecting.

Was he only dating Cherise because she happened to be an exotic angel from paradise? Were all his kisses and gifts insincere? If so, then he had fooled her for weeks.

And what if he grew bored with his alien girlfriend?

Then Cherise would be an outcast among the cave dwellers, too foreign for most of them.

Ma had abandoned her. Thomas had abandoned her. Cherise kept wondering what Flen saw in her.

If he abandoned her, too, it would break her.

"I'm going with my friends," Cherise decided. "I'm sorry, Flen. I just can't stay underground."

Vy threw her arms around Cherise in a hug. Cherise hugged her foster sister. She might die fighting Torth, but at least she could count on Vy and Kessa. Her friends would never abandon her to death.

And even if Thomas was a Torth hybrid . . . well, somehow, Cherise trusted him. He would not underestimate dangers. He would not misjudge people.

He was a good companion to have on a journey.

Jinishta twirled her spear, looking bored. "Okay." She shifted her gaze to Flen. "Are you staying underground?"

Flen glared at Cherise as if she had deliberately humiliated him.

As if she had abandoned him. Betrayed him.

Cherise swallowed her own sudden guilt. Maybe she was a bad girlfriend.

"I only want willing warriors," Jinishta said in a warning tone. "If you're not willing, Flen, then stay behind."

Haz swaggered to the front of the knot of warriors surrounding them. "I'll take Flen's place," he offered.

"I want his place!" Orla complained.

"Choose me," Shevrael offered. "Someone else can babysit the warriors who remain behind. It doesn't have to be me."

More warriors volunteered, babbling over each other. Haz raised his voice, trying to boast about how many cannibals he'd slain. His story sounded concocted. He was similar in age to Flen, and he had tried to woo Cherise with that same braggart confidence.

Flen looked flabbergasted by the competition. He glanced around, and he seemed to firm up his inner resolve.

"I'll accompany Cherise," he said.

The other warriors fell into a resentful silence. Haz glared at Flen with friendly exasperation.

"Are you sure?" Cherise searched Flen's gaze. He had spent half the march complaining about how the messianic army were a bunch of fools, marching to almost certain death.

"You must take this mission seriously." Jinishta studied Flen. "Our civilization depends on it."

"I hadn't realized how important it is." Flen stood straighter and clasped Cherise's hands. "And I hadn't realized how much you wish to accompany your foster sister. If that's why you're going? Then it is my duty—and my honor—to go with you. To protect you."

"Really?"

"I love you." Flen squeezed her. Then he nodded to Jinishta. "I can't let my angel walk into danger alone. Besides . . ." He gave Haz a helpless grin. "If the messiah is going to restore the Alashani to light and glory, how can I refuse to partake in such a momentous event?"

"Then prepare." Jinishta gave him a nod. "Dress in blacks."

She walked away, twirling a spear and issuing commands.

No one else seemed to see the tightness around Flen's eyes. He was hiding a lot of fears and doubts, but Cherise could respect him for that. One thought stood out: Flen loved her.

He valued Cherise. He valued love, and loyalty, and all the qualities that made humans great.

CHAPTER 5

INFINITE COMPLEXITY

Vy surreptitiously tucked a blaster glove into her black wraps. The weapon was bundled so no one could tell what it was.

"That won't save you if a Torth spots Ariock," Thomas said weakly. "And they will."

He lay on a bedroll, skeletal and frail.

"It's better than being defenseless." Vy tried not to flash back to the Swift Killer aiming at her legs. She was grateful to Pung for the weapon. He had brokered a deal to smuggle a few blaster gloves out of the Yeresunsa monastery.

Vy nearly offered to give Thomas one of the secretly smuggled blaster gloves.

Then she remembered his suicide attempts, and she decided to hold off. She just wasn't sure what he was thinking these days.

"Any ideas on how we can help you?" Vy asked.

Thomas looked ambivalent.

The neuromuscular disease that he had fought valiantly against for his entire life was defeating him. And no one but Vy seemed to care how hard he fought. No one else seemed to remember the years during which he had defied the disease. How human he'd been. He used to help kids with homework. He used to have a wry, sardonic wit.

Vy felt defeated.

She had asked him a lot of health-related questions during the trek, and he answered readily enough. But he didn't seem interested in gaining a refill of his medicine, or much of anything else. Death loomed large for him.

Nowadays, he asked about Alashani religious matters. Their pantheon. Their prophecies.

He refused to reveal what Migyatel had foreseen or imagined just before she died, but it seemed to trouble him. The fact that he would not outright denounce Migyatel as a fraud . . . that bothered Vy. Thomas was precise with words. He never spoke direct lies.

Part of him believed in prophecy, it seemed.

On top of that, Thomas seemed preoccupied with the weeping apparition who had appeared to him in the prison. He didn't know whether or not she was the Lady of Sorrow the Alashani worshipped. So why did he insist that she was real? And that she needed to be rescued?

"Um, Lady Vy?"

Vy turned at the timid voice. Orla stood there, dressed in black wraps as if she was prepared to visit the surface.

"Will you, um, allow me to attempt to heal the *rekveh*?" Orla looked queasy.

Vy moved aside, presenting the fragile bundle that was Thomas. "Please!"

Thomas watched the teenager as if she held the key to the universe. Orla moved into his range and knelt, sucking her lips inward like she was struggling not to vomit. Thomas had a hungry look of fascination.

Orla visibly forced herself to touch his sunken chest.

The air between her and him sparkled with healing energy. Thomas's torso lifted off the ground, like he was magnetized.

Vy watched intently. Perhaps Orla understood physiology in a way that Ariock did not?

Thomas fell back. His breathing sounded clearer.

"The *rekveh* is a mess, internally." Orla leaped up and backed away, unwilling to be within Thomas's range for a second longer than necessary. "I am sorry. It is impossible to save such a wretch."

Vy struggled to hide her disappointment. She shouldn't have gotten her hopes up.

"Thanks for trying," Thomas said.

Ariock was using his powers to armor himself, padding his body in leather plates and black-dyed woolen wraps, mummy style. It made him even more massive than he already was. Vy marveled that he could walk around without knocking over people or wagons.

Soon he was ready to march, outfitted like the other warriors, with a scarf and cowl. He even wore a custom-size quiver with huge spears.

"Ready?" Ariock approached. He used his powers to detach a wagon bed from its axles. "You won't have to worry about keeping up. Climb aboard."

Vy stared at the detached platform, which floated like a crude version of a hovercart.

Ariock gently lifted Thomas and placed him onto the makeshift travois.

"Won't you get exhausted?" Vy stepped aboard, but she felt ashamed. The absence of her leg was a loss in so many ways. She had already wrapped her ivory peg leg in black-dyed bandages so it wouldn't stand out.

"I don't get exhausted," Ariock assured her.

But he looked tired. Vy wasn't sure if she believed him.

She reminded herself that Ariock wasn't suicidal, and he wasn't stupid. Not really. He was foolhardy, sure, but he would turn around if they faced truly impossible odds.

Earth might not be out of reach. This was feasible.

Torth pilots needed to rely on the Megacosm in order to leap across the galaxy using their network of temporal streams. Thomas, however, could make do without the Megacosm. He was able to rapidly crunch equations to generate the requisite input vectors, which were staggeringly complex.

The rest of them had no hope of thinking that fast.

If Thomas fell unconscious, or if he died, they would be unable to enter a temporal stream and escape the local solar system. But her foster brother was a fighter. This could work.

Final goodbyes were being made.

The departure group gathered. Kessa, Weptolyso and Yuey, Varktezo, Cherise, and a bunch of Yeresunsa warriors, including Flen and Jinishta. They all wore woolens rubberized with waterproof tar. The two nussians had coated themselves in blackness. Despite their rhinoceros-like size, they might be mistaken for debris in the dead city if they held still. Only their small red eyes stood out.

They were ready for the rainy night above.

Vy stepped onto the detached wagon bed. Like most Alashani pieces of furniture, it was made from soft timber planks, like cork, carved from tree-size mushrooms. She sat next to Thomas and put her arm around him.

"Fare well." Ariock gave a small wave to the messianic army, who watched him with worry. They probably felt abandoned by their messiah.

They would make camp and await his return.

Meanwhile, Ariock walked across the crumbling bridge toward the exit. The travois floated behind him, controlled by his Yeresunsa awareness. Vy rode the platform along with Thomas and several travel packs.

She understood why Ariock was taking such a huge risk.

He needed to be able to live with himself.

Besides, she would never ask him to cower in too-small cave apartments for the rest of his life. He was unhappy underground. He needed a place with weather.

The tunnel became steep and rocky. Black-wrapped warriors leaped from one treacherous ledge to the next, as agile as gymnasts, despite the supply gear they carried. Flen used his powers to lift Cherise whenever she needed help.

Orla had apparently earned permission to come along. She leaped past the travois and caught up to Ariock, puffing from exertion.

"Messiah," she said. "I want you to know, I did attempt to heal your *rekveh*."

"Oh?" Ariock gave her an appreciative glance. "Thanks. Would you please do it again?"

Orla struggled to keep pace. She had to step over stones or leap from boulder to boulder. "A more permanent healing is theoretically possible."

Ariock stopped walking. He waited for an explanation, and Vy saw fierce hopes and doubts at war on his face.

"Only theoretical," Orla hurried to clarify. "We would need a lot more time."

"What do you mean?" Ariock asked.

"Let me try to explain." Orla glanced back to make sure the travois stayed at a distance. "A body is made up of many small structures. Tiny structures within structures within structures." She pinched her fingers to demonstrate.

Cells? Vy wondered if the cave-dwelling teenager actually knew the rudiments of biology.

"Each of those structures has a natural inclination," Orla went on. "A mode of behavior that is innate to it."

DNA? Vy wondered.

"When I heal," Orla said, "I nudge the tiny structures to follow their innate nature. That is what allows the body to defeat its problems and strive toward health."

Ariock seemed to be following the explanation.

"But," Orla said, "if the innate nature of the small structures is wrong?" She gave him a knowing look. "That is the problem with your *rekveh*. The nature of his structures is unhealthy. Too many of them are inclined toward death instead of rebirth. Altogether, his body is striving toward death instead of life."

Vy turned to Thomas and saw him nod, confirming that Orla had given a very crude—but accurate—description of spinal muscular atrophy.

"How much time would you need to fix it?" Ariock asked hopefully.

Thomas laughed. He sounded bitter.

"I would need many lifetimes," Orla admitted with a giggle. "I could heal anything with enough time. I could heal old age, or blindness, or all the problems with your *rekveh*." She seemed proud, almost smug. "Because I can fix those tiny little structures. I know how to do it."

Vy suppressed a surge of hope. She might be grasping at straws, but if the problem was mere complexity . . . well . . . that was Thomas's expertise.

"She can't do it," Thomas said in his weak, raspy voice. "She would have to replace every cell in my entire body."

A replacement body?

As far as Vy knew, not even Torth technology could grant an artificial body. The Torth had robotics, but even with their longevity drugs, Torth still grew old and died. The Commander of All Living Things was a skeletal horror. She might have superhuman strength, but every knobby bone was visible in her skintight armor.

"No one can do what Orla is talking about," Thomas said.

Ariock still looked hopeful. "You healed my wound." He touched his chest, where black woolens hid his biggest scar.

"Mmm-hmm." Orla nodded agreeably. "But remember, that was very draining for me, and very hunger-inducing for you."

Ariock considered that.

"Your *rekveh* would require many magnitudes greater treatment." Orla clenched her fist to illustrate, moving it up her torso, bit by bit. "His small structures need to be reworked and birthed anew. Each tiny structure is unique, and they all interact in precise, intricate ways. Like an aqueduct factory. Only it is nearly infinite in complexity."

Thomas looked thoughtful.

"Even if I had a god's capacity for knowledge," Orla said, "even if I could weave a thousand tapestries with one hand while operating an aqueduct and dancing at the same time . . ." She laughed at the absurdity. "Even so, the trauma and lengthy duration of such a healing would kill your *rekveh*. No one could withstand a process like that. Not even you, great one."

Ariock looked frustrated, like he wanted to solve a puzzle.

"It is impossible," Orla said.

Vy looked at Thomas.

"If Ariock was a mind reader," Thomas said, "it would be possible. Then I could guide him. I could show him blueprints, so to speak."

That was frustrating. Vy rotated the puzzle pieces in her mind. Ariock and Thomas had such complementary traits, it seemed that a solution should be within their grasp.

"But she's right," Thomas said. "It's impossible."

CHAPTER 6

STRATOWER SKY

A massive boulder blocked the exit. Ariock paused, assessing the blockage.

A step below him, Jinishta said, "You cannot move the entrance boulder while also carrying that platform. You are carrying too . . ." She trailed off, agape.

Ariock had already expanded his awareness into the boulder. He shifted its immense weight and levitated it up and away.

A humid reek wafted down, along with the hiss of rainfall.

"You don't think I can do two things at once?" Ariock spoke with dry sarcasm. Conversation was supposed to be difficult, if not impossible, for an overly strained warrior. He made power look effortless, and he knew it.

"You could have let me do that," Jinishta said without much fight.

"Remember," Ariock said, "I'm in charge now."

He pulled up his warrior's veil so that his face blended into shadows and boosted himself out of the hole, into the world above. He had already set down the boulder and shifted his attention to the makeshift travois that carried Vy and Thomas.

He ducked out from an overhang—and paused to stare at Stratower City.

The sky was multicolored.

Holographic billboards and airborne neon traffic shimmered less than half a mile away. The riot of lights illuminated the base of a shape that was too large for Ariock to take in all at once. The Stratower did not just fill the sky.

It was the sky.

It was larger than clouds, larger than a mountain range. Darkness and mist cloaked its astronomical midsection and hid its summit, but reflected neon lights swept up its surface in baleful diagonals, implying a curvature. Its rotund base blocked the entire horizon.

"Light!" someone whispered.

"Glory!" That person sounded reverential.

The Yeresunsa warriors had joined Ariock. Some fell to their knees in the muck. Neon lights reflected in their wide, astonished eyes. They had probably never dared to venture this close to the Torth-ruled city until now.

Ariock ignored their awe and reverence. Alashani did what they did. He had more important things to think about.

He healed Thomas again. It had an insignificant effect.

Then he stood, attempting to size up the Stratower.

The largest skyscraper in the known universe exhibited hints of frilliness. In contrast to the dull, geometric structures nestled against its girth, the Stratower looked ornate. But there would be eyes everywhere.

Ariock figured he could locate hidden routes by stretching his awareness. Instead of climbing up the outside, it would be safer to sneak up an interior elevator shaft or something like that.

Despite his size, he was camouflaged, warm and dry in his wraps. Jinishta had taught him how to move like a shadow. He hiked over sludge-covered rubble, pausing every so often, allowing his companions to stay close. He used his powers to levitate the travois. It was almost as easy as moving his own legs.

Thomas claimed that the Stratower was closed to the public. It was solely for Servants of All and visitors whom the Servants chose for promotion to their ranks.

What mysteries did it hide?

Ariock recalled the Yeresunsa monastery, with its power crystal. He had accidentally shattered the crystal. Perhaps the Stratower hid similar relics? If so, Ariock guessed that he should be extra careful. He didn't want to trigger objects with unknown magical properties.

"That is the Border River ahead of us," Jinishta whispered. "Be careful. Its waters are toxic."

Her voice should have been drowned out by rainfall, but she used her powers to direct her whisper so Ariock heard her.

Everyone heard the torrential sound of the river. Black sludge flowed, with chunks of debris bobbing in the morass.

A wall loomed beyond the Border River, smooth and very tall. It seemed Stratower City was protected by a wall and a moat. How medieval.

According to Alashani lore, no one could cross the Border River. There were no bridges or tunnels.

Ariock supposed that he would have to levitate everyone for quite a distance. Otherwise he would have to collect debris in order to build a noticeable bridge. The Border River was wide, perhaps as much as a quarter of a mile with that wall.

Kessa hissed a warning. "A Torth watches us!" she whispered fiercely.

Everyone went motionless except for their eyes.

Ariock frantically scanned the rubble. He squinted against the glare of lights, searching the top of the silhouetted wall.

His eyesight was inferior to that of an ummin. He knew he must be missing something.

He might expand his awareness and search for unwelcome life sparks, but he didn't like the idea of abandoning his shielding around his friends.

"I see it." Jinishta drew two of her spears. Her luminous eyes were fixed on a target.

Ariock followed her gaze, and at last, he noticed a faraway, solitary lump. It looked like a piece of nondescript equipment left atop the wall. But when the wind blew, the thing shifted and drew its cloak tighter.

Someone was definitely kneeling atop the wall, obscured by rain and distance.

The entire Torth Majority could peer through one lone Torth's eyes.

"Jinishta, no," Ariock whispered, flowing air to make sure she heard. "I'll handle this. Let's stay hidden."

A spear would be obvious murder. A gust of wind, however, could be mistaken for random happenstance.

Ariock divided his attention. Part of him remained with his human body, keeping it breathing and balanced. The rest of him sped through rain-drenched air. That extension of himself leaped over the toxic Border River, then sped up the metal wall. He swirled around the life spark of the watcher.

It was alive, all right. Ariock sensed more vibrancy than any life spark he had ever encountered. Not even Yeresunsa warriors felt this potent.

Was the watcher supercharged in some way? Or was it just full of Torth audience members? Ariock had no idea.

Time to die, Ariock thought.

He ballooned his awareness into cold, humid air, compressing it. An unseen whirlwind gathered.

The idea of murdering someone in cold blood—even a dangerous Torth—felt a little bit shameful. Slaying enemies in battle was unequivocal self-defense, but this faraway sentry showed no overt signs of threat.

It is a major threat, Ariock reminded himself. Murder should never be easy, of course, but one lone Torth could summon an army. He had to get rid of it.

He funneled his whirlwind until it was refined into a pressurized force, easy to aim.

Ariock slammed his gale-force wind into the watcher.

The lone Torth plummeted off the wall, flailing toward the toxic river of sludge. It had been hit by raw strength equivalent to a speeding freight train. Mortal terror would probably drive away its inner audience.

Ariock slammed back into his body, satisfied.

"Done," he told his friends. Hopefully the Torth Empire would chalk up the sentry's death to a freak accident.

Ariock began to scan the rubble for anything that might serve as additions to the wagon bed platform. If he was going to levitate his friends over the Border River, it would be easier to group them onto a makeshift—

"That Torth is back!" Varktezo said.

Ariock stared at the top of the wall in disbelief. For a second, he figured Varktezo must be joking.

But no. The watcher stood undefeated, cloak rippling in the wind.

Its cowl had fallen, revealing white hair and a white beard. An old man? The watcher held what looked like a twisted, silvery cane.

Ariock extended his awareness with frantic desperation. He had to make sure the death worked this time.

The old man leaped off the wall before Ariock could smash him with a hurricane-force gust.

The shadows along the wall were too great, and Ariock lost track of where the watcher had gone. He widened his awareness in order to scour the area. He needed to find that potent life spark. Every second the lone Torth survived brought greater danger.

What had the watcher reported already? Strange phenomena? Or was he trumpeting an alarm about the Giant's return?

"We should return underground," Flen said in a low, terrified voice.

Ariock located the brilliant life spark. It was close. Much closer than it should be, and approaching at a swift pace.

This enemy made unexpected moves. As far as Ariock knew, Torth could not fly. A Servant of All could do strong acrobatics, like Yeresunsa warriors, but this old man lacked the empty white eyes of the highest rank.

And why would one lone Torth rush to confront the Giant all by himself? Why not wait for a horde of kamikaze nussians, plus a fleet with nuclear bombs ready to drop?

Something wasn't adding up.

Ariock had no time to investigate. The old man was rushing up the slope toward him. Torth were never supposed to show emotion, but this one looked exultant.

"Kill it!" Jinishta whispered. She drew three spears and hurled them in quick succession.

Her warriors followed suit. Spears hurtled at the old man, bullet-fast, from all eight of the albinos.

The volley should have skewered the old man. Instead, he spun faster than humanly possible and whipped his staff to thwack the spears aside. He moved with the speedy grace of a Yeresunsa.

But an Alashani would never reveal his face aboveground. The face displayed here was definitely not albino, in any case. The figure's cloak hid his clothing, but Ariock caught glimpses of armor.

A Servant of All. It had to be.

"Let's run!" Flen begged.

The shortest warrior, Orla, used her powers to levitate all her spears simultaneously, like missiles ready to launch.

"It sees us, you fool!" Jinishta used her powers to gather the spears, trying to be as unnoticeable as possible. "Never show your powers to the monsters. You know this, Orla!"

Ariock sped his focus outward, this time forming a solid hammer of air. He swung the invisible sledgehammer with enough force to kill a charging bull.

The old man raised his staff.

The force of Ariock's impact blew his cloak back, and the rubble around him got scoured from the shock wave—but the target himself remained unharmed, feet planted firmly on the ground.

Yeresunsa.

Ariock gaped, because a Torth with Yeresunsa powers was supposed to be impossible. Yeresunsa Torth were always destroyed as fetuses on baby farms. A secret hybrid might survive, hidden on Earth, like himself. Like Thomas. And like Jonathan Stead. But here, on this planet? The Megacosm made secrecy among Torth impossible.

Then Ariock remembered the story of Thomas's nameless mother. Hadn't she kept a massive secret, even under torture in the Isolatorium?

Hadn't Thomas himself kept his human kindness secret and buried while he cruised the Megacosm?

So some Torth could keep secrets.

How many? Were there actually Torth who were going about mundane business, torturing slaves or slurping nectar smoothies, and secretly hiding illegal Yeresunsa powers?

What a horrifying thought.

"I'm Garrett Dovanack!" the old man shouted. "Your great-grandpa!"

Ariock blinked and stared anew. Could it be?

The old man did resemble the family portraits Ariock had grown up around. Old Garrett had died when Ariock was a baby, but anyone could recognize those bold features and deep-set eyes, similar to his own.

"Torth will imitate friendly voices," Jinishta said in a warning tone. "You must not believe it."

"Die, Torth!" Orla screamed. She hurled spears.

The other warriors joined in, but the old man—Garrett?—moved so fast, it seemed he flickered.

"I am Jonathan Stead!" he yelled in the slave tongue, whamming spears out of his way. His motions blurred from superhuman speed.

He was nearly close enough to read their minds.

Nearly close enough to disable Ariock with a pain seizure.

And if he was a Torth, that was exactly what he must be angling to do: distract or defeat the Giant until the fleet could arrive. Such a "heroic" act would win any Torth a place of honor in the Megacosm, to be revered for all eternity.

The old man was clad in Torth armor. He had eyes like a Blue Rank, rather than the vivid purple that Garrett was said to have had.

Anyhow, Garrett was dead. If this was him—at the ripe old age of one hundred and eleven or so—why would he spend his dotage lurking on a miserable planet full of enemies? Why leave the comfort and safety of his fortified mansion on Earth?

Why abandon his family when they had most needed his protection?

In the years since Garrett had passed away in a nursing home, his daughter and grandson had been murdered by the Torth Empire. Ariock had grown up in a mansion haunted by the family that should have been there.

Where had his great-grandfather been during those lonely years, if not dead and buried?

What about when the Torth had abducted Ariock and his mother? They had forced Ariock to fight alien monsters, they'd enslaved his mother, they'd crucified him in an alien desert. It had not been Garrett who saved them, but a frail renegade.

Garrett Dovanack had cherished his family on Earth. He had built them a fortune and a fortress. He'd protected them for a century. He never would have abandoned them to suffer torture and death.

This could not be him.

Ariock gathered energy, brewing it into crackling electricity. He reached back and drew two of his enormous spears.

This lying imposter needed to die.

CHAPTER 7

GOODWILL

Sparks flew as the imposter shielded himself with ionized air. "Idiot!" he bellowed in a deep, booming voice. "Do you want every Torth on the planet to know you're here?"

Ariock was so furious, some of his power had whipped out in dual white-hot bars of electricity, along with the spears he'd thrown.

Well, rainfall might obscure what was happening here.

Then again, perhaps millions of Torth were already tuned in? The old man was trying to be distracting. Ariock dared not let up his attack. He connected to more of his oversize spears and sent them hurtling at his opponent, too quickly for anyone to dodge.

His attack should have pummeled the old man into a bloody pulp.

Instead, the imposter shielded himself, all the while shouting that he meant no harm, that he was Jonathan Stead. He clearly had power to spare. More raw strength than any Alashani warrior and, judging by his acrobatics, he seemed Alashani-trained.

Ariock had never faced such a tough opponent before. A killing blow would require all his focus.

He had already let go of the wagon bed that carried Vy and Thomas. Now he released his air shield. He couldn't worry about shielding his friends until this battle was over.

"I'm family, I swear!" The old man sounded genuinely desperate. "I didn't come here to fight you. I came to help you!" He thwacked aside a volley of spears thrown by the warriors.

Ariock stood at his full height. He continued to grow beyond the scope of his body, into the rain-drenched night. He had once decimated a spaceport. He could kill an old man.

"Here, does this help?" The opponent waved a hand in front of his eyes and pointed to the result. "Purple. The Torth never display this color, right?"

The old man no longer had blue eyes. Now they were a luminous purple, somewhat like Alashani eyes.

"I'm not a Torth!" His voice boomed. "I am Garrett Dovanack!"

Ariock figured it was all a monstrous lie designed to make him hesitate. Yet he hesitated anyway. Why would a Torth put so much effort into playing pretend?

Was it possible . . . ?

"Kill it!" Jinishta hurled her last two spears.

The warriors used their powers to regather their weapons. In the pause, Ariock sent razor whips of air along with his own spears, and he prepared a spiked shock wave.

The old man desperately forked lightning his way.

Ariock shielded himself just in time. Sparks fizzled into the night like supercharged fireworks.

"Stop!" the old man yelled. "Won't you just hear me out?"

Maybe his vernacular English was supposed to set Ariock at ease. It didn't. The old man threw a shock wave even as he spoke, shattering Ariock's imminent attack and forcing him to refocus on defense.

One of Ariock's huge spears slammed into the old man's chest. It bounced off, but it did send the old guy spinning and staggering. That had to hurt.

Ariock slammed an immense shock wave at the imposter, splitting the ground. Then another. And another. His opponent dodged and leaped so fast, he seemed to flicker in and out of existence. But Ariock was relentless, not allowing the old guy any chance to rest. Debris sprayed everywhere. Electricity rippled like lightning. The ground began to look chewed up, unsettled by impact craters.

It was too late for stealth.

Possibly too late to protect the Alashani civilization.

And if Thomas lay unattended in the toxic rain for much longer, he could die.

Ariock raised his hands, each finger extended with energy, ready to smash the old man between two tidal waves of force. He had to end this battle and get his friends to a safer location. Either he would flee back underground to the Alashani, or he'd fly into the Stratower. One or the other. But he had to destroy this imminent threat before he could do anything at all.

Snapping bars of electricity disrupted his concentration.

An electric barrier sprang up, breaking Ariock's lines of focus. While he regathered energy for a renewed attack, the old man approached with pained weariness. He limped, as if stricken with arthritis, like he had not just been doing acrobatic leaps and somersaults. Muck streaked his armor and his neatly trimmed beard.

He was coming too close.

At this close a range, any Torth had a decisive advantage over nontelepaths. They could read minds. They could give pain seizures.

Jinishta held spears ready to throw. But she aimed at Ariock instead of the old man, and her mournful look made her intentions plain.

The Pact.

It was suicide time.

Each of the warriors looked ready to murder Thomas, Vy, Kessa, and his other friends.

Desperate, Ariock blasted his awareness through the electric bars, forcing them to fizzle and die. At the same time, he slammed air around the old man, lifting him off the ground, trapping him so that he could no longer leap away or worm elsewhere. Buffered by Ariock's air shield, perhaps the imposter would have trouble extending his own awareness?

The old man spoke in a panicked frenzy. "I can heal your friend Thomas! I promise. Let me prove my goodwill!"

That was what a Torth would say.

It must be a ploy. It had to be just a way to get Ariock to let down his guard, so this superpowered Torth could flip the battle and win.

And yet.

Even so . . .

Whenever Ariock sensed Thomas's life spark, it was a mere ember. His friend no longer had weeks left, or even days. Thomas needed more healing than Ariock could give. And wasn't his well-being the whole reason Ariock had rushed up into this dangerous night?

"No one can heal him."

The admission tore something inside Ariock. He was so angry at himself. He had made a promise and proved himself to be colossal failure.

He let the old man go. Why not? It didn't matter who won anymore. They were all doomed. Everyone had a weapon out. The lightning bolts must have rousted a Torth army. A fleet would descend upon this place, and Jinishta and her warriors would try to murder Ariock and his friends, because that was their way.

Rain poured down.

"I'm doing everything I can," Ariock admitted, shoulders slumped. "And it's not enough."

The old man wiped sweat and grime off his forehead. "Well," he said, leaning heavily on his staff, "I might know a trick or two you haven't tried."

CHAPTER 8

ALIVE IN HELL

"We don't have time to waste." The old man limped toward Thomas in a dignified manner. "If I'm going to heal your friend, it needs to be before the Torth show up. And you'll need to allow me close enough to touch him."

Jinishta used her powers to get Ariock's attention, turning his head. "You cannot trust a Torth," she whispered urgently in the slave tongue. "It will say anything to make you lower your guard. Do not let it get any closer!"

She prepared to hurl spears. The other warriors took their cues from her and aimed their spears, ready to throw at a command.

The old man froze. He seemed uncaring about the spears, but he aimed a politely questioning expression toward Ariock.

My call, Ariock realized.

He had to decide whom to trust. Jinishta? Or the powerful stranger who claimed to be Garrett Dovanack, otherwise known as Jonathan Stead?

Rain hissed around them. As the damp chill seeped through minuscule vents in Ariock's wraps and padded armor, he realized that he *wanted* to believe.

He desperately wanted a hero he could look up to.

According to slave legends across the galaxy, Jonathan Stead was supposed to return someday and free all slaves. Maybe this old man would turn out to be the Alashani messiah? And heal Thomas? And become the father Ariock wished he had never lost? And make the universe a better place?

"Do what you can," Ariock said.

The old man limped toward Thomas, leaning on his cane. Was he trying to look harmless and endearing? He had just been leaping around like an acrobat twenty seconds ago.

But maybe he was genuinely arthritic. Ariock could defy gravity despite his size. Jinishta could lift a boulder twenty times her weight. Perhaps it wasn't so far-fetched that an old man could infuse his geriatric body with power in order to speed up his motions.

Jinishta hissed through clenched teeth. "Ariock, this Torth will have summoned many more of its brethren. Don't you understand? It is buying time! We cannot stay here!"

"I have not called any Torth," the old man said. He switched to English, speaking to Ariock. "They'll come anyway, thanks to this kerfuffle. But I'll help you escape."

He turned to Jinishta and spoke to her directly, fluent in her native language. Jinishta's eyes narrowed with suspicion. She looked feverish with outrage at the mention of Eidelwen. Ariock recognized the name of her ancestral family member.

Eidelwen was Ariock's ancestor, as well. His great-great-grandmother.

The old man must be claiming that his mother was Eidelwen. That would make him an Alashani and therefore not a Torth. Family connections mattered more than anything in Alashani society.

"No," Jinishta said in the slave tongue. "I do not accept a vile *rekveh* as my family."

But she looked deeply rattled. She must be wondering how a Torth could know so much about Alashani society and her family in particular.

Garrett spoke just like an Alashani.

Maybe he really was Jonathan Stead returned.

Maybe he had a good explanation for his absence for all these years.

Ariock struggled not to cave completely to his childish longing for help.

He knelt next to Thomas. When he expanded his awareness, he could sense the catastrophic failures throughout the boy's body. Fragile, under developed lungs hardly drew breath. Thomas seemed asleep. Maybe he was too weak to wake up. Vy cradled his head in her lap.

"We'll argue later." Ariock stood, ushering the old man closer to Thomas. "I'm warning you." He held his hands out to either side. "If you hurt anyone here, I'll crush your skull."

Ariock knew that his own size and strength were intimidating. He might be evenly matched with the old guy, but this close? He could probably tackle this opponent.

"How friendly." The old man sized up each huge hand. "My. You've grown a lot less trusting since the last time I saw you."

Ariock tried to ignore that statement. He tried.

As far as he knew, he had visited old Garrett once, when he was a baby. Not that he remembered. His mother used to speak of that trip to the senior care facility with bittersweet sadness, mourning the man who had acted as a father to her beloved husband, Ariock's father. "*Everyone loved old Garrett,*" she had said.

"All righty." The old man knelt in the muck beside Thomas, every movement pained. "First, I need to know, where is his medicine case?"

Ariock could not guess why the battered, empty case would be of any use. He supposed it was still underground, back with the stripped wagon and the rest of the disbanded army—

He lost his train of thought, shocked when the NAI-12 briefcase appeared in the muck.

He blinked. It had just *appeared* there.

"And now," the old man said, "I need someone who is aware of the last known location of his extra supply on Earth. Vy? May I probe your mind briefly?"

Vy looked taken aback that the old man knew her identity. The black veil hid most of her face, but she nodded. "I guess."

"*Rekveh!*" Jinishta bared her teeth at the old man. "It is not even trying to hide its evil power!"

Ariock wondered what his own thoughts were giving away. At this range, the old mind reader could fish out any detail of his life.

The NAI-12 case popped open, manipulated by Yeresunsa powers.

Ariock stared in fascination as the vials magically filled with liquid. Upside-down vials popped out of their pockets, righted themselves, and inserted themselves into orderly rows. One by one, each vial filled with greenish serum: NAI-12.

Thomas's battered injection pen floated up into the rain-soaked air. A refilled cartridge popped into it.

"Vy," the old man said. "Will you do the honors?"

Vy reached for the injection pen with uncertainty. It flew into her grasp as if magnetized.

"Hold that a moment." The old man turned to Ariock. "Now I'm going to explain what happens next, since I'd rather not get murdered by you in the middle of it."

Ariock gave an uncertain nod.

"Once Vy injects him with the medicine," the old man said, "I'm going to give it something like a supercharge. It will go straight to his spinal cord and halt all cell death. At the same time, I need to wake your friend from his coma."

"His coma?" Ariock was horrified to hear that.

Vy nodded. She looked unsurprised.

"The waking will draw on his last reserves," the old man went on. "It's going to look bad, like he's dying, but it's necessary." The old man spoke as if soothing a frightened animal. "In order to push his body to reverse some of its atrophy, I need access to his supergenius consciousness. He should be capable of mapping out a blueprint, so to speak. I'll use that for targeted healing of his worst organ failures."

A wave of hope battered Ariock. This healing sounded like what Orla had spoken of. "You mean you're going to give him a new body?"

"No." The old man held his gaze. "No power in the universe can do that. All I can do is reverse the worst damages. I will grant him a few extra weeks of life. Is that okay?"

"Great. Do it." Ariock was impatient, ready to heal Thomas again if the old man delayed much longer.

"All righty." The old man gave Vy a nod. "Dose him up."

Before Vy could unwrap one of Thomas's arms, his arm raised on its own, as if held by an invisible hand. The wraps unraveled ultrafast.

Exposed to polluted rain, Thomas's arm looked as thin as a twig and likely to snap under the barest pressure. His skin became streaked with grime.

Vy spoke as if she was at her job in the hospital. "Do you have any alcohol swabs?"

Garrett nodded toward Thomas's arm, and a portion of skin became magically clean.

Vy gently planted the pen there, in the crook of his elbow. She delivered an injection.

"It's showtime." The old man spread his gnarled hands, like a maestro prepared to conduct an orchestra.

The wraps spun around Thomas's arm, faster than humanly possible, sealing his skin against the rain. The lid of the NAI-12 case snapped shut and latched. At the same time, Thomas gasped. His eyelids fluttered, the whites of his eyes showing.

The old man leaned forward until his forehead nearly touched Thomas's.

A second later, Thomas dropped into unconsciousness again. Black rain pelted him.

The old man moved from one task to the next with smooth efficiency. A dazzling array of healing took place inside Thomas. The air around him writhed in transparent snakes, and the force of the healing lifted Thomas halfway off the ground. The outpouring of energy seemed equal to a thousand Alashani aqueduct factories. Ariock sensed vital organs regaining health, cells repairing, and billions of microscopic operations taking place all at once.

It was like watching a city constructed in time-lapse video. Too many steps to keep track of. It must require astronomical feats of concentration, far more than Ariock thought he could ever be capable of. Thomas's eyelids were fluttering. Perhaps he was subconsciously guiding the work?

It went on for at least a minute. Toward the end of it, the old man began to look ancient. He grunted and wheezed with effort.

At last, the healing ebbed, and Thomas dropped back down into the muck. He immediately curled up, sobbing.

That was more motion, more liveliness, than he had shown in months.

Ariock hastily examined Thomas with his powers, forgetting the old man for the moment. Thomas's life spark was strong again! Almost healthy! As healthy as Thomas ever got, anyway.

Vy cradled his head, staring down at him with disbelief. "Thomas?" she said.

"Am I dead?" he whispered.

Vy brightened. "How do you feel?"

"Ugh." Thomas sounded miserable. "Can you not ask me nurse questions?"

Ariock connected to Thomas's life spark, but his refresher healing was pitiful and useless after the dazzling orchestra the old man had performed.

The old man sagged with exhaustion, shoulders slumped. Now he looked like he really might be over one hundred years old.

He flourished, and a cigarette popped into existence between his gnarled fingers.

The end of the cigarette flared cherry-red.

The old man inhaled and breathed smoke with immense satisfaction. "Mind if I smoke?" He closed his eyes in bliss. "Ahhh. I missed these things so much."

Vy stared at the old man as if wondering how real he was. Ariock felt much the same. He had so many questions.

Then he remembered that he had a friend who could gain all the answers they needed. Thomas was within range of the old man. He just needed to be fully focused. It would be best not to overload his telepathic perception with extra minds in the vicinity.

"Come on." Ariock knelt to offer Vy his hand. "Let's give them space."

Vy gave him a questioning look, but when she saw his certainty, she caught on. She gently propped Thomas on the soft part of a supply pack and allowed Ariock to guide her beyond the telepathy ranges of the old man and the boy.

"Thomas?" Ariock said.

Thomas opened his yellow eyes. Bleary, he took in the sights of Ariock, Vy, Kessa, Weptolyso, Jinishta, the rainfall, the old man with his cigarette, and the circus-bright skyline of Stratower City.

All traffic was gone. The holographs had shut down, although the Stratower windows still emitted their baleful glow. An ominous, buzzing roar came from the distance.

"Is this hell?" Thomas whispered.

"No." Ariock pointed to the old man. "Hey. Can you please tell me who that is?"

CHAPTER 9

TASTER OF SECRETS

Thomas had had a passive, yet successful, suicide.

He had tolerated sensory deprivation in a foul dungeon, barely eating, sick, so that he could finally die. He had rejected the temptation to ascend into the Megacosm. He hadn't even ignited a flame for warmth. He had, in fact, rejected an unexpected power surge granted to him by the weeping apparition known as the Lady of Sorrow. None of his friends had guessed that his supply of NAI-12 was dwindling until months after it was all gone.

All of that was a success.

He should be deceased.

This black downpour felt like hell, but he recognized the Torth Homeworld. Someone had magically healed him. On top of that, he felt as if he'd been receiving regular doses of NAI-12. Some of the damage to his organs was reversed.

Which was impossible.

He patted his hands down his body, checking on what other impossibilities had taken place. He felt like himself. Same skinny, underdeveloped torso. Arms and legs that he could barely move.

"Who is that?" Ariock repeated. Even at a distance, he towered. He pointed to a man who sat nearby, within telepathy range, silhouetted against the artificially bright skyline.

Thomas didn't feel ready, quite yet, for a barrage of answers. He was damp and cold, and he felt as if he'd just recovered from pneumonia. And he was exasperated. What was he going to have to do if he wanted to die?

The old man began to speak, but Ariock cut him off. "Don't say a word."

The old man took another drag on his cigarette. Which was incongruous. Cigarettes were an Earth thing. No one on this planet should smoke them.

His thoughts puffed toward Thomas like his acrid smoke, encoded in Torth patterns. *I am Garrett Dovanack (Jonathan Stead). My great-grandson (Ariock) needs to hear it from you. Tell him.*

Those rapid thought patterns marked the old man as a Torth. Yet his impatience seemed human.

Thomas squinted against the black downpour. Direct lies were impossible in telepathy, yet this man's claim was pure fantasy. Garrett Dovanack had had a funeral. Twenty years ago. Thomas contained Delia's memory of the open-casket viewing. And sure, this old man did look like him, but it was dark. Maybe it was only a passing resemblance.

The old man snorted. "I do have some experience with faking my death, you know." In his mind, he urged Thomas, *Come on, kid, hurry up and ID me. We don't have all day to luxuriate here. A Torth army will bomb this place any second.*

Thomas found himself intrigued, even curious.

So he dug into the old man's memories.

He followed veins of buried emotion, like a miner seeking gold. Mind probes were considered rude, but Thomas hardly cared. He had to learn what secrets this old man might be hiding.

He did have an identity. He was a Blue Rank known as the Credible Witness. A relics collector, specializing in ancient scrolls and scripts. But . . .

No. He had another identity.

Garrett Olmstead Dovanack had cradled a sweet toddler in his arms and fervently wished he could stay on Earth to help his great-grandson grow up.

Long before that, a much younger Garrett wept with joy, cuddled up against his wife, as she cradled their infant baby girl.

Thomas shoved himself upright, eager to soak up more. This was incredible. Judging by the memories he had tasted so far, this old man was the hero he claimed to be, and his mind did, indeed, contain tantalizing hints of rich complexities. He had secretly hunted and killed Servants of All. How many? Dozens, at least. Maybe more.

As a Blue Rank, he was researching a slave legend known as the weeping woman. He thought of her as the Lady of Sorrow, and he believed she was more than just a myth. He wanted to find her and set her free.

Wow.

Overcome by insatiable curiosity, Thomas leaned closer to the old man, drinking delicious secrets, one after the other, as fast as possible.

Before he had invented his Garrett identity, he had been known as Jonathan Stead. Indeed, he had been carried, on the backs of freed slaves, into that lamplit, secret underground city. The cave-dwelling Alashani had, indeed, worshipped him as their messiah.

Fascinating.

As a pretend human, Garrett had once stood on the caldera of a volcano with his wife. Poignant. But those wife memories were tinged with sadness, because she was dead.

Thomas skipped to a more recent memory. The elderly Blue Rank was compiling a valuable book, full of scraped-together copies of parchments from the archaic predecessors that predated the Torth Empire. He had needed to barter away one of his favorite slaves for his most recent acquisition. He regretted transferring that kind, attentive ummin to a new owner—

YOU'RE DONE.

The forbiddance slammed into Thomas with a jolt of pain. At the same time, Garrett leaped up and scrambled backward. He left Thomas's range so fast, his motions blurred.

Ariock gave Thomas a perplexed, questioning look.

"Yeah." Thomas fell back. He no longer had the strength to hold himself upright. "That's Garrett Dovanack. Or Jonathan Stead. It's really him!"

He yearned to feast on more of those fascinating memories. Perhaps he shouldn't have dug in quite so ruthlessly, uninvited? Garrett must contain the answers to thousands of mysteries. He must know all sorts of unique secrets. How had he survived for so long? How was he able to fool the Torth Empire? Why was he here? Why was he searching for the Lady of Sorrow?

Thomas gaped at the old man. It would be worth staying alive, just to maneuver his way back within range to soak up more knowledge from Garrett. What a treasure trove!

"Impossible!" Jinishta looked outraged and disgusted as she turned from Thomas to Garrett. "Jonathan Stead cannot be a vile *rekveh*!"

"Think again." Garrett spoke to her in the slave tongue, tapping ash off his cigarette. "I was never stupid enough to tell the Alashani that I have that particular power. But I'm telling you now." He stuck the cigarette back in his mouth and puffed with smug defiance. "I'm a mind reader."

Tears shone in Jinishta's luminous eyes. Rage, disgust, hatred. Thomas guessed the Alashani would never accept a mind reader as their legendary hero.

"Deal with it," Garrett said callously. "Telepathy is just another Yeresunsa power. Now, I suggest you brave Alashani warriors go run back to your little hidey-holes"—he made a running gesture with his fingers—"and let me aid my great-grandson in getting free from this nasty planet."

"But . . ." Ariock sank to his knees, putting himself closer to eye level with everyone. "How . . . ?" Questions filled his eyes. One did not need to hear his thoughts to guess many of the things he wanted to know. "How are you still alive? I mean, where have you been?"

Simple questions. Thomas knew that Garrett could offer a few sparse facts, enough to ease Ariock's curiosity. Instead, he puffed on his cigarette and said, "I'll explain later."

Something about that assurance seemed insincere.

Thomas had not taken his gaze off the old man, scanning for facial microexpressions, and Garrett had similar facial giveaways as Ariock. He didn't want to explain where he had been or what he'd been up to.

Garrett steamrolled over any other questions that might pop up. "For now, you need to exit this hellhole of a planet. You got your pilot." He pointed to Thomas. "You'll find a neon-blue transport on the far side of that wall, over there." He pointed. "Have your pilot fly it up the Stratower, to a specific launchpad. Here are the car keys plus a map." He tossed a slim data stick to Ariock, who caught it by reflex. "The route is preprogrammed. I'll distract the Torth by pretending to be you. As long as you don't dawdle, and you don't draw attention to yourself, you'll have a safe trip."

Ariock gaped.

"Oh, and there's a slave inside the transport," Garrett added. "I'd appreciate it if you take him with you. All right?"

Ariock gawked even more.

"One more thing," Garrett said. "Don't go to Earth. The place is crawling with Servants of All on the lookout for you."

"They're not invading Earth, are they?" Vy begged to know.

"Nah," Garrett said.

A lie.

Thomas knew that Earth was slated for conquest, even though the old man betrayed no hint of it, not even a microexpression. The upcoming invasion of Earth was big news in the Megacosm. Thomas had ascended when he was a prisoner in the dungeon pit, just long enough to be kicked out, but he had learned that much.

"Earth is just a bad place for you in particular," Garrett said easily, although he had to know that he was being deceptive. "Head toward a reject planet. I don't care which one. I'll find you. I promise."

If that was true—if Garrett could truly find Ariock anywhere in the galaxy—it begged the question: How? Was he working with invasive tracking implants? Was it some unknown Yeresunsa power? Thomas itched to find out.

Garrett pushed Ariock, trying to make him budge. "Time to go. Get moving."

Searchlights fanned through the rain-soaked air above Stratower City. The clouds looked pregnant with artificial lights.

Fortified transports began to break through, into sight. Transports swarmed, crisscrossing each other's paths in choreographed motions. Their searchlights scissored across the dead city.

"But . . ." Ariock was clearly struggling with a lot of emotions and even more questions. To him, the future must seem brighter and more optimistic than it ever had. But that sudden change raised questions.

"Are you going to be all right?" he asked his great-grandfather.

"I'll be fine," Garrett said.

"Who is the Lady of Sorrow?" Thomas asked, not daring to blink as he observed Garrett's face. He wasn't going to stop learning unless someone forced him to stop. "Why are you searching for her?"

"Is that really important right now?" Garrett skittered farther away from Thomas's telepathy range. "We're about to be attacked by the biggest, baddest army in the universe. Dig down and be honest with yourself. Is now the best time for chitchat?"

"How were you able to lie in the Megacosm?" Thomas asked. That was a key question, right there. Garrett must have buried his emotions, his personal history, even his core values and beliefs, whenever he cruised the Megacosm. And he could not exist as a Blue Rank unless he was doing just that. Keeping major secrets while in the Megacosm was supposed to be impossible.

Garrett gave him a threatening glare.

"Megacosm?" Ariock reassessed his great-grandfather with a hurt look. "Are you . . . are you a Torth?" He hesitated before making the accusation, as if it was too horrible to contemplate.

"Nope," Garrett said. "Your supergenius friend just jumped to a wrong conclusion."

Thomas narrowed his eyes. He had absorbed enough of the old man's recent history to know that he was currently a Blue Rank who went by the moniker the Credible Witness. He owned a penthouse on the outskirts of Stratower City, with a heated swimming pool and nineteen slaves to serve him. The transport and slave on the far side of this wall belonged to him.

If Thomas was able-bodied, he would have trapped Garrett, or used powers to trap him, just to get some answers. Vocal speech was too painstakingly slow.

"Look," Garrett said to Ariock. "I can give you a safe window of fifteen or twenty minutes, but only if you get moving *now*." He whacked Ariock with his staff, then looked chagrined as the impact shivered through his arm. Ariock was unaffected by the blow and did not budge.

"Run!" Garrett regained his balance.

Still, Ariock hesitated, concern etched on his face. It must feel unreal to him that someone else was offering to protect him. He had always been the protector. He'd always been self-reliant, with no one else who could shoulder his burdens.

An ominous rumble overcame the sound of rain. The rain itself was blocked from above, cut off by an increasing mass of armored transports.

"*Aonswa?*" Jinishta said. "Let's retreat underground. It is too dangerous here."

The Alashani warriors cowered and watched the fleet with terrified eyes. They had to squint against the increasingly bright artificial lights.

"Let's go to the spaceport!" Vy yelled, tugging Ariock's wraps.

They might never get another chance to interrogate the old man or learn his secrets. What if the Torth destroyed Garrett? This might be his suicide.

It was plain that Ariock had similar concerns. "It just doesn't seem right," Ariock said, "to—"

Garrett interrupted with impatience. "I can hold my own against an army. Don't forget, I'm a storm god."

He swept his silver staff upward, and a shock wave spread throughout the clouds.

Transports careened into each other with a horrendous screeching of metal. Sparks rained down, and in the distance, a few twisted chunks of metal plummeted in a shriek of wind. Wreckage shattered in the tarry ruins of the dead city.

"Don't make me waste my efforts," Garrett growled over his shoulder. Wind whipped back his grime-streaked white hair. "Get going!"

The wind picked up, pushing debris across the ruination of the dead city.

Garrett lifted one hand, threads of excess energy whipping off him. The invisible extension of his hand became a dark mass of swift-moving clouds. The clouds sagged toward the ground in a dark funnel that gained speed, transforming into a monstrous pillar of debris.

The tornado sucked transports into its vortex. It spat them out as wreckage.

Garrett raised his staff, and missiles froze before they could strike him. Violent jabs of lightning stabbed more transports.

No doubt about it. He was purposely holding off the fleet, risking his life to help Ariock. The Torth Empire knew of only one living person who could make storms. They would assume that their opponent was Ariock.

At least for a while. They would get close enough to see the truth, eventually. Their bombardment was only going to get worse.

Vy and Jinishta were both yelling, trying to urge Ariock in opposite directions. It almost looked like the prophecy Migyatel had foreseen for the messiah—except Thomas was certain that Jinishta was not part of it. He had absorbed countless prophetic visions from Migyatel. Among them, he had seen what she predicted for Ariock: a high-stakes existential crisis that involved Vy versus another woman.

A winged woman.

In any case, this was just an ordinary crisis, and Ariock's gallant indecision was putting everyone in danger.

"He's right." Thomas resented Garrett for putting them in a situation with so few options. Couldn't he have shown up earlier, in the Alashani underground, rather than out in the open? Sure, Jinishta's people would have attacked him, and a battle like that might have caused a cave-in or some earthquakes . . .

"Ariock," Thomas called. "He's giving us this chance. We have to take it."

His piping voice rattled Ariock out of his uncertainty. Thomas was alive because Garrett had healed him. Garrett had proven his goodwill.

Bombs rained down, and explosions painted the night with fire. Ariock used his powers to levitate the wagon bed platform. Vy hopped aboard, securing the battered NAI-12 case and Thomas as well. Kessa and Varktezo joined them. Ariock gestured toward Stratower City and took off running in that direction.

Thomas expected the Alashani cowards to run the other way. He was pretty sure that Flen, at least, wouldn't dare to follow the messiah any farther.

But Orla led the charge.

She magically gathered her spears and ran downslope, toward the Border River, alongside the levitating platform. Jinishta adjusted her veil, hiding her face, and followed. So did Shassatel, Aral, Tavish, Yavin, Henshta, and finally Flen. He scooped Cherise up in his arms, no doubt boosting his own meager strength with Yeresunsa power.

Weptolyso and Yuey loped on all fours. They kept pace with the flying wagon bed platform and everyone else.

Varktezo watched the receding silhouette of Garrett as he flung lightning at the fleet. Thomas mentally peered through the ummin's eyes. He needed to meet that old sorcerer again.

He was going to find a way to soak up every tidbit of secret knowledge that Garrett was hiding.

CHAPTER 10

WINDSWEPT FURY

Ariock figured he could use his powers to part the roiling moat at the base of the wall.

But how long could he hold back thousands of tons of sludge? He didn't know. He had never tried anything on that scale. He didn't know if he could manage it while simultaneously scaling the wall and carrying his friends.

Rib cages and other rotting matter floated in the breakneck current. It really must be toxic, if it killed wild zoved.

A temporary bridge over the Border River might be more prudent than parting its waters.

Still running, Ariock slid his awareness into the debris field, seeking any object flat enough to offer traction. Layers of muck cemented ancient debris in place. Ariock pried loose each useful bit, then flew each item into his field of view. He shoved them together in a haphazard way.

The wall loomed like a frozen tidal wave, possibly built from the same indestructible material as starship hulls. Delicate electronics perched on spiky parapets. Those might be motion detectors or cameras, so Ariock smashed the nearest ones with hammers of air. Garrett was expecting him to be sneaky.

Explosions rocked the borderland. One fiery bomb blew up dangerously close by.

Ariock skidded to a halt and poured all his focus into his makeshift walkway on top of the wall. The wind was becoming a hurricane, so forceful that it might hurt his smallest friends. He reinforced the narrow causeway, using his powers to wedge interlocked pieces tighter together.

"I can carry Vy," Weptolyso offered, halting next to Ariock.

"And I will carry the ummins," Yuey said.

Ariock gave them each a grateful look. He supposed he would carry Thomas himself.

Vy climbed onto Weptolyso's back with aid from Yuey. She held on tight, determined. The big nussian moved with care.

"I will take Thomas, too," Weptolyso offered.

"Really?" Ariock hoped he wasn't expecting too much.

"It is my honor." Weptolyso sounded like he meant it. He tucked Thomas against his immense chest plate, careful not to crush the fragile boy.

Ariock made his way up the creaking surface of his makeshift bridge. He tested each interlocked piece before he stepped onto it, ensuring that the bridge would hold together with scant concentration from him.

A shrieking gale of wind threatened to topple him.

Ariock widened his bubble shield. He kept his balance while shoring up the ramp. His warrior training enabled him to focus on many critical problems at once. Soon he was atop the wall itself. He made room for his friends.

They hustled up the walkway, single file. Weptolyso, Yuey, then Cherise and the warriors.

As Ariock waited, he glanced back at his mysterious and powerful great-grandfather. Lightning superbolts branched from Garrett's staff, snaking horizontally across miles, electrocuting everything in their path. Missiles screamed toward the lone figure. Garrett threw the fury of the Torth right back at them.

Like me, Ariock thought.

He no longer had any doubt. This was Jonathan Stead, the hero who had freed a thousand prisoners from the Isolatorium. Garrett webbed lightning and summoned ropy tornadoes, each strike timed with precision.

Ariock felt small in comparison. He could learn more efficient methods of winning just by watching Garrett's movements.

Someone tapped his shoulder. He looked over to see Vy, perched on Weptolyso's spinal ridge.

"The ladder down is there!" she shouted over the wind, pointing.

Cherise was already on her way down, hand over hand on the rungs. About four stories below, a lone transport waited in the shadows, parked behind an industrial-looking bulkhead. Two dimmed neon-blue racing stripes made it visible. Otherwise, its running lights were off.

Ariock gestured for his friends to hurry down the ladder. "I'm right behind you."

Jinishta paused. She sized up Stratower City like it was an impossible opponent in a sparring match.

"You can go home, Jinishta," Ariock reminded her, hoping she would. "This is your last chance."

Jinishta tore her gaze away from the sky-blocking immensity of the Stratower to focus on Ariock. "We will not flee. We are with you, no matter what."

Flen wilted. He probably wished Jinishta hadn't said that.

Well, whatever. Ariock figured the time to talk them out of it was past. The silly warriors were going to need to confront daylight for the first time, once they all got to some foreign planet.

Not Earth.

Poor Vy. She just wanted to go home, to see her mom again. She daydreamed about it a lot.

Deep down, Ariock knew that he wasn't a part of her daydreams. He wasn't dating material. He probably wouldn't fit through the door of the Hollander home unless he ducked and twisted. Vy found excuses to sit near him, to casually touch him, but anyone could guess why.

She loved his protection. She loved his powers.

But she wasn't crazy. Vy wasn't going to get intimate with a giant. Ariock knew that. Once she felt safe, she would probably push him away and hook up with an Alashani or someone else who might be considered normal.

Like Cherise. She had entirely quit her relationship with Thomas, and her trust issues were probably just an excuse to escape alien weirdness. Ariock figured that deep down, Cherise didn't want intimacy with a mutant who was many degrees removed from being a standard human. She had chosen Flen because Flen acted like a normal guy.

Buildings groaned as a shock wave rolled through Stratower City. The wall quivered. Ariock glanced back at his only living family member. Was Garrett sacrificing himself just so that Ariock could survive?

Why?

And what did Ariock have to look forward to, if he made it to the safe haven of a reject planet? A boring retirement where he felt lonely and rejected?

A waterspout lurched out of the toxic river, sucking muck and rain into itself and swelling at an alarming rate. Garrett sent it crashing over transports. Amid all the explosions and wreckage and thunder, the old man seemed to be bellowing with manic laughter.

Ariock knew the giddy joy of battle. When he was a giant of wind and lightning, he was unconstrained by mortal limitations.

How would that freedom feel if he didn't need to worry about accidentally hurting friends nearby?

Part of Ariock yearned to leap down and join Garrett.

Really, it seemed wrong to abandon his great-grandfather in such a vicious battle, so soon after meeting him. It was his fault that Garrett was getting hammered. He had been idiotic to attack the old man with lightning and shock waves. Shouldn't he have guessed the truth?

This whole situation was his fault. The Torth wanted to kill him, not Garrett.

What if he lost his only family?

Ariock thought of his mother's body, lightweight in his arms, dead because of his stupidity. Garrett had protected three generations of the Dovanack family. Did he need to sacrifice himself like this now? Just for Ariock?

I'm not willing to lose him, Ariock realized. Not like this. Not when they'd just met, with so many unanswered questions.

His friends waited at the getaway transport. They had opened the door, a rounded triangular hole, and a terrified four-armed govki emerged. Cherise appeared to be speaking to the furry slave, calming it down.

Ariock didn't need to use the rung ladder. He jumped to the ground, infusing his body with enough strength to absorb the shock of landing.

People jumped in surprise at the impact.

When Ariock straightened, unhurt, they resumed a worried conversation. The sporty-looking vehicle was too small for so many passengers. Weptolyso and Yuey weren't even going to fit through the open door.

Ariock wondered why Garrett had provided him with the equivalent of a Lamborghini. Why not something practical, like a cargo truck? The nice upholstery was bound to get ruined, anyway, between muck-drenched wraps and nussian thorns and spikes.

Ariock reached inside with his powers and crumpled luxury seats.

He gripped the door frame and weakened a section of the metal hull so that he could twist and snap that whole side of the vehicle away. He hollowed out everything, including bolts and flooring. That should make enough room to fit two nussians.

Ariock gently took Thomas and placed him on the pilot's seat. It was built for an adult pilot, but maybe Vy could hold Thomas on her lap or something?

"Go ahead," Ariock said, gently helping Vy to climb off Weptolyso. "Pack inside."

Unburdened, Weptolyso wriggled into the transport through its ruined doorway. He had to crawl on his armor-plated belly to fit. Nussians rarely went horizontal—they even slept upright—but Weptolyso did not complain as he squirmed to make room for Yuey.

She grumbled, but she managed to fit next to him. At least both nussians understood the need. This wasn't about blind faith in the messiah. It was about doing what was best to help their friends.

Everyone else packed in with grimaces of discomfort. The warriors sat as far from Thomas as they could get, huddled next to the nussians. Vy lifted Thomas onto her lap.

Ariock tucked the NAI-12 medicine case into the seat well near her leg.

Vy's worried gaze met Ariock's. "Can you keep up?"

Vy must realize—they all did—that Ariock wasn't going to fit inside the overcrowded transport.

Ariock sensed life sparks hidden behind fortified walls. The Torth had not evacuated their city, and he imagined overconfident civilian Torth creeping about their usual business, getting massages or having feasts or watching gladiators tear each other to bloody shreds.

Why? Because Torth always won.

At their core, most Torth were lazy, smug cowards. They would not expect their enemy to suddenly gain a powerful partner.

"I'm going to help Garrett," Ariock decided.

Vy gaped at him.

"No!" Thomas pleaded from her lap. "Please don't! You're supposed to help us escape this planet! Garrett told you to!"

Ariock patted the roof of the transport reassuringly. "I'm tired of hiding and running away."

That was an understatement. He was sick to death of it. Prisoners cowered and hid and ran. He didn't want to spend his life with a prisoner's mentality.

"Thomas will get you to the spaceport," he assured his friends. "And into a ship."

With a supergenius who had Yeresunsa powers, plus eight Alashani warriors, they should be able to defeat a few surprised Red Ranks, or even some Servants of All. They could surely stay safe for twenty minutes on their own.

"Oh." Ariock had nearly forgotten the car keys Garrett had given him. He dropped the tiny data stick onto the dashboard.

"I'll meet you at the spaceport on top of the Stratower," he said. "With Garrett."

"He's giving us this chance to escape!" Thomas cried with desperation.

"How will he escape, himself?" Ariock pointed out.

Thomas sputtered. There was no answer. Garrett was probably sacrificing himself in some noble, heroic way.

Once Ariock joined him in battle, however . . . this could turn into something better than a desperate fight for survival. Ariock could double or even triple the amount of force that Garrett was outputting. He was sure of it. He could turn this battle into a victory. A victory for slaves and prisoners and nontelepaths. Maybe something with long-lasting repercussions.

Ariock longed to put himself into the unbridled rage of six-hundred-mile-per-hour winds. He and Garrett together could probably stop an armada.

Vy gave Ariock a look of wounded betrayal. "Don't abandon us," she begged.

Ariock had never seen her look that way before. Angry and hurt, because of him.

"I'm not abandoning you," he said. "I'll catch up in fifteen minutes. Or…" He needed to learn Garrett's mysterious tricks. "I'll find you, no matter where you are in the universe. I promise. If I don't show up fast enough, just do what you need to and get off this planet."

Everyone stared at him with disbelief.

Ariock didn't have time to find the right words. "Thomas?" he said. "Please keep everyone safe."

With that, he left, springing toward the rung ladder. He couldn't look at their shocked faces any longer or else he would lose his bloodlust to kill Torth. And that wasn't fair to Garrett.

Enough people had sacrificed their lives to protect Ariock Dovanack. He couldn't let Garrett be another casualty.

He pulled himself to the top of the wall in flying leaps and vaulted over the toxic river. As he landed on the far side, he spread his awareness, billowing into wind and rain and ionized energy.

His last human thought was a realization that he'd forgotten to tell the Alashani why he had put a mind reader in charge. They had no idea that Thomas, the disabled child whom they had held prisoner, had Yeresunsa powers.

Oh, well. They would figure it out.

CHAPTER 11

NOT THAT EVIL

Thomas gazed at the blank, powered-off dashboard and struggled to cordon off his infuriated feeling of helplessness, apart from everyone else's. The nearby brew of emotions was overwhelming. Nobody wanted to be in this situation.

Especially not him.

"*Please keep everyone safe.*" Ariock had no right to dump that on Thomas. In a crisis amid people who mistrusted or hated him, Thomas was supposed to . . . what? Perform admirably? Turn into a hero? Thomas just wanted to curl up and let other people handle the problems.

"Is this machine supposed to levitate?" Orla asked with hesitance. Her people lacked words for hovering, flight, or anything to do with skies.

"Yes." Vy searched for a place to plug in the data stick. "I just need to figure out how to use the ignition key."

"Torth are coming," Kessa warned. She sat up front with them, wedged next to Varktezo and the extremely confused govki slave. She pointed at armored figures in the distance, running through rain-soaked darkness toward the wall.

Red Ranks.

One of them must have spotted the parked transport, because a few dozen swiftly changed direction, like a flock of birds. They were going to investigate. Thomas estimated they would arrive within the next forty seconds.

Vy swore. "Thomas?" She showed him the data stick. "Help?"

Well, no one else was going to learn how to pilot a transport in the next thirty-eight seconds.

Thomas snatched the data stick and tossed it into the ignition pan. The dashboard lit up, holographic displays materializing near his face. Vy adjusted him on her lap, giving him easy reach of the controls.

A mapped route to the spaceport lit up, with an autopilot option, and a highlighted destination docking bay.

It seemed Garrett Dovanack had preplanned this rescue. He had saved Thomas's life in the bargain, and he had managed to do it all without endangering the Alashani civilization. A masterful plan.

Except Garrett had failed to take a few things into consideration. He had failed to imagine an escape crew that included two nussians, judging by the size of the vehicle he'd provided. And Garrett had completely underestimated Ariock's reckless streak and heroic savior complex.

Thomas would have helped him to avert these pitfalls, had he been consulted.

Red Ranks swarmed toward the transport. The Yeresunsa warriors readied their spears, exuding a dark willingness to kill or be killed. They were fatalistic. They were ready to chew poison if they found themselves defeated.

Fascinating.

Thomas engaged the hoverdisk, so their vehicle levitated a few feet off the ground, which allowed clearance for the thrusters. He couldn't help but savor the Alashani memories coming from the back seat. These albino warriors lived in sumptuous underground palaces, and they studied arcane mysteries. Sacred relics? Oh, he had to learn more about that. Torth historians collected relics from preconquest eras—Garrett was apparently one of those historians—but ancient history was a niche subfield within the Megacosm. Thomas yearned to dive into Jinishta's memories and explore everything she knew.

Later.

"Everyone hold on tight," Thomas said in the universal language of the slave tongue, "since we're missing a wall."

He pushed the transport up into the rainy night. It had a high-performance engine, and even overloaded, it flew faster than most people were comfortable with. One of the Alashani screamed in fear.

Varktezo, the adolescent ummin, was grinning. He watched every move Thomas made while also watching the city spin below them.

Thomas took care not to bank too hard as he followed the mapped route. But he flew fast, aware that the Red Ranks had probably glimpsed him. News of the Betrayer would spread through the Megacosm like wildfire.

His companions assumed that the big target was Ariock.

Even Ariock forgot that Thomas was just as much of a target—if not more so. The Torth Empire held collective memories of hunting and killing rogue Yeresunsa, but Thomas was their first and only rogue Yeresunsa who also happened to be a renegade supergenius. Many Torth, if not the Majority, would upvote the Betrayer as the top threat, even worse than the Giant. Never mind that he couldn't walk.

So Thomas flew low, minimizing their target profile. He skimmed over an endless-seeming rooftop, between slanted, twisted towers. He threaded through an archway bearded with stalactites. The ping-pong maneuvers made their vehicle hard to hit, and all the while, he tracked potential emergency landing sites.

He whipped around a curved tower, and his overclocked brain registered several threats. Armored white figures. With missile launchers.

Guided missiles arrowed toward their transport from thirteen different directions.

If Thomas possessed storm powers like the Dovanacks, he would have blasted the missiles backward and shielded their vehicle. But he had no shielding power. He was unable to create storms or manipulate electromagnetic energy, and he wasn't telekinetic. He had not practiced his fireball power. Anyhow, extra fire would not save them from fiery explosions.

Thomas mapped trajectories and calculated maneuvers in the split second before things exploded. Avoidance was impossible.

"Tighten your grip on everything right now," he said.

Then he nosed their transport downward in time to avoid two missiles, which collided with each other instead of with their vehicle.

The explosion slammed them with a bone-jarring impact and a cloud of fire. Vy held Thomas tight enough that he didn't tumble off her lap and out the ruined doorway.

He fixed his entire focus on the holographic controls, measuring altitude changes against velocity, struggling to keep them aloft.

A missile slammed into the altitude thruster.

Thomas saw it coming through the eyes of Kessa, who did not have time to cry out. He got just enough warning to set up an emergency landing routine. Momentum would carry them over that drainage canal. They would plow to a stop in the muck along the next slightly curved roof.

People screamed as the transport spun and dropped from the impact. Thomas spun menu options, setting up a landing glide and finalizing their trajectory, with wind and wobble taken into account.

Then he buried his face against Vy and braced for the impact.

He felt cheated. He hadn't really wanted this second chance at life, so unexpected and undeserved, but he did want to rescue the Lady of Sorrow. And he did want a chance to soak up the rest of Garrett's secrets. He wanted to learn things. Instead . . .

Was he fated to die the way his nameless mother had died?

He almost wished Migyatel's final prophetic vision would come true. Better that than the Isolatorium.

Her dying vision had unnerved him more than he wanted to admit, even to himself. Migyatel had foreseen hordes of zombified Torth under his absolute command. The Megacosm cracked and burned in the presence of a monstrous new sort of Commander of All Living Things: an older version of Thomas, able-bodied and teenaged, and still a supergenius. His future self shadowed the galaxy and changed planets. He was a master of beasts and a master of mind readers.

It can't happen, Thomas reminded himself. Even if he somehow survived today, he wasn't ever going to become able-bodied. Nor would he ever use armies of mentally enslaved people as his own personal meat shields. He wasn't that evil.

Their crippled transport slammed against a sludge-slick roof.

They bounced, careened sideways, and screeched through a half a mile of muck. No one dared to speak. Their broken vehicle stopped at a drunken angle.

There was nowhere to hide and no time. Armored Torth flooded onto the rooftop around them, leaping out of bulkhead doors or jumping down from cargo carriers. Red Ranks surrounded the crashed vehicle before it slid to a complete stop. They took aim, and judging from the lack of blasts, Thomas knew they were going to capture rather than kill their quarry.

"Spears won't penetrate their armor," Thomas said, speaking to the Alashani in the back seat. "They will try to inhibit our powers with microscopic darts, and they'll throw grabber balls that can turn into nets to trap you. Our best chance of survival is for you to use your powers to strip off their weaponized gloves. You can—"

Jinishta interrupted him in an icy tone. "Who made you the premier?"

"We do not take orders from a *rekveh*," Flen added.

All the Alashani glared at Thomas with disgust and hatred. One of them crossed her middle fingers in a sign to ward off evil.

Superstitious idiots.

But not a surprise. Thomas shrugged and gave up.

"Your messiah put Thomas in charge for a reason." Vy twisted around, glaring at Jinishta.

"To haul the vehicle," Jinishta retorted. "Now that the *rekveh* caused us to crash? A warrior needs to be in charge. I am our only hope of survival."

"We could silence the *rekveh*," Yavin suggested, drawing his curved knife.

"Don't you dare." Kessa put herself between the warriors and Thomas, protective.

Cherise emanated shame, but although she wanted to speak in defense of Thomas, she remained silent.

Thomas gritted his teeth and endured her love for Flen. He had no right to feel jealous or resentful. He had no right to feel anything for Cherise. So what if he would never meet anyone like her again—a person whose beautifying worldview helped lift away his own cynicism? And so what if Flen was a less-than-ideal boyfriend for her?

Anyone was a better boyfriend than Thomas. The toxic rain was healthier.

"We must kill these Torth," Jinishta commanded. "Spears!"

All eight warriors poured out of the transport, hurling their spears as fast as possible.

It didn't go well for them. The spears bounced off armor. The Red Ranks glanced at each other, faceless due to their helmets, but no doubt expressing surprise in the Megacosm.

Smoky clouds churned in a tower over the horizon, strobed by lightning. The Dovanacks were causing a major storm.

The Red Ranks began to throw grabber balls at the black-clad figures. Soon they were netting Alashani warriors and circling closer toward Thomas.

If he survived this battle . . . ? Well, if he could survive this, then maybe he would give a little bit of credence to Migyatel's version of his future.

CHAPTER 12

DUAL DOVANACKS

Ariock was the size of a storm. His shoulders towered as clouds, and his voice was thunder. His limbs were ever-morphing curtains of wind and rain. Against him, the Torth were puny weaklings, barely noticeable as individuals.

They forbade their slaves and victims to have voices. So he would enjoy squashing Torth. No mercy. Let them throw all their force at him. He was a force of nature. Unstoppable. Invincible. He wasn't going to rest until every last Torth on this planet was dead.

Very distantly, as if heard through a wind tunnel, a tiny voice screamed words into his mortal ear.

A friend?

Well, he was busy. Transports kept replacing the ones he swatted down, adding to the heaps of smoldering wreckage. Metallic underbellies spewed missiles. Would the pests ever give up?

The human part of Ariock recalled that this planet was specifically a training ground for Servants of All, the military ranks who hunted and killed rogue Yeresunsa like himself. They had herded him here. Trapped him here.

He would make them regret it.

The nearby man continued yelling at him. Ariock struggled to identify the voice.

Ah, right. His heroic great-grandfather.

Ariock downsized, keeping half his attention on the storm and the enemy missiles while shielding himself with air.

"I told you to run!" Garrett screamed at him. "Get out of here! Go, go, go!" He used his powers to shove Ariock repeatedly, with enough force to cause a train wreck.

Ariock rooted himself to the ground. With the ever-increasing number of enemies to fight, it was asinine to waste energy on an argument. Annoying. "I'm not leaving without you," he explained.

"You idiot!" Garrett seethed.

Ariock tried not to take offense. His ancestor was overreacting, but soon enough, Garrett would calm down and understand that victory was within their grasp. They could defeat this army together. As a family.

"We are not invincible." Garrett huffed out angry, measured words. "Every Torth you kill gets revered in the Megacosm as a heroic martyr. That's the whole point. They're wearing us down. Their army stays fresh while we don't!"

Garrett certainly looked tired and worn down. Judging by the grime that streaked his hair, his personal shielding had faltered.

But Ariock felt as strong as ever.

He swelled his awareness across the battlefield. Thousands of life sparks brushed through him, like feathers on his skin, revealing where he needed to get to work on killing Torth. He raised a thick arm, and electricity crackled around the invisible extension of himself.

"They're going to change tactics!" Garrett yelled. "Trust me. I spy on the Megacosm, and they're sending nuclear bombs this way."

Was Garrett trying to scare him? It only made Ariock more determined to protect his great-grandfather. He wasn't going to leave an old man alone to face a nuclear arsenal.

"I gave you fifteen minutes for a perfect escape," Garrett said. "Now that's gone. You wasted it! Agh. Let's just think for a second."

Ariock took a step, making the ground quake. Red Ranks fell. Ariock found fissures underground. He heaved them apart as easily as splaying his hands, and the toxic river overflowed. Red Ranks slipped and drowned.

"I'm helping you," Ariock patiently explained.

"I had this handled." Garrett glared. "Now we're trapped, you idiot. What were you thinking? You can't retreat underground, because the Torth would chase you into the Alashani realm. So what is your escape plan? Are you going to wreck your way through Stratower City? You'd end up killing millions of innocent slaves."

That was, unfortunately, a valid criticism. The dreary towers of Stratower City hid opulent innards. Millions of hopeless slaves lived and suffered there, serving cruel Torth masters.

"How were you planning to end the battle here?" Ariock asked.

His reasonable question seemed to stoke Garrett's fury. "I was going to escape!" Garrett fumed. "But I can only save myself! I can't take anyone with me!" His voice went higher, like he was strangling. "If you had just— Agh! Where are your friends?" Garrett looked wild. "Where did you leave them?"

"They're heading toward the spaceport." Ariock figured that all the Torth attention was focused on himself and Garrett. His friends would stay safe.

He was rain. He was clouds. He was microdarts and smoldering destruction. When he swept his arm, transports smashed into each other, falling to crush enemy soldiers.

Did the Torth think they could wear him down? His strength was as endless as an ocean. Let them batter themselves against his power. They would erode.

"You can't wear down the Torth Empire!" Garrett yelled, his wet hair plastered to his head. "You're not a force of nature. You're a person. And your buddy Thomas is a bigger target than you are! In fact, he's in trouble. They got shot down! The Torth are taking— Agh!"

Ariock waited for more. He couldn't spare much attention for a conversation, but a mind reader such as Garrett should realize that. No doubt he would continue as soon as he got over his apoplectic rage.

But Garrett did not go on.

Silence stretched out, and it occurred to Ariock that maybe Garrett had interrupted himself for a more serious reason. His great-grandfather stood in the downpour, gray-faced with shock.

He held one gloved hand clamped to the back of his head.

"Garrett?" Ariock redistributed his awareness into an amorphous shield that encompassed the old man as well as himself. "Are you hurt?"

Garrett pulled his hand away. His voice was as gray and tremulous as he looked. "My powers . . . are gone."

The inhibitor.

It was a disappointment, but Ariock straightened, relieved that Garrett was unharmed. It could be worse. With the Torth fleet pounding them both, he couldn't spare the full focus needed for a healing.

"They hit me with the inhibitor." Garrett sounded dazed, as if trying to make sense of his own words. "I thought they were too far away. I let my shield go."

"It's okay. I'll protect us." Ariock pumped more focus into his own shield, extra wary of the invisible microdarts flying through the air.

"I got distracted," Garrett whispered hoarsely. "I'm so sorry. I was focused on . . . ugh. It doesn't matter now." He swayed, as if he might keel over from old age. "We're doomed. It's all over."

"What were you saying about Thomas?" Ariock thickened his shield as a missile smashed into it. Fire plumed around the perimeter, leaving him and Garrett cool and untouched. "Are my friends all right?"

"No, you dolt. They're in terrible danger." Garrett leaned on his staff, shoulders slumped in defeat. "I gave you simple instructions. Instead, you mucked everything up. You were supposed to—"

"Where are my friends?" Rage rippled through Ariock, snapping out in electrical spikes. Vy and Thomas, Jinishta, Weptolyso and Kessa and Cherise... if the Torth captured them, they could be injured or worse.

And the Torth would learn about the Alashani.

They would invade the beautiful lamplit cities and destroy millions of people. All his albino cousins. All those free-born nussians and ummins and other species.

"We can't save them," Garrett said. "I'm sorry. Let's find somewhere to hide, and we'll rescue the survivors later. If we can."

If?

Ariock stared at his supposedly heroic great-grandfather. Had Garrett forgotten how to take risks?

"Let's go," Ariock said. "I'm saving them. Show me where they are. Lead the way."

Garrett gave him a look as if he'd lost his mind.

But Ariock couldn't imagine giving up. Not while he wielded immense power. He had spent most of his life feeling helpless. He wasn't going to abandon Vy and everyone else at the first hint of a problem. He wasn't that fragile.

"Take me to my friends," Ariock demanded.

"I don't have powers right now." Garrett demonstrated by hobbling a few steps, leaning on his staff as a cane.

It seemed the arthritis and crooked leg were legitimate.

Ariock picked up his frail great-grandfather in one arm and sprinted toward Stratower City. He arrowed lightning through the mob of Red Ranks, knocking Torth off their feet like bowling pins. Helmets muffled their screams.

Missiles exploded against his shielding.

He began to shove missiles away with counterforce, making them explode against Red Ranks.

"I can't believe I let you distract me." Garrett was muttering to himself. "I can't believe I let my guard down like that. We're going to die."

That sounded like a melodramatic overreaction to Ariock, but he had no time to criticize. He threw himself into a mighty leap and sailed over the toxic river. He grabbed the lip of the wall with one hand, levered himself up, and landed on his feet.

"You're a target!" Garrett shouted to be heard over the wind and the explosions. "If you drop your shield even for a second, they're likely to hit you with a microdart."

Ariock leaped to a long rooftop, jarring Red Ranks out of his path with his impact.

A missile exploded against his shield in a shower of sparks and billowing flames. He thickened his shield against the heat and black smoke.

"If you lose your powers," Garrett shouted, "try to get a visit from the Lady of Sorrow. She might be our only hope."

"Isn't she just an Alashani myth?" Ariock took a running leap and landed on another building. He skidded in muck and kept running, shielding himself from microdarts and blasts, slightly off-balance with Garrett tucked under his arm.

"She'll come to you," Garrett said, "if you're dying and alone and utterly hopeless. That's when she's most likely to show up."

That sounded like nonsense to Ariock.

Life sparks ran at him, and he had to throw all his focus into self-defense. If only he had bandwidth for a conversation.

He did recall Thomas swearing that he had been visited in the dungeon pit by a weeping mind reader. Thomas claimed that he had rejected her offer of mystical powers. Ariock secretly figured it must have been a fever-induced hallucination.

Garrett kept talking. "She lent me the power to break free from the Isolatorium. She saved me. It was all her. She gave me the power to free all those prisoners."

Ariock tried to process what Garrett was saying. Someone else was responsible for his great feats? Someone else—the Lady of Sorrow—had freed a thousand slaves and killed a thousand Torth? She was the great hero?

The entire legend of Jonathan Stead was a lie?

Why had Garrett taken credit for it?

Maybe the old man was just babbling nonsense in his terror. Maybe he was senile. How could a mythical deity like the Lady of Sorrow be a real person?

Ariock wished he could suck up the truth, like Thomas. Guesswork was nothing without trust, and he simply didn't know Garrett well enough to get a sense of how trustworthy he was.

"Am I going the right way?" Ariock demanded, annoyed that he had to ask. Thomas would have given directions without needing any prompting.

"I told you," Garrett said, "we can't win here. It would be smart to hide. We could rescue your friends later, when we get a chance to be sneaky about it."

Ariock wasn't going to cower in a sewage shaft while his friends were murdered and hauled to the Isolatorium. How could Garrett think that was acceptable? What was wrong with him?

Not a hero.

"The Torth won't kill Thomas right away," Garrett said. "I'll bet they'll keep Vy alive, as well."

For torture.

Maybe Garrett, aka Jonathan Stead, had never been a hero. Maybe he had lied and cheated his way into legend status, taking credit for what a truer hero had done. Maybe the Torth armor he wore reflected his true persona.

After all, Garrett was a mind reader.

Their kind all seemed corrupt. Anyone who looked at the Alashani underground and compared it to the galactic Torth Empire could see which was more wholesome.

Ariock slowed down, trying to control his rage. He wanted to fight everything in sight. He could cause towers to buckle, canals to crack, but that would kill too many innocent slaves.

Missiles slammed his shielding.

One part of him struggled to figure out where Vy and his other friends were, while another part fretted about protecting Garrett and getting directions. Meanwhile, he was the rain-soaked air, and the missiles, and the storm above.

He felt battered. More than anything, he had to stay aware of every life spark that came close to his core self. Microdarts and missiles were dangerous, but Torth were the biggest danger. He must not allow anyone within striking range. Half a second of a pain seizure could disable him long enough for his shield to dissolve. Then he would get hit with inhibitor and be powerless. Like Garrett.

Except he would lose everything if he fell. More than just his life. Everyone he cared about would suffer and die.

"That way." Garrett pointed with reluctance. "They're behind that tower."

Ariock lowered his head and ran. Between the mad dash and his personal shielding, his awareness was stretched very thin.

He jumped a chasm and kept running, not winded, his muscles infused with Yeresunsa power. The bombardment was reaching an uncomfortable threshold. It felt like working the steam-powered aqueduct. He had no room in his mind for anything extra.

"We're dead anyway," Garrett said. "This is one big, fat failure."

Red Ranks vanished into hatches. Was it Ariock's imagination, or were the Torth suddenly running away from him?

Overhead, transports lifted higher, vanishing into cloud cover.

Torth raced through vault doors, disappearing from sight. The wind grew colder from the lack of fiery explosions.

"We need shelter!" Garrett screamed. "Go inside! We can't be out here!"

At that moment, Ariock caught sight of a desperate battle on a distant rooftop, around the crashed transport. His friends were trapped by hundreds of armored Torth.

He flooded his awareness toward them, desperate to shield everyone from the nuclear detonation he sensed was sure to come. He had no choice at all. If he failed, no one else would save them.

Perhaps now, under pressure, Garrett would share his secret defense? He had implied that he could escape the Torth.

"How were you planning to escape?" Ariock no longer needed to shout quite so loud.

"I can teleport!" Garrett yelled.

Teleport.

It took Ariock a moment to decipher that word, to recall movies and books with characters who could vanish and reappear elsewhere.

No wonder Garrett was hard to kill. That was a useful superpower. As a telepath, Garrett could sense attacks coming, and he could vanish on a whim.

But not now.

His powers were disabled.

Garrett sounded close to tears. "We're doomed."

Several thoughts flashed through Ariock's mind. Teleportation was feasible. But the Torth weren't going to ease off their attack, so there was no time for a lesson.

In fact, the Torth must have seen the Giant and his famous ancestor fighting together, with double the storm power. They would try to destroy both Dovanacks with every weapon in their arsenal.

That was why those distant Red Ranks were still hammering Ariock's friends, even as he sensed an impending heaviness in the sky. The Red Ranks fought on, seemingly oblivious to the shrieking hum that echoed between thunderheads. They were counting on Ariock to absorb a nuclear bomb while they got their job done.

Because that was what Torth did. They strove to appease the Majority no matter what. Winning was their only acceptable outcome.

Ariock realized, with a sinking feeling, that this battle was only just getting started.

CHAPTER 13

TARGETED

Thomas hurled wildfire. Or he tried to. Either he had not properly mastered the Yeresunsa trick of extending awareness, or his range had a limitation. His wildfire burned whatever solid material it encountered first. With the cracked windshield in his way, he had to aim his attacks through the torn-off door.

And his flames died quickly in the humid air. Golden plumes did engulf a couple of the Red Ranks, but it hardly fazed them.

Their armor was fireproof.

All he could do was his best. He raised his small hands and aimed wildfire at Red Ranks whenever he had a clear shot.

Jinishta hurled herself inside the transport and leaned over the pilot seat's backrest, staring at Thomas. "You're a Yeresunsa?" Her eyes bulged with shock as she reassessed everything she thought she knew about him. Bewilderment radiated off her.

"Yep," Thomas confirmed.

Red Ranks tossed grabber balls, netting black-clad warriors. Their own armor emanated signals that repelled the balls.

Thomas wished he had prioritized learning warrior skills instead of absorbing Alashani cultural traditions. Crafts? Theater? Stonemasonry? What frivolities! He dug through Jinishta's memories, learning how to kill.

Intense emotions helped Yeresunsa go into killing mode. Hm. Thomas tried to work up a sense of justified outrage, but he just wasn't feeling it. He was too concerned about tracking the ever-shifting melee. Although he could predict much of the action, even the raindrops, the warriors moved unpredictably. He didn't want to cook one of them by accident.

One of the netted warriors busted free.

Then another, and another. They somersaulted to collect their spears.

The Red Ranks hesitated in unison. Helmets hid their faces, but Thomas could guess at their surprise. How were their black-clad opponents so mighty? Did the little warriors magically have the strength of nussians?

The warriors were revealing too much about their powers.

And too little. Superstrength and superagility could be dismissed as a quirk of nature. The Alashani dared not use telekinesis or lightning here. They would rather die than alert the Torth Empire to the fact that rogue Yeresunsa were surviving in secrecy.

Vy yanked on her blaster glove.

That was more effective than spears. When Vy took aim and shot a Torth in the head, he stumbled backward into his comrades. His helmet was a metallic mess. A charred hole gaped where his face should be.

Jinishta squeaked in shock. "How . . . ?" She definitely had not expected a useless cargo person to be more effective than a troop of Yeresunsa warriors.

"I figured we might need these gloves," Vy explained, her tone apologetic.

"Sorry, Premier," Varktezo added as he pulled on his own blaster glove. He blasted two Red Ranks in succession.

Jinishta's veil hid her face, but Thomas sensed her gaping shock.

There was a lot for her to process. She hadn't known that anyone could smuggle items out of the Yeresunsa monastery, let alone that the blaster gloves had that much firepower. She never would have expected a former slave to be handy with the evil weapons used by Torth.

And how had she missed the fact that the *rekveh* who had nearly died in her care had hidden a deadly power? A power that involved flames? She had never heard of such a thing.

Jinishta emanated a frustrated, overwhelming curiosity. "How . . . ?" Questions brimmed in her mind and threatened to spill over.

Thomas answered her topmost unspoken question. "I never tried to escape," he said, "because I promised Ariock and Kessa that I wouldn't cause trouble."

Jinishta's mind reeled. Mind readers were supposed to be the most selfish and greedy creatures in existence. She could not imagine why a *rekveh* would honor a promise that did not include any benefit for himself.

"I have more honor than most Alashani," Thomas said, mercilessly contradicting her wrong assumptions. "And if you want to win this battle, you'll need to fight smarter. How about if your warriors try to knock Torth off the edge of this building?"

Jinishta recognized a good idea when she heard it.

She hesitated for a moment more, still struggling against her own wrong assumptions. Then she leaned outside and bellowed the command to her warriors.

It wasn't exactly a stalemate out there. The Red Ranks tried to avoid the superstrong warriors, and most of them succeeded. They flung themselves toward the wrecked transport, hungry for the personal glory of capturing the Betrayer.

Amid the mob, Thomas caught glimpses of a woman in white armor. Her white cape rippled in the wind. Toothy nubs heightened the silhouette of her shoulders.

A helmet hid her curly blond hair and pouty facial features, but Thomas guessed who it was. No other Servants of All were risking their superior lives. This one prowled the perimeter of the battle like a moth drawn to flame.

The Swift Killer must yearn to stand victorious over the Betrayer.

She wanted to prove that her genetic pedigree wasn't as tainted as every Torth assumed it was. She wanted to vanquish the spawn of her disgraced clone sister.

Thomas attempted to cook her alive in her armor.

There were too many obstacles in the way. The Swift Killer merely swiveled to face the broken windshield of the transport. Had she sensed his thwarted attack? A bit of excess heat, perhaps?

A warrior screamed, suffering from a pain seizure.

That was bad news. If a Torth was close enough to torture one of the Alashani, then that Torth was close enough to read his mind. Close enough to gain an inkling of what sort of sapient he was.

The remaining warriors pressed against the hull, outnumbered and surrounded. Thomas sensed the minds of the nearest two. A throbbing headache emanated from both. They had been using their powers nonstop, hurling spears with bullet-like force and then retrieving those spears, while infusing their bodies with extra speed and strength, to shove Torth over ledges or to break free of telescoping nets. They were close to depletion. Their raw power was drained.

"We need Ariock." Thomas spoke his frustration out loud.

Weptolyso snorted from the far rear of their broken transport. "I will defend us."

He roared like a bear. The rear of the transport erupted, its shell splintering as Weptolyso and Yuey burst free to join the fight.

The pair of nussians picked up startled Red Ranks and threw them off the building. They bulldozed Torth away from the exhausted warriors.

But nussians made for big targets.

Within seconds, Yuey was grappling with a net. Mechanical legs gripped her and telescoped outward. Constricted, she toppled, slamming into muck.

Weptolyso bellowed his rage and tacked a Red Rank. Grabber balls stuck to his spinal ridge and began to hamper his movements.

Cherise saw how exhausted Flen was. She leaned over the seat. "Do you have any more blaster gloves?"

Vy handed her a packaged weapon.

"Don't," Thomas pleaded, but Cherise thought he was a coward. She thumbed the trigger and blasted a Torth's helmeted face, cratering it.

Several warriors struggled in nets. One of them, Orla, seemed to be suffering a pain seizure. She gave a mighty yell and busted free.

As she did so, bluish electricity snapped along her black-clad body.

"NO!" Jinishta cried in anguish.

It was too late.

The Torth saw the use of Yeresunsa powers. Every Red Rank in the vicinity stopped moving and swiveled their helmeted faces to stare at Orla. Even the Swift Killer was paying attention.

Thomas didn't need to ascend into the Megacosm. He knew that the Torth Majority must be abuzz, swapping replays of the lightning power display. They would make educated guesses about the black-clad primitives who possessed illegal powers.

It was over for the Alashani civilization. They were discovered.

Or they would be soon, probably by the end of today. All the Torth needed to do was probe the minds of their newly acquired prisoners. Shassatel. Yuey. Henshta.

If any supergenius Torth got a chance to probe Thomas's mind, they would learn quite a lot.

"Take this." Jinishta offered Thomas a carefully wrapped pellet. "Swallow it."

A suicide pellet.

During the past few months, Thomas would have done anything to earn a swift death. He had fantasized about it. Jinishta had no idea what a treasure she offered.

He nearly opened his mouth to accept the precious gift.

Only . . . well . . . Thomas was no longer sure that he wanted death. He wanted answers from Garrett Dovanack. He wanted to find the Lady of Sorrow, to ease her suffering. He wanted to learn more about the Alashani.

"Nope." Vy snatched the pellet. "Thanks, Jinishta. I'll give it to him if it's warranted."

Vy was lying. It was obvious.

Jinishta glared, but she had no time to argue. Her people were getting overwhelmed. Metallic nets tightened around Aral and Yavin, tightening in automatic jerks. The warriors writhed helplessly in the muck. They were too depleted to burst free.

Red Ranks approached them. If any Torth came too close, the warriors were likely to eat their suicide pellets, which they stored in their veils for easy access.

"Your suicide pact no longer applies." Thomas spoke quickly, trying to communicate a lot in a few seconds. "You can't protect the Alashani by dying anymore. You need to fight!"

Jinishta was no longer certain what to think of the creature named Thomas, or the cargo people. She gave up on trying to figure it out. Their broken vehicle was hardly enough shelter. She understood that the Torth were very likely going to scour the dead city and invade her homeland. What could she do?

She lunged outside with a snarl of despair.

A grabber ball hit her. Jinishta tore it away with power-enhanced strength, but another grabber ball snagged her wraps, telescoping into a bendable cage.

Cherise's cry of anguish was nearly lost amid the bellow of nussians and the downpour. Had she actually leaped outside?

Thomas extended his awareness, trying to locate her, but enemies and allies were a mess of indistinguishable data. He could not sense life sparks. That seemed to be something only Ariock was capable of.

The Torth began to spray the warriors with microdarts of inhibitor. Now that they understood what sort of opponents they faced, they were merciless.

Tavish drew his arm back to hurl a spear, but his arm disintegrated in a spray of blood.

Orla attempted to heal Tavish. She shrieked in primal rage as she lost access to her powers.

"Ariock will save us." Vy said it with feverish certainty. She curled around Thomas, shielding him with her body, ready with her blaster glove.

Thomas sensed her mind. Nothing he could possibly say would shake her faith. Vy trusted Ariock the same way the Alashani did. The only difference was that she didn't call him *messiah*.

Some of the captured warriors went silent and still. Had they swallowed poison? Fools. Didn't they realize that their suicide pact no longer applied?

"Thomas," Kessa said. "Can you not use your power to turn the Torth to our side?"

His other power.

His dark power.

Thomas didn't bother to explain the catch-22 problem. Zombification required all his vast concentration. He was helpless while twisting a mind. If any Torth got close enough for Thomas to turn it into a zombie, the victim would also be close enough to victimize Thomas with a pain seizure.

He was outmatched.

Invisible microdarts sprayed toward Thomas, over the netted bodies of his friends. Thomas seared them with superheated air. But more came at him, and more.

He would not be able to keep up his self-defense forever. Sooner or later, he would become just as depleted as the Alashani warriors.

Only one warrior remained in the fight. Thomas sensed Jinishta's mind, and she was exhausted, like an athlete forced beyond her limit of endurance. The warning headache was like lactic acid buildup in muscles or shortness of breath. It was a problem that required rest. Jinishta would collapse soon.

Red Ranks closed in.

CHAPTER 14

NEWSWORTHY

The Upward Governess ignored her breakfast buffet. She floated on a well-cushioned hoverdivan, overlooking her private indoor lake, where the wildlife was most active. But she hardly noticed the colorful mating displays or the exotic young animals playing in the marsh grass. Slaves in crisp gray uniforms paraded past her, offering savory and delicious delicacies. They were surprised by her rare obliviousness.

She was unwilling to peel even a sliver of her attention away from the faraway battle.

Her warnings to the Torth Empire had proven correct. The Betrayer and the Giant were alive and in a fighting mood.

But that wasn't the biggest shock to the Torth Empire.

Imposter! the Majority hissed.

The bearded visage of an old man—the Imposter!—bounced from mind to mind. His former associates shrank under the scrutiny of thunderous mental audiences.

He hid among Us!

Like a malignant tumor!

The Imposter!

But who would distrust a respectable historian? How was anyone supposed to know that the Credible Witness—a false identity!—was actually a traitorous rogue?

He had been so normal.

The Blue Rank heretofore known as the Credible Witness had been a law-abiding and, quite frankly, boring citizen of the Torth Empire. He had owned a typical number of slaves. He had spent a typical amount of time trading in forums, sleeping, and eating. Sure, he might have kept to himself, but so did everyone of his rank. Yes, he regularly took a few private minutes to think by himself after he woke up every day, but so did almost everyone in the cool color ranks, the Greens and Blues.

Throughout the Megacosm, Torth began to size each other up with newfound suspicions. If one renegade traitor could live among them . . . might there be others?

None of the supergeniuses had predicted this.

Not a single one had guessed that Jonathan Stead was still alive and hiding among Torth in plain sight.

I am certain that such traitors and rogues are rare, the Upward Governess assured anyone who cared to tune into her mind. Disunity was dangerous. Torth must remain largely in harmony, trusting one another, or else the whole Megacosm would grow unstable.

Fresh news from the battlefront interrupted the widespread suspicions. It seemed that a troop of Red Ranks had shot down the getaway vehicle. They had the Betrayer cornered. They had netted his protectors, and now they feasted upon those minds.

And what a smorgasbord it was.

!!!

There were underground cities full of free sapients.

With aqueducts.

There were entire cities populated by runaway slaves and savage primitives.

One of the veiled savages crackled with electric energy.

!!!!!!!!!

  Yeresunsa?!

The revelation slammed through the Megacosm like a volcanic eruption, destroying all other conversations in its path. *These cave primitives are rogue Yeresunsa!!!*

No wonder the savages were so supernaturally strong, so preternaturally agile. They had illegal powers! Were they Torth hybrids?

This news eclipsed everything else. Never mind the preparations to invade Earth. Humans were old news. Who cared about seven billion primitive humans when there was an unknown number of cave dwellers who had spread, cancer-like, within the very planet of origin of all Torth?!

How long had these pesky albinos existed?

A Red Rank eagerly dug into the mind of one of the captives. But even as the savage's memories began to yield tantalizing secrets, it died, gnashing a poison pellet.

It seemed the so-called Alashani cave dwellers had survived for unknown multitudes of generations.

Perhaps they had always been breeding and burrowing beneath the capitol homeworld of the Torth Empire? If so, they had gone undetected for far too long.

How many were there? No one had accurate estimates, but it seemed like a sizable population. More than one small city.

How powerful were they, as rogue Yeresunsa? No one knew. No one could even make an educated guess.

Altogether, the Megacosm was quaking with shock. This was like when the Betrayer escaped with the Giant, or when Jonathan Stead had escaped from the Isolatorium. This was an Event. And it was happening right now.

Every Torth wanted to participate. Comments zoomed back and forth, each striving to outshout the others. Torth quit whatever activities they were doing—shopping in forums, racing each other on hoverbikes, getting massages from multiarmed govki slaves—and paid attention. Some Torth were even generous enough to visit their sleeping neighbors and shake them awake. It would be a shame to sleep through news that changed the course of history.

Yet although the Torth Majority was enraptured, the Upward Governess found that she hardly cared about savages with powers. She hardly cared about runaway slaves hiding underground, or the existence of the Imposter, or the upcoming conquest of Earth, or the threat of the Giant. Those things did not affect her. The Giant was about to get smashed with a nuclear bomb, anyway.

All her focus was on the Betrayer.

He huddled in the shell of a ruined transport, barely protected by super-human primitives and runaway slaves. His wildfire attacks were feeble when compared with the feats the Giant was capable of. Perhaps he was holding back? But probably not. The way he kept trying the same ineffectual attacks implied a slave-like degree of frustration.

The Upward Governess used to try lifting her own plates and nectar cups, when she was very young, in a futile effort to prove, to herself, that she wasn't losing her physical strength quite as fast as everyone believed. She had long ago given up on that folly. It was a sign of desperation.

He was as good as captured.

Any second now, he would be hit with the inhibitor serum.

The Upward Governess nestled inside the minds of the Red Ranks who were creeping closer to the Betrayer and his remaining friends. They were so weak. So unprotected.

She could hardly wait to sense the Betrayer's despair as he got dragged to the Isolatorium. That would be a treat.

She wasn't interested in watching him scream from torture. Pain was never entertaining to her. But maybe, if she begged the highest ranks of the Torth Empire, they would grant her permission to travel to the Torth Homeworld so she could visit the Betrayer in person?

And then she would suck up his delectable mind one last time.

She could contain everything he had learned since he'd *(abandoned her)* left. It would be such a shame to lose the crumbs of his knowledge.

Too few people valued knowledge. They would just throw it away, the way they threw away excess food. Wastefulness, the Upward Governess thought, was why so few Torth bothered to rise in rank. They didn't care enough about acquiring more material luxuries and gardens and aquariums. They believed they already had enough.

They had small minds. Small imaginations. Very few Torth truly appreciated the wonders of life, the delicious flavors, the beauty, enough to collect those things, the way she did.

The Upward Governess selected a truffle from a tray of delicacies and took a chewy bite. She didn't want to distract the Red Ranks with her gargantuan mental presence. So she stayed in the background, passive. She was content to simply enjoy the show.

For now.

CHAPTER 15

ALL OF THEM

Ariock stretched his awareness toward his friends on that distant rooftop. It was hard to concentrate with Garrett screaming at him. "They're dead! We need to hide!"

Something strange tickled the uppermost zone of Ariock's awareness. An object fell toward him, and it seemed too fast, too heavy, too hot. It twisted in the air, unbalanced, too dense to be a missile.

Ariock heaved all his awareness upward. He understood what this was, and he slammed a fist of hurricane-force wind against it. The Torth would not win. Not while he—

The night flared brighter than a thousand suns.

The detonation shredded his thoughts. Bridges shattered like exploding glass. Canals dried up. Their muck peeled away like dead skin.

A scorching wind suctioned everything upward, adding to a vast cloud of radioactive debris. Ariock spread himself into a massive dome of protection a split second before the shock wave hit. He was air. He was buildings. Thousands of life sparks filled him, moving within him, but he could not guess who they were or what they were doing. His awareness was flayed.

He felt just as scorched as those canals and rooftops. It was all he could do to hold everything together. His lungs were on fire. He was on his knees. He couldn't breathe.

Radiation. He had to do something about the air. Otherwise they were all dead.

Over the roar of the nuclear column, someone faraway was screaming nonstop. An Alashani warrior? Ariock hoped the screams were from terror rather than a serious injury, because he had to maintain his superdense shield while finding clean air.

Cautious, he pushed part of his awareness outward, inhabiting wind and rain. He was nuclear fallout. He was sizzling vapor. He blew over smoldering debris, and he accidentally fanned unnatural flames, but it didn't matter, because he finally found cold and relatively normal air.

He pulled the clean air toward his core self.

At the same time, he shoved searing, irradiated air away. Lightning danced and thunder roared, but he couldn't allow flashes and thunder and screams to distract him.

He didn't know what else to do. This wasn't like the last time he'd been bombed. Last time, the nearly indestructible hull of an interstellar streamship had shielded him. Now his only protection was his rudimentary leatherwork armor and rubberized woolen wraps. He might as well be naked on the surface of the sun. He wanted to curl into a ball.

Instead, he forced himself to keep at it, second by second.

He was one distraction away from a catastrophe.

"Ariock?" Garrett touched his shoulder, concerned. "They're coming at us. Shooting microdarts."

Sure enough, armored Torth poured out of hatches, thumbing their blaster gloves. They came at Ariock from every direction.

They had taken a rest break, hadn't they? They had rested while he worked. The Torth had cowered, safe inside hull walls, when the nuclear bomb detonated.

It had never hit the city, thanks to Ariock. The buildings were undamaged. Had the Torth assumed that Ariock would risk his life to shield everyone?

Of course they had. They had supergeniuses who could guess exactly what the stupid Giant would do.

"You have to recover," Garrett said. "Quick."

Trillions of Torth must be watching him with unseen grins, swapping triumphant commentary in their minds. All silently judging him. Eager to see him pulverized. Just like the audience in the prison arena.

"We can hide in the slave Tunnels," Garrett was saying. "Drop us down into a canal, and we'll find a drainage pipe. You can yank off the grate and use your powers to get us through the sewage, and then we'll hide in a slave zone."

Running and hiding. Again.

Defeat. Again.

Was that his life?

Ariock got to his feet, although his body screamed in protest and his exhausted mind balked. He thickened his shield so nothing could touch him. No microdarts. No nuclear fallout. Not even rain.

Faraway screams added to the thunderous roar of the mushroom cloud. A sea of armored Red Ranks surrounded his friends. It looked like they were dragging people away in nets.

"They're baiting you," Garrett warned. "Don't go over there. Please, for once, just listen to reason."

A distant part of Ariock realized that his great-grandfather was right. His attention was stretched to its limit. The nuclear column roared, black and strobed by lightning, threatening his shield. The Torth were as fresh as ever, whereas Ariock . . .

Well. A couple more bombs like that would destroy him.

"No one ever wins against the Torth Empire." Garrett's tone was tinged with sympathy. "Believe me. A lot of people have tried."

Ariock sensed thousands of life sparks hidden within the nearest buildings. Were they enjoying the show?

The audience here had pitted Ariock against nuclear weapons instead of alien monstrosities, but it was the same thing as the arena. He was entertainment. Just a game. The Torth must see him as a rabid monster, lunging around with their wranglers while the audience stayed safe.

A few particularly intense life sparks clustered in a cupola atop a tower. Most people—humans, Alashani, slave species, and even Torth—had a certain vibrancy. This group seemed excessively potent. They felt like Garrett had when Ariock had first encountered the old man.

This group was at full strength. Healthy. Powerful.

On top of the world.

They had a good vantage point to view the battle.

Ariock imagined them as a bunch of Servants of All, smug, watching his friends get netted and dragged through muck. They were probably inwardly chuckling while the Giant did dumb things, falling for their tricks.

"We need to hide," Garrett urged. "I promise, we'll find your friends later. But we have to survive first. Don't you get that? If you do what the Torth expect, they will kill you."

No doubt that was true. They expected Ariock to rescue his friends. They expected him to exhaust himself.

And they must feel so safe, invisible to him because of those walls.

Radioactive fallout couldn't touch them. Why should they worry about atomic bombs or a mad Giant? They were safe, fresh and armored, ready to leap into battle when needed. They would stand triumphant over Ariock when he fell.

He didn't glance at the cupola. He showed no interest in that direction. Instead, he gathered his strength and watched his friends.

His big hands yearned for a weapon. Not the slender spears in the quiver on his back, but something heavy. Something that would knock down indestructible walls.

Ariock filled his hands with ionized, pressurized air, extended along his awareness to form a gigantic hammer.

He compounded the air until it became dense and heavy. Electrical energy crackled throughout its crude shape. The war hammer might be unwieldy, but it would wreck things. Ariock relished its deadly weight. He aligned his extended self with the weapon.

Garrett was pleading. Ariock ignored him and swung the enormous war hammer.

He aimed for the troops who were netting his friends—and then changed his trajectory at the last second. None of the Torth were close enough to read his intentions. Garrett probably couldn't pick up on his unformulated plan, either.

Ariock's hammer smashed into the cupola with no warning whatsoever, in a shock of superbolts.

Chunks of armored wall exploded and vaporized. Internal structures shattered.

A white-armored Torth fell, flailing.

The teetering tower shouldn't even exist anymore. It was wrecked, yet even so, a gang of armored Torth balanced on the ruined platform, exposed to rain and wind. Servants of All. And Ariock recognized the skeletal frame of the Commander of All Living Things, with the horns that twisted upward from each of her armored shoulders. Her shroud undulated in the wind.

This gaunt lady had presided over Ariock's crucifixion in the desert. Her holographic face had been one of the first things he saw upon entering New GoodLife WaterGarden City as a chained-up prisoner.

As the elected leader of the Torth Empire, she had sent the agent who murdered his father. His family.

She had stepped on Ariock when he'd fallen, defeated, after crash-landing in the dead city.

She had a habit of watching the worst events of his life, always from a safe distance.

Like now.

Something inside Ariock clicked, like a key turning in a lock. He knew, with deadly certainty, that the Commander of all Torth would never stop pursuing him. Their feud was personal. Other Torth served the Majority, but she represented the Majority. She had to please her people, or else they would kill her and elect a new Commander of All Living Things.

She had to die.

Ariock hardly cared about who would be elected to replace her. The expression of distaste on her skeletal face betrayed how vulnerable she felt right now, in this moment. That expression was the Torth equivalent of sheer terror. She had nowhere to go, unless she wanted to jump, and Ariock would see wherever she landed. The tower's elevator shaft was a shattered mess.

He kept up his shield, fending off a barrage of microdarts. At the same time, he gathered his extra focus.

This time, Ariock didn't bother with misdirection. The commanding ranks of the Torth Empire were terribly exposed, trapped on that shaky remnant of a lookout tower.

Ariock let them see his smug look.

He swung, and his pressurized war hammer of air and electricity smashed into the top ranks.

Sparks exploded as his hammer blow met a shield of molten wildfire.

The Servants of All remained in place. They did not get knocked off the ruined tower or obliterated in a spray of bloody vapor and bone fragments. They were unexpectedly shielded.

The whole battle stopped.

Faceless helmets turned toward the Commander of All Living Things and her ring of Servants atop the tower. Red Ranks ignored prisoners enmeshed in nets. Garrett gawked. The blasts and microdarts stopped.

Silence hung between storm gusts.

Ariock had the impression that Torth must be exchanging superfast communications with each other. And he understood why. Deep down, he knew.

Yeresunsa.

One or more of those elite Torth must have powers no Torth was supposed to have. With his focus attenuated, Ariock couldn't guess which one was the problem.

He tried to force his way through the unexpected shield, but it was too intense. He had to keep up his personal shield at all costs. The Torth might act stunned, but he did not trust that. One enterprising Red Rank might manage to creep close enough to disable him with a pain seizure. He had to stay vigilant for his personal safety.

Garrett ought to keep a lookout. Instead, the old man looked thunderstruck, gaping at the Servants of All behind their wildfire shield. Was he trying to guess which one was dangerous?

Ariock let his lightning hammer devolve into thick, jumpy bars of electricity.

Lightning poured from his wrapped hands, vaporizing toxic rain, searing cold air. He would find a weakness in that dazzling shield of liquid wildfire.

"It's all of them," Garrett whispered. "Every single Servant of All." He looked stunned. "They're all Yeresunsa."

That was when Ariock finally understood the depths of danger he was in.

He was trapped in an arena with too many monsters and no way out.

CHAPTER 16

MINDS BLOWN

!!!!!!!!!!!!!!!!!!!!!!!!!!!

The battle on the Torth Homeworld had just taken a turn that no one expected.

Befuddled slaves watched the Upward Governess, awaiting commands, but her mouth simply hung open. Her mind reeled from the hammer blow tearing through the Megacosm.

When the Giant had packed air and energy to form a quasi weapon, she had barely paid attention. She had assumed—like all the viewers, both firsthand and in the Megacosm—that the Giant was going to hammer a few Red Ranks into pulp, like a stupid savage. It would work only until he got slammed by more nuclear warheads. In the meantime, he would be lucky not to hammer his friends by accident.

But he had changed his trajectory at the last second. Instead of throwing the huge hammer at Red Ranks, he had swung it in an unexpected direction, toward the most elite ranks on the battlefield.

He should not have known they were there.

Even with the Imposter by his side, the Giant should not have any way to guess where the Commander of All Living Things stood, because the Imposter had lost all his advantages when he'd revealed the truth of who he was. Surely he could no longer enter the Megacosm without a mob pointing him out?

This Commander of All liked to take risks, so of course she was near the battle, ready to leap out as soon as the Giant got neutralized. She was ready to bask in victory. But she was supposed to have been hidden and safe inside that armored tower top.

Now that the cupola was a smashed ruin? She ought to be dead.

!!!!!!!!!!!!!

The Majority struggled to process what had just happened. The Commander of All Living Things—elected leader of the Torth Empire, and representative of the Torth Majority—stood atop an obliterated tower, under direct attack by a monster.

And she was unharmed.

Elite Servants of All ringed her. They flickered in and out of the Megacosm, as if unsure whether or not to admit certain truths to their inner audiences. The Swift Killer had dropped out of the Megacosm entirely. Anyone could see her, balanced on the broken tower with the rest of them . . . while wildfire spewed from her armored hands.

Sickening conclusions ripped through the Upward Governess a microsecond before the rest of the Torth Empire began to run through the same deductions. She connected facts in an undeniable framework that challenged the very foundations of civilization.

Was it possible the Swift Killer was one lone freak?

If so, then her fellow Servants of All should be attacking her with microdarts. They weren't.

Instead, while the Torth Majority reeled, the highest strata of Torth society merely imitated the reactions of their inner audiences. They struggled to feel shocked. Any Torth could recognize their insincerity. The Commander of All Living Things herself was unsurprised by wildfire gushing from one of the most elite Torth in the empire.

How had the Commander of All and her coterie kept their balance while the Giant smashed the cupola into a shattered mess?

How were they still alive, when armored walls were torn asunder?

They must all have Yeresunsa powers. It was the only explanation.

The Giant increased his attack. He forced a sprawl of crackling energy past the wildfire. A few of the white-armored Servants of All screamed, cooked alive in their armor. That was when the surviving Servants lifted their armored hands and joined the Swift Killer's defense.

The conspiracy was revealed. They had nothing left to lose by defending themselves. Together, they emitted a continuous gout of wildfire that was strong enough to combat the Giant's bars of lightning.

Even the Commander of All Living Things joined in, although she was reluctant. She had to exit the Megacosm in order to use her powers—they all did—but before she descended, the Upward Governess tasted her dusty displeasure. The Commander was disappointed in the Swift Killer. She thought the Servant of All should have died rather than reveal this secret.

It would have been better to let the Giant kill Us, she thought.

She was probably right.

There were tens of thousands of Servants of All in the Torth Empire. It seemed incredible that such a large number of Torth could keep such a huge secret, but now that the conspiracy was undeniable, the Upward Governess began to tally up verifying hints of how it must have worked.

Only Servants of All were allowed the "privilege" of hunting and killing rogue Yeresunsa. Everyone assumed they must be best qualified to hunt monsters because they often rose through the military ranks, Red and Crimson. If they received mysterious training, well, so what?

Persistent questions about illegal Yeresunsa powers could mean death. So no one bothered to get too curious about it.

But how was it possible that so many Yeresunsa passed the tests on baby farms? Fetuses with defects, such as illegal powers, were terminated before birth. Everyone knew that.

If a Yeresunsa baby slipped through a crack in the testing process . . . or was secretly allowed to pass . . . its powers must lie dormant throughout childhood. It must never think of its powers consciously.

Perhaps it never even knew it was a Yeresunsa until it was inducted into the conspiracy.

The conspirators chose the most promising Torth, the ones groomed to rise fast in the ranks.

The Upward Governess had risen fast, herself. But she knew, from her own bitter experience, that she could not rise above her hard-won rank of Indigo-Blue, because the highest ranks were required to meet standards of physical fitness. Servants of All met an array of difficult requirements. They had to be intelligent and ambitious and combat-hardened. Dozens of strict requirements were emphasized all the time . . . emphasized so much, in fact, that worthy rejects got disregarded.

Everyone assumed that a Crimson or Indigo-Blue who never rose higher must be slightly deficient in some way. Maybe they were a little lazy. Maybe a tad unhealthy. Maybe somewhat gullible. Perhaps they had a slightly off-putting pedigree or an overreliance on tranquility meshes.

Except it was really none of those factors. There was a secret requirement.

The Upward Governess would never have risen higher even if she were physically fit and perfect in every way. Because she was not a Yeresunsa.

The Betrayer could have met that secret requirement, though. And perhaps . . .

Perhaps that was why the Commander of All Living Things had agreed to allow Thomas Hill to join the Torth Empire in the first place.

It had nothing to do with augmenting the collective knowledge of the Torth with a new supergenius. It wasn't about catering to the whims of a valuable Indigo-Blue Rank engineer. No.

It was about power.

Some Servants of All must yearn to use their powers openly, to quit the pretense of being humble public servants. That was why they had welcomed

Yellow Thomas, making him the first openly Yeresunsa person in history to be accepted by the Torth Majority.

They gave all sorts of justifications. He was a valuable supergenius. He was on the inhibitor patch. A lot of high ranks vouched for him, including the most respectable supergenius alive. Those were good reasons. Persuasive reasons.

If Yellow Thomas had remained tame and harmless . . . ? Well, eventually the Majority would have been amenable to reconsider the ancient law against Yeresunsa.

The Upward Governess found even more hints, now that she knew to look for them. It was obvious in hindsight. Newly raised Servants of All received strenuous combat training in the Stratower. Why was their training such a big secret? It was rude to ask. Torth never wanted to relive their Adulthood Exams, or any unpleasant personal experiences, so no one asked questions about things like that. The highest ranks were supposed to be perfection made flesh. No one dared probe the mind of a Servant of All.

Maybe they were even chosen for their discipline in keeping secrets. That might be part of the secret requirements.

How long had the clandestine cabal of Yeresunsa ruled the Torth Empire? How many generations?

No one had ever put the subtle clues together because Torth inherently trusted one another. That was what it meant to be a Torth. The Megacosm was a place of harmony. There weren't supposed to be Betrayers, or Imposters, or a conspiracy among the most prestigious rulers of the galaxy.

Or a rogue Servant of All who had given birth to a hybrid baby on Earth. The mother of the Betrayer had managed to conceal her pregnancy and childbirth from everyone in the Megacosm, even under intense torture.

The father of the Imposter had been a similar rogue Servant of All. He should not have been able to mate with a primitive cave dweller, impregnating her. He should not have been able to keep such an intense secret, let alone have a chance to flee to Earth along with his albino concubine. He never should have had enough leeway to raise the abominable hybrid baby, enabling his illegal offspring to grow up amid the savages of Earth and become the outlaw known as Jonathan Stead.

The Upward Governess had believed she was the only living Torth with a true secret, squirreled beneath layers of trivialities.

She'd been wrong. Secrets were downright commonplace, at least among high ranks.

All those thoughts flashed through the Upward Governess within a second. It took her another second to compile implications, then process and evaluate how those implications might impact her own future, and to formulate a course of action that could greatly benefit her.

She sat up against her pillows, no longer remotely interested in snack time. Here was an opportunity to regain all the authority she had lost, and then some. She would likely never see such an opportunity again.

TRAITORS.

The outraged sentiment was in many minds, harmonized by the Majority, but the Upward Governess made sure that her weighty mental voice was among the loudest. Her allegiance could not be doubted. She was with the Majority on this issue.

CRIMINALS AT THE TOP.

CORRUPTION.

THE GOVERNMENT IS ILLEGAL.

Implications slammed into the Megacosm like an asteroid hitting a planet. Civilian Torth throughout the galaxy dropped their food, or tripped and fell, or choked, or sat up in bed, gaping. Planets seemed to shift from the weight of so many Torth jerking in dismay.

The news continued to spread to remote space stations and outposts. Children on baby farms huddled together, unsure why so many adults felt stunned and betrayed.

Anger seeped into the furrows left by shock. The Megacosm began to buzz. And then it seethed.

Get rid of those traitors.

Execute them.

Replace them.

I will make a good (new) Commander of All Living Things, a stately governor declared. *Pick Me.*

(No) Pick Me, a popular plantation manager announced, gaining new fans amid the unrest. *I promise, I am not (corrupt) a dangerous Yeresunsa.*

More would-be commanders flooded the Megacosm, clamoring for the Majority's attention. Confused lower and middling ranks turned this way and that, unsure which outlandish promises to trust. Whom should they vote for?

All other news faded to insignificance. Who cared about conquering yet another primitive planet or invading a nest of pesky cave-dwelling savages? The Giant would surely be dealt with soon. Once he was vanquished, the Imposter and the Betrayer would be captured easily.

All those problems were tiny in comparison to the massive corruption at the heart of the Torth Empire.

The Megacosm boiled with emotions strong enough to border on illegality.

Torth dropped out, embarrassed by their own emotions. Others desperately tuned their tranquility meshes to maximum tranquility. No one wanted to deal with a problem of this magnitude. No one had expected it.

Supergeniuses began to weigh in. As the Majority writhed with uncertainties, the Twins rode the crest of one wave.

We ought to (immediately) demote everyone who shares significant genetic material with any Servant of All, the girl Twin thought.

Right, the boy Twin quipped. *Especially those who share a lineage with the Swift Killer.*

And the Betrayer! their inner audiences roared.

>*Get rid of babies who are clones of Servants of All!*
>*Get rid of babies who share their pedigrees!*

The pair of supergeniuses known as the Twins were close in age to the Upward Governess. They were widely respected as the second- and third-wisest beings in the known universe. No one dared contradict their wisdom.

Except for the Death Architect. *Can We (the Torth Empire) afford a major revolution (new government) while We face the Betrayer and the Giant?* she thought idly. *I propose that We legalize Yeresunsa and legitimize the current government.*

As if that would not tear apart the very fabric of society.

NO! the Majority thundered.

The Upward Governess wondered how her young peer remained serene and uncaring, even in the face of Majority disapproval. The Death Architect seemed unruffled all the time. How did she manage it without the aid of drugs, therapies, or a tranquility mesh?

We cannot trust the Servants of All, the girl Twin pointed out.

They have deceived the Majority, the boy Twin added.

The Twins were not genetically related—one was ebony-dark and fat, the other milk-white and bony—but their minds were mirrored. That was because they cohabitated. They had moved in together, and they sat together so often, soaking up each other's thoughts, that they were practically one mind. Their thoughts twined in and out of each other's statements.

The Servants of All deserve punishment—
—not a reward.

The Upward Governess used to fantasize, in secret, about twinning her mind with Yellow Thomas. Too bad that opportunity was gone forever.

She threw her support behind the Twins. *The top ranks kept a major secret from the Torth Majority. We need a new government.*

A better government, the Twins agreed in unison.

More Torth joined the simmering conversation, like dust streaming into rings around a supermassive planet. Soon all the ripe supergeniuses were present. Besides the Upward Governess, the Twins, and the Death Architect, there were the Geodesic Flux and the Rind Topographer. Several unripe supergeniuses were also present, including the Spin Overture and the Mechanized Meeter.

Hm. I suppose Yeresunsa should remain illegal. The Death Architect changed her stance with the ease of an eel switching direction. Hardly anyone blinked or wondered why she had changed her mind so easily. *So*, she went on, *We need to remove the current corrupt regime. Will the inhibitor serum be enough of a weapon? I imagine there must be secret loyalists (secret Yeresunsa) buried among the color ranks. We would need to root those out, as well.*

Suspicion erupted throughout the Torth Majority. No one could trust their neighbors.

I am (safe) trustworthy. The Upward Governess reached into the pocket of her vest and pulled out her blaster glove. She wriggled her pudgy fingers into the glove. Sharing her perceptions with as many Torth as possible, she switched her glove from blaster mode to microdart mode. Like all blaster gloves in her city, she was armed with plenty of inhibitor serum.

I don't have powers. She aimed the glove at her chubby arm and injected herself with inhibitor.

That earned her some respectful attention. The masses cheered.

Distant governors and governesses hurried to imitate her. They shot themselves with microdarts or had underlings inject them.

But they were too late. The Upward Governess had proven that she was genuine. The rest of them might be fakers.

We need a better way to root out traitors (Yeresunsa), the Death Architect opined. *I have ideas. Simply give Me Your permission, and I can (I will) invent weapons that will save Us.*

The Torth Majority trembled with uncertainty. Supergeniuses were not allowed to invent weapons. That was a long-standing ancient law. Certain people *(certain minds)* needed constraints.

The Upward Governess inwardly admired the Death Architect's audacity. In her opinion, supergeniuses ought to be permitted to do whatever they wished. They should be able to invent cures for their own ailments. And weapons. Whatever.

But now was not the time to throw more scary decisions at the Majority. People were half paralyzed with indecision and fear. They wanted reassurance.

Get Me an inhibitor patch, the Upward Governess demanded from one of her local underlings. *Every Torth should wear one, from now on.*

The Twins agreed. *We must discover who has been deceptive and false for years—*

—versus who is trustworthy.

The Twins had never been pioneers, never truly ambitious. They seemed to already have everything they wanted in life. It must be nice to feel so satisfied.

The Upward Governess welcomed her swelling audience. *I understand what it feels like to be betrayed. We are All betrayed.* Her massive mind towered in the Megacosm, like a beacon of reassurance. *I will do whatever it takes to bring justice for Our Empire. But let Us solve this peacefully.*

No one wanted a civil war. No one wanted to fight a battalion of telepathic Yeresunsa. The Majority flocked toward the Upward Governess, because she wasn't threatening to invent new weapons or overturn ancient laws. Instead, she offered reliability, empathy, and a mind smart enough to solve any problem.

If anyone smarter (and healthier) than Me proves worthy of a leadership role, the Upward Governess thought, *then I will throw My full support behind that person.*

She meant it. Harmony had to take precedence, even above her own desires, or else there would be no Megacosm and civilization would fall apart.

The Giant's hammer blow had shattered the Torth sense of security. Aftershocks continued to spread throughout the galaxy, shaking even the most obscure subthreads of the Megacosm. Potential commanders popped up here and there. Anyone who had enough admirers could gain a platform and spew promises of a more trustworthy government.

All Torth agreed on one point: without a unifying agenda, the Torth Empire would fracture into individual factions.

They demanded a leader everyone could trust.

The Upward Governess felt more alive than she ever had before. The only time she had ever felt this excited was the day she had met Thomas and absorbed everything in his mind for the very first time. That was a feast she would treasure forever.

For now . . . The Upward Governess paused, waiting for her audience to reach maximum size. She used her superfast processing speed to acknowledge every one of those trillions of Torth as worthy individuals.

Then she volunteered.

How about if You let Me be Your temporary Commander of All Living Things?

PART TWO

"You elected Me. You adore Me. I live to serve all mind readers. But since mind readers rule all life forms, I am more than a mere humble public servant. As Your foremost Servant of All, I actually command All Living Things."

—Audavian, the first Commander of All Living Things

CHAPTER 1

SERVANT OF ALL

The Swift Killer grinned as she leaped several stories down. She landed with ease, thanks to her musculoskeletal enhancements. Who cared about uncouth facial expressions? Who cared about laws anymore?

Red Ranks leaped out of her way as she strode toward the enemies. Lesser ranks ought to show respect to one such as her, but instead of bowing and groveling, the soldiers aimed blaster gloves her way.

Traitor.

They considered her an enemy. Ha. They had no concept how weak they were. The Swift Killer spiked out her awareness, enveloping her upper body in a shield that would melt microdarts before they could touch her. Most of her body was already armored. She might as well be invincible in comparison to these lowly soldiers.

She kept wanting to laugh, wildly, like a primitive. The awful strain of self-control was finally gone. She was free!

All her life, she had wanted to do forbidden things. Show off her powers. Burn impertinent lesser Torth to death. It would have been wonderful to singe the Upward Governess instead of allowing that fat girl to humiliate her.

And she was so, so sick of guarding her every thought. Someone as accomplished as herself should not have to feel constrained by society. That was so unfair. She served the empire well. She was entitled to act and feel more unfettered than an average citizen.

Using her powers was sheer delight.

Delight! Out in the open!

Despite the looming threat of the Giant, the Swift Killer giggled. Common Torth had no idea what joy or delight felt like, but Servants of All knew. She knew. Yeresunsa powers and emotions were linked, so the secret training sessions in the Stratower actually encouraged forbidden indulgences. One could not grow as a Yeresunsa without some base-level understanding of one's emotions.

In private arenas and in orgy pits, Servants of All reenacted savage, primitive behaviors.

They went on missions to Earth, ostensibly to police the planet for renegades, but really to study and to experience primitive pleasures. Even the sour old Commander of All Living Things must delve into taboo behaviors every once in a while. Not that she would admit to it.

It pleased the Swift Killer to shove her awareness into the rainy night and set the very air on fire. She sent golden flames swirling, just for fun. Let the Majority stand in awe of how very free she was. Free to feel. Free to be unguarded in her own mind. She was special. She was better than a lowly color rank, superior in every—

STOP.

The message exploded inside the Swift Killer. Obedience to the Majority was ingrained, so she skidded to a halt as if whipped.

A second later, she wondered why she should care if her stupid inner audience refused to acknowledge her superiority. The Torth Majority belonged under her boot heels. They should be worshipping her, not ordering her around!

You (Swift Killer) are out of control. Her audience bolstered the message, but it originated from the Commander of All Living Things and her loyalists.

Of course. The Swift Killer rolled her eyes. She liked that gesture. It was so in-your-face primitive.

Other Servants of All were always trying to curtail her. They treated her like a nuisance, like she carried a taint. Raw strength in power ought to make her a leader among them, but unfortunately, they didn't value strength at all. They valued self-restraint.

You have always been too impulsive, many Servants of All chorused.

Bad trait.

Obey Us—

—or submit to death by torture.

You are in violation of the law.

Their minds felt thin and withered. They were no longer supported by the Majority. Minds rippled throughout the Megacosm, seeking a strong leader to replace the current corruption.

How could so many people consider voting for the Upward Governess?

Ugh. That freakish child, doomed to die within a few months, could not possibly command respect. The Majority must feel desperate.

We are at the dawn of a new era, the Swift Killer announced to her inner audience. *The Empire needs a strong leader to take charge in these troubled times. You (the Majority) need someone (like Me) who can battle monsters and win.*

It was an impractical risk to nominate herself. The public was still reeling from a sense of betrayal. But they were weak-minded fools, and they clearly needed someone decisive to lead them. Perhaps raw strength was finally going to matter?

I will triumph over the enemies, the Swift Killer promised. *Elect Me.*

The only time she had come close to feeling this exhilarated was when she'd disguised herself among the primitives of Earth. She had collected muscly brutes in secret, men she'd made sure no one would report missing.

Other Servants didn't quite dare to think about their missions to Earth, but they probably raped and savaged humans, too. Why not? It was easy and fun. The Swift Killer had commanded her human slaves to dig their own graves when she was done using them.

Her clone sister had been stupid. She should have castrated her plaything rather than letting him impregnate her as if she was nothing but a beast. Of course she had gotten caught and executed. She shouldn't have gone native.

The Megacosm seethed. Torth debated, suggested, nominated, and spun from thread to thread. Aftershocks of the latest news continued to ripple in obscure subthreads, shaking Torth in the most remote outposts of the galaxy.

The Commander of All leaped off the wrecked tower, her shroud billowing as she fell. She used her powers to cushion her landing, and her upgraded body absorbed the impact with ease.

She straightened and strode toward the battle, skeletal and majestic. *Would You immortalize Me?* Her thoughts echoed throughout billions and then trillions of minds. *Would you make Me the last true Commander of All Living Things?*

She had the attention of the Majority.

We (Torth) can argue and debate, the Commander of All Living Things went on. *But if We break Our unity, then it doesn't matter whom You elect to replace Me . . . because that person will not command all living things.*

Her oration coated every mind with frost. It was true. The Megacosm required harmony, or else it would fracture into individual factions and cease to be a cohesive unit. Civilization would dissolve.

I would die to protect You. The Commander blocked a lightning strike with smooth efficiency. *I would rather be dead than exacerbate the divisiveness among Us.*

Noble. Possibly disingenuous. Yet many Torth believed her. Many Servants of All backed her up.

Let Us continue to serve You, Servants of All begged the Majority.

Let Us kill Our mutual enemies.

We do not rule. We never have.

We live to serve.

The Torth Majority yearned to trust their elected commander and public servants. Many agreed: they wished they had never learned about the malignant secret among the highest ranks. Ignorance would have been preferable.

My predecessor in office had Yeresunsa powers, the Commander of All let the masses know. *So did his predecessor. And the one before.*

We have kept the secret for many generations, Servants of All chorused.

A strain, they all agreed.

The Torth Majority listened with suspicion, with speculation, and with hope.

Frost formed wherever the Commander's boots touched tar. She must be freezing the microdarts aimed her way. *If I (We) pursue Our individual self-interests*, the Commander assured her massive audience, *instead of pleasing the Majority, then We are no better than slaves. I was elected to serve All. That is what I intend to do.*

The Swift Killer felt an urge to laugh. Sometimes she had inappropriate urges like that.

What would happen after the enemies were vanquished? A great many Torth wanted to know if the Commander and her loyal inner circle would submit to execution. If these deceptive Servants of All truly served the Majority, then they must submit to punishment for possessing illegal powers.

I live or die at Your whims, the Commander of All assured everyone. *If I serve You well, and You wish to kill Me all the same, then it is My duty to submit. I obey the Majority. I always have. I always will.*

Thousands of Servants of All echoed her, bleating their eagerness to serve and obey.

The Swift Killer found herself sickened by their willingness. Why should any Yeresunsa obey obsolete laws meant to subjugate them?

All We have to do is torture a few low ranks to set an example, the Swift Killer urged her peers. *Or how about if We enslave the Giant instead of killing him? I bet I can train him . . .*

No one was listening to her. All of a sudden, the Swift Killer was alone in her own mind.

She was so astonished, she nearly got cooked by a streak of wildfire from none other than the Betrayer. She had to spike out her awareness and fend off attacks.

A nearby Servant of All hissed in her mind, his message private. *It is beyond idiocy to defy the Majority. We are grossly outnumbered, and they are armed with the inhibitor. We cannot win through force any more than the Giant can.*

Civilization matters more than Us, another Servant of All added. *Maybe, if We are lucky, they will let Us live.*

Our only chance is to prove Our worth, the first Servant thought.

Beggars. Grovelers.

The Swift Killer ground her teeth, and then she allowed herself to scream her rage. She whipped heat through an extension of her arm, channeling it into a massive wall of flames aimed at the Giant's allies.

Let the others be suicidal. The Majority would try to round up Servants sooner or later, to execute them in the Isolatorium. The Swift Killer would flee before that could happen to her. She was not disposable.

Perhaps she would invite other rogues to join her? Together, they might found a new empire somewhere else.

Like Earth.

The idea excited the Swift Killer so much, wildfire snapped off her in wild waves, and she was unable to hide her vulgar grin.

Power had benefits.

CHAPTER 2

CHARMING THE HYDRA

The battle died all of a sudden, all at once.

Thomas uncurled a bit. From his vantage point on the pilot's seat of the broken transport, he could see Ariock in the distance, facing off against the Commander of All Living Things, against the backdrop of a broken tower and a nuclear cloud that strobed with lightning.

Why had the battle paused?

Thomas ascended into the Megacosm, almost unable to stop himself. He trembled with longing. And really, he no longer had any reason to resist. His promise to safeguard Alashani secrets was obsolete. The Torth had already probed the minds of Orla and others. They had learned about the lamplit underworld full of rogues and runaways.

That revelatory news would have shaken the Megacosm at any other time.

Now it was a blip. Ariock's hammer blow had slammed the very foundations of Torth civilization.

Ariock, naturally enough, was totally oblivious to what he'd achieved. He couldn't sense the metaphorical gnashing of teeth in the Megacosm. While the Upward Governess and the Swift Killer nominated themselves for supreme leadership, and while the Commander of All Living Things strove to prove that she still had value, Ariock hurried over to his friends.

"Are you all right?" Ariock set Garrett down, then used his powers to release Vy from a net. She had thrown herself outside in order to shield Thomas.

"I am now." Vy let Ariock haul her upright. Judging by the way her eyes sparkled with renewed energy, Ariock must have sent a wave of healing energy through her.

Or maybe that was just love. Thomas knew that Vy had never even considered swallowing her suicide pellet. She'd trusted Ariock to show up and rescue her.

A couple of the shani warriors had lost faith in their messiah, however. Yavin and Shassatel lay dead with their veils in their mouths. They had swallowed their poison pellets.

Tavish lay dead in a pool of blood. No one had been able to make a tourniquet in time to save him.

Flen wrapped Cherise in his arms. Orla moaned in pain. She curled around a blood-soaked gut wound.

Ariock knelt by the teenage healer. He used his powers to pull dirt and cloth away from her wound, cleaning it, the way Orla herself had taught him to do.

"Ariock, heal her later." Garrett sounded exasperated as Ariock ignored him.

Thomas thought the old man should save his breath and recognize futility when he saw it. Orla had saved Ariock's life when he was on the verge of death. No doubt Ariock blamed himself for the dead and injured warriors. He would not let her suffer.

"We need to get out of here!" Garrett said.

That was true. A few daring Torth orbited Thomas's mind, and through their perceptions, he sensed the entire Megacosm thrashing.

The Torth Empire was wounded.

Vulnerable.

It would grow new heads, like the monstrous Hydra of human mythology. It might even grow more dangerous than ever. But right now, in this moment ... ?

Thomas thought the Torth Majority might be open to a bit of psychological manipulation.

He peeled himself away from the Megacosm in order to ponder potential opportunities. It hurt, to cut off that wonderment, that feast of endless knowledge, but the Torth had enough advantages without being able to sense his pounding heartbeat or his sweaty fear.

Let them guess his intentions. Let them see him as mysterious.

Thomas finally understood why the highest ranks had welcomed him into the Torth Empire all those months ago. The fear of being discovered must have weighed on them. Yellow Thomas could have paved a path toward legalization and acceptance of powers.

That was all over with now. The top ranks would be hunted and persecuted. They must be panicking on the inside.

They must be feeling desperate to validate themselves, to prove their worth to the Torth Majority.

Thomas riffled through his mental library on game theory. Should he go for delay tactics? Stall for time?

Given a few extra hours, Ariock and Jinishta might be able to organize the Alashani into a real fighting force.

But they would not win a protracted war. Not in their current condition. Ariock could likely annihilate all the Servants of All in the vicinity, but more would show up, hacking away at his defenses. Eventually, Ariock would make a mistake. It was inevitable.

For a long-term or permanent win of any sort, Ariock required a bigger advantage than any he currently had. He needed a secret weapon. He needed something—or someone—who would catch the Torth completely by surprise.

Like the Lady of Sorrow.

Thomas glanced toward Garrett. The old man seemed to know a few things the Torth could not guess or predict. He had proven to be adept at survival. He was likely here, on the Torth Homeworld, in order to dig up an advantage or two.

An idea began to sketch itself in Thomas's mind. It was chancy. It was a gamble, for sure. But it was light-years better than their current trajectory of fighting and losing.

"My powers are disabled," Garrett explained to anyone nearby. He dived beneath the broken transport. "Ariock? You have to protect us!"

Ariock finished healing Orla just in time. A wall of wildfire rushed toward him, fast as a train. It slammed into Ariock's dome of protection. Fiery glory enveloped them.

Thomas mentally tested his plan for the potential flaws.

He needed to lure the Torth into a false feeling of superiority and comfort. He would make them an offer—something with mass appeal, something even the most powerful Torth believed they could spin to their own advantage. Lazy minds would overlook the hidden barb.

Satisfied, Thomas ascended into the Megacosm.

Only a handful of minds dared to orbit his. He was a pariah, and besides, most of the wakeful empire was wrapped up in lofty debates. They wanted to replace their government. They wondered if they could trust the Upward Governess as a leader. The Giant still posed a threat, so maybe they ought to keep the current deceivers in power until the enemies were vanquished?

Hey, Thomas thought to any Torth willing to listen. *I'm willing to surrender to the current Torth regime—if they agree to My wager.*

He waited for his offer to leak its way upward, through the orbiters of orbiters and onward. Meanwhile, the battle raged. A few Servants of All had telekinetic powers. They joined the Red Ranks, using their powers to drag shani warriors away from the Giant's protective bubble.

Thomas kept demanding attention in the Megacosm. *I could be Your willing slave.* He included sparkly subtext filled with wondrous promises. He had the power to brainwash people. Wouldn't the Servants of All like him to experiment with becoming a top social influencer? Didn't they want to gain his willing help without a costly battle?

I could ensure that You keep all Your prestigious authority, Thomas promised them. *I think You'll like My wager.*

He had their attention.

The explosions and wildfire died down. Thomas sensed the weight of a universe inside his mind. It came suddenly. A few thousand Torth orbited his mind, but they had audiences of their own, who also had audiences, and so forth.

Thomas took the opportunity to absorb fresh life experiences. He grabbed more and more, completely unable to stop, quivering with joy. Oh, the knowledge! Such a feast!

His orbiters increased in number. Thousands became millions.

Let's talk. Thomas used his TV-interview frame of mind. Confident. Competent. He did not muddy the feast by revealing what he'd deduced about the Upward Governess. Her illegal emotions were petty and minor compared with a conspiracy of illegal powers among the top ranks. The Torth Majority was already reeling. Thomas figured he could find a better moment in which to accuse his nemesis.

The attention of a galaxy was pinned on him.

"Psst," Garrett whispered in a futile attempt to avoid Torth notice. He huddled in the ruined rear of the transport, wrapped in his cloak. He eyed Thomas with suspicion. "What are you doing?"

Thomas beckoned. If Garrett wanted to be clued in, then he would need to come closer. Their telepathic ranges needed to overlap.

The old man tightened his mouth. At least he took the hint, and he began to get closer, climbing over the remains of seats.

Outside in the rain, Ariock turned around with wary suspicion. He had no idea what was happening in the Megacosm, so he couldn't guess why the Torth had quit their attack.

"Ariock," Thomas called. "Be on guard, but don't restart the fight. I'm giving negotiation a try."

Ariock grew more baffled as the Commander of All strode out of a tunnel of billowing smoke, flanked by Servants of All. They wore no helmets. They all stared at Thomas with their empty eyes.

"W e e e ' r e l i s s s s t e n i n n n g."

It sounded as if the rain was hissing words. It was actually an aggregate of Torth voices, all creaky from disuse. Their vocal cords were atrophied.

"Excellent." Thomas felt like a dust mite exploring the galaxy. The Commander of All Living Things watched him, along with dozens of Servants of All, and they all had massive audiences. Popular Torth peered through their eyes, with their own multitudes of followers.

The Torth Empire had more than thirty-eight trillion citizens, spread over thousands of different solar systems. At least 50 percent of them must be tuned in. Watching.

Thomas yearned to spend eternity basking in their collective knowledge.

It was painful to peel himself away from the Megacosm. He wanted to cry from the loss of access to all that glorious knowledge.

Instead, he forced himself to remain steady. He could not afford to show weakness. Nor could he afford to give the Torth too many hints of what he planned. It was best to keep them guessing.

"I have a wager," Thomas said in a cold, steady voice. "If you prove me wrong, you'll get both Ariock and myself. We would go to you willing. Without a fight."

Ariock was a titanic shape in the rainy night. He glared at Thomas with disbelief.

So did everyone else. Kessa, Varktezo, Cherise, Jinishta, Vy . . . none of them felt the turmoil in the Megacosm. They could not imagine why the Torth would even consider making a bargain with their Betrayer.

Thomas wasn't going to explain the logistics in front of the Torth Empire. They had to swallow the hook.

So he ignored his friends and focused on the Commander of All Living Things. "Agree to my terms," he urged, "and you'll likely get everything you want. Then you can go back to arguing about more important things, like who should rule your civilization."

No doubt a lot of Torth were impatient to get back to such important matters, as well as the conquest and enslavement of Earth and the Alashani.

"W i l l i n g l y." The Commander of All Living Things tasted the word she found most salient. Others whispered along with her.

"Willingly." Thomas shuddered, but he meant it. He had to. Facts were important to Torth, and he would not deceive them even if he could. Lies were distasteful.

He simply was not giving them any hints that he had a plan—or that he reserved the right to change his mind. If his plan failed, he would finagle a suicide pellet or two from his friends. Maybe.

It was strange. The notion of suicide no longer excited him.

Thomas supposed that he had wrongly assumed there was nothing new to learn. Now he knew otherwise. Who was the Lady of Sorrow? How could she be rescued? What arcane knowledge was Garrett hiding?

Thomas wanted to learn. He hoped the old man would hurry up and slide into his range of telepathy.

What about after he learned all the secrets of the galaxy? Thomas realized that he still wanted to live. Retirement might be nice. He envisioned a secluded cottage in a wilderness, on a planet where no one would think to look for him.

Yes. Retirement.

It seemed like a meager goal, like something a boring human might save up for. Thomas used to want a lot more out of life. He used to yearn for status, for approval, and for loads of respect from adults. He had wanted family and friends. A future. Billions of dollars, while he was at it, and a happy relationship with Cherise.

None of those things seemed important anymore.

Half of them were beyond his reach, anyway. To keep trying and failing was a recipe for misery. Thomas decided that he would be happy with a meager retirement. That was a decent goal to aim for.

Whispery voices came from his left and right. "N a m e y o u r r r r r t e r m s s s s."

Thomas buried his new goal for now. Retirement was a long way off. He would earn it. First, he needed to avoid a death sentence by doing the equivalent of snake charming.

Except he wasn't charming a cobra.

He was about to lull and fascinate the many-headed Hydra. He had to fool a few trillion mind readers, and he had to do it well enough so that no one suspected what he was scheming.

CHAPTER 3

WHISPERED BARGAIN

Garrett hid in the back seat, just behind Thomas. His thoughts were brusque. *All right, boy, what are you planning?*

The old man guarded secrets almost as well as a supergenius. Thomas groped past misdirections, digging past screens of useless trivia. Garrett's mind was a labyrinthian obstacle course.

Full of incredible treasures.

Thomas confirmed his own guesswork about the Lady of Sorrow. He spoke out loud to the listening Torth even while he continued to root through the old guy's memories. "My wager is this." He spoke loud and clear. "We will find the Lady of Sorrow."

"What!?" Garrett jerked away, all sneakiness forgotten.

"If we succeed," Thomas told the listening Torth, "then you let us go free. If we fail . . . ?" He let that option dangle, teasing. "Then we will hand ourselves over to you, as willing prisoners."

The Commander of All cocked her head to study Thomas. Smoke unfurled along her armored body as she considered his terms.

"Bad plan!" Garrett snapped.

Thomas wordlessly disagreed. He scooped up heaps of delectable memories, wishing he had time to savor all the amazing things he was learning.

Garrett's mind was sour with fury. *No one knows how to find the Lady of Sorrow!* he thought. *She's a phantom! You're promising something you cannot deliver!*

Thomas smirked inwardly. The old man didn't have enough imagination to consider all the possibilities of his own research. Nor did he see the opportunities presented by a fractured Megacosm. Not only was Thomas buying time, but he might gain a new ally who could actually—

YOU'RE DONE. Garrett flung himself out of Thomas's four-yard range.

—surprise the Torth Empire.

Thomas gobbled up as many tidbits of knowledge as he could in the microseconds before Garrett exited his range. He was left unsatisfied, yearning for more.

For one dangerous second, he considered corralling Garrett back into his range by using blasts of wildfire.

Nah.

Thomas forced himself to settle back. If he used his powers to coerce an arthritic old man, that would be like lying to people who could not detect lies. Too easy. It was bullying. Unfair to the victim.

The Servants of All exchanged considering glances. Creaky voices synced up all around him. "T h e G i i i i i i a n t—"

"—m u s s s t a l s s s s o o o a g r e e e e e."

"O r r r n o o o o d e e e e e a l l l l l."

Thomas gave Ariock an urgent look through the open wall of the wrecked transport. "Tell them you agree, Ariock."

Ariock's deep voice was as brittle as iron. "What am I supposed to be agreeing to?"

"We'll surrender to the Torth," Thomas explained patiently, "willingly if we fail to find the Lady of Sorrow within a reasonable amount of allotted time."

Garrett scrambled over a seat, cowering away from Thomas. "His plan is guaranteed to get us killed. Don't you dare agree to it! Say no!"

Thomas dared not reveal any hints. Garrett's alarm might be real, or it might be faked, but it was helping to sell his bargain. The Torth had to believe that Thomas and Ariock would fail. They had to buy it.

Ariock gave Thomas a searching look. "Why do we want to find the Lady of Sorrow?"

"I'll explain later," Thomas said.

"The boy is just making things up out of desperation," Garrett said. "You can't trust a word he says. He's a Torth. And he's being deceptive."

Thomas stared at Garrett. Deceptive? Him? How absurdly hypocritical.

"Trust me." Thomas gave Ariock a significant look.

"He had you crucified." Garrett thrust a gnarled finger toward Thomas. "How can you trust a word he says?"

Maybe Garrett was playing up the melodrama, but Thomas tried not to show how much the words hurt. Ariock's uncertainty was painful to see.

"I'm your family," Garrett said. "I have your best interests at heart."

"D e c i i i i i i d e." Echoed whispers sliced the air around them. The Commander of All Living Things shifted her bony hips. She would not wait long.

"Come on, Ariock." Thomas nodded encouragement. He resisted an urge to point at Garrett and shoot some truthful accusations his way. *Your great-grandpa is a compulsive liar who will lick anyone's boots if he thinks it will get him somewhere better. Also, we're dead unless you ignore him and trust me.*

Garrett aimed a disparaging look toward Thomas. "He's convinced of his own brilliance, but he has zero comprehension of what he's offering the Torth. His bargain will doom the universe! Mph!"

The Swift Killer made a throwing motion, and something smacked Garrett in the mouth. It looked like a piece of plastic, but it melted into Garrett's mustache and beard while he struggled to yank it away.

That looked like binding glue, except it was being molded with telekinesis.

Just what powers did the elite ranks have? They likely had all kinds of tricks and advantages, but they'd kept them hidden. Just like Garrett, their Imposter.

Garrett made incoherent sounds. His eyes bulged in outrage.

"S s s s s s i l e n c e," many Torth said.

"G i v v v e U s s s s s t h e I m p o s s s t e r r r—"

"—a l s s s s s o."

"We need him with us," Thomas said, over Garrett's convincingly desperate whines. "You'll get him, too, if we fail to find the Lady of Sorrow."

Garrett made frantic muffled sounds. Thomas would have been more sympathetic had Garrett not resorted to over-the-top lies against him. Doom the *universe*? Really. The Torth Empire only encompassed a galaxy.

"D o e s s s s t h e G i a n n n t a g r e e e e e?" the fractured Torth Empire whispered from every side.

"H e e e w i l l l l c o m e w i l l l l l i n g l y?"

"H e e e e w i l l b e O u r r r r s l a a a a a v e?"

Servants of All stood like mannequins, runnels of muck streaking their armor. Ariock stared at his would-be masters.

Their fates and their futures hung by a thread.

Thomas felt guilty for forcing Ariock into this huge decision armed with so little information. Ariock had no clue about what was being discussed. As a nontelepath, he was always missing information and therefore easily misled.

Garrett clawed at the gag, making desperate noises in his throat.

Ariock looked toward Thomas. *I want to trust you,* his gaze seemed to say.

Surely he understood that Thomas would not lie? Was he worried that Thomas was just grasping at straws?

Maybe he was right. Thomas's bargain was composed of stolen memories and half-baked ideas. It might not work. It did seem arrogant to believe he could outwit the entire Torth collective, including their supergeniuses.

But it was better than the alternative.

Please agree, Thomas internally urged, although Ariock could not hear his thoughts. Maybe the fate of the galaxy did not hinge on Ariock agreeing to a temporary ceasefire. Maybe. Yet Thomas felt as if billions of lives rested on the fulcrum of this moment.

The Torth Empire was fractured and in upheaval. Ariock had a real chance for victory. If he refused to bend . . . if he let this chance slip through his fingers . . . Cherise would die under torture. Everyone in Stratower City would probably die.

So many futures were tied to this negotiation. The Alashani civilization. The human population of Earth. Thomas suspected their fates were bound to this moment, as well. And their children's children. There was a chance to rescue the Lady of Sorrow, with all her power, and make her an ally. She probably had enough power to change the galaxy.

Ariock seemed to reach an internal decision. "All right. I agree." His shoulders slumped in resignation.

The Servants of All exchanged blank glances, and Thomas sensed their silent speculation. They were ready for next steps.

"W e e e n e e e d a s s s u r a a a n c e."

More whispers came from a different cadre of Servants of All. "W e n e e e e e d a w a y t o t r u s s s s s s s t y o u."

The Swift Killer trotted toward Ariock.

Thomas didn't need the Megacosm to guess her intentions. The Torth Majority would insist on scanning the Giant's mind. They wanted his memories, of course, but they were using Thomas's offer to pretend that this was a way they could trust his word.

Ariock tensed. The Swift Killer had destroyed Vy's leg. Her clone sister—Thomas's mother—had murdered most of the Dovanack family, including Ariock's father.

"Not her," Thomas said. "Pick someone else."

The Swift Killer stopped and turned a flat stare on Thomas.

"Choose someone who isn't a Yeresunsa," Thomas said.

After a considering moment, the Swift Killer retreated. Another Torth stepped out of the crowd.

Most of the Red Ranks had fled the battlefield, but this broad-shouldered man was among the brave ones who remained. He clanked in metallic armor, his face hidden by a helmet.

"This Red Rank is going to read your mind," Thomas told Ariock. "He won't attack you. All right?"

Ariock did not look all right with it. Any Torth could be dangerous to him at close range. A pain seizure would disable Ariock long enough for a shot of the inhibitor. What guarantees did he have that this soldier meant no harm?

Thomas ascended into the Megacosm, scanning the local news. He dropped out as soon as he was satisfied.

"He just wants to probe your mind," Thomas told Ariock, trying to sound soothing.

The Red Rank removed his helmet, allowing everyone to see his unnerving red eyes—and his apparent fear. He flinched at every slight movement. Ariock looked ready to smash the soldier, or smite him with lightning, if he made the slightest threatening move.

"Please don't kill him," Thomas said. "Please? Just let him read your mind, Ariock. It's important."

Ariock stood, tolerant and alert, while the cringing soldier probed his mind. Although the Red Rank was a hulking man, he was childlike in size compared with Ariock. And a lot more twitchy.

After a few seconds that stretched out like eons, the Red Rank dashed away in a mad rush, clanking.

"All right?" Thomas asked the Torth.

But really, he didn't have to ask. He could see their greed. They believed.

The Servants of All were ready to negotiate for terms that might win them some respect from the Majority.

CHAPTER 4

WITH THE GALAXY AT STAKE

Ariock held himself still, rainwater soaking his hair. He wished he understood more of what was going on. Why were the highest ranks willing to speak to "inferior" beings? Why not simply drop more nuclear bombs?

None of the mind readers offered clues. Garrett could not speak with that gag over his mouth. He looked wild with angry frustration.

Thomas, in contrast, radiated confidence. The wrecked pilot's chair where he sat, propped up against the backrest, might as well be a throne.

"We need carte blanche of this planet while we search," Thomas said. "No place is off-limits. And no one can attack us, or harm us, during our search."

"W e e e w i l l d o o o O u r r r b e s s s s t," many Servants of All whispered.

"T o p r e v e n t t t m i s s s h a p s s s."

Perhaps the Servants of All didn't like costly battles? Ariock had killed a lot of Torth. Forked lightning illuminated a city littered with wrecked transports and the mangled corpses of Red Ranks.

Or maybe they had lost the support of their people when they'd revealed their secret Yeresunsa powers?

Were they trying to win back respect? Maybe they wanted to prove that they could triumph without wrecking their capital city in the process.

Ariock could only make blind guesses. Thomas offered no hints.

"You can't shoot at us," Thomas clarified to the Torth. "You can't attack us, or even aim a weapon toward us. Otherwise the deal is off."

The wind picked up, joined by overlapping whispers. "W e e e e e h a v e c o n d i t i i i i o n s s s s, a l s s s s o."

"Y o u u u u u m a y n o t h a r r r r m a n n n y T o r t h h h."

"O r i n t e r f e e e e e r e w w w i t h U s s s s—"

"—o r r r s s s s l a v e s s s s s s—"

"—w h h h h i l e y o u s e a r c h h h."

"That's acceptable," Thomas said, "as long as it's true both ways. We search unmolested."

The Servants of All turned their blank-eyed gazes toward Ariock.

"Ariock agrees to those terms as well." Thomas gave him a coaxing look. "Right, Ariock?"

Ariock felt as if spikes should pop out of his forearms, like he was a nussian. He couldn't guess why the Lady of Sorrow mattered to Thomas, or really, why the Torth wanted to make a bargain in the first place. Lying was supposed to be foreign to mind readers. But Ariock didn't trust them.

"Right," he forced himself to say.

"You mussst brinnng proooof to Ussss—" many Torth breathed.

"—that thhhe Laaaady offf Ssssorrow exiiiissssts."

Thomas nodded. "Of course."

The Servants of All exhaled. "W w w e e e e give you onnne hooourrrrr."

"Sssssstaaaarting nowwww."

Thomas went red-faced with anger. "That's not enough time," he snapped. "We need twenty-four hours."

"O n n n e." That came from one direction.

"O r n o o o d e e e a l." That came from the opposite direction.

Thomas seemed to weigh some inner options. "If you refuse to give us the time we need," he said, "Ariock can fight you to the death right here. We have nothing to lose."

Ariock prepared for a battle to the death. He would almost welcome the straightforward nature of killing enemies. It seemed safer than trusting their whispery words.

On the other hand, he was all too aware of Vy leaning against the wrecked transport, scuffed and dirty, but beautiful nonetheless. She was bathed in light from the nuclear column. Dead warriors lay around her, but Vy was safe.

Unless battle erupted again.

No one's safety was guaranteed with nuclear detonations, walls of wildfire, and Ariock's gigantic powers in play. Battle meant death for a lot of people. His friends would likely not survive, and neither would he.

"We just need more time to search." Thomas softened his voice, enticing. "That's all. You know I've never spoken a lie in my life. I will be your slave if we fail. I promise. I will take an injection of inhibitor and hand myself over to you if our search for the Lady of Sorrow doesn't pan out. Just give us an adequate amount of time. How about twenty hours?"

Twenty hours without Torth interference.

A lot could happen with that much time to work with. Ariock and his friends could warn the Alashani to prepare for war. They could launch off this planet. At the very least, Ariock could design better armor, better weapons, and a better course of action.

Time. Thomas was buying precious time.

The wind sighed, or the nearby Torth sighed collectively. The Commander of All Living Things stepped forward, as thin as a corpse. "T w o o o o   h o u r s s s s."

"A n n n d   W e e e e e   w i l l   t a k e   h h h h o s t a g g g g e s s s."

"A a a s   c o o o l l a t t t e r a l."

"O n n n e - l e g g g   g i r r r l." The Servants of All held out their gloved arms, as if expecting Vy to walk into their collective embrace.

All the relief Ariock had experienced in the last few minutes snapped away.

He had been the world's biggest fool. He never should have allowed a Torth to absorb his mind, to learn whom he cared about.

"A a a n d   s s s s s i l e n t   g i r r r l."

Cherise looked shocked, and no wonder. Thomas showed no interest in her whatsoever. He had not spoken to her in months, and even now, he didn't glance her way. Why would the Torth Empire value her as a bargaining piece?

Flen wrapped his arms protectively around Cherise.

"Unacceptable." Thomas sounded like he had everything under control, but Ariock suspected that he must have run out of leverage. The Torth Empire did not love anyone. They had nothing of equal value that could be taken from them.

"We've made enough concessions," Thomas said. "If you want collateral, then you need to give us fifteen hours to find the Lady of Sorrow and show her to you."

The Torth paused, no doubt debating in silence.

Deep down, Ariock knew hostages were a reasonable request. If the Torth Empire allowed him to walk away free, with all his friends and powers intact, why would he bother to waste time on a quest for a mythical lady? Why would he return? He would never willingly submit to the Torth—unless Vy was in their custody.

The Torth knew that, of course. They knew that Ariock would swap his freedom for Vy's.

Thomas must know it as well. He tried anyway. "Three hours," he said. "And we get to pick the hostages. Not you."

"U n a c c c c c c e p t a b l e." The Torth hiss was like snakes slithering through dry leaves.

"G i v v v e U s s s s t h e h o s t a g e s s s s We a s s s k e d f f f o r—"

"A n n n d—"

"W w w e g r a n t y o u t h r e e e e h o u r s s s s."

"T h a t i s s s s a l l."

The Servants of All readied their blaster gloves, and it was clear that they were done bargaining. Ariock steeled himself for a final battle.

CHAPTER 5

SEALED WITH A KISS

Clouds churned as Ariock's awareness expanded. He was the sky. He was the ground. The building shuddered as he shrugged his way into bedrock.

Before he could start killing, Thomas spoke in a cold tone.

"Wait."

The Torth stood like statues. Curiosity did not show on their waxy faces, but they must be listening—and with their ears rather than their minds, Ariock realized. Thomas and the Torth were withholding secrets from each other. Otherwise neither of them would have bothered to speak out loud.

Maybe Thomas really did have a viable plan.

Please, Ariock thought. With so many friends in danger, with the entire Alashani underground facing ruination, he had to trust Thomas. Any plan was better than none.

Everyone focused on the frail boy, even Garrett.

"I will be your hostage." Thomas's voice cracked. "If you take just me instead of anyone else."

Ariock stared in disbelief. The Torth were fighting to defeat "the Betrayer" and "the Giant." Perhaps Thomas had a perfect scheme, or a grand plan, but how could he simply hand the Torth one-half of what they wanted?

"A g r e e e e e e d." The Torth did not hesitate. They all shared a greedy look.

Torth always grabbed more than they deserved.

"Not Thomas." Sparks crackled up Ariock's massive chest as he gathered his power, coalescing it into lightning bolts. If he had to die in battle today, so be it. The Torth would not get what they wanted. Not this time.

"C o m e t o U s s s s." The whispered words blended with the toxic rainfall. "B e t r a a a y e r r r."

Garrett made desperate sounds in his throat. He yanked the sealed glue over his mouth, to no avail.

Ariock wasn't going to listen to protests. He prepared to smash as many greedy, soulless Torth as possible. Thomas should have known that he would never—

"Ariock." A feminine hand touched his.

Ariock came back to himself. Vy stood close. Far too close.

That was dangerous for her. His friends needed to be in a safe place before he released all his fury.

"I'll be their hostage," Vy said.

Ariock felt blindsided. He let his electrostatic war hammer evaporate and stared down at her, trying to process why she wanted to sacrifice her freedom.

Thomas watched as if he'd expected this.

The Torth began to hiss disagreeably, but Thomas interrupted them. "If you try to take me," he said, "you'll get a slaughterfest right here and now. Or . . ." Thomas milked the pause. "You can take the original hostages you asked for and gain the leverage you want. Plus we all get three hours."

Leverage. As if Vy and Cherise were just bargaining chips.

"I'm sure you can make elaborate plans if you have three hours to work." Thomas shrugged like he didn't care. "It's up to you. You've got to do what's best for your people."

The Servants of All exchanged blank-eyed glances.

Ariock could imagine the vicious debates they must be having. If they pressed for the Betrayer, they risked everything. Every Torth in the vicinity, including the Commander of All Living Things, would almost certainly get slaughtered by Ariock.

Or they could back down and accept the two human hostages.

Vy and Cherise held value. With Vy, especially, they could control the Giant. They could manipulate Ariock like he was a puppet on strings.

"Obviously," Thomas said, "we'd have to trust you to keep the hostages safe while we search for the Lady of Sorrow." He gave the Torth a challenging stare. "That should go without saying. If we win the bargain, then you'll need to release Vy and Cherise. Unharmed."

Ariock realized that Thomas had never intended to hand himself over. That had been a bluff. He'd counted on Vy being . . . well, Vy.

"Three hours." Vy lowered her voice. "You need that time." Her blue eyes shone through the grime on her face. "I know you'll win. And you'll come back to rescue me."

How could she feel so certain?

And how could Thomas be so self-assured? Ariock studied the boy with frustration, trying to figure out all the things he had not said and all the hints he had not given. His face betrayed nothing.

"This is something I can do." Vy rapped her knuckles against her prosthetic leg. "Otherwise I'll slow you down."

Ariock didn't care about being slowed down. He knew what sort of torture his enemies were capable of, from firsthand experience. How could he fight Torth if Vy was tortured whenever he made a threatening move? The Torth were guaranteed a win if they had her.

"We can't—" he began to say.

"The alternative is death. For all of us." Vy sounded like she was begging him to see a simple truth. "Whatever Thomas is planning, it's a way for us to win. I trust him." She gave Thomas a look of respect and turned back to Ariock. "And I trust you."

Ariock knew that if he battled the Torth Empire, he would eventually be worn down and slain. It might take a few hours. It might cost millions of lives. But it was inevitable. He could not defeat a galactic empire all by himself.

Thomas's secret plan had to be better than that. Any plan was better than a pointless slaughter.

And someone had to be the hostage.

But not Vy.

"I'm pretty sure you need Thomas." Vy looked ashamed. "You don't need me."

Ariock took her hands, but she pulled out of his gentle grasp and backed away from him. "Also—" She nodded toward the surviving warriors. "Three hours could make a huge difference for the Alashani. Please. Send someone to warn them that they're going to be invaded by Torth."

Trust Vy to prioritize people who regarded her as cargo. How could Ariock let her enter danger alone, without anyone on her side?

The Torth seemed to let out a collective breath. "W w w e e e a c c e p p p t."

"I want a way to monitor the hostages," Thomas said. "So we know they're safe. If you try to break the bargain, or cheat, then all bets are off."

"A g r e e e e d."

One of the Servants of All began to calibrate a data tablet. The Torth Empire might be disappointed to gain two humans rather than the Betrayer, but they were still willing to play the game.

"I guess I don't get a choice?" Cherise said.

Flen held her protectively, but her expectant look went past him, to Thomas.

"You get the same choice as Vy." Thomas met her stare.

That was all he gave her. No explanation. No acknowledgment of the danger. No loving reassurance. Just a curious stare.

Would Cherise willingly put herself in danger for the sake of everyone else? Or not?

Cherise glided toward the Torth, proud and stiff.

Flen seized her shoulder, but Cherise gently pulled his hand away. "Go to your parents and sister." She gave him a sad, sweet look. "Give them a chance to escape the coming invasion."

She left Flen behind. He stared after her with anguish.

"Remember," Thomas said. "If any harm comes to the hostages, or if they vanish, this bargain ends immediately. You can't touch them."

"G r a a a a n t e d."

"W w w w e e e e e w i l l n n n o t h a r r r m t h h h e m—"

"—a s l o n n n g a s y y y o u h h h o o o l d—"

"—t o y y y o u r e n n n d o f t h h h e b a r r r r r g a i n n n."

Their creaky reassurances meant little to Ariock. He figured they would interfere with the camera feed or exploit some loophole. Even if they were civil enough to wait the whole three hours, they would use that time to set up some kind of awful trap.

They would torture Vy and Cherise at the first chance they got.

A brutish Red Rank strode forward with a calibrated data tablet, presumably programmed to surveil the hostages.

"Give the monitoring tablet to Kessa," Thomas ordered.

The Red Rank stopped in his tracks and looked from the two ummins to Garrett's govki slave. Slaves were interchangeable to the Torth.

Then a look of surety came over his face, and he headed toward Kessa. Someone must have fed him the correct answer in the Megacosm.

It was illegal for slaves to learn or use technology. Kessa accepted the tablet, wary, with her blaster glove on hand, but the Red Rank simply turned and walked away. It seemed the Torth Empire did value this bargain, at least enough to bend a few of their own laws.

Flen glanced toward his premier Yeresunsa, searching for instructions or commands.

Jinishta looked defeated.

Flen removed his quiver and offered it to her. "The monsters have robbed me of my powers," he admitted, his cheeks pink with shame. "I am useless in battle."

Jinishta ignored the quiver. So Flen offered it to the other warriors, and one of them accepted it.

"Will you go and warn our people, Aral?" Flen asked. "And protect my family?"

Aral nodded.

"You don't need to—" Cherise began to assure Flen, but he cut her off.

"I am useless without my powers. If I am to die, I will die with you." Unarmed, Flen sprinted to catch up with Cherise. "If you will accept me?"

Ariock understood. Flen would not want to risk watching, helpless, while his family was enslaved.

Cherise softened. "Of course." She gripped Flen's hand.

The Servants of All stood there like uncaring mannequins. Ariock half wished that Flen had kept his spears, although the Torth would probably have confiscated them.

Garrett kept making urgent, muffled noises. Judging by his furious glares at Thomas, he disagreed with the plan.

Maybe Ariock should rip that gag away and let the old man say what was bothering him?

But when all was said and done, Thomas was the one who had rescued Ariock from crucifixion in the alien desert. Not Garrett. Ariock could not guess why his great-grandfather had abandoned him for decades, or where he'd been while Torth assassinated his family on Earth. But in the short time Ariock had known Garrett, he had seen him as both a swashbuckling hero and a cringing coward.

He didn't know Garrett. He had no idea how to trust him.

Thomas, on the other hand, had a steely glint in his yellow eyes. That glint had been there when he'd plotted the Torth massacre in the village of Duin. He'd looked that way when piloting their stolen streamship past countless enemy vessels. When Thomas got that look, things got done.

Vy seemed to think so, too. "Three hours." Her gaze included both Thomas and Ariock. "I trust you."

Many Torth whispered. "T h r e e e e e e e h h h o u r s s s s s."

"S s s s s s t a r t i n g n o w w w w w."

"S h o w w w w w U s s s s s p r o o o o f f f—"

"—o f t h e L a a a a d y o f S s s s s o r r o w w w—"

"—o r r r e l s s s s e—"

"—g i v v v e y o u r s s s e l v v v v e s t o U s s s s."

"W w w w i l l i n g l y y y."

Vy limped toward the waiting Servants of All.

Weptolyso made a growling sound deep in his throat. He loped after Vy. "I will ensure that the Torth respect this bargain, Son of Storms."

Yuey joined Weptolyso with a look of determination. Nussians were variable in size, but she was nearly as large as the former hall guard, albeit less scarred and scuffed up. "Where Weptolyso goes, I go."

Ariock shook his head, wondering if his friends had lost their minds. Did they have a death wish? If Ariock got lost, if he failed, if he made any mistakes whatsoever, there would be no rescue.

"There's no need to give the Torth extra hostages." Thomas sounded frustrated.

Ariock stared hard at the boy. Whatever secrets he was hiding, he had better have an excellent reason to pin his hopes—and Vy's life—on a wager about the so-called Lady of Sorrow.

Orla twirled a spear. "I will—"

"The Torth have enough hostages," Jinishta cut in sharply. "More than enough. Do not go."

Perhaps Orla was feeling her own shame. She put her spear away.

Ariock could cover a lot of ground in three strides. It seemed boorish to sweep Vy off her feet without warning, but if she was going to trust Thomas and the Torth Empire to keep her safe, then she needed to know that she could count on Ariock, as well. She needed to know that he cared.

"I love you," he told Vy, holding her.

Once Vy got over her initial surprise, she smiled. Her face was soft against the stubble of his cheeks.

Her kiss was deliberate and tender.

For a time, they were the only two people in the universe. Rain was the only sound.

Or so Ariock wished. He dared not let his extended awareness dissipate. As long as Torth were nearby, he could not afford to let down his guard, not even in a moment like this.

"I'll come back for you." Ariock's voice sounded too rough, too abrupt, but he couldn't say it softly. "I promise."

Her smile was special, just for him. "I know."

The last thing Ariock wanted to do was leave Vy among enemies. But the clock was ticking. The Alashani underground needed to be warned to prepare for war. And the Lady of Sorrow needed to be found.

"I promise."

"I know," Vy said again, with that smile, as if she had absorbed everything he thought about her.

Ariock set her on the ground. "Within three hours. I promise."

"I'll be waiting." She brushed his hand with hers.

Then she limped away, toward the waiting Torth army.

CHAPTER 6

TRIANGULATING SORROW

Ariock knew he couldn't waste time. Every second hung with the weight of a mountain, then dropped into an abyss of no return.

"Kessa?" Thomas beckoned Kessa over to his seat in the wrecked transport. "Let's shut off the spyware on that tablet. We don't want Torth listening to us."

Kessa handed over the device, and Thomas began to swipe and tap the screen.

"We must prepare for war," one of the four remaining warriors said. "Let us go. Let us warn the army."

"Ariock and I have another task," Thomas said. "But anyone who wants to return to the Alashani should go now. Run, and try to stay out of sight, or the Torth will scoop you up."

The warrior, Aral, looked disgusted to receive advice from a *rekveh*. He glanced at his premier for advice.

Jinishta looked bleak. "Go," she said. "Take Henshta and Orla with you."

Aral and Henshta looked surprised, but Orla was horror-struck. "No!" she cried. "I must stay with the messiah!"

"You've doomed our people." Jinishta's tone was cold and merciless. "You broke the Warrior's Pact."

Orla hung her head.

"There is no way Orla can atone," Jinishta went on, speaking past her, as if the petite warrior no longer mattered. "But if she cares for her family, or anyone outside herself, then maybe she will help defend our people." Jinishta pulled down her veil, revealing a haggard, mournful expression. "Maybe she can help our people escape slave collars."

That was unlikely.

Did Jinishta believe that a handful of exhausted warriors could fend off endless troops of Red Ranks? The messianic army might hold off Torth troops for a while. They might be able to defend a bottleneck.

For a while.

Three hours, Ariock hoped. *Let the Alashani stay safe for at least three hours.*

He needed to make good use of the time Vy and the other hostages were buying for him. As he watched, Red Ranks herded Vy and the others into a floating prison cage. Its hooded overhang dripped with sludge. The toxic rain of this planet streaked everything it touched.

Ariock turned toward Thomas. He had better have a solid plan.

"You'll need to conserve your powers," Thomas said to the warriors.

They turned hateful stares toward him.

"I'm just saying." Thomas shrugged. "Aral, Henshta, and Orla are suffering warning headaches. Maybe you can recover somewhat if you don't use your powers at all on the way back. But you'll need to work together if you want enough strength to lift the entrance boulder."

The warriors exchanged looks of concern.

"Also," Thomas said, "would you mind taking Dyoot with you?" He indicated the govki. "Garrett's slave could use an introduction to freedom."

The furry creature huddled inward, all six limbs hugged tight around a stout, blue-speckled body. It seemed Dyoot had been doing his best to avoid notice, not interacting with anyone, except for a few incredulous glances toward Garrett.

Ariock resisted an urge to stare at his muffled great-grandfather the same way. Why did a supposed hero, someone who had freed a thousand slaves . . . why did he own a slave?

Had Garrett acted as a typical Torth slave owner? Had he been abusive?

"I would like to go underground as well," Varktezo said, although he gazed longingly at the data tablet Kessa held. "Is that okay?"

The warriors offered grudging acceptance. They probably appreciated Varktezo's motive. All his countrymen were enjoying the lamplit city of Hufti, oblivious to danger. Someone had to devastate them with the news that they would likely be reenslaved.

Or tortured to death for being runaways.

Ariock wished he had been stealthier. He should have tried harder to avoid Torth notice. If there was any way to save the underground cities, he knew he had to try.

"Come on, Dyoot." Varktezo spoke to the slave in a friendly tone. "I can take you to a place where there are no Torth. By the way, how would you like to wear your very own blaster glove?"

The govki loosened up as the adolescent ummin spoke to him. A good thing, Ariock thought, since he did not want to waste time on long explanations about how freedom worked.

"Aren't you coming with us, Jinishta?" Orla sized up her premier with resentment.

"No." Jinishta lowered her head in shame. "My powers are gone. The Torth stung me with some sort of evil." She touched her long neck, where a microdart must have injected her.

"The inhibitor," Thomas explained.

"I cannot stretch my awareness," Jinishta admitted to her remaining warriors. "I have no headache, but I am as helpless as a cargo person. I do not know if my powers will come back."

"They will," Thomas said. "In a few orbits."

Henshta held out her black-wrapped hand. "Then let us take you to safety."

"Go home without me." Jinishta backed away, refusing the offer of help. "I will see this quest through, even though I am cargo." Her fierce gaze locked on Ariock. "I must see what the death of our people has wrought."

That was fair, Ariock figured. Jinishta, of all the Alashani, had suspected that Ariock was just a big human with flaws. Now she was learning that she had been right. The messiah myth was just that.

Maybe she would even begin to respect Thomas a little bit.

Anyway, it would be good to have her along. Jinishta was more able-bodied than Thomas, Kessa, or Garrett. Even with her powers inhibited, she had an innate understanding of battle tactics. She might be helpful.

"Fare well," Aral said.

"Good luck," Henshta added.

"I will await any sign from you, Messiah," Orla said fervently.

"Take care of the Teacher," Varktezo said.

The three warriors ran into the night, along with the adolescent ummin and the govki slave. Their black wraps should help them hide from enemies. Even so, they would need to find their way through the mazelike outskirts of Stratower City, and then they needed to get past the toxic Border River. Finally, they needed to travel through the ruins of the dead city and lift an entrance boulder, avoiding wild zoved and sludge serpents.

The people left with Ariock made for a strange crew. There was Jinishta, morose. Garrett made frustrated sounds behind the gag.

Thomas sat awkwardly inside the wreckage of the transport, lacking a powered chair. "That should do it," he told Kessa, nodding for her to take the data tablet. "The Torth shouldn't be able to track us now."

Kessa accepted the tablet, its screen illuminating her beaked face.

"You can toggle the square window to see the hostages," Thomas said. "The circular window is a city map."

Kessa tapped something and seemed fascinated by the result.

The Torth were departing also, riding hoverbikes or hovercarts. The hostage cage floated in their midst, probably by remote control. At least the hostages seemed safe. No shackles. No slave collars. For now.

With the Torth heading indoors, Ariock figured he could let his guard down a little bit. Not completely. The Torth had agreed to leave him in peace for three hours, but Torth had been known to change their minds.

And they held too many advantages.

Ariock figured that if a Torth decided to break the bargain and shoot at him—even if they failed to hit him—other Torth would murder Vy before he had a chance to slaughter his way across the city in order to rescue her. He would never get to her in time.

And if a Torth succeeded in hitting him with the inhibitor? Then he would be unable to rescue anyone. He and everyone he cared about would be as good as dead.

"What's the plan?" Ariock demanded, irked that he had to ask.

"We find the Lady of Sorrow," Thomas said. "And we rescue her."

Ariock waited impatiently for Thomas to reveal the real plan. The supposed quest for a phantom must be a facade for a brilliant, secret scheme.

"Here's what I didn't tell the Torth," Thomas said, self-satisfied.

Ariock leaned closer.

"The Lady of Sorrow is a Yeresunsa," Thomas said. "The Torth don't believe she exists, except as a slave legend. But she's real. She's powerful, and I have reason to believe that she'll be on our side."

Ariock concealed his impatience. Surely Thomas knew that they didn't need yet another hapless warrior to look after.

"Her power is in your league, Ariock," Thomas said. "She might even be more powerful than you. It's possible she can wipe out all the Torth on this planet."

Unease wormed through Ariock. He recalled the dank, pitch-black labyrinth and the smell of the dungeon cave. Thomas had been dying in that pit. His charcoal scribbles, so macabre, had showed his disturbed state of mind.

How real was the Lady of Sorrow?

"Mrmph!" Garrett made a grinding, insistent noise in the back of his throat. He yanked at the gag.

"I saw an opportunity," Thomas went on, as if to drown out Garrett's drama. "The Torth Empire is in upheaval. You fractured them with your hammer blow." He gave Ariock a warm look, full of pride. "I figure we have a good chance to escape this planet by playing Torth factions off each other. The Majority no longer trusts its own leaders."

Ah. So that explained why the Servants of All had been receptive to a bargain.

It was easy to be brave with armies at their beck and call. Bereft of all that firepower . . . ? From the perspective of the shaken Torth leadership team, it was far better to defeat Ariock through a peaceful bargain rather than through a costly battle.

"And I guarantee that the Torth aren't expecting two Ariocks," Thomas said. "With the Lady of Sorrow on our side, we'll effectively double our power. She might even help the Alashani."

"I see." Ariock tried to imagine the Lady of Sorrow as a real person. Demented from eons of imprisonment. Possibly immortal. Haunting. And powerful enough to annihilate a planetary population.

"And she's a mind reader." Thomas made that sound like an added bonus. "So we won't have to waste time explaining things to her."

Ariock wasn't sure he wanted to encounter the Lady of Sorrow, even if she did exist.

Garrett glared at them, making frustrated "Mmph!" sounds.

Ariock extended his awareness with a mixture of shame and reluctance. He didn't want to hear whatever whinging Garrett wanted to insert, but the old man didn't deserve to stay gagged.

Ariock used his powers to rip the plastic glue away. Garrett grunted in pain and clapped a hand to his jaw. The gag took a few white beard hairs with it.

"Also," Thomas said, "I figure we can rally the Alashani into an army, and—"

"Idiot!" Garrett rubbed his bearded jaw, quivering with rage.

Thomas faltered. He shot Garrett a quizzical look, clearly uncertain whom the "idiot" comment was directed at.

"Stupid. Stupid. Stupid!" Garrett pounded his staff against the ground each time, emphasizing the word.

"What are you talking about?" Thomas said.

"Oh, look at me!" Garrett shrilled in a mockery of Thomas's voice, his eyes wildly childish. "I bet I can outwit the Torth Empire! No one can outsmart me!" He glared at Thomas, and his tone returned to its normal deep gruffness. "You have zero concept of what you promised."

Thomas looked stung. "I saved us. The Torth would have slaughtered Ariock."

"This is worse!" Garrett snapped. "You gave them collateral! Now they're guaranteed to win and rule the universe forever."

"We don't have time for this." Thomas drew himself up. "I read the truth in your mind. You know where—"

"I was bluffing!" Garrett laughed raggedly.

"You can't bluff to me." Scorn dripped from Thomas's tone. "Tell us where she is." Embers glowed in the air around him. "Or I will get the truth out of you."

Ariock felt like a riled dog on a frayed leash. Seconds trickled past, each one a reminder that Vy was getting farther away.

"I have no idea where she is!" Garrett threw up his hands in disgust. "I've spent my entire life searching for her and I never succeeded!"

"He's a liar." Thomas's yellow eyes blazed. "Don't trust him, Ariock. He knows where she is. I'm sure of it."

"Oh, for Pete's sake!" Garrett began to hobble farther away. "I saved your miserable neck, and this is how you repay me? If I knew where to find the Lady of Sorrow, I would have freed her decades ago. You idiot!"

"Put him in my range." Thomas pointed imperiously to Garrett. "I'll dig out everything he's hiding. Trust me. He knows."

Garrett growled and hobbled faster.

Ariock stared from one mind reader to the other. One of them must be wrong, or lying, but he couldn't tell whom.

He reached out with his powers. He really didn't want to manhandle his elderly great-grandfather, but there was no time for coddling or coaxing. He gently pushed Garrett into Thomas's range, solidifying the air to trap him in place.

Thomas frowned.

"Oh, you can't find what you're looking for?" Garrett said with savage sarcasm. "What a shocker."

A shadow of worry crossed Thomas's face.

Garrett's fury was all directed at Thomas. "You arrogant child. Did it not occur to you that I can lie to mind readers in the Megacosm?"

Ariock didn't like Thomas's reaction. He looked stunned.

"I've had a lifetime of practice at fooling Torth," Garrett said. "How do you think I survived for twenty years among them?"

"That's—"

"Impossible?" Garrett broke into Thomas's protest. "Boy, you can't guess half of what I'm capable of. You don't get to be my age, with my powers, unless you've learned to run mental circles around the average Torth."

Ariock struggled to keep his awareness tight, although it wanted to leap out in electric sparks. Had he let Vy walk into danger—torture and death— for a flawed plan?

"The reason you think it's impossible," Garrett went on, ruthless, "is because you're a sniveling coward. You'll never have the guts to do what I do. You let the Torth make you into one of them. But I never caved in. I never became one of the monsters!"

Ariock released his extended awareness, no longer willing to force Garrett and Thomas into proximity of each other. He had never seen Thomas so upset. The boy's shoulders were hunched up. He looked like he was enduring a physical attack.

Garrett hobbled backward, still hurling words at Thomas. "So yes, I broadcasted a lie. Of course I wanted the Torth to fear that I might have a secret weapon! I wanted to seem cocky. But it was an act!" He gave Thomas a look of disgust. "It didn't occur to me that you would fall for it. Seeing as how you're a supergenius and all."

"You could have given me a hint," Thomas said tersely.

That was an understatement, Ariock thought. Thomas picked up on details that no one else noticed, and he could process information in nanoseconds. A subtle hint would have been enough.

"Or you could have considered every possibility," Garrett said, backing farther away from Thomas's range. "I guess I shouldn't be surprised that you fell for it, since you are one of them."

He made *them* sound like a cuss word, the way most albinos said *rekveh*.

Thomas refocused on Garrett with newfound suspicion. "So, what's the secret trick? Just how do you fool mind readers, without actually becoming what you're pretending to be?"

"It's a lot of hard work," Garrett said imperiously.

It seemed the two of them had had a tragic misunderstanding. But shouldn't Garrett take some of the blame?

The cage was out of sight now. Indoors. Ariock couldn't guess where Vy was or what was happening to her, but he knew they no longer had three hours. They must have wasted ten minutes already.

"Do you have a plan?" Ariock looked from Thomas to Garrett, grasping for a shred of hope. "Any plan at all?" Surely one of them would provide answers.

His deep voice got their attention, and they quieted.

"We're at the mercy of the Torth now." Garrett turned away with a growl of disgust. "Way to go, genius."

"I bought us time," Thomas said. "And I thought I'd bought us more than that." He shot Garrett another frustrated, almost perplexed look.

Ariock's frustration needed an outlet. He forced his awareness to stay small, to think. Thomas had truly believed that he could ally with the Lady of Sorrow. Or weaponize her.

And it seemed Garrett actually believed that, as well.

Why did both Thomas and Garrett seem obsessed with a weeping phantom?

"What can you tell me about the Lady of Sorrow?" Ariock asked. "Do you have any hints? Anything to go on?"

Garrett slumped, looking defeated. "I've spent a hundred years trying to find her. All I can tell you, for certain, is that she must be somewhere in this city." He gestured vaguely. "Maybe the Stratower. Maybe the Isolatorium. I've never been able to figure out exactly where."

Ariock turned to Thomas.

"She appeared to me in that dungeon." There was a haunted look in Thomas's eyes. "I just . . . I figured her power would help us." He looked ashamed. "And Garrett knows how to summon her. Or so I thought."

Whenever Thomas spoke of his time in the sensory deprivation pit, he stopped looking like a child. Ariock understood scars like that.

Garrett gave him a sharp look. "The Lady of Sorrow appeared to you?"

Thomas nodded.

"Hmm." Garrett frowned in thought. "In all my years of research, I've never heard of her appearing to a Torth."

Thomas gave him a level look.

Garrett studied Thomas with newfound speculation. Then he straightened in a sudden, decisive movement. "Tell me where the Lady of Sorrow appeared to you."

Thomas looked cautious.

"Where?" Garrett demanded. "Was it in the dungeon labyrinth of Hufti?"

"Yes." Thomas observed Garrett's reaction with curiosity. "Beyond the gear gate and past the spike pits. I was in the lowest level."

Jinishta stared at them. She couldn't be happy to hear mind readers discussing the secrets of her home city.

Garrett used his staff to scrape marks in the muck, a series of dots and dashes that looked haphazard. "You saw her here." He scraped a line through one of the dots. "I saw her here." He scraped through another dot.

Ariock folded his arms, annoyed by the prolonged discussion. But at least they seemed to be collaborating.

"Did she offer you her power?" Garrett asked Thomas.

Thomas nodded.

"She only does that within this alignment." Garrett scraped connections in the muck, crossing lines until they resembled an off-kilter asterisk.

"She did it to you, too." Thomas sounded certain.

"Yup." Garrett hacked more marks. "There's a dungeon here. And a dungeon here. And here."

"That's how you escaped the Isolatorium, all those years ago," Thomas said in a tone of realization. "You channeled her power."

"I did." Garrett drew a circle around the lopsided center of a messy asterisk.

"She inundated you with power," Thomas guessed. "And you used it to crack Bloodbath Plaza, and free a thousand slaves, and kill a thousand Torth."

"That's right," Garrett confirmed. "I've never been that powerful before or since." He etched more lines in the muck. "If only I'd known what I was doing. With her power surge, I could have done so much more. I could have cracked the Isolatorium wide open. Maybe I could have taken over this planet. For a short time, anyway. Until her power surge left me."

Ariock gazed at the lines, not quite willing to let Jinishta or Kessa meet his eyes. He was descended from a fraud. Jonathan Stead had borrowed someone else's power. He'd used it to bust out of prison, and he hadn't even tried to create an opening for other escapees.

His heroism was an accident.

But Garrett had purposely tricked the Alashani civilization and put them in danger.

He had abandoned his daughter and grandson and other descendants.

And he had owned slaves instead of freeing them.

A fraud.

"Most sightings of the Lady of Sorrow happen near rivers," Garrett went on. "In dungeons near rivers. Particularly the River of Blood, in the Isolatorium. My encounter with her happened there. But so many people die horrible deaths in that place, I figured it skewed the data. Now, with some new data . . ." He etched a new asterisk, then stood back from his handiwork. "It's rough, mind you. But this has got to be where she is."

Ariock tried to make sense of all the lines. "Where?"

"I suspected. But now I'm certain." Garrett lifted his staff and pointed toward the immense shape that dominated the sky. "She's near the center of the Stratower."

CHAPTER 7

A NEBULOUS THRUM

Ariock could have run and jumped his way straight to the Stratower, as easy as a thrown spear. But it was the largest building in the known universe, larger than most cities just around its base. It extended beyond the atmosphere. For all he knew, it plunged deep into the planet's core as well.

"Where inside the Stratower?" he asked, not really expecting an answer.

Garrett shook his head.

"It would take lifetimes without end to search that building," Jinishta observed. Her tone was utterly devoid of hope.

Ariock considered other ways to give himself an advantage over the Torth. There must be something more practical than searching for a weeping phantom. Could he create improved armor for himself? Or . . .

"Garrett, can you teach me to teleport?" He looked to his great-grandfather.

Garrett looked taken aback, then thoughtful. "I've never taught anyone to use powers."

Ariock tried to look like a ready student.

"Teleportation is intensive," Garrett said. "It's more draining than healing someone with a fatal injury. It wears me out right away." He assessed Ariock. "It's dangerous for you to experiment with something intense right now. We need you at top strength."

"I'll be fine." Ariock had never gotten worn-out. He did have trouble multitasking, and he couldn't hold an important conversation while healing sick or injured people. Still . . . "I think I can handle it," he said.

"All right." Garrett stroked his short beard. "Let's see. Can you put yourself in a clairvoyant trance?"

"What?"

"It's complicated." Garrett spoke as if the explanation was a burdensome chore. "It's like . . . traveling without a body. Have you heard of astral projection?"

Ariock nodded.

"That's what it is," Garrett said. "And then, once your ghost self is where you want to be, you yank yourself inside out, body to mind, instead of the other way around." He illustrated with hand gestures.

Ariock stared, trying to comprehend.

"Oh, hell," Garrett said. "You'd get it if you could read minds."

"I could help," Thomas offered. "I can translate anything in your mind into eloquent words."

Garrett glared a warning his way.

Ariock had been keeping his awareness puffed out. The life sparks of his companions brushed through him, like static electricity on skin, but one was far more vibrant than the others.

Thomas's spark was no longer weak and guttering. It was a blaze of potency. In contrast, Garrett, Jinishta, and Kessa were all equal.

The sparks of the Servants of All had glowed like Thomas was doing now. It hadn't mattered when a thick wall had hidden them from sight.

"I can detect Yeresunsa," Ariock said, realizing the implications. "You say the Lady of Sorrow is ultrapowerful?"

Thomas and Garrett both reassessed him.

"I'm going to find her." Ariock closed his eyes to maximize his focus and pushed himself further than he ever had.

Life sparks ghosted through his awareness. He tried to ignore all the low buildings between his core self and the Stratower, but it was impossible. Thousands of unseen people trundled within him. More than thousands. They might as well be his blood cells, his inner workings, as numerous as stars in a nebula.

Some glowed a little more vibrantly. Some were dim and faint. But they were such a multitude, the differences seemed inconsequential. Even with his eyes closed and his full focus on their tickling presence, he would not have known if a handful of sparks winked out, or if any new ones appeared. There must be tens of thousands.

He pushed his awareness into the Stratower itself.

The Lady of Sorrow, if she existed, ought to glow bright. She should be like Venus on the clear winter nights when he'd peered through the sky room window.

Ariock wondered if he glowed more brightly than other people. Was this how Garrett had located him?

The Stratower was bigger than a mountain range and wider than a storm. The most powerful shani warriors could barely inhabit a one-block neighborhood of their underground cities, but Ariock could encompass many miles. In fact, he had never found his limit. He had no idea if he could inhabit this much complex space.

Carefully, gently, he expanded through level after level of the Stratower.

It seemed dangerous to incorporate so much into himself. A wrong eye blink and walls would shatter. A twitch or a sneeze would ripple through the entire Stratower and likely get thousands of innocent people killed.

He was grateful for all the times he'd practiced stillness around his mother, trying not to call any attention to himself. That was crucial here. He had no room for casual guesswork about the chambers and arteries of his vast new body.

There were oddities. A viscous river flowed within the Stratower, its liquid too thick to be water. A cold abyss stretched from the astronomical heights to the lower basement. If that was an elevator shaft, it must be terrifying to behold.

But overall, as Ariock filled floor after floor of the immense building, he sensed an unremarkable honeycomb of offices, forums, ramps, corridors, vehicles, and people. The Stratower was a vertical city. Millions of lives filled him. Some of the life sparks glowed with Yeresunsa vibrancy, but none particularly stood out.

Perhaps, if the Lady of Sorrow existed at all, her life spark was only a faint ember? Poor health or the inhibitor serum would do that to a Yeresunsa. Maybe she was undetectable.

Frustrated, Ariock explored his crown, which was surrounded by spaceship traffic. He explored his lowest depths, a water-soaked tomb that was devoid of life.

Ancient granite blocks shifted and ancient struts groaned, responding to small shifts in his mood, no matter how delicate he was. The tiny life sparks within him paused. The city traffic must be wary.

Frustration was dangerous.

His own monstrous awareness unnerved him. How could he be so vast?

He had to extricate himself before he caused a disaster. Bit by bit, Ariock rolled himself out of countless rooms, out of miles of ornate stonework.

As he retreated toward his distant core self, he became aware of a powerful thrum.

It was like a life spark, but diffuse, lacking any source. It seemed to exist everywhere. Ariock had detected this thrum when he'd first arrived on this planet, but he had gotten so used to it, the weirdness had stopped registering. It had become mere background noise whenever he extended his awareness.

He did not dare furrow his brow in thought. That would destroy buildings. Before he could allow himself to think, first he had to return to his natural size again. So he focused on taking himself out of walls and floors with the utmost care, trying very hard not to break anything.

At last, after several tense minutes, Ariock let out a trembling sigh of relief. His change in stature left him feeling vulnerable, but at least he had not accidentally murdered millions of innocent people. He had not harmed anyone. That mattered.

He inwardly decided to never go huge like that again. His size limit ought to be a storm, no bigger.

"You know, that's really dangerous." Garrett sounded gruff. "Anyway, I've tried it before. I can encompass a whole city when I have access to my powers."

Ariock's shoulders drooped as he realized that he had needlessly risked a city population. He should have asked before he went exploring. What made him think he could succeed where everyone else in history had failed?

"It was a good idea." Thomas watched Ariock with a thoughtful expression that bordered on respect.

"If the Lady of Sorrow could be found that way," Garrett said, "I would have found her. I tried everything. Mind probes. Clairvoyant trances. Years of research. Scanning for life sparks. It's all futile."

Ariock figured they should give up on this mad quest. Tales of the Lady of Sorrow stretched back for millennia. Other people who were smarter than him, and more resourceful, had tried to find her. And failed. The mysterious specter might be insane, and really, she might not even exist at all.

"You sensed something." Thomas was still assessing Ariock, perhaps probing his mind. "A nebulous thrum."

"A what?" Garrett said.

"Ariock senses raw power on this planet," Thomas said. "Like an ultrapowerful life spark without a focal point. Without a corporeal form."

Garrett began to look interested again.

"Maybe," Thomas said, "when she lends her power to a fellow prisoner, her power is able to gain a body and a focal point. But otherwise, she's trapped outside of time, or outside of space."

"Or both." Garrett stood straighter, leaning on his cane. "But if she has no body, then how can anyone find her?"

"She appears to people who feel what she feels," Thomas said. "The darkest despair."

"Yeah." Garrett looked like he wanted a cigarette. "So?"

"So she can be summoned," Thomas said.

"Not easily." Garrett's heavy tone drew Ariock's attention. Whatever secrets Garrett was hiding—whatever his reasons for masquerading as a Torth, whatever his reasons for pretending to be a great hero—he had suffered in the Isolatorium. He had battle scars.

And he was family.

Ariock knelt and grasped Garrett's lumpy hands, careful not to squeeze. "I'll do anything to rescue Vy." He met his great-grandfather at eye level, purple eyes to purple eyes. "How did you summon the Lady of Sorrow? Can we try it?"

Garrett hung his head. "I wish I could help."

"I'm desperate," Ariock pointed out.

"No." Garrett chuckled in a sad way. "You're not."

"You have to be suicidal." Thomas shared the same haunted look as Garrett. "And worse. You need to have no hope whatsoever."

Ariock sank to the ground, aware that he likely wouldn't survive the conditions necessary for an encounter with the Lady of Sorrow.

He traced the suicide scar hidden under his black wraps and leather armor. That night in the sky room, when he had knifed his arm open . . . well, he had been drowning in his own darkness. Beauty and wonder never would have registered. If a weeping ghost had appeared to him? He wouldn't have cared. He would have kept slicing.

Jinishta whispered something lyrical in her own language.

Thomas translated. "If the Lady of Sorrow permits you to return to the realm of the living, then you are a hero. But consider yourself warned. If you see her a second time, she will drag you unto death."

"Right," Garrett said. "That's just a fancy way of saying that she never appears to the same person twice." He gestured to himself and Thomas. "As far as I know, it's true. I expect that anyone who sees her a second time dies."

Kessa glanced up from a Red Rank corpse, where she was scavenging an extra blaster glove. "Jinishta and I have never seen her. Neither has Ariock."

Therefore, they had three chances to make her appear.

But who wanted to suffer a near-death ordeal?

It was all so far-fetched. Even if the phantom did show up, why would she agree to help Ariock slay Torth? Did he think he was some kind of hero in a story?

Really, Ariock knew he would be lucky to escape this planet with his life. Never mind the Alashani underground. It hurt to think of his cheerful albino cousins and his wrestling partners in the nussian quarter. And Pung. And the refugees from Duin. And Chaniyelem and Deschuba. And everyone else who would be slaughtered or enslaved by Torth.

But what could he do? Ariock avoided looking at Jinishta. He needed to just focus on rescuing Vy.

"I was able to communicate with the Lady of Sorrow," Thomas said. "Without words. She read my mind."

"Same," Garrett said.

"Blasphemy," Jinishta said, but her heart wasn't in it. She seemed to realize that hurling insults at mind readers accomplished nothing, especially when she was powerless and without backup.

"She only communicates through emotions." Thomas seemed to be thinking out loud. "She detects despair. She's attracted to it. So it's possible we can create a resonance with her."

Garrett was listening. Ariock wondered if that was a sign that Thomas was onto something.

"As telepaths, we can do more," Thomas said. "Especially me. I might be able to scan her mind and find out how to free her. I can work fast. I just need her to be summoned nearby, and maybe a few minutes where she stays with that person."

Garrett rolled his eyes. "Oh, I've had the same idea. I just haven't been able to recreate the right conditions for her to show up."

Thomas gave him a skeptical look.

"I've tried everything," Garrett said. "Believe me." There was darkness in his tone. "I've had twenty years to try things."

"Have you revisited the Isolatorium?" Thomas asked.

Garrett looked appalled.

"If any place is full of despair," Thomas said, "it's there. It's right near the Stratower. It could be a gateway to where she is. And this time, you have some new factors."

A look of dawning realization—and fear—came over Garrett's face.

"I can take any memory and recreate it in my imagination," Thomas said, "so it seems indistinguishable from reality to a mind reader." He hesitated, letting the conclusion sink in. "I can relive your ordeal."

Garrett looked intrigued as well as unsettled. "Do you really want to?" He sounded disbelieving.

"I'll do anything to rescue her," Thomas said.

The plan, such as it was, sounded insane to Ariock. If they did manage to summon the Lady of Sorrow, what came next? Hopes and prayers? Were they going to trap her? Make a deal with her?

Thomas turned to him. "I know it's a long shot. But I swear, you won't win any other way. We need to take the chance."

He sounded certain.

Ariock wanted to disbelieve Thomas, but it was impossible to dismiss the truthfulness in his yellow eyes. Besides, Garrett looked like he was searching for a valid reason to reject the plan—and failing.

"You want to go to the place where I was tortured?" Garrett said.

Thomas nodded. "It's where she shows up most frequently. Seems like the ideal place to start."

"Well, our transport is kaput." Garrett gestured at the wrecked vehicle.

Ariock extended his awareness to encompass the sporty transport. He might not have brilliant ideas, and he would probably never defeat the Torth Empire, but at least he could lift heavy objects. "I'll fly us," he said.

CHAPTER 8

RIVER OF BLOOD

As a slave, Kessa never would have imagined that she would meet legends such as Jonathan Stead. No one back home would believe her unexpected adventures, even if she told them without a single embellishment.

But they might believe her a little bit if they could see her right now.

The blaster glove fit loosely over Kessa's three-fingered ummin hand, and she had an extra one tucked into her wraps. She had scavenged them from dead Red Ranks. She also carried a data tablet. With a few finger taps, she could explore a wire-frame representation of any part of Stratower City. An interactive map enabled her to locate her hostage friends, represented by a glowing circle. A magical window enabled her to see their very faces, through an artificial eye that Thomas called a "camera."

Kessa used to take ignorance for granted. She had assumed that technology was too mysterious, too complex, for mere slaves to comprehend. But now that she could play with a data tablet without fearing a deadly punishment . . .

She was amazed by how easy it was to learn Torth glyphs. It did not require godlike intellect, as all slaves assumed. Really. An ummin child could figure it out.

She kept using it to check on Vy, Cherise, Flen, Weptolyso, and Yuey. They filled the onscreen window. There was no sound, but the hostages seemed able to speak to each other. The Torth were keeping their promise so far, treating the hostages better than most slaves or prisoners.

A string of changing numerical glyphs warned that their safety had a time limit. Kessa had studied Thomas's digital wristwatch, so she knew how humans symbolized numbers. She'd learned how to read Alashani pendulum clocks, as well. But she still didn't know the Torth way. She figured a few moments of study would solve that.

"I'll take the pilot's seat." Garrett spoke in an imperious tone. "Move the boy to the cargo hold, in back. I don't want him reading my mind."

"I don't want to risk falling out," Thomas said.

The transport was a wreck, with most of the wall panels destroyed. Any edge meant being exposed to the stormy air.

Garrett turned to Ariock. "I want him out of range. That means he sits in the far back."

"If you put me near an open wall," Thomas said, "I could fall out. It's not like I have functional muscles." He indicated his twiglike limbs.

"We don't have time to make you a kiddie seat," Garrett said. "Just yell if you fall out. Ariock will make sure you don't die."

"I don't want any *rekvehs* near me," Jinishta said.

Ariock glowered. The rain turned to ice, pelting them like tiny rocks. His concerns were clearly for civilizations and for survival, not for who sat where.

Kessa defused the tension. "I will hold on to Thomas." She scooped up the NAI-12 case first and tucked it into an elastic cargo pocket inside the rear of the transport, along with the data tablet. Then she hurried to the pilot's seat and picked up Thomas.

Lifting him was a bit of a struggle, due to her own frailty. At least Thomas made it easier. He clung to her.

"I will make sure you don't fall out," Kessa assured him.

Thomas tightened his grip in acknowledgment.

As Kessa made herself comfortable in the cargo hold, Jinishta launched herself toward the front of the vehicle with a dramatic sigh. Then she froze, even more resentful as Garrett settled himself into the pilot's seat.

Jinishta paused in the center, jaw clenched, caught within range of two mind readers.

Kessa almost hoped she would decide to go home and help her beleaguered people. There was enough tension between the Yeresunsa in this vehicle.

Ariock squeezed into the transport.

He had to use his powers in order to rip out the last passenger seat so he could scrunch up his long legs in its place. The warped ceiling was too low for him, so he leaned his head out one side, with one huge shoulder pressed against the ceiling, holding him in place. His position looked uncomfortable.

"Tell me where to go," he said in a commanding voice.

"The Isolatorium is that way." Garrett pointed with his staff. "Around the right flank of the Stratower."

Their misshapen wreck of a transport began to levitate, wobbling. Ariock must be familiarizing himself with the vehicle.

Jinishta sat cross-legged on the floor next to Ariock. She stared at her overgrown cousin with a look that was full of wonderment. "Are you . . ." She swallowed as the transport levitated higher. "Aren't you afraid you might, uh, drop us?"

"Ariock isn't an Alashani weakling," Garrett said with scorn. "Although he should be a little more conservative with his power usage." He aimed that insinuating remark at his great-grandson.

Their wreck of a transport flew. It moved as silently as rain, held aloft only by Ariock's will.

"Is everyone holding on tight?" Ariock asked. "I'd rather not have to save anyone."

Kessa gripped a mounting bracket that was firmly attached to the transport. She kept Thomas safe with her other arm wrapped around him.

"This should be impossible," Jinishta murmured.

When Kessa glanced into the interior of the transport, she saw the premier rigid with alarm, gripping seat brackets. Apparently Jinishta did not trust Ariock to carry a loaded vehicle. She had seen him operate an entire aqueduct factory, but perhaps this involved a more intense level of strength?

"Head a little more that way." Garrett gestured.

Their vehicle banked, sailing above black crevasses and mysterious rooftops. Sludge oozed off overhangs in muddy waterfalls. Covered bridges resembled hungry mouths, with toothy stalactites fed by eons of toxic rainwater.

Jinishta gazed at the ethereal glow of city lights in slack-jawed amazement. The concept of flying, and weather, and skyscrapers . . . it was all alien to an Alashani.

"You fly well," Garrett said.

Ariock had no room to straighten with pride, but his shoulder pressed against the ceiling a little bit more.

"But you ought to let go of your shielding," Garrett added. "You don't need to stretch your focus so thin. There's no reason to strain yourself when you don't have to."

"I'm not feeling any strain," Ariock said.

It seemed true. Their transport sailed above a labyrinth of chasms and rooftops, carried with surety and strength.

They banked. Jinishta shouted with dismay, and one of her spears clattered to the floor, bounced, then tumbled into darkness.

"If you hit your limit, then we're all in major trouble." Garrett's tone was sharp, perhaps in response to Ariock's attitude. "You saw how helpless Orla became? That could happen to you. Even Yeresunsa of our caliber can get depleted. And I guarantee, if you lose your powers, it will be when you need them most."

Ariock made an uninterested sound.

If he was dismissive, Kessa couldn't blame him. Jinishta and other warriors had given Ariock frequent admonishments about the warning headache, yet he never ran out of strength.

"You don't need to shield us." Garrett was insistent. "Kessa will keep a lookout with her sharp eyesight. She'll warn us if the Torth send missiles our way." He turned in his seat to peer at her. "Right, Kessa?"

"I will do my best." Kessa made herself sound confident, although she already had plenty to concentrate on, holding Thomas and glancing at the screen of the data tablet from time to time, through the mesh pocket of the cargo holder. The hostages looked safe.

It felt strange to soar above Torth buildings without being attacked. No missiles. Kessa imagined millions of unseen Torth, warm in their luxurious beds, or soaking in their spas, tended to by slaves who considered today to be just another dreary, ordinary day.

But those Torth were watching Ariock right now. Biding their time. Waiting for him to fail. Waiting for him to run out of strength or out of luck.

If there was any way for Ariock to triumph, then Kessa would make sure he saw it. She studied the city. She surveyed the monumental darkness of the Stratower.

"Even if the Torth do break their word," Garrett said, "the rest of us are not entirely helpless." He patted his cloak. "We're armed with blaster gloves. Except for Jinishta."

Ariock glanced at his great-grandfather. "What were you doing, as a Torth?"

Jinishta sounded stressed. "Should you be talking while you fly us, Ariock? Be careful!"

"I'm fine," Ariock told her dismissively. He turned back to Garrett. "Why were you living as a Torth?"

"I was gathering intelligence," Garrett said, his tone self-important and a little defensive. "My goal is to destroy the Torth Empire."

Grandiose.

It sounded like a lie, but Kessa kept her doubts to herself. Garrett did not quite match her heroic vision of Jonathan Stead. He seemed petty. He hid things. Like that blaster glove. Kessa had the impression that Garrett performed every word he spoke.

"Exactly," Thomas whispered, low enough so that only Kessa could hear. "He's a habitual liar. I need to get close enough to absorb his memories. I didn't manage to soak it all up, and I need to."

Jinishta had scooted away from Garrett. That put her near the cargo hold, and she cringed back, away from Thomas.

"I won't hurt you," Thomas said.

Jinishta looked even more scared.

Kessa wrapped her arm around Thomas as the transport banked, trying to show that he was a child rather than a monster. "Migyatel said the messiah shall have three advisers," Kessa pointed out. "Three mind readers." She indicated Thomas and Garrett.

Jinishta tightened her mouth with misery. Perhaps she was losing her faith? And maybe she felt vulnerable without her powers.

"If you would like a blaster glove," Kessa said, "I have an extra one. It would be more effective than your spears."

Jinishta jerked back with revulsion. No doubt she considered Torth-made equipment to be evil. Her people stowed stolen Torth gear in their monastery, but it was all untouchable.

After a moment, Jinishta looked reluctantly curious. "How is it that an ummin knows how to kill like a Torth?"

Her tone was almost respectful. She must have noticed that the "cargo people" had slain as many Torth as the Yeresunsa Alashani warriors. And they had done it without telekinesis, enhanced agility, or electric zaps.

"Everyone in Duin learned how to shoot blaster gloves." Kessa wondered if the premier had forgotten the tales told by Duin refugees. "Thomas taught us." She indicated the boy in her arms.

Jinishta looked like she was reevaluating a few misconceptions.

"Most of my friends are better at shooting than I am," Kessa admitted. "Irarjeg would be a good teacher. Also Pung."

Someone in Hufti should have asked the Duin ummins to teach blaster glove lessons. More than one hundred ummins could give a lot of lessons. Such training could save lives in the upcoming invasion of the underground cities.

But, of course, no one had asked. The Alashani thought very little of former slaves.

Jinishta looked like she was grappling with new ideas. She frowned at the rain-soaked city, and the enormity of the Stratower, and then at Thomas.

"That's the Isolatorium." Garrett pointed with his staff. "That building there."

A long, low structure spidered against the endless curvature of the Stratower. Sheets of black rain obscured its spiked hoods. Every opening was barred with lumpy pillars, like black runnels of saliva, frozen in time.

Ariock must feel some trepidation, because their transport slowed.

Kessa scanned the skies, then the ground, searching for threats. The place looked dead. But her gaze was drawn to what looked like a frothing canal, shielded by walls and imposing statues. The canal emerged from one hood of the Isolatorium. It crossed a rain-drenched plaza and plugged into the Stratower like an obscene artery.

Were those colossal guardian statues supposed to be Torth? But Torth did not sculpt or carve, as far as Kessa knew. They did not worship gods or admire anything. If they owned statues, they were stolen from a conquered civilization.

The artistry looked vaguely Alashani.

But these figures were eroded and broken, unlike the shrines to the Lord of Thieves or the Maiden of Candlelight. Heads and limbs were missing. The grime of eternal rainfall caked them, obscuring their features.

"No one knows who sculpted those statues," Garrett said. "They've stood for tens of thousands of years, since before the Torth existed."

He must be answering someone else's thoughts. All the same, a chill ran through Kessa. She remembered Thomas saying that slaves used to rule themselves.

The Torth Empire was not eternal.

The Torth used to be nothing. Perhaps someday, they would be nothing once more.

"That canal down there is known as the River of Blood." Garrett pointed with his staff. "So many unfortunate would-be rebels are tortured in the Isolatorium on a daily basis, their blood feeds a river."

Blood sopped over the canal walls, washing the feet of the ancient statues. A coppery odor saturated the air. Half-glimpsed chunks of torsos and limbs floated in the torrent.

Kessa didn't have enough tears for every dead slave. She almost wished she did, like the mythical Lady of Sorrow. But she had already wept a lifetime of tears for Cozu, her mate, who had died as a rebel.

She didn't want to see what became of brave souls like him.

"I have to warn you," Garrett said in a quiet voice, "the Isolatorium is a bad place even to visit. The sights we'll see will be unpleasant. And we're not allowed to intervene, thanks to your friend's crackerjack negotiating skills."

Thomas sank lower in Kessa's embrace.

Kessa clicked her beak, annoyed at the old man. She figured Thomas had done well, considering the circumstances and what was at stake.

"We have to ignore whatever atrocities we see, no matter what." Garrett gave Ariock a meaningful look. "Got it? Otherwise the Torth will do something harmful to Vy."

Ariock made a growling sound that might have been assent.

"Take that entrance." Garrett pointed. "That's where I escaped, years ago."

Their transport descended, soaring over the River of Blood. The enormity of the prison filled Kessa's field of view, grim and spiky.

Directly below them, the plaza was cracked, as if heaved by some long-ago calamity.

Jonathan Stead, Kessa realized.

The Lady of Sorrow had lent him her power. Jonathan Stead had slain a thousand Torth and broken a wall of the Isolatorium, even though he had been completely trapped and powerless at the time.

As powerless as a slave?

They glided into one cavernous hood of an entrance. Its overhang cut off the rain. The air remained cold and damp, and Kessa shivered, peering into black shadows, and bracing herself for the worst atrocities imaginable.

CHAPTER 9

PROPHECIES AND NIGHTMARES

Thomas felt exposed as they entered the Isolatorium. Glow strips ribbed the distant walls, giving the gloom an eerie, baleful illumination. Chain gangs of filthy alien slaves trudged between mold-caked pillars. Nussian guards herded the prisoners. The Torth guards were harder to detect, in dull crimson armor, but their red eyes tracked Ariock.

None of them took aim with their blaster gloves. Yet.

Thomas was all too aware that one nearly invisible projectile would end Ariock's ability to hold their wrecked transport aloft. If Ariock got hit with inhibitor serum, the rest of them would be pretty much helpless.

"Garrett," Thomas called. "Make sure Ariock is keeping himself shielded."

"On it." Garrett murmured to Ariock, and their transport slowed down. Ariock must have added an air shield to his mental load.

Thomas sensed Jinishta marveling at the strength of her overgrown cousin. She could not imagine how Ariock was doing so much at once. It seemed impossible from her perspective.

"Which way?" Ariock demanded.

"That direction." Garrett gestured down a gloomy indoor street.

They floated above slaves with protruding rib cages who seemed too exhausted to look up.

"Torth are monsters," Jinishta said.

"We can't help them," Garrett said softly, coaching Ariock. "Remember Vy. We can't get distracted here."

Thomas sat against Kessa, inundated with her sympathies, but he really wanted to be in proximity to the old man. He stared at the back of Garrett's head. Why had he showed up at the Border River just in time to rescue Ariock? He had been standing on the wall, watching. Waiting.

How much did he know about prophecies?

What were his motives?

"So." Thomas made his tone conversational. "Garrett Dovanack. What made you decide to leave your comfy home on Earth?"

It was the best place to begin an interrogation, because Ariock was listening. He must be extremely curious to learn the answer to that question.

Garrett snorted. "It's a long story. Now isn't really the best time."

"We may never get a better time," Thomas replied. "We could be dead later today."

Garrett was silent.

Ariock spared enough focus to look at him. "Please answer," he said tersely. "I want to know."

Garrett must realize that Ariock was straining his protective focus. In reply, he said, "I told you already. I wanted to learn more about the Torth. I wanted to figure out how to defeat them."

That was unsatisfying.

"Did you learn anything useful?" Thomas prompted.

"I'm surprised you didn't suck it out of my mind already," Garrett said.

"I'm surprised you're not volunteering the info," Thomas retorted. "If there's a way to defeat the Torth Empire, you should share it with us. Or at least tell the Bringer of Hope."

"Mmm." Garrett hesitated. "Go that way." He pointed.

Ariock turned their vehicle down a narrower street, gliding past bloodstains and downtrodden slaves. But he seemed to want more than the weight of their transport on his mind. "Tell me," he said.

"Now isn't the right time," Garrett complained.

Curiosity radiated off Kessa. She knew how much was at stake, for Ariock as well as for the whole galaxy. Humankind was on the verge of being conquered and enslaved. The Alashani were about to be invaded. The Torth seemed unstoppable. If there was any chance, no matter how infinitesimal, of wrenching apart the machinery of the Torth Empire, then that was a secret that ought to be shared right away.

"Yes or no?" Thomas called out. "Is there a way for us to defeat the Torth Empire?"

"Yes," Garrett said.

Thomas sensed Kessa and Jinishta exchange glances. He wondered if Garrett was trying to be funny. If so, his sense of humor needed a lot of adjustment.

"I don't believe you," Thomas scoffed.

"Well," Garrett said, "if you hadn't wasted your time as a Torth with your head up your ass, you probably would have found it, too. I guess I'm just more resourceful than you are."

Thomas blinked at the unexpected insult. Did Garrett have a problem with him?

"If there's a way to defeat the Torth Empire," Ariock said, "I want to hear it."

Garrett heaved a reluctant sigh. "I can't tell you. There are repercussions if I say much more."

That was evasive.

The transport wobbled as Ariock's focus shifted with frustration. He had to regain control of it.

Did Garrett have a valid reason to be infuriating? Maybe his alleged solution for destroying the Torth Empire was a cure that was worse than the disease? Or maybe he was afraid the Torth would pick up the secret and reverse it? Even if that was the case—

A nussian bellowed in pain.

A loose group of filthy nussians occupied an arena off the main avenue, hollow-eyed. A Crimson Rank lounged in a crystal hoverchair, holding a weapon that looked like a cattle prod. It seemed he was forcing one of the exhausted nussians to whip a smaller one.

It was a child, being attacked and beaten by its own mother.

"There is no justice here." Jinishta clenched her black-wrapped fists.

The indolent Crimson Rank watched their wreck of a transport sweep past. His eyes were demonic.

Ariock's tone was a threat. "Talk."

Garrett winced. "Okay. Fine." He seemed to realize that he needed to distract Ariock from the torture scene, and the best way to do that was to give the big guy some hope of justice. "You're aware that the Alashani believe in prophecies, right?"

Ariock did not dignify that with an answer.

"Well," Garrett said, "the predecessors of the Torth believed in prophecy, too. I found relics from that era, copied and recopied. Specifically, I found copied depictions of ancient paintings that foretell the future."

"A *rekveh* should not speak of prophecies," Jinishta said.

Thomas struggled to rein in his impatience. Garrett had better make his point soon.

"There was one prophet in particular," Garrett went on. "Her name was Ah Jun. And she painted something like a step-by-step guide on how to defeat the Torth Empire."

Ariock slowed to a stop. The transport hung in midair as he processed those substantial words.

Thomas's mouth hung open.

He had met a prophet. He had absorbed Migyatel's entire life—which meant he had absorbed many lives. Prophetic power was a lot like telepathy in that way. Migyatel had known far too much. Whenever she touched an item, any item, she saw its origins and its future. It was the same when she touched people. The past and the future were nearly as visible as the present. To Migyatel, life held few mysteries. She had been able to see years into the past and into the future. She could see the next generation of her own family.

How much greater was Ah Jun, if she could see entire millennia into the future?

The power of Ah Jun must have been many orders of magnitude more powerful than that of Migyatel. It seemed impossible. Ah Jun might have been driven mad by near-infinite knowledge. But Thomas believed it was possible, because he had met the Upward Governess, who contained millions of lifetimes. He had met Migyatel, who had known so much, even though she'd died from shock upon being inundated with Thomas's own future.

There was something to this.

Garrett was a liar, but his emotions were honest. And he was a true believer. Thomas heard it in his voice and saw it in his eyes. Garrett believed that he had stumbled upon a way to defeat the Torth Empire.

Ancient paintings. Prophecies.

Perhaps that was how Garrett had known where, and when, to intercept Ariock. Unless Garrett was a prophet himself?

"Where are these prophetic paintings?" Thomas's tone trembled with eagerness. "What do they predict?"

"I'm sorry," Garrett said. "But that's for me to know and you to figure out on your own."

Thomas made an undignified squawk of outrage.

Ariock aimed a glare at his great-grandfather. He demanded answers without saying a word.

"I trust you, Ariock," Garrett said, unruffled. "But I don't trust the boy. And if I were to tell you, he would suck it up from your mind."

Thomas gaped. He was too offended to speak.

"This is how it has to be," Garrett said. "Ancient prophecies are delicate things. If events get skipped, or if they happen in the wrong order, then the whole thing could blow up in our faces."

"I would take that into account," Thomas pointed out, stung from the insult. What was Garrett's problem with him? A supergenius could be trusted to handle ancient prophecies with caution and care.

Garrett turned in his seat to glare at Thomas. He spoke slowly, as if speaking to a dim-witted child. "I don't trust you."

Thomas ran through retorts in his mind. Should he point out the fact that a legitimate prophet had labeled him an adviser to the messiah? How about the fact that he never spoke lies? Never mind that the Torth Empire had rejected him as their Betrayer. Thomas was the most trustworthy person in the galaxy! If some ancient paintings showed even a hint of a suggestion about how to destroy the Torth Empire, then surely it was worth allowing Ariock's supergenius companion to take a look?

"I trust him with my life," Ariock said, his tone dangerous.

"Well, there's your mistake," Garrett said.

Thomas had trouble keeping his power reined in, he was so furious. Sparks of indignation flared. Kessa had to move back.

"If I'd wanted to screw over anyone here," Thomas said, his tone tightly controlled, "don't you think I would have done so by now?"

Garrett drummed his fingers on the armrest of the pilot's seat. It seemed like a lazy, unconcerned gesture . . . but Thomas detected tension in the set of Garrett's shoulders, and in his furrowed brow, as glimpsed through the eyes of Jinishta.

Rage simmered just beneath Garrett's surface.

Rage toward Thomas? But why? Where did it come from? What was this about? Did it have to do with something in the future—a deed Thomas had yet to do? Was it related to the vision Migyatel had foreseen?

Weird.

"The boy is a schemer," Garrett said to Ariock. "No one can fully probe what's in his mind. That makes him inherently untrustworthy."

"I rescued Ariock from crucifixion," Thomas said. "I saved his life. More than once. Where were you when we all needed help? Pretending to be a Blue Rank?"

"I was doing more than you can comprehend." A vein stood out on Garrett's brow. That looked like explosive rage, barely restrained.

Kessa seemed to hear the tension. "Um," she said carefully, "aren't we trying to find the Lady of Sorrow?"

"I would never hurt Ariock." Thomas needed to make that clear. "Or any of his friends. I'm not a monster."

"But you did hurt him." Suddenly Garrett whirled out of his seat, and his rage was naked. "You let your friends suffer. You would have killed Ariock! *I* had to save him!"

"What?" Thomas felt more perplexed than angry. What alternate reality was Garrett talking about? "You weren't there. I was. *I* was the one who saved him."

Garrett stumped toward Thomas, leaning on his staff, apparently having forgotten that only one of them had viable powers. "You spent three months as a Yellow Rank, right there in the same city where Ariock was forced to fight in gladiator battles. You had every chance to rescue him. But you didn't! You let the monsters torture him."

Thomas flushed red. "You know what it's like to live with an audience inside your head, sharing everything you think and do. There's no privacy. I couldn't make rescue plans! I had to wing it!"

"You could have found a way," Garrett insisted. He stopped just beyond telepathy range. "Admit it. You were having too much fun wearing tranquility meshes and ordering slaves around."

That was so unfair, Thomas's rage became curling tendrils of heat vapor. "It must be nice to teleport," he said. "You could have been the hero. But you weren't there! What were you doing? Ordering *your* slaves around?"

Garrett gripped his staff as if he meant to hit Thomas with it. "I was in the middle of a crucial task on Athpinar, but I was there in the Megacosm. I saw the whole crucifixion ceremony. You were going to let him die. I had to intervene!"

"What are you talking about?" Thomas begged to know. "I was completely alone. No one helped me."

Kessa stared at him, fascinated. She had never heard Thomas make these confessions.

"I took the biggest risk of my life." Thomas wished he had clarified these things earlier. Ariock and Kessa ought to know what he had gone through in order to rescue them. "I threw away everything I owned, including a possible future, to rescue my friends. I did it without help, without praise, without resources, without anything. I did it knowing that Ariock's power could wreak havoc and possibly end innocent lives. I was torn, but I did it anyway." He glared at Garrett. "So why are you trying to steal credit from me?"

"You did it because of nightmares," Garrett said.

Thomas closed his mouth.

He had, indeed, suffered vivid nightmares on the night of the rescue. One dream had been the Upward Governess eating his brain. Another had showed his nameless mother, eyeless and damaged. She had sacrificed everything in order to give Thomas a chance to live and make a difference.

The worst nightmare had been an abused version of Cherise, still in love with Thomas even though he'd tortured and abandoned her to slavery and death.

"That's right." Garrett went on like a steamroller, glaring at Thomas over his staff. "I stirred your subconsciousness. It's one of my talents. I gave you those nightmares. And I'd be happy to give you more!"

Thomas shrank away. "What kind of sick . . . ?" He was so overwhelmed with uncertainty, he didn't bother to finish his accusation. Just how much did Garrett know about him?

Far too much.

Garrett must have studied Thomas. He knew him. Somehow, Garrett had watched Thomas in his luxury suite, tossing and turning on that enormous bed. If he was telling the truth, then he was as much of a hero as Thomas.

Or more so.

"I had to do something," Garrett said. "You obviously meant to have yourself a peaceful night's sleep after sentencing your friend to death. So I went ahead and risked everything—the future of the universe—because you were too much of a coward."

Ariock's doubt was painful to see. "You freed me," he said to Thomas, "because of nightmares?"

Thomas looked away from Ariock's searching gaze, overcome by shame. Had he acted solely because of those nightmares? Was he really that much of a coward?

Garrett's voice was huffy and self-righteous. "I gave the boy some incentive to do the right thing."

It hurt. Thomas felt as if he was confronting his own shortcomings for the first time.

He wasn't entirely sure if Garrett was being truthful, but there was something to his accusation. Thomas had struggled to sever himself from the Torth Empire. He had been reluctant to leave. Was he too reluctant to do the right thing?

Was there something inherently wrong with him, morally?

Was he tainted by his Torth genetics? Was he too much of a Torth?

"Garrett was not there," Kessa said, her voice low. She was close enough to hug Thomas. "You were." She touched the ring of scar tissue around her neck, and Thomas sensed her memory of the collar falling away. He had done that for her. "You were the one who took all the risks."

CHAPTER 10

INFILTRATION

Kessa wasn't sure what to think of Garrett. He clearly wanted to take credit for Thomas's bravery.

It seemed he did that a lot. He had told the Alashani that he was their messiah, long ago. He had claimed to be a hero. And he had just assured Ariock that he alone knew secrets that could lead to the defeat of the Torth Empire.

Big claims.

Perhaps Garrett could live up to his boasts? He was Jonathan Stead, the legend.

But without his powers, he was also somewhat feeble. He leaned heavily on his staff. "We don't have time for this." Garrett stumped back to the pilot's seat and plopped into the chair. "Drive." He pointed.

Ariock looked wary. He did not defend Thomas, but Kessa guessed that was due to the urgent time pressure. They simply did not have time for drawn-out arguments.

A glance at the tablet showed the countdown. In that distant cage, Weptolyso and Yuey hunkered protectively around Cherise, Flen, and Vy.

Kessa wrapped her arms around Thomas. He avoided everyone's gaze, but he wasn't fast enough to hide the glisten in his eyes.

He was weeping.

Garrett's accusations had dug at an unhealed wound. Unfair accusations, Kessa thought. Thomas was no coward. And he was not loyal to the Torth Empire in any way. Otherwise he wouldn't be capable of tears.

Kessa instinctively chastised herself for speculating about Thomas and Garrett. Slaves were not supposed to speculate about mind readers. Her thoughts could get her killed.

Then she gave herself permission to keep thinking.

It was allowed. Thomas was not going to punish her.

He was a friend.

It was strange to consider a mind reader a friend. Kessa had never thought of Thomas in such warm terms before. But she realized that he had never shown vulnerability to her, or to anyone else, until now. This was the only time she had ever seen or heard about him crying. He had suffered in a dungeon pit without much complaint. He had seemed able to turn off his emotions, and that had made him seem alien. Like a Torth.

But he did have emotions.

Like a slave.

Everywhere Kessa looked, she saw reminders of the difference between slaves and mind readers. Chain gangs trudged below them. Slave masters watched the transport in a way that made Kessa want to check her blaster glove.

Ragged prisoners stared up at the transport, mesmerized, because voices were unheard-of in this place. They would not imagine that the spoken argument had been between two mind readers. That would seem impossible.

"Which way?" Ariock asked.

They floated into a nexus of corridors. A canal full of putrid blood sloshed out from one dim tunnel and into another.

"Um." Garrett peered at one opening, then another. "That way." He pointed. "I think."

Ariock's tone was critical. "You think?"

"Look, it's been ninety-four years since I was here." Garrett hunched his shoulders defensively. "They've repaired the damage I caused. Everything looks different."

"I can find the way." Thomas's eyes were still wet, but his tone was steely. "If Garrett will step into my range. I can fish it out of his memories."

"No!" Garrett said immediately.

"I'll need your memories anyway for this whole thing to work," Thomas said pointedly. "Otherwise, why are we here?"

Garrett seemed unable to come up with a counterargument. Everyone's gaze fixed on him.

"Could you—" Ariock began.

Garrett cut him off. "Nah, the boy is right. The Torth won't do anything to help us. It has to be me." He stood, grumbling. "This whole endeavor is a long shot. No one's ever been able to summon the Lady of Sorrow at will."

"She deserves a chance," Thomas said.

Garrett limped closer, leaning on his staff. He halted as soon as he was within Thomas's range. "Hurry up, boy."

"Come closer," Thomas suggested.

Garrett snarled like a cornered animal. "You shouldn't need any extra time. I'll give you three more seconds."

Thomas leaned forward.

Garrett said, "Three, two, one." As soon as he finished the countdown, he scrambled out of Thomas's range, nearly tripping over his robes in his haste. Jinishta had to move aside to make room for him.

It seemed Jinishta and Garrett shared more than a familial bond. They shared a fear of Thomas.

Garrett was like a blustery nussian who was trying to convince everyone that he wasn't afraid, Kessa realized. He disparaged Thomas because he didn't want to admit how scared he was.

"We're at the wrong nexus," Thomas said. "Backtrack to the last intersection, Ariock. I'll point you in the right direction."

Their vehicle sped back the way they'd come. Ragged screams echoed from dark tunnels.

"The Torth Empire has no concept of who or what the Lady of Sorrow is," Garrett said. "At least we have that going for us."

Ariock side-eyed his great-grandfather. "I'm not sure I understand what she is, either."

A phantom. A dungeon spirit. Kessa silently agreed with Ariock. She felt foolish for even considering that the goddess of life and death would show up and be helpful. Perhaps Thomas and Garrett were like children who believed in sand spirits?

"I'm not sure we can count on all Torth being totally ignorant," Thomas said. "It turns out they're pretty good at keeping secrets, on an individual basis."

Garrett snorted. "The whole Torth government: a bunch of Yeresunsa. I have to admit, I did not see that coming."

"I should have," Thomas said. "Turn right at this corner, Ariock."

Ariock followed the directions.

"Well," Garrett said, "hopefully the Majority will be in anarchy by the time that timer goes off. They'll probably slap the Commander in chains and torture her to death right here. Plus as many Servants as they can get their hands on."

"I doubt it," Thomas said. "Take the leftmost branch up ahead, Ariock."

"The Majority won't allow Yeresunsa to rule them," Garrett said firmly. "Guaranteed, they'll elect a new government by the end of today."

"Unlikely," Thomas said.

"It's happened before." Garrett spoke as if that should end the debate.

"Twenty-two thousand years ago," Thomas said. "This is a different era, and a different situation."

"How so?" Garrett sounded annoyed. "All those millennia ago, the Majority discovered a conspiracy of Yeresunsa among the top ranks, just like now. They rooted them out and destroyed them using the inhibitor. Then they elected a whole new government within a few hours. This is the exact same situation."

"Except," Thomas said, "now everyone knows it didn't work the first time."

Garrett turned to look at him, troubled.

The discussion held Kessa enthralled. In her life as a slave, she had never been privy to Torth history or politics. Slaves had no way of guessing what motivated their masters and owners. But Garrett and Thomas were exiled from the ubiquitous Megacosm, and since they refused to sit near each other, they had to speak out loud, like slaves.

"During the last twenty thousand years," Thomas said, "Yeresunsa secretly rose to the top again. And secretly took control. Again."

"They'll be ousted again," Garrett said.

"The last time it happened," Thomas said, "during the seeding of Paleoterra and Firmament, the Majority was wrestling with major challenges. They were still conquering Algyp. Nowadays? It's been millennia since the last time an average Torth had to make an important decision. And they're comfortable. They don't want the shake-up of an entire government overhaul."

"Hmm." Garrett sounded dubious.

"Make a left at the next intersection," Thomas said. "And bear to the right after that."

As Ariock followed his directions, Thomas went on. "I'm betting they'll let the Yeresunsa rule them for a little bit longer. Just until the threat is eliminated." He indicated Ariock.

"Well, I guess you've bet our lives on that supposition." Garrett sounded grudging. "But the Commander is scrambling to hold on to her shreds of power. What's to stop someone from straight up usurping her while she's weak? Like your former mentor. What's her title, the Really Fat Governess?"

"The Upward Governess knows better than to upset the Majority," Thomas said. "She's predictable. I'm more concerned about how other supergeniuses might exploit the current situation."

"What do you imagine they'll do?" Garrett spoke with grudging respect.

"I could see the Death Architect teaming up with disenfranchised Servants of All," Thomas said. "Mm, maybe the Twins. I wouldn't put it past the Spin Overture, either."

Garrett frowned. "The Death Architect. Is she that little girl who keeps coming up with torture experiments that kill slaves in gruesome ways?"

Thomas nodded.

"Agh," Garrett said. "She gives me the willies."

"Head down that passageway that branches to the right," Thomas told Ariock.

Kessa wished Pung or Weptolyso could hear this conversation. If only Cozu were with her. She had two magical windows: one through the data tablet, and one through this glimpse of Torth politics. It was like a view into the Megacosm.

"Do you think a supergenius will try to team up with the Commander of All Living Things?" Garrett stroked his short beard.

"Not her," Thomas said. "But the Swift Killer? She could be used as an assassin or some other type of pawn. She'd be easy to manipulate."

"Who?" Garrett looked annoyed at the gap in his knowledge.

Instead of replying, Thomas hesitated, as if holding an inner debate with himself.

"Oh, right." Garrett snapped his fingers. "The one who's your aunt. What a loose cannon. She's the one who spilled the beans and showed off her Yeresunsa powers, thereby ruining the conspiracy for her comrades." He laughed. "They'll turn on her first thing."

"I agree that she's shortsighted," Thomas said with pensive care. "But that's what makes her vulnerable to manipulation. Go down that ramp, Ariock, and make a sharp right at the bottom."

Cracks webbed the ribbed walls. Old bloodstains marred the floor, which was dusty rather than polished. This part of the dungeon had a musty odor, as if abandoned.

They glided through a chamber decorated with rubies and rotting aliens, all hanging by their wrists. Skeletons twisted in the air. Many were common slave species, but there were a few exotics that Kessa did not recognize. She'd never seen anything like the tall, stalklike creature with a brightly hued face. Nor did she recognize the shiny black alien with wispy antennae trailing from its head.

One skeletal ummin was still alive.

His feverish gaze tracked the transport. Kessa pulled her cowl close, embarrassed to be flaunting freedom. That poor victim must be here because he'd had idealistic notions about freedom.

Like her long-dead mate, Cozu.

"Is this what will happen to my people?" Jinishta whispered, staring at the horrors.

"No." Kessa attempted to offer some optimism. "The Alashani will be enslaved, not murdered. Obedient slaves do not end up in the Isolatorium."

"Obedient?" Tears rolled down Jinishta's face. "Slavery is not living. I don't care what you say. Obedience is not truly living."

Kessa did not argue. She had seen theater performances and craft bazaars in the Alashani underground, and she privately suspected that slaves did the same things, albeit in poorer ways. Freedom was as vital as food and air. Slaves found ways to obtain scraps of it.

"Take the leftmost fork," Thomas said.

Kessa wanted to beg Ariock to stop and rescue the tortured ummin.

She hated herself for looking away. No wonder the Lady of Sorrow wept. Perhaps even a goddess could feel helpless in a place of so much suffering.

Jinishta spoke in a tone of realization. "This is why slaves obey their masters." She stared at the corpses. "This is why."

"Yes." Kessa did not need to embellish the cold truth. Had Jinishta never fully imagined the consequences for rebellion? Here in the Isolatorium, the consequences were obvious.

"My nieces and nephews." Jinishta sounded tortured, herself. "My sisters and brothers. My mother and father. We must defend the Alashani realm."

Since Kessa did not wish to imagine her friends in chains, she tried to picture the Lady of Sorrow. A kind and loving human figure. Someone like Vy, but with powers. Someone who would solve all their problems and free all the slaves in the galaxy.

"Oh, look," Thomas said. "We can skip the rest of the maze and go directly to the room where Jonathan Stead was tortured."

Kessa turned to where he was facing. A jagged hole in the stone wall tunneled into darkness. Its broken edges did not match the entrances and exits elsewhere in this dungeon. When Kessa peered in the opposite direction, she saw more punched-through walls. Each was more explosive-looking than the last. Support beams leaned inward or had buckled and fallen.

Garrett spoke in a hoarse voice. "Looks like they only fixed the damage to the outer walls."

"Our transport can fit through, Ariock," Thomas said.

They headed farther into the Isolatorium.

"How can Torth stand to be Torth?" Jinishta whispered as they left the lone prisoner to his lonely fate.

Kessa had theories. A lack of emotions must feel like having sand instead of internal organs. Every experience must feel alike.

She could only fantasize that someday, more Torth would be like Thomas.

CHAPTER 11

FOR LOVE

Despite the urgency of their task, Ariock found himself challenged to stay on target. It was hard to fly past so much suffering without rescuing the victims.

And questions needled his mind. Questions made it hard for him to maintain an unbroken shield while levitating a laden transport. He speculated about his friends' motives in painful new ways.

"So." Ariock tried to sound casual. "Garrett, you've been around for a long time. Over a hundred years?"

"I'm a hundred and eleven," Garrett said crabbily. "Feeling every minute of it."

"Does your long life come from Torth genetics?" Ariock asked.

"I'm just good at avoiding death," Garrett said.

Thomas made a derisive sound. "He takes longevity pills. That's how Torth extend their life spans."

"Oh." Ariock tried not to feel dismay. His great-grandfather could read his mind.

He sneaked a glance toward Garrett. This was the old man who had protected him in the desert. He had done . . . well, something . . . to Thomas's mind, perhaps. Ariock wasn't entirely sure about that. But he guessed that Garrett had actually caused the sandstorm that drove away millions of Torth spectators. That storm had buried Torth cameras and lasers and whatever else they'd had pointed toward him in the desert.

It had opened up the chance for Thomas to succeed in his rescue.

Everyone believed that Ariock himself had caused that storm. But he knew the truth. He had hardly been conscious. And he'd learned, through lessons with Jinishta, that one could not shield oneself while unconscious. Ariock had been in such a weakened state during that storm, it should have killed him. Lightning should have zapped him, again and again, on that metal cross. If not lightning, then sand. He should have been flayed alive.

Instead, Ariock had been untouched.

Someone had shielded him during the sheets of lightning and scouring winds.

Garrett stared into the gloom. He must have been there, as much as Thomas. Two different mind readers had rescued Ariock. They had watched over him and protected him.

Had old Garrett shielded Ariock during the plane crash that killed his father?

Just how long had Garrett watched over Ariock, protecting him? Delia, Ariock's mother, used to say that he must have a guardian angel.

Ariock really wanted to have a long conversation with Garrett about his motives and intentions. Why had he protected Ariock, but not Delia, not Will, not Rose, not anyone else in their family?

At any other time, Ariock would have insisted on having the conversation. But the clock was ticking down. Vy was waiting for his rescue.

The tunnel dead-ended in a meager room.

Ariock slowed their transport to a stop because there was nowhere left to go. Flickering light strips provided a desultory sort of lighting for the emptiness. Plugs hung from the ceiling. There was a rusted table. It looked more like an abandoned, forgotten junk closet than a torture pit.

"This is it," Garrett said. "This is the room where I encountered the Lady of Sorrow."

Ariock set the transport on the dusty ground. Metal parts sagged and clanked as he allowed himself to fully withdraw his awareness. It almost felt good to be wholly himself again instead of an overcomplicated collection of extended limbs and artificial parts.

Jinishta watched him the way one might assess an unknown beast. Clearly, she had not believed he could carry the transport all this distance.

Otherwise she was wondering how Ariock could be the messiah, after his decisions had doomed her people.

He had to look away.

"They handled me like your average rogue Torth," Garrett said, his gaze hollow. He limped out of the transport, leaning on his staff. "The room was on fire when I was here last." He touched a grated tabletop. "And there were alien bugs, designed to torment the flesh." He traced a puckered scar along his withered cheek. "They tortured me for what felt like weeks. I had no strength left. I was in chains, wounded, and dying. And this was where they would burn me alive. It was supposed to be my death."

Ariock extracted himself from the cramped vehicle, glad to straighten his back.

The soot-blackened ceiling loomed a scant inch above his head. He was so used to low ceilings from the Alashani underground and the tiny cell where the Torth had confined him, it actually felt spacious.

"The worst thing," Garrett said, "wasn't the pain. It was the mystery. I had no idea who, or what, the Torth were."

Jinishta gave him a disparaging glare. She disembarked and assessed the wreckage of the wall Jonathan Stead had punched through, measuring it with her gaze. She compared it to Garrett with skepticism.

"It's true." Garrett gave her a level look in return. "I am a mind reader, yes. But I grew up on Earth. I thought I was human. When the Torth brought me here, they almost never entered my range, and of course they never showed me how to access the Megacosm. So I was in the dark."

Ariock could relate to that.

"The Torth seemed demonic to me," Garrett said. "So I thought that they must be demons. What did I know? I was only seventeen."

Ariock could understand that, too. The vast majority of mind readers were dangerous enemies who did not deserve their many luxuries.

"Also . . ." Garrett released his breath in a rush, like he was releasing long-held pressure. "My wife was pregnant. I needed to get back to her."

Ariock blinked. He hadn't known Grandma Rose had been born to teenage parents.

It was hard to envision Garrett as a bright-eyed teenager. All his portraits throughout the Dovanack mansion showed him as an old man, or in late middle age, with balding temples and a grizzled appearance. With his bold features, young Jonathan Stead had probably looked a lot like Ariock. Only normal size.

"Who raised you?" Thomas asked, eyeing Garrett with suspicion. He sat propped against a panel of the transport. Kessa had arranged him there so that she could wander the room, examining bolts and plugs as if she was a tourist in a museum.

"Julie's family adopted me." Garrett's tone dropped several degrees.

Ariock had never heard that name in relation to his family tree.

"Julie?" Thomas asked. "Who was that?"

"My wife," Garrett said.

Ariock eyed him askance. Had Garrett married his adoptive sister?

As far as he knew, Garrett's wife had been named Sarah. She had died long before Ariock was born, but portraits of her hung in the Dovanack mansion—a pretty woman with dark hair and a mischievous look in her eyes.

"Sarah and Julie were the same person," Garrett said with impatience, apparently reading Ariock's confusion. "I used to be Jonathan, and she was born Juliette Stead. I took her last name because I had none of my own."

"Oh." Ariock tried to imagine how that was possible on the world where he'd grown up.

"I wasn't supposed to exist," Garrett explained. "Like him." He jerked his thumb at Thomas. "I wasn't Torth. I wasn't Alashani. I would never be accepted in either culture."

Ariock had all but forgotten that Garrett was a Torth-Alashani hybrid. He acted like a human, but he wasn't human at all.

"Were you a street orphan?" Thomas sounded fascinated. "How did your parents die? How old were you when the Steads adopted you?"

"Shouldn't we attempt to summon the Lady of Sorrow?" Garrett glared at Thomas. "How do we begin? What's your brilliant strategy?"

Thomas looked chagrined. "You're right." He eyed Garrett. "I could use more of your memories. Come closer."

"You have enough," Garrett snapped. "Make do with what you already have."

Thomas let out a put-upon sigh. "I'll try. I'm not sure you gave me enough." He closed his eyes.

Ariock glanced around the decrepit room. Thomas could probably use his powerful imagination to reconstruct the sorrow and despair this room had once contained, but it wasn't so easy for the rest of them.

Ariock tried to put himself in the mind-set of young Jonathan Stead. Hurt. Confused. Tormented by Red Ranks who looked like demons to him. Desperate to return to Earth. Desperate to go home and protect his wife.

His pregnant teenage wife who was also his adoptive sister?

"You're getting hung up on details that don't matter, Ariock," Garrett said. "And I had all kinds of worries about the baby, believe me. I feared that I was half demon and that any baby of mine would be, uh . . ." He trailed off, his face creased with pain.

Ariock could guess what Garrett was reluctant to say. The baby might be a freakish monster.

Like Ariock.

Grandma Rose had turned out normal, hadn't she? So had Will. But Torth genetics left their mark even three generations later.

"I don't care that you've inherited heavy-G adaptations and a growth disorder." Garrett rolled his eyes, as if he thought Ariock was way off track. "Who cares about that? No. I was afraid the baby would inherit dangerous superpowers like mine."

"Oh." Ariock wondered if Grandma Rose had been born with such powers.

Probably not. Otherwise he would have heard about it.

Garrett gave him a strange, almost pitying look. "Anyway, I figured the Torth would hunt and murder my offspring. I could read their intentions enough to pick up on that danger. So yes, I was desperate to get home. I had sworn to Julie that I would always be there for her." Garrett looked burdened. "But she knew I told lies sometimes." He trembled, avoiding everyone's gaze. "And then I vanished."

It must have seemed as if Jonathan Stead had abandoned his young wife.

"That is why you risked the Alashani civilization," Kessa said in a tone of realization. "That is why you would do anything to get home. It was for love."

"Yes," Garrett admitted. "I loved the Alashani, and I recognized them as my mother's people. But at the same time, I knew that Julie must be hiding, penniless, running from place to place, while Torth agents hunted her. For all I knew, they had already murdered her. I had to protect her."

Ariock heard the anguish in Garrett's voice. His great-grandfather had taken a reckless gamble with the fate of the Alashani civilization, but he had done it for the sake of his family. He had done it because he loved someone with all his heart.

Ariock would have done the same.

Jinishta kept comparing the hole in the wall to the old man. She was listening intently, even though she did not understand much, if any, English. Now she turned to glare at Garrett. "Jonathan Stead?"

Garrett laced his gnarled hands on top of his staff and peered at her. "Yes."

Jinishta glared at him with unspoken accusations.

"Of course I lied," Garrett said in the slave tongue. "Your people skewer heads like mine. My goal was to live, not to get myself decapitated."

Jinishta continued to look furious.

When Ariock considered how well Garrett had masked his abilities— not only from the Alashani, but from humans, as well—he couldn't help but be impressed. Garrett must have feigned ignorance every time he held a conversation. He would have laughed at jokes when he already knew the punch line. He would have acted surprised whenever someone intended to surprise him.

It was all an act.

And he had done it for years. Decades. A lifetime. Even Thomas would have trouble maintaining a facade like that, Ariock suspected.

"You let us believe you were our messiah," Jinishta said.

"Well." Garrett waved dismissively. "That's neither here nor there. What does it matter now? It was nearly a hundred years ago."

It clearly mattered to Jinishta. Her eyes blazed with indignation. "My people believed you."

"Your people believe a lot of silly things," Garrett said.

Jinishta's luminous eyes glistened.

Ariock recalled her worry that the new messiah would turn out to be yet another selfish liar who put their civilization at risk. Unfortunately, her fears had proven to be very valid. Thanks to Ariock, all the Alashani would be wearing slave collars by the end of today.

He would save them if he could.

"In hindsight," Garrett said, "could I have been more diplomatic? Sure. I could have been as reluctant as Ariock and rejected every boon your people gave me." His tone made it clear how foolish he thought that would be. "But I had to get home to Julie. I loved her. She was my world." He gave Jinishta and Ariock a sour look. "I'm not sure that's something either of you can understand."

Jinishta bristled, hurt. She never spoke of romance or lovers. Ariock had the impression that she was too duty-bound to get distracted by love.

But so what? Did one need to be in an ideal relationship to understand the power of love? Jinishta had that big, cheerful family. She understood why they existed.

Ariock had never done anything intimate with anyone, other than that kiss with Vy, but he thought he understood love, too. He'd read books. He'd watched TV. Even if he hadn't, he wasn't about to abandon Vy.

He would rescue her no matter what it took.

The countdown was still ticking away. Ariock could not forget how many people were in danger of being enslaved or massacred because of him.

Thomas looked troubled, eyes closed. Dried tears had made tracks in the grime on his face. There was no sign of hope.

"Why did the Lady of Sorrow choose you?" Jinishta seemed angry about that. "Why did she grant her power to a *rekveh*?"

"I would very much like to ask her that question." Garrett sounded sincere. He began to pace, planting his staff to offset his limping gait. "I was terrified and exalted. And she was full of rage and sorrow. It was as if we'd merged. We were one entity for a short time."

Cracks webbed the broken wall. Garrett had punched his way through the entire Isolatorium, freeing prisoners and making himself into a legend. And he wished that he had done a lot more.

He could have taken over this planet with borrowed power.

"With her enormous power," Garrett said, "I was able to break the Bloodbath Plaza in half and kill a frenzied army of Torth. It wasn't like the storm you saw me throw earlier. I mean a real wrath-of-God storm."

Ariock had trouble imagining that.

"I should have fled to the spaceport," Garrett said. "And I would have, if only I'd known what space travel was." He shook his head, rueful. "I was just an ignorant kid."

That made Ariock wonder how Garrett had gotten home to Earth, eventually.

"Instead," Garrett said, "I headed into darkness, away from searchlights and bombs. I didn't know where to go."

"And her power left you?" Kessa asked. "Why?"

"I don't know," Garrett admitted. "I passed out somewhere in the dead city. Liberated prisoners carried me farther."

Ariock could identify with that. His friend Weptolyso had carried him through the dead city.

"Then the Alashani found us," Garrett said. "When I woke up, I was in a luxurious bed, and the slaves who'd come with me agreed that I must be the messiah. They spoke, in awe, of the way I'd slain a thousand Torth. So then the Alashani figured I fit their ancient prophecy."

Jinishta's anger melted a bit, mitigated by shame. She knew her people. Garrett had taken advantage of them, but they had likely made it very easy for him to do so.

Ariock wondered what else the legend of Jonathan Stead was missing. He wanted to know how his great-grandfather had figured out how to get home to Earth. Did teleportation have something to do with it?

Teleportation might be the key to saving Vy.

"I tried to summon the Lady of Sorrow again," Garrett said. "And again." He touched his chest, as if he was missing a piece inside himself. "But she never returned."

In the transport, Thomas looked grim.

"So I was stranded on this planet," Garrett said. "I played along with the Alashani while I recovered my strength and healed from my injuries. But secretly, I was experimenting with my powers. I needed to get home, and—"

Thomas interrupted. "This isn't working. I need more memories."

CHAPTER 12

THE SOUND OF SORROW

"This is pointless." Garrett blew air through his mustache. "I don't think my memories are the key. She isn't a genie. No one summons her. She either appears on her own or she doesn't. That's why people worship her."

Ariock could see despair in Thomas. In Jinishta. Even Kessa was losing hope. The countdown timer continued.

But when Ariock pondered the mysterious Lady of Sorrow, he realized that he owed her a lot. In a roundabout way, she had given Ariock his chance to be born. By empowering Jonathan Stead's escape from this prison, she had enabled him to go home to protect his family, which had led directly to Ariock being born.

And to Thomas's existence, too.

She mattered.

The Lady of Sorrow had made an enormous difference here, in the Isolatorium. She might matter again. Everyone else might be ready to give up, but Ariock wasn't.

Please. Ariock closed his eyes. He tuned out his friends, his surroundings. He leaned his forehead against the cold metal wall. *If you can hear me,* he thought to the unseen, unfelt presence, *please let me find you.*

"Ariock." Garrett made a noise of pity. "She doesn't answer prayers."

Maybe not.

Yet Thomas swore that she had read his mind. Because she was a mind reader.

We need you, Ariock thought. *Everyone on this planet needs you.*

Nothing.

Ariock tried speaking out loud, just in case she could hear him better that way. He forced himself to voice his worst fears. "Vy will die if you don't help us. The Torth will torture her to death. I love her, and I won't be able to stop them."

The room remained shabby and still.

Garrett sighed. "Slaves pray to the Lady of Sorrow all the time. Look how much good it does them."

"Blasphemy," Jinishta said, but without vehemence. She didn't believe that prayers worked, either. She had told Ariock as much, in between lessons.

"Maybe we should . . ." Thomas hesitated. "We could all try to feel despair?"

Jinishta gave him a disconsolate look.

Ariock rolled his shoulders to relieve the stiffness that had settled there. He didn't need any extra prompting to feel desperate.

"Tap into your worst memories," Thomas urged. "Or whatever makes you feel suicidal. Try to amplify your despair."

Ariock had plenty of bad memories he could dredge up. Like allowing Vy to walk into Torth custody. That was bad.

Or the moment when he'd learned how sick Thomas was from the dungeon pit.

Or his mother. Dead in his arms.

His father, dead in the plane crash that should have killed Ariock.

Oh, and learning that the Alashani were doomed. That was his fault, too.

He could not rescue anyone in his memories. But maybe he could save people who were alive and in need?

Ariock peered through the hole in the wall, which led to other rooms of despair. How many runaways and rebels were undergoing torture in this monstrous building, right now? Within his reach?

"Don't." Garrett gave Ariock a sharp look. "Don't you dare waste your strength."

"We can't get sidetracked," Thomas added in a warning tone.

Surely they had at least two hours left? Ariock wanted to rescue someone. He desperately wanted to be a . . . well, a savior. A hero. He was sick of accidentally killing people.

"People beg the Lady of Sorrow for help all the time." Thomas spoke quietly, but in the stillness of the room, his words seemed large. "They beg her for hope. For rescue. But I think she is a victim herself."

"Blasphemy," Jinishta said. But her tone lacked certainty. Perhaps she was beginning to believe that Thomas knew what he was talking about.

"Maybe she's suffered for so long," Thomas said, "she's forgotten what hope is. Maybe all she can understand is despair that's as large as her own."

Ariock traced the knife scar on his forearm, hidden by wraps and armor. He understood isolation. He had grown up without friends. Not so long ago, he had known weeks without speech, without hearing a human voice.

"I don't think she listens to people who beg for salvation," Thomas said. "She's seeking someone like herself. Someone who understands the pain of isolation."

A black cloud had filled the desert sky around Ariock, sinking to engulf him. That was loneliness.

The Lady of Sorrow only showed up in dark places. Only for brief moments.

She never appeared to Torth.

Ariock reached out with his mind, unfurling his awareness. He listened with every fiber of his being. *You don't have to be alone*, he thought. *I promise, I want to meet you. I would move mountains just to meet you. Can you show me where you are?*

He sent himself further and further away, until the Isolatorium structure became his body.

His backbone was steel. His heart was a river of blood from tortured slaves.

Lives sparked through him, little bursts of static electricity. None were supercharged, but Ariock was no longer looking to borrow her power. He didn't want someone else's power coursing through him, anyway. The prisoner could be utterly powerless, and it didn't matter. He only wanted to rescue her from whatever prison she was trapped inside.

Was that a stir of air?

Maybe it was his imagination.

"How long has she been imprisoned?" Kessa asked.

"Millennia," Garrett said.

Let me help you. Ariock reached ever further.

A frozen, dead-silent world surrounded him, with nothing and no one to witness who he was. Names were meaningless. The Lady of Sorrow was a title, but she had probably not chosen it for herself, any more than he had chosen "the Giant." That was not her true identity.

She was not a goddess.

Not a phantom, either.

You are alone, Ariock silently acknowledged, inviting her to read his mind. *But I am here. I know you're trapped. I know you exist.*

He spread his awareness ever further, like fingers uncurling, opening for a touch.

"Ariock, this won't—" Garrett began to say, but Thomas cut him off with a loud "Shh!"

A breath stirred the hair on Ariock's head.

It was slight, but enough to cause a breeze through multiple tunnels and indoor streets of Stratower City. Ariock felt none of it with his bodily senses. But he was the city. His monstrous awareness encompassed far more than his core self.

"We can help you," Thomas whispered.

Garrett peered around the room, as if he expected to find a woman hiding underneath a grated table. Ariock could have told him there were no extra life sparks nearby.

He sensed plenty of life sparks lurking in nearby tunnels and corridors. Torth were creeping close, probably eager to spy on what he was doing.

Let me help you, Ariock thought, aware that the prisoner might be listening to his thoughts and fully aware that she was a real person. *The universe has forgotten you. But I know that you exist.*

Despondent weeping echoed up the tunnel, as if from a great distance.

Ariock got chills. This was no mockery of sorrow. The wordless sobs hinted that this person, this prisoner, needed rescue even more than Vy did.

Her voice faded fast.

She lacked strength on her own. She might be trying to reach out and failing. Ariock held his breath and tried to figure out which direction the echoing sobs had come from.

Please, he offered in his mind. *Let me help you.*

The weeping voice returned, directionless.

Or so it seemed. Ariock had his awareness extended, so he sensed something that no one else could detect. Some of the air in the tunnel seemed to have a . . . weight . . . or its own gravity.

There was no one there.

As Ariock peered down the tunnel, searching for a humanoid form, he sensed the phantom presence retreat, almost too fast for him to register its departure. The weeping voice faded to nothingness.

Yet Ariock glimpsed strange, fleeting reflections in the dull metal of the walls.

His eyes could not track the fast-moving gleams. They might be his imagination. But when Ariock expanded his awareness, searching, he caught hints of that strange, nonliving presence, whipping away from him faster than any creature could move.

Dust particles?

Dust should not be able to steer. The particles whipped around sharp corners and through dark, warped shafts, unlit even by flickering lights.

Ariock took an uncertain step.

Only someone with his monstrous awareness could track those particles. They were about to leave his scope. They were so tiny, so insignificant, Ariock would never find them again. Not in the vastness of the Isolatorium.

He arrowed his awareness to chase vanishing particles and strange reflections. If they were signs of the Lady of Sorrow—and he felt certain they were—then she must have used a supreme effort of focus to make herself audible, to make her presence known.

She did not seem to exist in the same reality that Ariock inhabited. She had very little power here.

Maybe she could merge with prisoners who straddled the line between life and death, but she could not escape her own prison. All she had been able to do was clutch at Ariock's offer of help, like a drowning victim reaching for an offered hand.

She might not even believe that Ariock was real.

The fleeting, barely existent presence continued to retreat. The distance was becoming dangerous. Soon Ariock would incorporate a huge swath of the Isolatorium, and if he blinked, if he twitched the wrong way, tunnels and torture arenas would collapse.

He needed to run.

There was no time to discuss the risks. No time to plan a route. The phantom presence was vanishingly distant, and Ariock was going to lose track of her entirely unless he tossed away all other considerations and decided, unequivocally, to rescue her.

He had to close the distance. If only he knew how to teleport.

He dared not split his focus in order to protect his friends while also chasing the phantom. He needed all his mental focus just to track the vanishing presence, and he would not risk spreading himself over too vast an area.

"Thomas," Ariock said in a rush. "Protect everyone."

Thomas was weak, but with his brainpower, he should be able to think of ways to keep everyone safe. Jinishta and Garrett would simply need to get over their mistrust of him for a while.

An eternally suffering prisoner needed Ariock's help. No one else in the universe could save her.

He began to run.

PART THREE

*"The Lady of Sorrow weeps for every slave.
Thus her tears are never-ending."*

—common belief on the Torth Homeworld

MAD FLIGHT

Kessa gaped at the space where Ariock had knelt a moment before. What had he seen or heard to make him race away so suddenly? How long would he take before returning?

"Crap." Garrett limped rapidly toward the broken wall, as if he meant to sprint after his great-grandson. His crooked leg hindered him. Judging by the stiff way he walked, Kessa suspected he had arthritis, like she did.

"Did he just abandon us?" Jinishta sounded outraged and anguished at the same time.

Garrett limped out of the room, determined. "We have to follow him."

Kessa stared in disbelief as the old man left her sight. It was one thing for Ariock to be reckless, but an elder such as Garrett ought to know better. How foolish was he? With his powers disabled, the Isolatorium was the most dangerous place for him to wander alone. No one would rescue him from angry nussian prison guards, or from any Torth who decided to flout Thomas's bargain.

She watched the hole in the wall. Neither Ariock nor Garrett returned.

Jinishta sprinted toward the exit.

"Where are you going?" Kessa said sharply. None of them, not even Jinishta, had any hope of keeping pace with a running Ariock. He could enhance his muscular strength with Yeresunsa powers, and he never seemed to tire. He had proved that on their march out of the Alashani underground. He could outpace a hovercart.

Wildfire flamed in the tunnel, forcing Jinishta to halt.

"It's dangerous out there," Thomas said in the slave tongue.

His tone was reasonable, not a threat, but Jinishta whirled around with an intense glare. "I know what you want, *rekveh*. Forget it. I am not your slave, and I am not going to carry you!"

Kessa tapped her fingertips together. If they wanted a chance to survive, then they ought to stay with the only person among them who had active Yeresunsa powers. It was foolish to split up.

"Let's go!" Jinishta urged Kessa.

As if the two of them could handle the Isolatorium. The premier Yeresunsa didn't even know how to shoot a blaster glove.

"We need Thomas," Kessa pointed out.

Jinishta's face hardened. "Let the *rekveh* fend for himself. Carrying him will slow us down too much. And we must leave! We cannot stay in a place where the Torth will easily find us."

It did seem prudent to leave this room and find a hiding place. The Torth must have seen Ariock galloping away. They would deduce that the rest of them no longer had the Giant's protection.

Kessa sighed. Most of her strength was leeched away from a lifetime of slavery, but she was going to have to be the one to carry Thomas. Oh, and the data tablet as well. And the NAI-12 medicine case.

"Jinishta," she began.

"Put the tablet in my hands," Thomas suggested. "I have enough strength in my fingers to carry it."

Kessa went to him and arranged the tablet in his grip. Then she struggled to find a comfortable way to carry him.

Jinishta made a sound of disgust. "In some ways, Kessa, you are still a slave."

Kessa flinched, surprised by how much those words hurt.

"Jinishta's a shortsighted idiot," Thomas said. "Like most of her people."

Jinishta threw them both a look of disgust. "You two deserve each other." With that, she whirled and hurried down the tunnel, leaving Kessa and Thomas alone in the echoing, damaged heart of the Isolatorium.

Kessa clicked her beak in frustration. Would they all be easy pickings for Red Ranks?

"I'll find a hovercart for us to use." Thomas tapped the data tablet. "This map shows available transportation in the prison. The only thing is, we need to grab the nearest one before the Torth grab it."

Kessa peered over his thin shoulder to study the glowing iconographic map. The little disks must indicate floating platforms. If that glowing white dot represented their current location, then there was a motionless hovercart a few corridors away.

"With any luck," Thomas said, pointing out the unmoving icon, "this one will be empty, awaiting a driver."

Kessa double-checked her blaster glove. The Torth might honor Thomas's bargain, but then again, they might try to seize an opportunity to grab Thomas while he was relatively undefended.

"Jinishta is right about one thing." Thomas sounded frustrated. "You can't move effectively, or defend yourself, while carrying me."

Kessa began to point out that there was no choice. Thomas did have impressive powers, but physically, he was as helpless as an infant.

The Torth did not deserve to win such a prize.

"I can fend off Torth if it's just for a couple of minutes," Thomas said. "Even if they happen to have powers. I've absorbed a lot of Alashani Yeresunsa fighting tactics."

That did not sound convincing.

"Let me give you a rundown on how to drive," Thomas said.

Kessa paid careful attention as he outlined the principles of operating a hovercart. The controls were much simpler than she would have imagined. A child could have mastered it.

The unlock procedure, however, was multilayered and mind-bogglingly complex. It involved multiple variables and dependencies.

"Are all hovercarts locked like this?" Kessa asked, incredulous. It seemed like an unnecessary, overcomplicated hurdle.

"Yes," Thomas said. "Your average Torth can simply grab the latest unlock code from the Megacosm." His tone held a hint of disparagement. "Slaves don't have that advantage. That's exactly why the Torth make it difficult."

"Ah." Kessa rehearsed the unlock steps in her mind. Deep down, she marveled at the lengths to which Torth went to keep slaves ignorant. Why? Surely slaves, even armed with technology, could not overwhelm the mighty power and collective knowledge of the galactic empire.

The Torth wanted to believe they were clever gods rather than simplistic hedonists.

She wondered if any of them actually felt shame about it.

A series of wet blasts echoed from a distance.

"Let's hope that was Garrett or Jinishta winning," Thomas said. "And not Torth slaughtering them."

Kessa peered into the flickering darkness. She had a lifetime of practice at blending into backgrounds and avoiding mind readers, but this dungeon was unlike the streets she was familiar with. The humidity was worse. The smells were fouler. She couldn't trust her eyes in a normal Torth city, riddled with holograms and ultrarealistic windows. What sorts of illusions would the Torth favor in the Isolatorium?

"You've got to hurry," Thomas urged her. "Good luck."

"I will try not to die." Kessa pulled on her blaster glove and crept toward the tunnel, pushing down her fears.

She crept from one ribbed alcove to another, listening intently. It seemed insane for an elderly runaway to sneak through a prison where rebels and runaways got executed on a regular basis. She would probably end up as a corpse in the River of Blood.

When she heard the ghostly whoosh of a hovercart, she flattened herself alongside a support beam, heart pounding.

She had no time to find a real hiding place. She barely had time to ready her blaster glove. Judging by the speed of the approaching hovercart, she would get only a second for a lucky shot. If she missed—

"Kessa!" a gruff voice said.

The platform skidded past Kessa, moving too fast for a quick halt. Garrett stood at the helm, and Jinishta skulked in the rear of the vehicle, as far from the mind reader as she could get.

"Hop aboard," Garrett said, slowing the platform.

Relief washed through Kessa.

"We need to pick up Thomas," she said, hurrying onto the platform. Running lights glowed dim and baleful around the perimeter. Spikes were hammered through its railing, matching the cruel aesthetic of the dungeon.

"You shouldn't have left him alone." Garrett slammed the controls, and the hovercart flew forward. The sudden acceleration threw Kessa off her feet. She grabbed a railing strut and hung on tight.

"I'm glad that you worked up the courage to leave the *rekveh* behind," Jinishta said in a low voice.

Normally, Kessa would forgive disdain aimed her way. She had endured worse. She understood that the Alashani had trouble comprehending slavery, just like slaves did not truly understand how freedom worked. Neither one was at fault for their ignorance.

But Jinishta ought to understand by now. She had seen disobedient slaves get tortured to death.

"I see that you are with Garrett," Kessa said, "a *rekveh*. Why aren't you bravely forging your own path through this prison?"

"I do what I must," Jinishta said, "in order to catch up with the messiah."

"If you hate the messiah's friends without troubling to know them," Kessa said, "then we follow different codes. I am a seeker of truths. The Code of Gwat is what allowed me to think my way free of beliefs that held me in thrall to Torth masters."

Jinishta's glare hid puzzlement. She was struggling to figure out what Kessa meant.

"I learned that humans are not my enemies," Kessa said. "And Thomas is not my enemy." Her tone turned sharp with bitterness. "Valuing knowledge gave me a path to freedom. Your rejection of knowledge—the Alashani avoidance of facts—is likely to make your people accept slavery very, very easily."

Jinishta puffed up, offended.

"Did Garrett rescue you?" Kessa was just guessing, but judging by Jinishta's sullen face, she had hit a nerve.

"Yup," Garrett said. "And she should thank her lucky stars I showed up when I did. Otherwise she'd be shackled and wearing a slave collar right now." He whipped the hovercart around the final curve of the tunnel.

Jinishta blushed.

"You did not break Thomas's bargain with the Torth?" Kessa asked Garrett with trepidation. "Did you?"

"Nope." Garrett slammed the controls, and the platform braked hard, fishtailing past Thomas. He looked relieved to see them, clutching the data tablet.

"It seems a few Torth do want to flout the bargain," Garrett said. "Others are obedient to the current galactic leadership team. So they had a little quarrel over what to do with Jinishta."

The hovercart shuddered to a jarring halt.

"I need one of you to grab the boy," Garrett said. "Hurry."

Kessa leaped down. Someone stronger ought to carry Thomas, but neither Jinishta nor Garrett seemed willing.

"So the Torth . . . ?" Kessa had trouble imagining Torth shooting each other to death.

"They did," Garrett said. "Four Torth blasted each other. I don't think they can blame us, so we should still be good, as far as the bargain goes."

Onscreen, the hostages looked safe, if rattled.

Kessa handed the data tablet to Jinishta. "Get over your fear," she dared to say, in response to Jinishta's disgusted reluctance to touch a vile Torth object.

Next, Kessa slid the NAI-12 case through the railing slats. Then she waddled aboard with Thomas in her arms.

"Put him in the far back." Garrett pressed against the railing. "And make sure he stays out of my range."

Jinishta also squished aside, as if Thomas smelled foul. "I don't want him near me."

Thomas gave no sign of being offended. Kessa supposed he was used to people fearing him.

The hovercart accelerated before Kessa and Thomas were fully settled on the floor. Their speed picked up until they whipped around hairpin turns, dangerously close to smashing into walls.

Kessa had to grab the railing and hang on. She held Thomas with her free hand, trying to protect him from wild turns.

"You're driving too fast," Thomas said.

"We don't have time to be piddly squeaking around." Garrett made a sloppy gesture at the controls, and they jerked in a new and unexpected direction. "The trick will be continuing not to harm any Torth. Especially since I really want to."

Kessa studied the old man. He seemed as reckless as a berserk nussian. All the same . . .

He had efficiently stolen a hovercart, despite his temporary lack of powers and his arthritic limp. And he had managed to rescue Jinishta in the process—without harming any Torth.

There might be something heroic to him, after all.

"I am not worried about being enslaved," Jinishta said imperiously. "I have poison."

"How noble." Garrett sounded sarcastic. "Good thing you're the most dispensable one of us."

That had to be hyperbole, Kessa thought. There was no way Garrett considered his premier Yeresunsa cousin to be less valuable than an arthritic ummin.

"Do you know where you are going?" Jinishta demanded.

"People tend to notice Ariock," Garrett said dryly. "I'll just skim some minds on the way. If that fails to point out his path, I'll ascend into the Megacosm and . . ."

Kessa tuned him out as she noticed a clogged intersection ahead. Nussians milled around. Garrett was going to barrel straight into them.

Even if the hovercart protected Kessa and the other passengers, the hapless nussians would be hurt. And then the bargain would be nullified. The Torth Empire would feel free to retaliate for Garrett's supposed interference with their slaves and their business. The hostages would be in terrible danger.

"The bargain!" Kessa cried. "We cannot interfere!"

"Oops." Garrett swerved at the last second. "We'd better take a detour."

Their hovercart whooshed through a torture chamber, past geysers of fire and waterfalls of gore.

"This way is a dead end," Thomas said.

"Not at all." Garrett did not change their direction or speed in the slightest.

"It's a drop," Thomas said with more vehemence. "Five stories down. We have to go back!"

"You'll cushion our fall," Garrett said, "using your powers."

Thomas's eyes bugged out. Kessa had never seen him look terrified, and it made him seem completely human.

"Make sure we don't drown in the River of Blood or whatever." Garrett slammed the control panel, and they slalomed past metal trees where dying slaves hung, impaled.

Jinishta cursed as she clung to the railing, trying to avoid sliding near Thomas.

"I can't!" Thomas sounded strangled with fear.

"You'd better," Garrett said. "Otherwise we're dead."

"My powers can't do that!" Thomas yelled.

"You have the climate control power," Garrett said. "You can add heat to air. Create a thermal airflow that gives us a cushion. Use your noggin."

"I'm not powerful enough!" Thomas said frantically. "I've never done anything like that before! I don't have the control or the training and I don't even know if I have the raw power—"

"Quit whining," Garrett said. "We're going over the waterfall in three." He held up three fingers. "Two." He folded a finger.

Thomas wheezed in terror.

"One." Garrett held up one remaining finger.

The floor ended.

Their hovercart sailed over a cascade of blood. Beyond it, far below, the River of Blood thundered through a vast forum. Ancient statues gazed upon the red water.

Garrett folded his last finger, making a fist. "Time to grow a pair, boy."

Their hovercart arced over the waterfall of blood, weightless. Thomas screamed. Jinishta screamed.

Kessa gripped Thomas and locked her gaze on his. They were plunging. She forced herself to focus, because she knew that Thomas needed a reassuring mind right now. Panic was unhelpful.

"You can do this." Kessa forced herself to beam confidence. "I know you can."

Hot air enveloped them.

She braced herself for a bone-shattering impact, and a bloodbath, that never came. Instead of plunging into the River of Blood, their platform skimmed on a hot red mist over its surface, zigzagging in a crazy way. Thomas wore a look of intense focus.

Their hovercart skipped over the low wall. They flew between statues on a current of hot air.

Then they were careening over solid ground again, tipping this way and that. One corner of the platform slammed against the floor. Metal screamed on metal, leaving a trail of sparks, and chain gangs of alien prisoners stared at them.

"Good enough." Garrett worked the controls.

Thomas sagged. His yellow eyes were wet with relief. Or maybe those were tears of rage-fueled triumph?

"Oh jeez," Garrett said, peering ahead. "I told him to be conservative with his powers."

The fortress-thick wall ahead was reduced to rubble. A juggernaut had barreled through the building, destroying ancient support beams and kicking through the rooms beyond.

Hundreds of Red Ranks were massing below the wreckage. Some poured through it, following the path Ariock had created. The rest guarded the way, and they looked prepared to kill any interlopers. Armor and extralarge blaster gloves made them seem almost as bulky as nussians.

Kessa realized, with a sinking feeling, that the Torth Majority must be second-guessing the bargain Thomas had negotiated. They had agreed only because it gained them leverage. With Vy in their custody, they expected the Giant to be docile and meek.

Instead, Ariock had damaged their prison.

The countdown numerals on the data tablet continued to flicker. Kessa tried to take that as a good sign. But why did Vy and Cherise and Weptolyso look worried? They peered at something beyond the edge of the screen.

"I hope you can feel anger, boy." Garrett thumbed his ornate, custom-tailored blaster glove into deadly mode. "We might need you to throw some fireballs. And remember, you need to protect yourself from the inhibitor, first and foremost. Otherwise we're dead."

CHAPTER 2

CRISIS MODE

Thomas doubted that he could single-handedly slay an army. He wasn't Ariock. If this encounter turned violent, he was pretty sure that the Torth would win.

"You're our only active Yeresunsa, boy," Garrett said with an edge to his voice.

The blockade of Red Ranks formed an impenetrable wall. They readied military-grade blaster gloves, while even more Torth glided out from tunnels and torture arenas. They were going to try to ensure that Ariock and Thomas remained split up.

Thomas raised his voice, trying to address the Torth Empire. "You promised not to interfere with our search."

No response.

Not that Thomas expected anything like guilt or shame from Torth. They might be holding fierce debates in the Megacosm.

That was where he needed to be.

"I'm going into the Megacosm," Thomas told his friends.

Jinishta looked disgusted, but no one tried to talk him out of it. They understood what was at stake. Nations depended on Thomas's success here. The long-forgotten prisoner known as the Lady of Sorrow needed help, and so did a lot of other people.

So Thomas ascended.

He heard the distant melodies of minds, chorusing in harmonious agreement, with some discord. Niche interest glimmered and gleamed, as multitudinous as star systems in a galaxy. The realm of pure imagination was sweet and soothing. This was paradise. This was undiluted knowledge.

Thomas wished he could dwell here like the Upward Governess and other supergeniuses did. They reveled in the Megacosm every waking moment of their lives, absorbing lifetimes of facts with every breath they took. Their knowledge would always be superior to his own. All he could do was visit paradise for a brief, blissful time.

Betrayer.

The Betrayer is listening.

Torth minds whispered to each other, nudging each other with warnings. A few brave Torth wanted to know the Betrayer's current power and health status. Wouldn't that help the empire? Plus, maybe they could soak up whatever knowledge he contained about the Lady of Sorrow.

Thomas gobbled up their knowledge just as they tried to gobble up his.

Of course, he could process things much faster.

He leaped from mind to mind, back-tracing conversational threads. He absorbed news about the impending conquest of Earth. About secret underground cities full of runaway slaves and sinister albino people. About the hostages *(Cherise) (Vy)* who were soon to become bait at the center of an ingenious trap that could potentially kill the Giant.

Unless the Betrayer gets in Our way, the Death Architect thought, warning her billions of listeners. *Now is a perfect opportunity to (get him) destroy him.*

A huge percentage of her audience chorused in agreement.

It would be easy. That came from the girl Twin. Her mind was like a nuclear column, sparking with inner thoughts and pulsing with calculations.

He is all but defenseless. That echo came from the boy Twin, whose enormous mind resembled that of the girl Twin so closely, they were nearly identical pillars in the Megacosm.

He is the most dangerous of Our enemies, the Upward Governess thought. Her gigantic mind was the largest, as complex as ever, but it seemed tinged with reluctance when she added, *He should be gotten rid of. But it would be nice if We could preserve him for interrogation.*

Red Ranks exchanged mental glances. They did not take orders from supergeniuses, but . . . well . . . whom did they take orders from anymore?

They aimed their blaster gloves.

Kessa shielded Thomas with her small body, her own blaster glove ready.

Thomas ignored his own overwhelming urge to cower. Instead, he recklessly invited the army to come closer. *Who among you wants to be brainwashed? Who wants to lose their mind?*

As he made the threat, he envisioned Red Ranks approaching him, vying with each other to be the first to disable the Betrayer. In his vividly imagined scenario, the stolen hovercart darted forward unexpectedly, bringing Thomas directly in range of a Torth. He would waste no time. He would seize that mind and give it a vicious twist. He would break it.

And then?

The unfortunate Red Rank would become a puppet, just a vessel for the Betrayer to ruthlessly dominate.

And what would he do with a Torth puppet?

Well, he could turn it into a proxy body. His own body couldn't do much, but he could certainly force a drone to kick, punch, kill, and drag other victims into his range.

If you want to be my drones, Thomas invited, *come closer.*

The Red Ranks sprayed microdarts. Thomas was ready. He had shielded himself with heated air, and the darts burned and dropped away, unable to touch him.

Step aside, Thomas urged them. *Let Me pass.*

He projected the countdown timer, reminding his listeners of exactly how much time remained in his bargain. Just enough time for a spa soak and a massage. Just enough time for a leisurely meal. Surely the Torth Majority could wait that long?

If I don't find the Lady of Sorrow within that time window, Thomas reminded his burgeoning audience, *then you (the Torth Majority) will get me, and the Giant, and the Imposter—all of us—without a fight. We will sacrifice ourselves willingly.*

The Torth supergeniuses tried to dissuade the listeners. They didn't trust the Betrayer, and as far as they were concerned, no one should trust him.

But the Red Ranks were reluctant.

This isn't Our fight, one Crimson Rank leader broadcast to the rest. *It is not (should not be) Our job to fight Yeresunsa.*

Right, many others chorused.

Leave it for the Servants of All (those traitors) to do.

Let Yeresunsa battle Yeresunsa.

The Servants of All in the Megacosm were largely silent. They were pariahs, suffering from a collective loss of authority.

Besides, they were busy building a trap around the hostages. A bomb. The Giant would try to save them, and once he failed, the rest of the threats (*like the Betrayer*) would be easy to collect.

Wait until the countdown ends, a Servant of All urged.

Yes, another agreed. *Let Us see if the Betrayer will honor his promise.*

Thomas didn't need to wonder why the Servants were so eager to wait. They wanted the remaining hour and half in order to perfect their bomb trap.

Many Servants of All assured each other that the Giant would throw away his own freedom the instant he saw the one-legged girl in danger. They thought the Giant was really just a powerful runaway slave—and blatant emotions made slaves easy to conquer.

Thomas screened his private thoughts beneath a landslide of trivia. He was inwardly amused by how easily the Torth leadership dismissed Ariock.

They were so tied up with their own civil strife, they had overlooked how many times Ariock had surprised the Torth Majority. He wasn't as stupid as they seemed to believe.

And the Torth leadership was driven by desperation rather than ingenuity right now. The Servants of All were too scared of the Majority, too desperate to prove their own value, to adequately self-evaluate.

Desperation would give them blind spots. They were likely to make a mistake or two.

Throughout the Empire, factories and chemical laboratories worked overtime to manufacture more inhibitor. The revelation of the conspiracy continued to tear riptides through the Megacosm, and neighbors and comrades eyed each other askance. Many Torth now volunteered to wear an inhibitor patch. Anyone who refused to adopt the new fad would be suspected of being a secret renegade.

Suspicion weakened the social fabric of the Megacosm.

The Commander of All Living Things was on her metaphorical knees. *Allow Me (Your elected Commander) to do what you have elected Me to do,* she begged her constituents. *Let Me destroy all threats to Our great and glorious civilization.* She flashed an image of the hostages. *I will make sure the Giant never leaves Stratower City.*

The Majority barely trusted her any more than they trusted the Upward Governess. They grumbled, silently arguing about who ought to lead the galactic empire.

Nobody wanted to take responsibility for thwarting the Betrayer and restarting a battle. Not right at this particular moment.

The countdown will be over soon.

We must discuss Whom to elect.

The Red Ranks were eager to help elect a new leader. They wanted somebody smart in charge, someone who wasn't a traitorous Yeresunsa. They exchanged glances, wondering if they should elect the Twins, the Death Architect, or the Upward Governess.

But should they really put the fate of civilization in the hands of a child?

Maybe they ought to elect one of their own? A competent Crimson Rank, for instance, might be better than any of the current options.

Thomas dropped out of the Megacosm. His skin felt clammy, and his guts were clenched, but he had a wild hope. The Torth Empire was truly in crisis mode.

"We can go," he told Garrett.

CHAPTER 3

ANTIHERO

"The Torth are planning to build a bomb around the hostages," Thomas said. He hesitated, then plunged ahead. "I wonder if you can get any secret details about that?"

"Are you talking to me?" Garrett steered past rubble.

"You claim to be an expert at fooling mind readers," Thomas pointed out. "If anyone can spy on secret Torth plans, it's you."

He was genuinely curious about how Garrett might respond. If it was truly easy to disguise oneself in the Megacosm . . . well, that begged some major questions. Like: How many other secret renegades might be hidden within the Torth Empire?

"Now that they know I can spy," Garret said, "they won't discuss top-secret plans in the Megacosm. I think we're out of luck."

That was true. But it did not satisfy Thomas's curiosity. He decided to go for a blunt question. "How did you do it?"

"I'm a lot more stealthy than you," Garrett said.

Thomas rolled his eyes. Of course a mind of normal scope was more stealthy than that of a supergenius. No matter how weak and underdeveloped Thomas was in reality, he was a freakishly huge presence in the realm of thoughts.

That was one reason why he identified so well with Ariock. They were both outsized, just in different ways.

Maybe Garrett had answered his question. Since Thomas could never disguise his own mind in the Megacosm, he had hardly considered the option. Garrett, on the other hand, had a normal-size mind, plus he'd had a lifetime to figure out how to blend in with average Torth and fish out information.

Hm. That might be an exceptionally useful skill, if, theoretically, one had to fight the Torth Majority.

"We'll deal with the bomb later," Garrett said, speeding around a bend. "First, we need to help Ariock rescue the Lady of Sorrow."

"Blasphemy," Jinishta muttered. She did not want to believe that her goddess was actually a prisoner, especially one who could read minds. Yet her insult lacked conviction. She was beginning to entertain unthinkable possibilities.

Garrett pushed their hovercart to its top speed. They flew through the outer rooms of the Isolatorium, flashing past Red Ranks and interrupted torture sessions.

The old guy acted like a reckless idiot. He had pretty much thrown Thomas off a cliff and expected him to instantly pull off a miracle. And then, when Thomas had actually succeeded, where was his gratitude?

Maybe Thomas should quit expecting gratitude? He had yellow eyes. He looked like a Torth.

But Garrett should know better.

Was old Garrett such an insecure braggart that he wanted to puff himself up in comparison to his younger and smarter rival?

Thomas really wanted to believe that.

Except his own mind would not permit callowness. He knew that a petty idiot would never have survived in the Torth Empire for long. The old man was wily. He had secret depths that Thomas had yet to plumb.

Unfortunately, Thomas could even imagine a few valid reasons for Garrett to despise him. Thomas had let the Torth Majority bully him into sentencing Ariock to death. He had accidentally killed a couple of his human foster parents. Sure, he had excuses and justifications, but such behavior was sort of evil.

On top of that, Thomas's pedigree might stir up old resentments.

Garrett's daughter and grandson had been murdered by the Lone Assassin, Thomas's biological mother. Had someone else in his ancestry destroyed Garrett's beloved wife? She had died under mysterious circumstances. It was no wonder the old man held on to so much rage.

Maybe Thomas should say something apologetic about the murders.

Except he didn't want to. None of those deaths were his fault! He hadn't even been born yet. Besides, Garrett surely could have intervened if he'd wanted—

Jinishta gasped at something ahead.

The abominable River of Blood writhed with moaning aliens, tortured at intervals along its rushing length. One of those tortured souls didn't look like an alien. Was that an Alashani child?

No.

Thomas gained a more comprehensive look through the perceptions of Kessa and Jinishta, and he wished he hadn't.

This torture victim was a little girl. Maybe a human, maybe a Torth. Whoever she used to be, she was now stretched on a torture rack, arms dislocated, crying.

"Ignore what you see." Garrett's voice was icy. "We can't interfere."

Jinishta aimed her angry incredulity from Garrett to Thomas and back. "What is it that I see? I do not understand."

But Thomas did understand.

It made a perfect, horrible kind of sense. The Torth Empire had trillions of citizens. Statistically, it was inevitable that a few Torth would be born with a full range of emotions. Some Torth would sympathize with slaves. Some of those sympathizers would attempt to free slaves.

Here was where they ended up.

"That's a renegade Torth." Garrett sounded bland, as if it was no big deal to see a child tortured and sobbing.

"But . . ." Jinishta sounded outraged. "It is a child!"

"They're almost always children," Garrett said, as if annoyed that he had to explain. "The testing committees do a great job of screening out deviant minds, so almost all the Torth who reach adulthood are sociopaths. But there are plenty of children who never pass their final exams."

"The Torth are worse monsters than I thought," Jinishta said faintly.

Thomas had never inquired too closely about what happened to baby farm rejects. When he was a Yellow Rank, the Upward Governess had given him a state-of-the-art scientific research lab. He had been careful not to harbor any curiosity about where the living tissue samples and organs came from. He hadn't wanted to know.

But deep down, he had guessed.

Now he saw the awful truth in the form of that tortured little girl.

He also saw another truth: that girl was supposed to be him. She was him by proxy. That torture rack was exactly where the Torth Majority wanted him to be. Thomas would have ended up here much sooner if not for the secret cabal of Yeresunsa who ran the Torth government, and if not for the Upward Governess advocating for his life.

"Stop the hovercart," Thomas demanded.

Wildfire ignited around him in a golden glow. He would melt those shackles. He would burn any Torth who thwarted him.

Garrett kept the vehicle moving at top speed. They left the tortured girl behind.

Thomas prepared to hurl a fireball to make Garrett stop.

"We. Cannot. Interfere." Garrett turned to glare at Thomas, the wind whipping his hair and cloak around him.

The bargain. The rules. The parameters, which Thomas himself had come up with, and which he'd approved . . . those rules now seemed like a tragic embarrassment.

Thomas, of all people, ought to provide a safe haven for renegades.

The universe hated them. Renegades had no friends. They were outcasts from Torth society, from slaves, and from Alashani. No one else in the universe would even think about saving that girl. Probably not even Ariock.

"I am sorry, Thomas." Kessa put her hand on his arm, wanting to give comfort.

The regret she emanated was real. She might not feel exactly the same way Thomas did, but she, too, wanted to rescue people like herself.

Kessa had seen a tortured ummin who reminded her of her long-deceased mate.

Even so, Thomas felt ready to scorch the air, to stop their speeding vehicle and turn it around. He had been unable to rescue his biological mother, but he wanted to make the difference for another nameless renegade.

"Do you want Cherise to live?" Garrett demanded. "Renegades and runaways die here every day. Believe me. They die every hour." He sounded haunted. "Let's rescue the Lady of Sorrow. We can worry about dying children and everyone else later. Okay? Lots of people in the universe are suffering. You won't help anyone if you get us all killed."

Right. There were countless victims who remained unheard and unseen whom no one knew about.

Kessa held Thomas almost as if to hold him down. "The Torth placed that scene in our path on purpose."

She was wise.

Thomas knew it was true. The Torth pretended to be gods. They would normally hide any evidence to the contrary. Instead? That poor child was on display where anyone could hear her cries and witness her torment.

Kessa had avoided the fate of most runaways only by a chain of improbable and fortunate circumstances. She was akin to Thomas in that way.

Their hovercart was flying fast. Damp, chilly air wafted from the rain-soaked night beyond the crumpled edges of Ariock's punched-out tunnel.

The rain smelled and tasted like freedom.

Thomas closed his eyes and tried not to imagine how many silent, nameless prisoners were being forced to die in horrible ways.

He actually wanted to borrow the immense power of the Lady of Sorrow. He would use her power to smite every torturer in this city.

CHAPTER 4

AN HONEST COWARD

Rain and gloom obscured the tallest terrestrial structure in the known universe.

There were space stations and starships longer than the Stratower, Thomas knew. There were factories and indoor cities that sprawled across a greater acreage. But this tower would dwarf them all, and it was more than a mere office building. It was the symbolic backbone of galactic civilization.

The Stratower filled his field of view as their stolen prison hovercart careened alongside the River of Blood. Most of its pointy windows were dark. Thousands of windows emitted just enough of an eerie glow to define its curved shape.

Thomas inwardly admitted to a certain amount of curiosity about what was inside the tower.

Had he been a loyal Torth—if he had been raised on a baby farm, if he had never gone renegade—then he would have yearned to visit this nexus of power. In another life, Thomas would have climbed the ladder of cool Green and Blue ranks, the engineers and thinkers. He might have been secretly inducted into the cabal of Yeresunsa at the top of Torth civilization.

His biological mother had done exactly that. The Swift Killer had done it as well. They had both trained within the Stratower. As clones, they would have possessed the same hidden powers.

Which left Thomas with a lot of questions.

For instance: Why hadn't his biological mother tried to wreck her way out of the Isolatorium, like Jonathan Stead?

The most likely answer was that her fellow Servants of All had secretly disabled her powers with the inhibitor serum. Perhaps a lot of Torth with Yeresunsa powers were tortured to death in the Isolatorium. Maybe it was downright mundane.

Thomas shivered and tried not to think about the little girl who was dying in an awful way, with no one to care about her and no one to rescue her.

The fact that his own biological mother had been a Yeresunsa opened up a more worrisome concern. Yeresunsa powers were highly heritable.

Thomas figured he had inherited his brainwashing power from . . . well, someone. Probably his mother.

Had she brainwashed an unsuspecting human into having sex with her? Was that how Thomas was conceived?

And then, to get rid of the evidence, had she killed the stud? Like a spider consuming its mate?

Were the top Servants of All socially influential because they could literally change people's minds by using their secret powers?

Thomas decided not to think about it. He would, however, be extra wary around the Swift Killer and anyone else who shared his pedigree. He would not let a Servant of All into his range.

"Y y y y o u   w i l l   n o t   f f f f f i n d   h h h h e r." Red Ranks streamed toward the Stratower on hoverbikes and hovercarts. Their overlapping whispers resounded throughout Bloodbath Plaza. "S h e e e e e   i s   n o t t t   r e a l l l l l l."

How encouraging.

Garrett ignored the whispers, steering past the colossal guardian statues along the River of Blood. He had to weave around Torth, and nussians carrying supplies, and overloaded hovercarts. There were even lone Torth in hoverchairs. Slaves waddled in their wake, burdened by luggage.

Whooshing sounds from beyond the clouds implied that airborne traffic was circling the docking bays, searching for parking spots.

"Why are so many people heading to the Stratower?" Kessa asked. "I thought it was closed to the public?"

"It is," Thomas said. "Normally."

"The Commander of All Living Things recommends a citywide evacuation," Garrett reported.

That did not bode well.

"Why?" Thomas asked. "Does it have to do with the bomb they're setting up around the hostages? Is it nuclear?"

Garrett shook his head. "They're not making any of that info public."

"When is the bomb set to go off?" Thomas eyed the countdown timer on the tablet. They had over an hour remaining. Surely the Torth would want to control the situation? He suspected they would rig the bomb to go off at a signal, probably from the Commander of All Living Things.

"All I know," Garrett said, "is that they've opened up the Stratospheric Spaceport to the public for anyone who wants to leave the planet ASAP. A lot of Torth are flying to the polar cities. But as you can see"—he gestured—"some local residents have opted to flee the planet."

"Maybe they fear the Lady of Sorrow," Jinishta said.

Thomas doubted that. Most Torth dismissed her as nothing but a slave myth.

"Or the messiah," Jinishta said.

Thomas was pretty sure it was the bomb. But Jinishta had no frame of reference for such destructive power, really.

"I'm guessing a good number of Torth are also here to chase Ariock," Garrett said. "They don't want to lose sight of where he is."

Ariock had left an obvious path. He had apparently punched a cave-in through an entryway in the Stratower two or three stories tall. The damage looked insignificant compared to the size of the ornate, monolithic skyscraper, but Thomas knew that even the Stratower's vault-like doors were considered impregnable. Traffic clogged the ragged hole.

"I do wish he would be stealthier," Garrett said.

"Maybe he's really found her." Thomas sat straighter, eager to meet the possibly immortal prisoner known as the Lady of Sorrow.

"Out of our way!" Garrett called.

The crowd of armored Torth and depressed slaves did not jostle aside. They behaved as if the approaching hovercart did not exist.

"Boy," Garrett said. "Make them move."

It wasn't worth an argument. Thomas concentrated, trying to gather his willpower into one projected area. He heated the air throughout the crowd.

Soon slaves were panting or sweating. Their masters shot Thomas a baleful collective glare.

Would this be considered interference? Thomas hoped not. He withdrew his power, unwilling to test it further.

"Don't be timid," Garrett snapped.

"There's another way in." Thomas gestured to the River of Blood. Maybe that canal had been crystal clear in the ancient past, before the Torth Empire arose. Now it burbled into an ornate maw of the Stratower, carrying toxic rain and filth and blood. It was no River of Tears.

"Hovercarts can't maintain lift over liquid," Garrett pointed out. "Are you planning on thermal currents?"

"Just trust me." Thomas hid his uncertainties. "I'll get us across."

He didn't think he could pick up the hovercart and make it fly. That waterfall save had been enough of a stretch for him. His atrophied muscles were twisted and useless. There was no point in infusing his own body with superstrength.

But liquids could freeze into solids. And Thomas could alter temperatures.

The hovercart's magnet needed a floor to repel against. Roughly two feet down ought to be sufficient.

Cautious, unsure what degree of control he might exert, Thomas reached out with his awareness. He sensed the rushing torrent. Next, he sank his focus into the blood water, sensing its ambient warmth. He sensed its kinetic force.

Now, to remove those things.

Creating ice was the opposite of creating wildfire. Instead of a wild burst of outrage, this was more like a smothering. A suppression. It was mathematical, and logical, and crystalline.

Glaciation came naturally to Thomas. He supposed he could understand why it seemed natural to the Commander of All Living Things, and probably to a lot of Servants of All, as well.

He started with the edge of the canal closest to him. He twined a latticework of blood ice across the surface. As liquid splashed over the frozen lacework, Thomas froze that as well. A raised latticework of frozen blood crept over the surface.

"Go over it," Thomas urged Garrett.

"It's not all the way frozen," Garrett protested.

"I'll handle it as we go," Thomas said.

The problem was the relentless force of the canal. Its warmth and pressure eroded his frozen causeway in progress. It was a fight. Thomas doubted he could keep it up for long.

"Hurry," he added.

Garrett slammed their stolen hovercart to full speed. They tumbled over the lip of the wall on a rush of thermal air, and soon they scraped against the icy latticework before bouncing up, regaining their smooth glide.

Trembling with the effort of maintaining so much ice, Thomas calculated the bare minimum of solid surface necessary to keep their hovercart aloft. Then he reconfigured his creeping latticework, allowing the river to melt and wash away unnecessary pieces. He let the river smash the used causeway behind them.

Anyone with normal mental processing capabilities would have been fatally inefficient. But Thomas created a perfect lattice of ice for their hovercart, a web just barely solid and wide enough to keep them gliding over the river.

They careened through the ornate opening that led inward. The interior of the Stratower was echoey and regally ornate. Orb lamps lit the way, giving the canal a romantic hue. Elegant sculptures of porcelain and stained glass screened the traffic jam of pedestrians.

It smelled like blood.

"Give us some lift, boy," Garrett said.

As if this magic was totally unremarkable.

"Ariock went that way." Garrett used his staff to point to a huge passageway. An indoor bridge arced over the River of Blood, but it had recently collapsed. It looked as if a giant fist had smashed it, preventing the crowd of Torth from easily following.

"Fine," Thomas said. They did need an updraft to fly past the remains of the bridge and into that passageway. But did Garrett imagine this was easy?

With a supreme effort of concentration, Thomas added thermodynamics to his current calculations and tasks. He cycled both icy and superheated air beneath the hoverdisk, creating a violent updraft.

Their vehicle arced upward instead of plunging away with the melting ice.

They soared over the broken stone lip. Thomas extended his awareness again, cycling the air enough to cushion their landing. Garrett steered them before they could careen into a heap of what looked like gemstones.

"Huh," Garrett said. Judging by his tone, he had not known what to expect.

They skimmed between forests of fanciful sculptures and mounds of crystalware, all of it strewn with gems. Thomas glimpsed his own pallid reflection, distorted, in hammered golden friezes and pearlescent goblets or bowls. This region of the Stratower looked like an endless cornucopia of loot.

Jinishta struggled to look apathetic, but her awestruck unease was plain to anyone who could read minds. She could not have imagined as much treasure as this hoard.

And no one she knew could freeze water.

"I suppose what you did was moderately impressive." Garrett sounded unimpressed.

"Come on." Thomas glared. "No one else could have done that."

"Don't be so sure," Garrett said. "It's a serious mistake to underestimate our enemies."

Thomas inwardly conceded that Garrett was probably right about that. The Torth Empire had conquered every alien civilization they encountered. The heaps of alien relics in this immense passageway attested to that.

"In ancient times," Garrett said conversationally, "novice Yeresunsa had to prove themselves worthy of having powers. Yeresunsa back in the day were like royalty. But they didn't allow just anyone to join. They had standards."

Thomas hoped the old man wasn't angling toward an insult. He was getting sick of those.

"Cowards weren't allowed to call themselves Yeresunsa," Garrett went on. "They were untrained scum. Even if they had powers, their betters considered them to be pathetic, fit only to obey orders."

Thomas wondered where Garrett got this information. Certainly not from the Megacosm. Had he read it in a moldering book? Perhaps from the prophecies of Ah Jun? Or was he just making things up?

"You know why?" Garrett steered around a glass sculpture of a gigantic alien antelope, draped in ornate linens.

"Why?" Kessa was as curious as ever.

"Because they were unwilling to examine their own emotions," Garrett said. "They were afraid to examine their own values and their inner selves. A Yeresunsa who lies to himself is dangerous. Someone like the boy, for instance, would have been considered a danger to himself and others."

Wrong! Thomas wanted to shout.

The lie stuck in his throat.

Was he afraid to examine his own emotions? Yes.

Was he terrified of his own powers? Yes.

Was he afraid to be honest with himself? Yes.

Was he less than human? Probably, yes.

Garrett knew Thomas all too well, and what he saw was . . . well . . . a pathetic coward of a scumbag. Thomas had earned the moniker "the Betrayer," hadn't he?

"He's emotionally unstable," Garrett went on. "The Yeresunsa of ancient times would have kept him only as an untrained novice. He would be a handy tool. Like an ice maker, or a flamethrower."

There was truth to that.

Thomas liked feeling useful. That was why he'd volunteered to manage investment portfolios for his foster families on Earth. He had been eager to serve the Upward Governess. And now he wanted to serve Ariock.

Obedience was so much easier than entrusting major decisions to his own damaged psyche.

"Thomas is keeping us safe right now," Kessa said. "I trust him."

But she could not examine his mind. She could not truly know him the way Garrett could assess and measure him.

Thomas and Garrett kept disagreeing with each other. Such clashes meant that one of them had to be subordinate to the other, or else they would fight and argue all the time. They could not both be in charge.

So which one of them was better suited for leadership?

Garrett felt confident enough to insult the boy who could burn him to a crisp. His prescience was scary. Maybe that was because he was self-actualized. He might be intellectually honest with himself in ways that Thomas was not.

How else could Garrett maintain his emotional well-being while immersed in the Megacosm?

The old man claimed that he had never forgotten his purpose in life, even when he was surrounded with Torth. That must require exceptional emotional maturity. Sure, Garrett told lies, but he was an effective liar because he could dissect people's hearts.

Thomas could only dissect the mind.

The biggest act of cowardice was to lie to oneself—to act on unexamined emotions.

That was what bullies did. That was what Torth did. And it was what untrained, immature, bratty novice Yeresunsa did, as well.

Thomas bowed his head.

He still intended to probe Garrett's mind if an opportunity arose, but he acknowledged the old man as his superior.

For now.

CHAPTER 5

GLAMOUR AND GLASS ELEVATORS

The trading forums of New GoodLife WaterGarden City had not contained even a fraction of the wealth stored inside the Stratower. Thomas stared at the endless wonderland of glittering treasures.

"They must have stolen all this from the Alashani." Jinishta sounded disgusted as she peered at cavorting statues, intertwined pillars, and elaborate tapestries.

"I don't think so." Garrett steered around crystal fronds edged with silver filigree. "The Torth Empire only just learned about the existence of the Alashani today." He pointed to an impressive red granite statue of a heroic-looking nussian. "These treasures come from conquered civilizations."

Indeed, Thomas recognized various styles of artwork from periods of antiquity, originating from various planets. He couldn't blame Jinishta and Kessa for their troubled looks. Thousands of artisans working for thousands of years could not have produced so much.

"Why lock it away?" Jinishta asked. "What is the point of stealing these . . ." She fumbled for adequate words. ". . . these marvels, if they are never to be admired? Or used?"

Thomas could not resist pointing out her hypocrisy. "Your own Yeresunsa monastery has a bunch of sacred relics that are locked away from the public."

Jinishta looked troubled and introspective.

"Many civilian Torth do own relics." Garrett shrugged. "But it makes sense that Servants would own more plunder than anyone else. They are—or they were—the highest ranks. Plus, they were the ones in charge of conquests."

His disdain was apparent in his word choices. *Plunder. Conquests.* Garrett considered the Torth to be nothing more than lowly thugs, thieves, and slavers. He didn't see them as the pinnacle of the greatest galactic civilization to have ever existed.

And he was probably right.

Thomas had spent too long fearing the Upward Governess and the Torth Majority. Maybe he ought to dump his last vestiges of respect for them.

"That statue over there." Jinishta pointed to a queenly woman sculpted from quartz, with stylized wings arcing out from her shoulders. "That was not made by aliens."

It was not made by Alashani, either, Thomas knew. The Alashani had no concept of wings or angels.

"That's a relic from the predecessors," Garrett said. "The people who used to exist before the Torth arose."

Very little was known about the predecessors. Thomas wondered what ancient secrets Garrett had unearthed in his quest to find the Lady of Sorrow. He might know a bit more than what was commonly known in the Megacosm.

Jinishta gasped. "You mean that is a sacred relic?"

"I guess so," Garrett said blandly. "The predecessors were Yeresunsa. Or, more likely, they were ruled by Yeresunsa. They built this fortress of a sky-scraper, among other things."

Jinishta looked suspicious. Thomas was close enough to read her mind, and he sensed her skepticism about the predecessors, because they seemed like Alashani to her. Yeresunsa? Creators of artwork and statues? People who existed independent of the Torth Empire? How could they be anything other than Alashani?

And, Thomas inwardly admitted, she had valid points. The style of art-work used by the predecessors and the Alashani had remarkable similarities.

To him, that made for a clear theory. The Torth had not wholly wiped out the predecessors. Instead, the Torth had driven them underground—and, over centuries and millennia, had forgotten their existence.

Meanwhile, the predecessors had changed. They had undergone an Age of Starvation and an Age of Chaos. They had suffered a population bottle-neck or two. Now they were albino and superstitious.

"Uh-oh," Garrett said, peering ahead.

A traffic jam of pedestrians blocked the crystalline passageway. Torth boots and nussian feet had tracked mud across the shiny floor. Some of the pedestrians gazed around with suppressed wonderment. Civilians were not normally permitted inside the Stratower.

The passageway curved into a grand archway.

That, in turn, opened into a lobby vast enough to swallow the largest skyscraper on Earth. Gilded glass cages zoomed up or descended silently on tracks that ran so far upward, they vanished to a distant point obscured by atmospheric haze. Thomas counted two thousand, one hundred, and ninety-seven elevators in a quick glance.

Ariock stood in the middle of the elevator lobby, towering in his inky-black wraps, nightmarish in comparison to the well-dressed sea of Torth. He wasn't waiting in line. He looked stymied.

A couple of Servants of All sprinted past the hovercart, their capes rippling. The traffic parted willingly for them.

"Did he lose her?" Garrett muttered. He nudged the hovercart into the crowd, attempting to get closer without running anyone over.

Ariock saw them and strode over. The crowd parted for him. It seemed the Torth feared the Giant just enough to move out of his way, although they also sized him up like predators preparing for a slaughter.

Servants of All dotted the crowd, cloaked in soft white. Their empty eyes were especially predatory.

Thomas felt as if he was trapped in the equivalent of an unlit stick of dynamite.

"What happened?" Garrett asked.

Ariock leaned down to answer in a low, embarrassed voice. "I lost her."

Garrett looked like he wanted details. Thomas understood, from Ariock's mind, that there had been particles. Dust particles, tenuously controlled by the Lady of Sorrow.

"She went . . ." Ariock made a hopeless gesture toward his feet. "I don't know. Down."

He assumed that a lowered voice would prevent the Torth from overhearing. He was wrong. Even if all the Torth were out of earshot, they would glean the conversation as soon as one of them crossed paths with Ariock or any of his friends.

"There's nothing down there except stone," Ariock said.

Baffled, Garrett peered at the floor, inlaid with iron filigree around quartz slabs.

Ariock leaned closer. "How are the hostages?"

"Unharmed." Kessa showed him the data tablet. "As far as I can tell."

"I'm sure they're fine." Garrett gave no hint that Vy and Cherise were bait for a trap.

Thomas tried to take comfort in the fact that none of the other super-geniuses were proactively involved in planning the trap. The Majority was freezing them out to some degree.

At least, Thomas hoped that was still the case.

If only he could swim unnoticed through the Megacosm. If he became desperate to spy on the Torth, he would need to beg Garrett for help.

"I'm open to ideas." Ariock's tone was gentle, but there was a strained undertone. Time was ticking away.

"Give me a moment." Thomas closed his eyes and tried to tune out the worries around him.

We are here, he silently told the prisoner. *We want to rescue you.*

The Lady of Sorrow offered no response.

Not that Thomas really expected any. Whoever she was, wherever she was, she could not easily communicate with people who were free to move in the outside world. That was obvious. Otherwise she would have gotten herself rescued generations ago.

Millennia ago?

Thomas considered the tales and myths about the Lady of Sorrow, stretching back into antiquity and earlier. He considered the heaps of relics in the Stratower. There was a lot of forgotten history here, and a lot of implications that the predecessors had been powerful Yeresunsa.

He riffled through his absorbed cache of knowledge. Did anything in this massive lobby resonate with ancient history . . . ?

The floor.

He opened his eyes to study the polished quartz stone. The inlaid tiles and iron filigree had been replaced dozens of times over the millennia, but its original layout was probably unchanged.

Thomas contained a sketchy overview of the entire lobby through the eyes of Red Ranks he had passed. The stonework formed the shape of a stylized eye, with a hook on either end. Thomas had seen that design elsewhere. Early Torth used to conquer planets under that ancient symbol of authority.

"Drill through the pupil of the stylized eye," Thomas said.

Ariock gave him a questioning look.

"The floor," Thomas explained. "It's an ancient symbol of telepathy or Yeresunsa, I think. Maybe both. I don't know what's underneath the solid stone. But I'm guessing it's an ancient dungeon."

Nobody knew all the secrets of the Stratower. The current shadow government had usurped its power from earlier Torth, and they, in turn, had usurped it from an earlier leadership. The collective knowledge of the Megacosm was indistinct when it came to their own early beginnings.

There must have been a lot of churn when the Torth Empire was newly formed. That was how the Alashani had slipped away and been forgotten. And that was probably why a powerful and mysterious long-ago prisoner had been forgotten.

"There is empty space far below us," Ariock said, his tone distant. "I sense it." Thomas sensed Ariock's awareness stretched downward, perhaps as far as a quarter of a mile. "I think there's a canyon."

"Break the floor." Garrett stamped his staff for emphasis. "Let's check it out."

Ariock got a determined look on his face.

Thomas became aware of the overcrowded lobby. Torth waited in turns to board elevators. Humans would have gotten pushy in such an overcrowded exodus scenario, but telepaths could operate a streamlined schedule through the Megacosm.

"Move back," Ariock said, loosening his arms.

"You can't harm any Torth." Thomas meant to sound like a voice of reason. Unfortunately, he sensed the gathering strength inside Ariock's mind, and his voice turned into a squeak. This lobby was as busy as any major train station or airport. And Ariock was about to get violent.

Garrett reversed the hovercart. They glided backward, but not nearly as fast as they should be going.

Ariock lifted his arms, and quartz slabs popped out of alignment. Cracks zigzagged beneath boots. Red Ranks began to shove each other, trying to escape the lobby.

"Protect us, boy," Garrett said casually. "Just in case."

CHAPTER 6

WHAT WAS FORGOTTEN

Thomas gave Garrett an incredulous look. How was he supposed to shield them? Sure, he could shift temperatures, but that would not protect anyone from a collapsing floor, or from thousands of blaster gloves or any sort of major disaster.

Ariock radiated visible waves of power. He stood in the now-deserted center of the lobby with a dangerous glint in his deep-set eyes.

If any Torth tried to slow Ariock down . . . if they attacked him at all . . . perhaps even if they did nothing . . . well, Ariock must want an excuse to slaughter Torth, after the atrocities he'd seen in the Isolatorium.

The bargain was hanging by a thread.

"I would protect us if I could." Garrett glared at Thomas, perhaps ashamed of his own helplessness. "Just . . ." He trailed off in a frustrated growl. "Agh. Just use common sense and keep us alive!"

Fissures split the floor in a crazy quilt.

"I'll do my best," Thomas said, "but we have to get the Torth out of here and make sure no one is harmed."

Jinishta yanked her scarf-veil over her nose. She leaped to her feet and brandished her spear, shouting, "Get out of the way, Torth! Out of the way!"

Her warnings had no effect. A few Torth aimed disdainful glances toward the noisy Alashani premier, but the rest continued to shuffle toward various exits. Some of them even continued to wait for elevators.

A deep rumble shook the lobby. Stone blocks shifted, and dusty pebbles rained down. The very walls gained a grinding, relentless voice.

"MOVE. TORTH."

The lobby cracked in a jagged ring around Ariock. A moaning wind arose from darkness below.

Torth began to run.

Garrett jammed their hovercart toward the nearest exit archway. Ariock balanced upon a levitating chunk of floor, like a floating island topped by a slab of quartz. The floor was crumbling, caving in, unsupported by anything below. Tension had held it in place for millennia. Now that tensile strength was gone, and connective sections of the floor tumbled into the jagged abyss.

The void looked infinite.

Red Ranks shouted, trapped on falling slabs. Glass elevators zoomed upward, packed to capacity. One Torth threw himself toward the crowd on solid ground, but his comrades did not bother to catch him, and he clung desperately to a crumbling ledge until it fell, tumbling and taking him downward.

Thomas could only watch with horror. The bargain was breaking. There was no way Ariock would take risks just to save a bunch of . . .

The fallen Red Rank levitated out of the abyss on a slab of quartz.

Another batch of Torth soared over the crowd, and another.

This was not the bludgeoning action of Ariock's first few battles. This was . . . well, it was masterful. Even Garrett gawked. It seemed he had not anticipated Ariock to be so dexterous with his powers, and so unflagging.

Thomas sensed a reluctant glow of pride in Jinishta's mind.

No doubt about it, these were her lessons paying off. She had challenged Ariock's weaknesses and built up his strengths. Now Ariock was a lot more masterful, especially in his capacity for multitasking.

He caught every at-risk Torth with invisible extensions of his awareness. He added them to levitating slabs, shoving them helter-skelter, and then he deposited the crowded slabs far away, safely on marble balconies or in antechambers.

Ariock surveyed his handiwork from his levitating chunk of rock. Once it seemed clear that no one else would fall by accident, he gave Thomas a nod, thanking him for the clue. "Will you be okay up here?" he called. "Should I bring—"

"Go!" Garrett made a shooing motion. "Find her."

Ariock floated downward into the rocky chasm. The remaining edges of the lobby floor collapsed as his awareness deserted them.

"Back away!" Jinishta clutched the railing.

"We've got to see this quest all the way through," Garrett said. "I just didn't want Ariock trying to protect us while he has an important task."

Thomas made a strangled noise, unable to figure out if Garrett was suicidal or insane. "We can't follow him!" He tried to sit straighter, to glare at the old man. "If we go over that edge? We're dead!"

Garrett worked the controls. Their stolen hovercart tipped toward the abyss. "You're a capable Yeresunsa."

"I'm not a miracle worker!" Thomas whipped his awareness outward. Could he sabotage their vehicle by freezing the hoverdisk? He needed to bring them to a halt, but momentum was a problem. They would glide.

"Control our fall, boy," Garrett said as the hovercart dipped violently vertical.

The depths below were dark, empty, desolate, and dead.

Jinishta and Kessa screamed, and Thomas screamed with them.

Hovervehicles required a floor. The magnetized hoverdisk needed a solid surface to repel against. Did Garrett assume that Thomas had the strength and stamina to levitate this vehicle indefinitely? Well, he was wrong. Thomas was a supergenius, not a superhero, and that mistake was going to get them all smashed to pulp at the bottom of this insane plunge.

A gnarled hand clamped over his mouth. Thomas's scream got muffled against callused skin.

"Get a hold of yourself," Garrett growled into his ear. "You're capable of saving us."

Wrong. Thomas struggled to draw breath around Garrett's hand, to scream again.

"You have all kinds of problems," Garrett snapped, "but you're a decently strong Yeresunsa."

Thomas struggled to form coherent thoughts. He was weightless. They were going to smash to the bottom of the abyss at any second.

Garrett's tone softened, almost kindly. "Do you want my secrets?"

Yes. Thomas really wanted that. Garrett was tantalizingly close. His mind was a ferocious swirl of complexities.

"You want to invade my mind?" Garrett asked, full of secrets that might change the universe.

Thomas sought out the most promising hints. He began to soak up what he could.

"Then pull yourself together and save us!" Garrett's mind spiked with rage, jarring Thomas.

Live. Yes. That sounded like a good idea.

Thomas extended his awareness and gathered friction from the air as they fell through it. He redirected the heat from their friction to a point below their platform, then created a thermal burst that bumped them aloft.

His stomach rolled over as the platform met him from below, scooping him up.

They leveled, gliding rather than falling. They might smash into a wall at any moment, but at least they were no longer plummeting downward.

He was actually doing it! They were flying!

The exciting novelty disrupted Thomas's focus. They wobbled in midair.

"Focus," Garrett said. *Like this.*

A cloud of helpful knowledge flooded Thomas. In his mind, Garrett mimed exactly how he would manipulate heat into a powerful thermal current. He would then loop the effect, turning it into a mental subroutine so that it wouldn't chew up all his brainpower. Also, he wanted to leave some focus left over in order to create a headlamp effect, so they could see where they were going rather than flying through unnerving pitch blackness.

"I know it's difficult." Garrett's condescension came across even as he shared his expertise.

Thomas wanted to defend himself, but he had to focus on thermodynamics. Teeth chattering from adrenaline, he calculated the optimal lift coefficient. He factored in his estimate of their velocity and the platform's angle of attack.

The air had a dank, echoing quality. So what? He set aside his observations for later examination.

He created a thermal lift subroutine more perfect than anything Garrett could have come up with. And he did it faster than Garrett would have done.

"How about some illumination?" Garrett said. "I know it's a lot to juggle, but I'm sure you can manage it." In his mind, he showed how to create a puny little fireball and maintain it in thin air.

As if Thomas hadn't already figured that out on his own.

Four disks of wildfire swirled underneath the hovercart, searingly white, like miniature galaxies. Thomas maintained one under each corner of the platform. It was a lot of subroutines to keep track of, but he could juggle this much complexity and still have enough idle brainpower leftover for multiple conversations.

"Good enough." Garrett sounded disappointed to have run out of criticisms.

Kessa clapped her hands in delight. Somehow, that made up for all of Garrett's opprobrium and left Thomas with a fragile sense of pride.

He dared to withdraw a smidgeon of his focus. Now was a perfect opportunity to probe the old man's mind.

Garrett pushed away from the railing and limped toward the prow. Thomas needed to hurry before the codger could exit his range. As he dived in . . . a granite cliff face loomed, startlingly close, at the edge of his makeshift light.

Thomas threw all his focus into veering away from the cliff face.

Had he imagined rows of windows? Surely the rocks were just mottled by shadows and ancient lichen.

Thomas fueled his wildfire disks to enlarge and brighten them. He peered through the gloom. He had to know what was down here.

Skyscrapers?

Row after row of stone buildings towered in the gloom, like stacks of mausoleums. A few were collapsed from the weight of untold years.

Thomas's firelight reflected on dim glassware inside buildings, dulled by age, yet untouched by rain or wind.

It was an entire city, lost beneath the Stratower.

Thomas scanned farther, unwilling to blink for fear of missing details. Here was a pristine archaeological site that predated the Torth Empire. How many secrets did this place hide, uncorrupted by rain or sludge or living things?

Never mind Garrett's memories. This treasure trove of secrets outclassed all others.

ABOVE TEARS

"Why are you slowing down?" Garrett asked.

Thomas refused to waste energy on an answer. He studied ancient buildings, ornate with pedimented sculptures, decorative battens, and other artistry. The builders had been technologically advanced. There were lichen-covered billboards and empty marquees where backdrops for holographs would have been displayed. Cobwebs festooned the remnants of spotlights and fountains.

Judging by depictions of lightning in the friezes, this had been a city of magic.

And aliens, as well, judging by a frieze that included a maned sapient of some sort. The long-gone inhabitants must have been cosmopolitan.

"That way, boy!" Garrett pointed imperiously. "Follow the river."

So that was why the air had a fetid quality. A ribbon of water frothed far below, dimly reflecting the glow from Thomas's white-fire disks. The abyss was as deep as he feared.

"Is that the River of Tears?" Jinishta peered over the edge of the railing, more at home underground than she had been in the world above. She gazed at the distant river with incredulity.

It did smell like pure, fresh water. Not blood. Not sludge.

According to mythology, the River of Tears was generated by the Lady of Sorrow, who wept for every slave killed. The Alashani believed that the life-sustaining river began in the land of the dead, a fabulous realm beyond imagining, full of grottoes and sparkling gems.

Jinishta seemed to think she had entered the Alashani equivalent of Shangri-La. Maybe she was correct.

Ariock had most likely traveled upstream, seeking the source of the river. That made sense. Even so, Thomas longed to take a detour, to explore a building or two. How many long-sealed cabinets contained data tablets from antiquity? Or even books? Paper might disintegrate at a touch unless handled with the utmost care.

If only he had weeks, or months, to explore this place. He practically drooled with yearning. He needed to learn everything that was forgotten.

"Pick up the pace, boy." Garrett leaned against the railing, like he was enjoying the breeze.

It almost hurt to move faster, to skim past endless entombed neighborhoods that were hiding unfathomable secrets. *Later,* Thomas inwardly promised himself. *I will come back and thoroughly explore this place as soon as I can.*

Garrett began to hum a jaunty tune, as carefree as a pirate captain on the open sea after too long languishing in a port.

When he caught Jinishta and Kessa staring, he offered them an unrepentant grin. "I miss singing. You have no idea."

They thought he was insanely reckless.

Thomas remembered that Garrett had spent the last two decades pretending to be a Torth. This morning, Garrett had awoken on a luxurious bed, thinking of himself as the Credible Witness, with slaves tending to his every need.

Now he was here.

Thomas remembered his own transition, which had felt like being doused with ice water and shoved back into reality. He still had trouble coping with the change. Emotions tended to erupt out of him.

"Did you own slaves?" Jinishta asked, challenging Garrett's jolly mood. She might accept that the old man was truly Jonathan Stead, but nevertheless, she considered him to be a liar, a braggart, and, worst of all, a *rekveh.*

Garrett stopped singing. He considered Jinishta for a moment, possibly weighing different answers.

He must have owned at least fifty slaves. After all, he had been a Blue Rank, the Torth equivalent of an elite intellectual.

"Yes." Garrett had apparently decided to risk the truth. "All Torth own slaves. I needed to blend in if I was to have any chance of learning their secrets."

Jinishta tensed with hatred. "Why didn't you free your slaves?" she demanded.

"That would make them runaways," Garrett said dryly. "Which is a death sentence. If I had set them loose in some alien wilderness, they would have been hunted down. They wouldn't stand a chance against all the technology of the Torth Empire. And I would be tortured to death in the Isolatorium for being a traitorous renegade."

Jinishta looked sickened but thoughtful.

"I did what I could to give them a better life," Garrett explained, speaking as much to Kessa as Jinishta. "Every slave I owned was a rescue case. I bartered with abusive Torth who murdered their own personal slaves for petty mistakes. I would trade goods or services until their slaves were mine, and then I gave them as much kindness as a Torth can give. Which isn't much, granted. I did not get friendly with my slaves. That would have been too obvious and too dangerous. Still, I promise, I made efforts to give them a better-than-average future."

Thomas had also attempted to treat his slaves well when he was a Yellow Rank. He had managed to pull it off—up to a point.

He could not guess what had befallen Nror, the tawny-yellow govki who used to serve him nectar drinks and give him massages. Was Nror serving another owner? Or was Nror murdered, punished for having served the Betrayer?

It was too bad the govki hadn't been able to escape along with Pung and Kessa and the rest of them. He had worked the wrong shift.

"What is happening to your slaves now?" Kessa asked, her eyes round with worry.

"I'm sure they're fine." Garrett spoke in a soothing tone that did not fool Thomas at all. "I wouldn't want any of them to get punished for belonging to the dreaded Imposter"—he gestured to himself—"so I bartered them to other semibenevolent Torth. I sent away the last few this morning, before I chucked away my Torth identity."

Jinishta looked suspicious. "You had a govki with you."

"Yeah." Garrett shrugged apologetically. "I needed to keep one slave so I could avoid suspicion as I flew away. Dyoot is cool. I figured he would enjoy adventuring with Ariock and the rest of you."

Thomas wanted to pick apart Garrett's claims, or drill him with questions. But he found that keeping the hovercart aloft was a growing strain.

The mental subroutines were relatively simple. It was no great stretch for Thomas to manipulate airflow while simultaneously burning air for light and fuel. Even so, he felt a growing sense of exhaustion.

It felt like physical therapy. Thomas used to dread those humiliating sessions, wherein he would exercise for five minutes, all the while aware of his own impending collapse. Sometimes the collapse would come sooner than he expected. Spinal muscular atrophy meant that his muscles could not build up. He had to fight every week, every day, in order to maintain what little mobility he had.

Thomas anticipated his own collapse here, too. The intense exchange of hot and cold air that buoyed their platform was, for him, the equivalent of weight lifting. Ariock and Garrett might be unfamiliar with power depletion, but the Alashani warriors knew it well enough, and Thomas had soaked up Jinishta's knowledge. He expected an incapacitating headache at any moment.

How much longer before he collapsed? Five minutes? Two?

"Who were the predecessors?" Jinishta asked, oblivious to Thomas's concerns. "You say they were not Alashani." She studied the dead buildings that faded into gloom. "So who were they? Did the Torth kill them all?"

"The predecessors," Garrett said, "were the ancestors of both Torth and Alashani. They gave rise to both the Torth and the Alashani."

Kessa looked curious. Thomas was so distracted by questions, he had to struggle to keep his subroutines going. Garrett must contain a fount of knowledge.

Jinishta gave him a challenging glare. "Alashani and Torth are not related."

"Wrong." Garrett was matter-of-fact about it. "Alashani and Torth both arose from a common ancestral species. I suspect that humans—and wild zoved, for that matter—belong to the same genus."

Jinishta moved so fast, Thomas nearly missed her intention. She whipped out her scimitar. Before Garrett could dodge or defend himself, the curved blade was against his throat.

"Liar," Jinishta said in a dangerous voice.

Garrett swallowed and leaned as far away as he could without tumbling over the railing.

"Jinishta!" Kessa pleaded.

Although the premier had moved beyond Thomas's range, he'd absorbed enough of her personality to guess what was going through her mind. Jinishta had spent all day reeling from facts that didn't align with her worldview, but Garrett's latest claim crossed a line. It was a direct attack to the root of her faith. As far as Jinishta was concerned, telepaths were unholy, no more related to people than sludge serpents or toxic rain.

Garrett tried to push her short sword away, but Jinishta held it locked in place.

"I'm living proof that Torth and Alashani can have viable offspring," Garrett said.

"No." Jinishta held the blade steady. She had tolerated this journey with two *rekvehs*, but if Garrett or Thomas showed any signs of becoming her enemy, then it was decapitation time.

"Alashani are people," Jinishta said. "Torth are not. They are *rekvehs*, which means they murder and enslave all that is good. They pollute, like the rain that turns everything black and dead."

"Mind readers are born among Alashani sometimes," Garrett said. "You know it's true."

Tears flowed down Jinishta's cheeks. "Those are flukes caused by toxins or curses. We are not related!"

"Just as nontelepaths are sometimes born to Torth," Garrett went on, relentless. "The Torth call those babies abominations and murder them." His tone heated up. "The same as your people."

"We are unrelated!" Jinishta howled.

"You and I are literally cousins," Garrett snapped at her.

"You are a *rekveh*!" Jinishta yelled in his face. "There is no relationship! We cannot be family!"

"My mother was Eidelwen!" Garrett bellowed back. "Premier Yeresunsa of Hufti!"

They all knew the story. Even so, Jinishta recoiled, apparently shocked to hear confirmation of the scandal that had devastated her family and sent her grandparents into humiliating poverty. Eidelwen had . . . done something . . . with a Torth. Something that made her pregnant. She had left her home rather than abort or kill the baby, and no one had ever seen or heard from her again.

"My father was a Servant of All." Garrett hurled Jinishta's scimitar out of his way. Suddenly, he was shouting. "Do you think I'm *proud* of that? Do you think I wanted a monster for a father? He tortured millions of people to death! He was the head of the Isolatorium!"

They all gawked.

"He raped my mother." Garrett stomped toward Jinishta, forcing her to back away. "He murdered her. And I . . ."

Garrett seemed to rein himself in, struggling to control his temper. But in his fury, he accidentally entered Thomas's range.

Thomas absorbed each horrific memory, fascinated and repulsed. What a unique upbringing! The wounds of Garrett's distant childhood were disturbingly raw.

The old man fixed him with a purple stare. "Get out."

His tone was low, like a wolf's growl. Thomas swallowed. His updraft subroutine vanished in a wave of fear, and the hovercart plummeted for a second until Thomas reestablished the updraft. They wobbled, as if in turbulence, and his wildfire disks flickered while he diverted resources to making sure they stayed aloft.

"Get control of yourself." Garrett stalked out of Thomas's range, cloak swirling behind him. His tone swung from rage-filled to completely calm.

And contemptuous.

Thomas had to make a supreme effort to keep his thermodynamic lift ongoing. He trembled, but not just from exertion.

He didn't mind obeying orders. That was peaceful. And he could tolerate distrust. Most people hated him on sight, and that was their problem. That was just how things were.

But Garrett was a hypocrite.

He thought Thomas had emotional issues? Ha. One of them was unhinged, and it wasn't Thomas. One of them was dangerously unhappy and emotionally stunted, and Thomas was pretty sure he was the more well-adjusted one. Garrett wasn't nearly as self-possessed as he pretended to be.

At one hundred and eleven years of age, Garrett still hated his long-dead father. That was some serious baggage. That was a whole other level of screwed up.

Thomas had not managed to absorb the entire story, but he could guess at the unknowns.

Garrett Olmstead Dovanack—a man who had chosen a false name with initials that spelled GOD—was not nearly as innocent and righteous as he wanted them all to believe. Maybe he hadn't abused slaves, but he was definitely ashamed of something. He was actively trying to prevent Thomas from learning whatever horrible thing he had done.

Thomas had his own problems, sure. But he wasn't consumed by shame.

Hadn't he engineered a slave rebellion? Hadn't he invented a treatment for spinal muscular atrophy?

Hadn't he struck a bargain with the leaders of the known universe?

And he was, after all, a supergenius with powers. That meant he was more than a sidekick. He was not someone to trifle with. Garrett wanted him to be obedient, to shut up and do whatever he was told?

Well, if Garrett wanted all that, maybe he should work on being someone worthy of respect first.

CHAPTER 8

FLOOD OF TEARS

Kessa could see that Thomas was struggling to keep the hovercart aloft. They drifted lower, then lower still, until the roar of water sounded loud and not very far below them. All but one of the white fire disks winked out.

Thomas's face was tight with concentration. That wasn't a look that Kessa had ever seen on him before.

The river smelled pure and fresh, but its frothing rapids were far more violent than the sedate River of Tears. Yet perhaps it was the same river? Kessa supposed that it might level off and broaden once it reached the Alashani realm. The carefully crafted shape of the channel in the Alashani underground would cause the water to calm down and smooth out.

This part of the river, however, was a deep gorge. Kessa searched for a road alongside the churning whitewater, some ancient boulevard, just in case Thomas's strength gave out. But the walls were steep cliffs on one side and moldering buildings on the other.

Jinishta, sulking on one side of the platform, gave a shout and pointed ahead.

They had caught up to Ariock. He stood on a glossy triangle of flat rock that poked out of the river, at the foot of an extremely tall and narrow dam. He had conjured electric orbs in order to illuminate the stonework.

Colossal statues formed the bottom quarter of the dam. Their shoulders were thrown back, as if to hold back the unseen subterranean lake. Water spilled out of the quartz eyes of the central figure: a woman with flowing hair.

A statue of the Lady of Sorrow.

But this statue had stylized wings.

The river seemed to originate from her unseeing eyes. Her enormous quartz head gazed into an eternal distance while streams of water eroded tracks in her cheeks. Each of her hands was raised in a pleading gesture, catching the water that spilled down her face. Water pooled in her cupped hands and poured between her eroded fingers in ribbons. Water rolled down her gowned body, glistening, until it splashed at her feet. Her wings formed struts that helped support the dam.

None of that was what caused Kessa's beak to drop open in shock.

She had seen plenty of statues on this world, but she had not expected a colossal quartz-stone ummin. He stood next to the Lady of Sorrow.

Kessa walked to the hovercart railing and gaped in wonder. The colossal ummin was just as eroded as the Lady of Sorrow, but even so, he exquisitely carved, his frame robust, his bearing noble, and his brow ridges elegant. His proud stance reminded Kessa of her deceased mate, Cozu.

Her throat tightened. Someone on this planet, long ago, had cared enough to commemorate her species.

And five other sapient species.

Next to the idealized ummin stood an idealized mer nerctan. There were also a few alien sapients that Kessa did not recognize. One was flat-faced, its intelligent visage framed by a thick mane, every furry strand painstakingly carved. Another had a long nose that drooped past its jaw. A third looked stumpy, with tufts of hair sprouting from its pointy ears.

Kessa had never seen anything like them. Why include totally unknown aliens while leaving out the common govki and nussians?

The galaxy must have been a very different place when these statues were carved.

Jinishta whispered something that sounded like a prayer in her native language. She knelt and bowed to the ancient colossus of the Lady of Sorrow.

"Ariock!" Garrett shouted to be heard over the thunder of water. "Is it a dead end?"

Ariock's electric orbs flickered as he turned in surprise. "You were able to follow me?" He sounded amazed. "I sensed your life sparks, but I thought you might be a bunch of Torth in a transport or something."

The hovercart settled onto the triangular island, which consisted of broad, eroded steps. Thomas slumped against the railing. He looked sick with pain.

Ariock hurried over to heal Thomas. Kessa saw the air writhe beneath his huge hands, sparkling with tiny lights.

"You can't heal depletion," Garrett said in a gruff tone.

Sure enough, Thomas remained slumped and exhausted.

"His powers are drained," Garrett said. "He just needs time. Save your strength, Ariock. The Torth will probably figure out a way to follow us down here." He peered back the way they had come, into the darkness of the entombed city.

"I don't know what to do next." Ariock looked ashamed. He gestured toward the dam. "She's just a statue. There's no one alive within miles except for us."

"Hmm." Garrett sized up the dam. He looked stumped but unwilling to give up.

Kessa turned to Thomas, hoping he might have an insight or two. But Thomas's eyes were squeezed shut in pain. He looked too exhausted to think.

Ariock and Garrett studied the dam with similar looks of frustrated bafflement.

"Great Lady." Jinishta stepped off the hovercart and onto the eroded stone steps. She knelt, cupped her hands, and tasted the water.

Judging by her blissful expression, it was pure.

"Help me find my faith again," Jinishta whispered, apparently in prayer. "Should I believe in the messiah?"

If the Lady of Sorrow heard, she was unmoved.

"Will you give me a sign?" Jinishta begged, despondent.

"There's a hidden passageway behind the statue of the Lady of Sorrow," Ariock said. "It's a tunnel beneath the reservoir."

Garrett gave him a look of inquiry.

"I sensed it." Ariock shrugged, embarrassed. "But I would have to destroy the statue in order to get inside, and it might just be a natural cave. It doesn't contain anything, as far as I can tell."

"Did you explore the whole passageway with your powers?" Garrett asked.

"No," Ariock admitted. "It goes on for a long way. But I searched for life sparks. There are none back there." He gestured. "And none down here at all, except for us."

Garrett leaned on the railing of the hovercart. He squinted up toward the distant, weeping head, which was surrounded by long, flowing quartz-stone hair and crowned by mist.

"Do you ever predict the future?" Garrett asked in a casual tone.

Ariock looked down at him. "Um, no? I don't think so." He paused. "What do you mean?"

Kessa kept her beak shut. She remembered a secret Delia Dovanack had whispered after a certain work shift, when her companions had had trouble falling asleep. Delia had begged Vy and Cherise never to remind her son about the traumatic nightmare that had predicted the death of his father.

They were honoring that promise. As far as Kessa could tell, Thomas was honoring it as well. So would she.

"I have hunches sometimes," Garrett said in a tone of admission.

Kessa recalled Delia mentioning that her son had been particularly restless during the week before the Torth abduction. She had speculated that Ariock must have sensed impending disaster.

"I wouldn't call myself a full-fledged prophet," Garrett said, resting against the railing. "But it's a pretty common trait among Alashani, to feel lucky, sometimes. You sort of get a sense that something momentous is about to happen."

Jinishta glared at him. No doubt she wanted to shout that an evil *rekveh* could not be Alashani.

At least she restrained herself this time. Perhaps she was inwardly accepting the fact that Garrett was half Alashani.

"Okay." Ariock studied his great-grandfather. "Uh, so, do you have a hunch about that statue?"

"I do." Garrett stroked his beard, thoughtful. "And I think you're feeling it, too."

Ariock studied the colossal winged statue with renewed interest.

Thomas spoke up, his voice pinched with pain. "I learned from Migyatel. The power to foresee the future is intertwined with a power to see the past. It could be that's what you sense. Something momentous might have happened here."

Jinishta glared at Thomas, no doubt blaming him for the death of her holy prophet.

"Oh, right," Garrett said. "You met a genuine prophet!" He studied Ariock with fresh interest. "When we have time, I'd love for you to show me, in your memory, everything about that encounter."

Jinishta sounded bitter. "Why do you care what Migyatel said? Do you have faith in prophecies?"

"I do," Garrett said amiably. "Anyway, that's interesting, what the boy said. Here we are in a place of undisturbed history." He gestured around. "We're surrounded by ghosts." He frowned up at the huge weeping statue. "It's possible we're picking up something that we should pay attention to."

They studied the dam in silence together.

Kessa's skin tightened from ambient humidity. She glanced at the data tablet and was unnerved by how different it looked. The hostages sat in dimness. And one set of digits on the countdown no longer changed.

Whether they found the Lady of Sorrow or not, Kessa felt sure the Torth would do something awful to the hostages once the timer stopped.

"Maybe there's a trigger or secret door or something." Ariock stepped off the island and slogged toward the dam.

"Careful!" Garrett clutched the railing and his silver staff, one in each hand, as if he needed extra support.

"Be gentle with her," Thomas said. "She's fragile." Despite his winces of pain, his tone was a warning.

Ariock reached up to caress the crystalline gown of the statue. Even with the cruel-looking spikes poking out from his thick arms, even with his inky-black wraps and armor, he looked the fragile one in comparison to that enormous statue.

But he must have used his powers. A splintery sound came from deep within the dam.

Cracks spiderwebbed up the quartz-stone gown from his black-wrapped hand.

"Oh no!" Thomas's wheezing cry of anguish was nearly lost as the sound of water grew louder.

Water began to spray from cracks in the quartz. Ariock slogged backward, holding up his arm in a shielding motion. His face was intense with focus.

"You just . . . !" Thomas sputtered.

Fissures appeared across the statue's arms and wings. Ariock might be using his powers to hold her together, but he seemed to realize that it was pointless to keep that up indefinitely. His goal was to get into the passageway behind the colossus.

So Ariock allowed her to begin to fall apart. One arm broke off. Her wings shattered in a thunderous crack of breaking stones.

Behind the statue?

An immense wall of water.

Kessa's eyes widened with fatal alarm.

The weight of water hammered the upper reaches of the dam, breaking off chunks of ancient stonework. Those massive waterfalls, in turn, hammered the enormous statues of aliens, which must have stood solidly while untold generations of slaves lived and died in misery. Water poured forth in a violent deluge. Ariock threw up his arms, and the flood slammed against his invisible shield of pressurized air.

The triangular island of eroded steps was shielded.

Everything else was an avalanche of frothing whitewater. It rushed overhead and all around them. Gigantic stones smashed against the barrier shield. One of those stones resembled a massive foot from the ummin statue. It spun away.

"What have you done?" Thomas sounded like he was about to cry. "You flooded the Alashani!"

Ariock's look of determination transformed to dawning horror and unfortunate realization.

Jinishta heard what Thomas said. She whirled around to stare toward the downriver gorge, which now overflowed with tumultuous froth. Her luminous purple eyes went wide with horror.

None of them had thought through the implications of where the river led, Kessa realized. Well, except for Thomas. And she had, herself. But the others? Either they hadn't recognized the choppy river as the same River of Tears that nourished the Alashani civilization, or the gorge had seemed so deep and endless, they'd assumed that a flood would peter out before it made its way to the Alashani underground.

"You've obliterated countless artifacts!" Thomas's voice cracked, anguished. "The things we could have learned!"

The enormous flood showed no signs of slowing. If anything, it was increasing. Gigantic rocks continued to break off into the deluge.

"I'm sorry!" Ariock sounded strained. His sluicing protection sparked here and there, shedding enough light to illuminate the whirling tunnel of water that engulfed them.

The darkness in front of them exhaled dry but foul air. Puddles remained on the ground, shining where light hit them.

Kessa saw, with astonishment, that a tunnel was, indeed, revealed where the dam had cracked away. The colossal statue of the Lady of Sorrow had been blocking this passageway.

A fancy corridor, really.

Rows of cracked marble pillars supported a ceiling cobwebbed with dust, lichen, and stunted stalactites. Mummified skeletons littered the dusty floor.

They were so ancient, Kessa mistook them for piles of dust at first. Fragmented skulls poked out of drifts of dust. Fibers from clothing that had long since rotted away formed a colorless carpet. Finger bones hinted at hands that might have clawed at quartz stone, seeking a way to escape.

The corridor made a slow exhalation, like someone dying.

Perhaps it was only an echo created by the rush of water, but Kessa thought that this place sounded like distant, faraway, ghostly voices. It emanated loneliness.

"I think we're on track to find the Lady of Sorrow," Garrett said, peering down the ancient corridor of mummified death.

Ariock looked anguished. He glanced behind him, at the floodwaters.

"We have to move forward, Ariock," Garrett said.

Water continued to roar over and around Ariock's invisible shield. A microsecond of distraction would be enough to get them all killed. Water would smash them, tear them apart, and drown them in a matter of seconds.

"My family." Jinishta sounded choked, drowning in hopelessness.

"What's our time schedule look like?" Garrett asked Kessa.

Kessa glanced at the screen, as if she could read the countdown. Did the bargain even matter anymore? If the Alashani were not already being collared as slaves, they would be forced to flee aboveground when their aqueducts were obliterated. Their lamplit cities would drown in surge waters.

"Thirty-eight minutes," Thomas said.

Garrett limped to the control panel and fiddled with the controls. The platform levitated. Now that they were over solid ground, it seemed Garrett was back in control as the driver.

"Will someone please get Jinishta?" he said.

The someone, of course, had to be Kessa.

She hurried to the premier Yeresunsa and gently hugged her, offering whatever inadequate solace she could give. Maybe some Alashani people would find a way to survive? Maybe the flood would take a while to reach them? Perhaps enough of them had that predictive power that Garrett had hinted at to make a difference?

"I have to save the Alashani," Ariock said, his huge voice heavy with shame. "This is my fault."

"We have to rescue the Lady of Sorrow," Garrett said forcefully.

Ariock shook his head, agonized and stubborn.

Jinishta looked at him, but she no longer looked friendly. Ariock had disappointed her one too many times.

"It's my fault," Ariock said.

"This sign is clear." Jinishta seemed to gather her inner strength. "He . . ." She forced herself to stand, still glaring toward Ariock. "He is not the messiah."

Kessa had nothing to say about that, one way or another.

She helped Jinishta make her way to the hovercart. The premier was burdened by sorrow and seething resentment, which she meted out with glares aimed at Garrett, Thomas, and especially Ariock.

"You'd better not abandon us," Garrett told Ariock. "Just think it through. If you run away now, Vy is dead and so are the rest of us. You can't save an entire planet while the Torth are dropping nukes and murdering everyone in sight."

Ariock looked unconvinced.

"We have a chance to free the Lady of Sorrow!" Garrett made that sound grand, like it was the same thing as saving the entire universe. "She has powers like yours. Come on. Everything else will wait a half hour!"

Still, Ariock hesitated.

Water roared and funneled past him, wreathing his silhouette in a chaotic deluge.

As soon as Kessa and Jinishta were aboard, Garrett made the platform leap into motion, deeper into fetid darkness.

"We have one chance to make a difference," Garrett said, perhaps trying to justify himself to the rest of them. "This flood will slow our enemies. We might actually be able to win and stop the Torth from enslaving the Alashani. We have to do this!"

They swerved around ancient skulls and the remnants of rib cages. Kessa wondered how long Ariock would stand behind with his indecision.

He might be able to stop the disaster if he could fly faster than whitewater.

If he got ahead of the flood and built a solid dam out of rocks, and if he didn't need to dodge too many blasts and inhibitor microdarts, and if the Torth did not sabotage whatever makeshift dam he built as soon as he turned his back . . .

A lot could go wrong.

If he failed—if he got depleted or shot by the inhibitor—he would be leaving his friends to die in various horrific ways, easy prey for monsters.

Ariock squared his huge shoulders, carrying an unseen burden. He followed the hovercart as if he meant to bash aside any and all obstacles. Behind him, the frothing water collapsed in twinned curtains that splashed into each other with a mighty clap.

Broken rocks piled up as a brace against the flood. Ariock used his powers to fit stones into each other, interlocking them into place.

Soon the roar of water became a deeper sound. It flowed over Ariock's makeshift dam. Kessa imagined the biggest river on this world, flowing with a smooth, deadly power.

The Torth would never find them.

They were sealed inside this ancient dungeon or tomb. They were buried.

Shadows clung to lofty archways. Dust fuzzed marble pillars. The traffic jam of death seemed endless, with mummified skeletons everywhere. Some disintegrated as the hovercart floated over their remains.

"How can a prisoner have survived down here?" Kessa wondered out loud.

"I don't know," Garrett said.

Thomas looked uneasy. He had no explanation, either.

Ariock strode alongside their hovercart, his long legs carrying him at a pace faster than most species could run. Tightly controlled spheres of electric light hovered around him, shedding a cold illumination upon cobwebs and desiccated bones.

"I'll save the Alashani," Ariock assured Jinishta, with more determination than Kessa had ever seen. "After I save the Lady of Sorrow. And Vy and the hostages. One crisis at a time."

He strode into the darkness ahead of them, illuminating the way.

CHAPTER 9

BETWEEN THEN AND NOW

If not for the life experiences Thomas had absorbed from Jinishta and other veteran Alashani warriors, he would have had to guess about the sharp, insistent pain in his head.

Instead, he knew all about warning headaches.

No one could heal them. Painkillers had no effect on them. The headache might subside within minutes, or it might take hours. That depended on how much he had overdrawn his raw power. Most importantly: If he attempted to use his powers while in this pain? He would fall into a coma and die.

But other things hurt worse than pain.

The staggering loss of knowledge gave Thomas a damaged feeling, much like the effects of his neuromuscular disease.

He would have been okay with Torth archaeologists and treasure hunters monopolizing the lost city. Someone ought to be able to learn about the final years of the predecessors. Knowledge ought to be valued and preserved.

If only he had had time to snatch a relic.

Ariock lit the corridor ahead, his shoulders weighted by guilt as he marched forward. Thomas couldn't really blame him for taking action. That was what Ariock did.

But there had been time to stop him. A couple of seconds, at least.

Thomas could only blame himself for the disaster. So what if he was wincing in pain from a headache? That was no excuse. It was obscene to lose so many ancient secrets.

Tears streamed down Jinishta's grimy face, her grief echoing his own. "Messiah," she said bitterly. "He is the opposite."

Thomas had no love for the Alashani people. But their culture? Their knowledge? He couldn't bear the thought of all that getting obliterated.

Millennia of isolation had gifted their culture with a lot of unique quirks. Folktales. Songs. A mineral-rich cuisine. Their loopy form of writing. Their techniques for dyes and weaving and gemstone cutting.

No one would care or remember any of that in fifty years.

Like the predecessors, and like all slave species, the descendants of any survivors would transform into a feeble iteration that no one recognized. The original civilization would fade into a background footnote of Torth history. Only inscrutable relics would remain.

It was abhorrent.

"I should have forced him to stay underground," Jinishta said.

Thomas sensed a worm of betrayal gnawing at Jinishta's heart. She believed that Ariock was a dangerous rogue. That was causing her to reevaluate all her dearest beliefs. If her own faith in the messiah was wrong, then what else was she wrong about?

Perhaps *rekvehs* were not evil demons, after all.

Jinishta inwardly admitted that Torth were undeniably cousins of the Alashani. It made her sick to accept the detestable family tree of her people, but she was even more sickened by the lies that her wonderful, caring, otherwise sensible people believed.

"Ariock may not be the messiah," Kessa said kindly. "But he is still our friend."

Jinishta glared with unvoiced rage.

"We promised to fight the Torth by his side," Kessa said with quiet conviction. "That matters more than ever."

Jinishta blinked back tears, emanating shame as she realized that Kessa—a former slave with a scar around her neck—had more nobility and honor than she herself, a premier Yeresunsa, possessed.

So slaves were not weak-willed cowards.

That was another Alashani belief shattered.

Garrett gasped. A hand flew to his mouth as he stared at a faded, lichen-covered mural.

At first, Thomas could not guess why the hovercart was braking. Why were they reversing and backing up? Garrett was frustratingly beyond his range of telepathy.

Ariock continued up the ancient corridor, oblivious. Thomas began to say something . . . but then Kessa got a good look at the mural, and her mind spiked with shock, and Thomas sensed what she saw.

His understanding of the world came apart at the seams.

"It can't be!" Kessa whispered.

Thomas studied the remnants of paint clinging to the wall. The light was fading as Ariock moved farther away. But there was enough light to see a depiction of a crowded amphitheater under a desert sky. A gaunt giant stood before the audience, his head bowed before a skeletal woman who wore the unmistakable twisted horned mantle of the Commander of All Living Things. And between those two figures . . .

Thomas gripped at the hovercart floor, desperate to touch something solid. That painted boy could not be him.

It could not be.

Yet Thomas recognized the way he'd been dressed that day, in gold-patterned yellows. He recognized his silver hoverchair. There was the Upward Governess in the front row of the audience. He even recognized his slaves, Nror and Pung, and the flat umbrella they'd held to keep him in the shade.

The passage of eons had leeched away the painted pigments. Spots and stains marred the brushstrokes, so that much of the painting appeared eaten away. But there was enough left to make it recognizable.

"The originals." Garrett moaned like an art collector who had found the greatest treasure imaginable.

"How is this possible?" Kessa recognized the painted scene. She had been in the audience that day. "Is this . . . is this prophetic artwork?"

Garrett pressed knuckles to his mouth, stifling a squeal of excitement. "These are the Prophecies of Ah Jun. The originals!" He stared down the corridor, enthralled by what seemed an endless march of murals on both walls. "Oh my stars."

Thomas stared down the corridor with even wider eyes. Prophecies.

Real, true prophecies.

Prophecies that must show exactly how Ariock could win against the Torth Empire.

The flood Ariock had unleashed might destroy countless secrets, but here was a mother lode that made everything else insignificant. Here were secrets beyond price, beyond compare. This corridor must display the solution to the galaxy's biggest problem!

Thomas needed this knowledge. He needed it more than anything!

He had to study every single mural in this corridor, because legitimate prophecies needed to be taken very, very seriously. Never mind Migyatel. These ancient prophecies would empower Thomas to turn the galaxy into a better place, no matter what the Alashani prophet had foreseen. It was best to be forewarned.

As Thomas studied the prophecy on the opposite wall—a queenly figure seated on a crystal throne—the hovercart sped into motion.

"What are you doing?" Thomas cried. "Slow down!"

"Nope." Garrett leaned over the controls like a race-car driver. Murals blurred past on either side. "We'll study them later. The clock is ticking."

That response was so wrong, it seemed nonsensical to Thomas for a microsecond.

Then he remembered that Garrett didn't want anyone else to know the future. Garrett didn't trust Thomas.

Because Garrett must be a blithering idiot.

The pain in Thomas's head was subsiding. It might be gone in a few minutes, but for now, he didn't dare use his powers. There wasn't much he could do to wrest control of the hovercart from the old man.

So he settled for using his eyes—plus the nearby eyes of Kessa and Jinishta—as scanners.

The wind from their passage disturbed mummified corpses. They tore through curtains of dust-coated cobwebs at a reckless speed. Unfortunately, those cobwebs covered far too many murals. Lichen and mold obscured the rest.

Thomas ground his teeth, frustrated by how few of the paintings were viewable. They needed to be carefully restored. This incredible corridor needed a lot of work.

Even so, hints leaped out to his hyperkeen awareness.

There was a mural that showed Thomas, not in a flattering pose. That was when he'd been crying on that tower top in the dead city, defeated by the Commander of All Living Things.

There was a painting that looked very much like what Ariock had just done, cracking the immense dam of statues and accidentally unleashing the flood.

Ariock paused in the corridor ahead. He was staring at a damaged mural that portrayed a storm god floating over a curved red planet amid lightning and thunderheads. The painted version of Ariock wore black armor with shoulder spikes, evocative of nussian physiology.

"Don't stop!" Garrett snapped at his great-grandson as they sped past. "The future will never happen if we stop now. Light our way!"

Ariock seemed to shake himself out of his own thoughts. He had to run to catch up. Soon he was jogging past their hovercart again, focused and determined.

Thomas decided not to spare any extra mental energy for events that had already happened, or for the present reality. He bent all his mental bandwidth toward soaking up every detail of the corridor, as much as he could.

The whole right-hand wall, he soon realized, wasn't worth watching. He did not recognize the queen with purple hair and wings who kept appearing in various murals on the right. Nor did he recognize the maned alien with its braided beards, or the child with a bald head and smooth skin where her eyes should be. That cast of characters appeared repeatedly on the right side of the corridor.

That side was an entirely different story, Thomas understood.

Maybe it was a different timeline. Or perhaps the two series of murals were interrelated? Might there be a clue in their deliberate placement opposite each other?

Thomas lacked the resources to figure out how, or why, the murals were arranged the way they were. He dared not even blink. He had to see everything. He had to know what would happen.

He turned his attention fully to the left-hand wall, where he kept glimpsing tantalizing hints about the future that concerned him. There was Weptolyso, at the head of a nussian army. There was a spaceship battle near a blue-white planet that might be Earth or might be Verdantia or some other habitable planet. There was Ariock again, smiting what looked like a group of begging, pleading Servants of All.

Was that a painting of Kessa?

The lichen-blighted mural showed an ummin dressed in queenly brocades and an impressive headdress, yet the curve of her beak, and that scar around her neck, made her recognizable. Were those Torth kneeling before her like supplicants?

Kessa stared at that mural just as hard as he did, struggling to soak up the details during the second while they flew past it.

They sped past a row of murals too damaged to reveal much of anything. Water must have seeped through the ceiling stonework here, ruining the ancient works of art. Thomas wanted to scream in frustration.

One of those severely damaged panels showed a boy that resembled Thomas, except he was standing up.

Like he could walk.

A monstrous beast loomed behind the painted Thomas figure, silhouetted by flames, with a hint of leathery wings and the toothy mouth of a gharial. Thomas hardly cared about the implied dragon. Had the painter imagined a wrong or fake version of him? An android, or a clone of some kind?

"Don't look!" Garrett growled over his shoulder. "It's not always healthy to know the future unless you're a prophet. Trust me. Shut your eyes!"

That sounded like bad advice to Thomas.

They were hurtling down the corridor, but Garrett had to slow down, because there was a dead end ahead. Ariock faced immense, ornate double doors, coated by verdigris and cobwebs.

He tested the doors. Judging by their immobility, they were locked and tightly sealed.

"Break through," Garrett suggested.

That might be more bad advice, but Thomas wasn't going to analyze the situation. His eyes were dry from wind and from his refusal to blink, yet still, he absorbed the sights of the left-hand wall. He searched mold stains for hints of the future.

There was one more tantalizing mural.

Lightning indicated a Yeresunsa battle. The painted figure might represent any warrior who was enhanced by thorny armor, but there was a silvery staff. And the decapitated head of that warrior, tumbling into space and spewing blood, had a recognizable white beard.

That looked like Garrett's head.

Kessa and Jinishta saw the disturbing image and remained silent. Garrett must notice the mural as well, but he made no remark.

He must have already seen it elsewhere.

On an ancient scroll? In the memory of an ancient digital archive? Thomas wondered how long Garrett had lived with that prophetic image in the back of his mind.

Maybe that explained why Garrett was so cavalier. Did he assume his own death was preordained? Thomas had so many questions. He absolutely needed to absorb the old man's wealth of secrets.

"I'm going to break the doors," Ariock warned.

"Good," Garrett said. "Do it."

Ariock raised his hands and used unseen powers. At his will, the moldy vault doors crumpled inward.

Noxious, stale clouds of rotten dust wafted outward.

Thomas knew, with a pang of despair, that no one could survive entombed here. Whatever lurked in the darkness beyond those ancient doors, it had been locked away and forgotten for eons.

There was no rational, sane way for it to be alive.

CHAPTER 10

PRISM PRISON

So much dust coated the ancient cobwebs, they looked like drapery. Pieces fluttered and disintegrated as Ariock stepped cautiously into the chamber.

His electric spheres seemed sacrilegious here, like a carnival inside a mausoleum. Ariock dimmed his lights, just in case the prisoner crouched behind dust-fuzzed pillars, or behind that impressive high-backed throne. Her eyes would surely be sensitive to light.

Dust eddied around his feet. The air tasted stale. It made him want to hold his breath.

This had once been a grand hall, judging by the glimmers of opulence. Now shadows clung to the lofty arches between pillars.

Ariock crept farther inside. He tried to ignore a desiccated mummy on the floor and the remains of another mummy slumped upon the throne. He didn't quite dare to speak out loud. His big voice would disturb more dust, and he already felt like an intruder.

So he spoke inside his mind. *Lady of Sorrow? I am here.*

He wondered if she could hear him.

The hovercart made a whispery, whirring sound as it entered the grand room. Ariock turned to his friends, expecting them to be underwhelmed and disappointed, like he was.

An inhuman shriek rattled the walls and pillars. Dust sifted down.

Ariock whirled around to face the darkness.

Identical shapes mimicked Ariock's motions with exactitude, going still when he tensed. They crackled with the exact same lightning that ran up his own arms.

In that light, Ariock saw what he was facing: this grand hall was paneled in mirrors.

Just as Ariock began to calm down, feeling like a fool, something indistinct slammed against the nearest mirror. It seemed to hurtle out of some dark universe inside the reflective surface.

Ariock twitched in surprise.

The shape seemed unable to exit the mirror. It pressed itself against the dusty glass, blurry face contorted in pain, with dark smears for eyes and mouth. Long hair floated like a dust cloud behind it.

The smear of a mouth gaped impossibly wide. The apparition shrieked in pure insanity.

"Oh." Thomas spoke in a tone of horror-struck realization.

A second later, Garrett gasped, apparently struck by the same realization, whatever that was. Both of the mind readers stared at the throne—or its desiccated mummy—with sick comprehension. Garrett covered his mouth with a trembling hand.

"What?" Ariock demanded.

"How can she still be alive?" Garrett sounded pained. "How is that even possible?"

"I don't know." Thomas looked like he was riffling through a mental library, noting topics he had yet to learn.

Ariock spread his awareness across the dusty floor, hoping to discover an unfamiliar life spark, or some clue.

The throne was solid crystal. It seemed macabre to inhabit the desiccated mummy upon the throne, but Ariock gave it a try anyway. The mummy was indistinguishable from the dust it was sunk into. Just dead matter. No life spark.

Ariock forced himself to sound calm and rational. "Where is she?" That countdown timer was still ticking.

"There." Thomas gestured with his chin to the mummy Ariock had just examined. "I hear her thoughts. I feel her sorrow."

Garrett rubbed his arms. "God."

Ariock stared at the mummified skeleton again. The corpse was so withered, he couldn't tell whether it had originally been a female. The skin was long gone. The clothes were fibrous dust.

The apparition drifted in one mirrored wall, then the next. She was an indistinct shape that sighed and moaned with inhuman sounds.

Ariock checked around the room, but there was no ghostly apparition floating in reality.

He sent his awareness into one of the mirrors. He didn't know what to expect, but he sensed a peculiar thrum. The pane of glass seemed almost like a live wire. Every molecule buzzed with energy that seemed unnatural to its state.

When Ariock examined the other mirrors, they all had the same low energy.

"This is freaky," Garrett said.

Ariock walked to the nearest mirror. He unraveled the wraps of one hand, intending to place his bare flesh against the dusty surface.

"Careful, Ariock." Garrett sounded alarmed. "We don't know how she got like this."

Ariock hesitated. His reflection filled the whole pane. He instinctively tried not to look at his own freakish silhouette.

Then he thought that if he could drag himself out of despair, maybe he could do the same for her.

Will you talk to me? he urged in his mind. *Can you understand me?*

A low moan shook the chamber. Ariock listened for words, for any familiar tones, but the duration alone was inhuman.

His friends looked as mystified as he felt.

Ariock was unwilling to stand idly while time ran out, and so, despite Garrett's warning, he attempted to grasp the phantom blur with his hand. But the mirror's surface did not yield.

"I suppose I could try breaking the mirrors?" Ariock tried to shrug off his uncertainties.

The indistinct shape emitted a piercing shriek, either rage or triumph. She slammed the mirror with indistinct fists, faster than a flesh person could have managed. The force of her blows should have cracked the glass, but the mirror only rattled. Dust sifted down.

"Don't!" Thomas shouted to be heard over her shriek.

Ariock stopped.

"The mirrors are keeping her alive," Thomas shouted. "We have to think about how to help her without killing her by accident."

Garrett clenched and unclenched his fists, as if trying to grip answers out of thin air.

"What are we supposed to do?" Ariock was aware that he sounded dangerous. Vy was counting on him. The Alashani must be drowning.

"Let me try communication." Thomas closed his eyes.

"I'm pretty sure she's not in a helpful mood," Garrett said. "There's something wrong with her mind." Judging by his wary look, that was an understatement. "A lot wrong," he amended.

The shriek went on much longer than any living being could hold breath. It devolved into anguished sobbing, like she was giving up.

"Okay." Thomas had gone pale. "Yeah, her mind isn't really . . . um, solid. Maybe we can solve her situation with logic."

"Oh, goody. Let's." Garrett folded his arms and regarded Thomas as if he was a performing monkey with an endless array of pointless tricks.

"She's alive," Thomas said. "But her body is not. There is an analogue in nature."

Garrett raised an eyebrow.

"The indigenous fauna of Mer Nerct," Thomas said, "evolved a way to transfer memetic material from a dying host to a new one."

"Not even remotely the same situation," Garrett said.

"The concept of transfer has relevance, I believe," Thomas said. "And I can think of another analogue." He stared at Garrett. "You spoke of being clairvoyant. That's astral projection, right?"

Garrett looked unnerved by Thomas's guesswork.

"You can leave your body." Thomas sounded certain.

"Yes." Garrett drew out the word with reluctance, seeming wary of whatever conclusion Thomas might be angling toward. "But I can't do it right now. I'm on the inhibitor."

"How does your clairvoyance normally work?" Thomas leaned forward, as if desperate to absorb answers. "Is it anything like the state she's in? How do you return to your body, when you're done spying on people in your disembodied ghost form?"

"I'm not sure how that matters." Garrett hunched his shoulders, defensive, clearly unwilling to share his secrets with Thomas.

He relented after a second, perhaps catching Ariock's impatience.

"It's always easy to come back to my body. I just snap back. That's my natural state. The effort is leaving my body. The longer I do it, the harder it becomes."

"Can you become separated from your body permanently?" Thomas asked.

The idea seemed to unnerve Garrett. He unfolded his arms, his weathered face grave. "I don't know if that would be possible. But it sounds like hell to me. It's not fun to be a ghost."

"Why not?" Thomas's tone was sharp with interest.

"Because when I'm in that form, I lack powers." Garrett made a hopeless gesture. "I lack a body and a voice. So I can't affect anything."

Ariock gazed at the pile of dust on the throne. If that was her body, then her condition was permanent.

"Nor can I read minds when I'm detached from my body," Garrett added. "Everything is muted. Colors. Sounds. Smells and tastes are nonexistent. Same with touch. I'll sense people's moods, but I can't hear their thoughts."

Thomas was alert, his gaze intense. "So . . . you can sense despair, when you're in that state?"

"Well, yes." Garrett sounded dubious. "I'll detect any intense emotion if I happen to be floating nearby that person. But it's not like I can communicate as a detached spirit. No one sees me, no one hears me, and I can't touch anything. And also, I can't do it indefinitely." He looked disturbed as he studied the shape in the mirrors. "Clairvoyance is draining in every sense of the word. It leeches away health and mental fortitude. My thoughts get fuzzy. It's exhausting."

Ariock wondered if the prisoner—the Lady of Sorrow—had been traveling around in that diminished way. She must have found a sad, very limited way to leave her cage from time to time.

"I can't imagine being trapped in that state for longer than a few hours," Garrett said. "It feels like dreaming. Very surreal. It's hard to hold on to any coherent thoughts."

"But you always snap back to your body," Thomas said, his tone musing. "Like you're tethered. What's the longest you've been able to go disembodied for?"

"Maybe a couple of hours?" Garrett sounded like he was guessing. "But I don't take risks like that anymore. It's not smart to do it for longer than ten minutes per day."

"Because your body is left unprotected?" Thomas asked.

Ariock saw Garrett's reflection in the nearby mirrors as he nodded. "That," he said, "and it's a drain. If I did that for an hour every day, I'd be feeble and bedridden."

The phantom shape in the mirror approached Ariock's reflection. She remained blurry no matter how close she came, and Ariock wondered, with sadness, if the prisoner had forgotten what she was supposed to look like.

Worshippers imagined her a certain way.

Perhaps that was why, whenever she showed herself to despairing prisoners, she took the form of a weeping woman with long, flowing hair. Was she merely a reflection of their expectations? Maybe their despair rekindled the prisoner's tenuous sense of self?

She was drawn to fellow prisoners in despair.

Because that was her state.

So was she an echo? A mimic? Perhaps she could not hold on to coherent thoughts.

"She's tethered to something in this room," Thomas said. "Probably one of the mirrors. Maybe the throne? I have no idea how it's possible, but somehow, her body died, and she got tethered to something inanimate. If we set her free . . ." His frustration increased. "She needs something to tether to. A body she can use."

"A vessel?" Garrett said.

The indistinct shape lingered in the mirrors, quiescent. Waiting.

Both of the mind readers looked at each other, apparently confirming that they each understood an unspoken implication.

They turned their speculative looks toward Jinishta.

CHAPTER 11
DUST TO DUST

Ariock expected an outburst from Jinishta. She would probably refuse to sacrifice her own body—her own life—for the sake of an unknown prisoner, thanks to a plan concocted by mind readers. Ariock couldn't blame her.

But Jinishta looked thoughtful. She might as well be choosing which quiver to wear.

"Jinishta," Thomas said, "if you serve as a vessel for the Lady of Sorrow, the process is likely to entail your death."

"Agh! Did you have to tell her that?" Garrett snapped in English.

Thomas glared at the old man. "The truth? Yes. It's called informed consent."

"Or," Garrett said, "you could say something to speed along the decision-making process." He switched to the slave tongue, so Jinishta could understand his words. "It won't hurt."

"We don't know that," Thomas cut in.

Garrett glared at him and switched back to English. "Do you mind? How about if you use your negotiating expertise to actually sell her on this?"

"I don't tell lies," Thomas said. "That's your forte."

While the mind readers argued, Jinishta looked inward, not listening to the language that was foreign to her.

Ariock could not imagine what was going through her mind. But he felt certain that Jinishta was not disposable. He knew that much.

"Jinishta," he said. "You don't have to do this."

Jinishta straightened. She drew her one remaining spear and stamped it down for emphasis, looking from Thomas to Garrett. "I will do it," she said.

Perhaps Ariock should have felt relief, with a decisive course of action. He only felt a devastating loss. For his mentor, his cousin, his friend to sacrifice her life . . . this was not what victory felt like.

"No," he said.

Jinishta faced him with resentment. "Ariock, I am prepared for an early death. That is what it means to be a warrior."

The Warrior's Pact. Ariock hated their self-sacrificial creed.

He understood fatalistic determination, which had carried him through battles he seemed sure to lose. That was what it meant to be a warrior. But life should not be cheap. No one should feel pressured to choose suicide.

"I am not sure I want to live, anyway," Jinishta said. "After what has happened." Her confidence slipped off, unmasking despair.

Because of Ariock. Because of what he'd done.

"I'm sorry." Ariock searched for a better apology and failed. Nothing he could say or do would right his wrongs. The only way he could atone was to triumph over the Torth and find a way to rescue and permanently protect the Alashani civilization.

"I am ready." Jinishta's voice was small but firm.

Ariock was aware of the time pressure. Ten minutes or less, he thought, to rescue the Lady of Sorrow.

Vy and the other hostages were doomed unless he gained a major advantage.

Ariock knelt in front of Jinishta and gently took her black-wrapped hands. "You're the bravest person I have ever known." She deserved a better friend. "I don't know if this will work, or what. But . . ." He searched for a way to show his respect. "I'm honored that you're willing."

"We will make sure that people remember your name," Kessa said.

Ariock thought that was the most eloquent thing any of them could have said. "Yes."

Jinishta smiled for the first time since they had departed her underground realm. Smiling, she looked like a different person, kind and beatific. "If my life can save my people," she said, "then I am glad to pay that price. And I consider it small."

The Lady of Sorrow breathed a hopeless gust, causing mirrors to rattle. It was one step away from a screech.

"How much time do we have?" Garrett asked.

"Four minutes," Thomas said.

"All right." Garrett's leisurely tone belied the urgency. "I'm going to move the hovercart back." He took that action even as he spoke, reversing the platform until it floated through the broken vault doors, back into the corridor of prophecy. "I can't guess how to retether her—"

"I might be able to direct her," Thomas said, "once she's free."

"Fine," Garrett said. "Let's get started. Jinishta?" He indicated that she should exit the hovercart.

Jinishta removed her quiver and gear. Unburdened, she strolled into the dusty chamber of mirrors, joining Ariock there.

"Go stand by the crystal throne," Garrett said. "That's probably the optimum place."

Jinishta cast a doubtful look at the mummy on the throne. She stood in front of it, displaying an impressive lack of fear.

"Ariock?" Garrett said.

Ariock could guess what was expected of him. "Break the mirrors?" He lifted his arms, ready to shatter every pane of glass in the huge room.

"Let's start with one pane," Garrett suggested.

"Just make a small chip," Thomas added. "If it seems to be working, you can shatter the rest."

The Lady of Sorrow floated in the mirrored panels, an indistinct blur who watched Ariock from dozens of vantage points.

A strange shiver of trepidation ran down Ariock's spine.

Despite everything, Ariock hesitated. He asked himself if this was truly the right thing to do. Why did he feel so . . . well, anticipatory? Like he was about to enter a battle? The hairs on his body were raised.

He had felt this way in the spaceport on Umdalkdul, just before he'd wrecked the place and killed his mother by accident. He had felt this way before every major battle he'd been in.

"Be careful." Garrett sounded wary.

Ariock had suffered many indignities when he was a gladiator. Among the worst were the iron hooks hammered into his forearms. The Torth had used those hooks to chain Ariock between arena battles. Since then, he had reshaped the hooks, turning them into jagged spikes.

He tapped one of his spikes against his own reflection.

Cracks radiated outward from where his spike hit.

The phantom within the mirrors shrieked with unidentifiable emotion, unconstrained by any throat or voice. Her wheezing scream filled his ears.

As the cracks spread, a chip of the mirror popped out.

The shriek abruptly changed, becoming gusty and more sinister. It hummed within the walls like an unseen flood.

A gout of energy surged out of the coin-size break in the mirror. To Ariock's extended awareness, the energy had the spark-like quality that he associated with life. But it also had the electrical energy of a storm and the kinetics of an avalanche.

"Control the flood!" Garrett yelled.

Both mind readers focused on the seething energy. It screamed toward the hovercart—then whipped in a U-turn before it could exit the chamber. It slammed into Jinishta.

The impact knocked Jinishta flat on her face. She had no time to brace herself.

An instant later, the energy plumed out of Jinishta's body, rising above her prone form to revolve around the throne. It lifted particles of dust into whirlwinds and screamed.

All the other mirrors rattled alarmingly. Cracks began to appear at their edges, as if the glass was struck by heavy blows from the inside.

"She won't accept Jinishta!" Thomas shouted. "She wants her original body."

Garrett seemed on the verge of making a sarcastic comment.

"I can help," Thomas cut in feverishly. "She wants resurrection. Ariock? Can you give her lightning? And water. But protect us from the cave-in that's about to happen!"

What cave-in? Ariock began to ask, but Thomas was still talking. "Also, she needs some of your blood."

The shrieking energy gathered itself, screaming, and slammed into Ariock with a force like a speeding truck.

It threw him across the chamber. He smashed against a mirror on the far side. As he struggled to regain his breath, broken beads of glass sprayed past him, and something fierce and alien inhabited his soul. That was how it felt.

Ariock wanted it gone. He levered it away, and the energy willingly scratched itself out through his skin, then punched through his armor and wraps. It roared away with red streamers.

His blood.

The mirror behind him exploded. Blood trickled over Ariock's body, but the stinging pain was unimportant, because the energy pouring into the room was more than this enclosed space could contain.

Lightning crackled. Pillars shook. Energy poured from two different broken mirrors, meeting and mixing over the throne. Gale-force winds forced their way past the opening Ariock had initially made, causing more glass to pop out and shatter, and as the holes widened, the gale thickened into a mixture of electricity, wind, blood, and life.

The gale suctioned up the pitiful remnants of the mummy on the throne, collecting its dust with the blood and other elements until it vaguely resembled a female form.

The form broke apart after a second. Her scream was prehistoric, like the hunting cry of a pterosaur.

A third mirror exploded. The rest of them were a webwork of cracks and coming apart.

Wind tore at Ariock's hair and wraps. He had to squint against the strobes of energy. He was unsure whether the chaotic electricity came from her or from his own pained alarm. He forced himself away from the mirrors. The air was so solid, it was like forcing himself through cement.

Two more mirrors exploded, one after the other. An ominous rumble filled the chamber, audible even over the shrieking wind.

Fine particles of dust swirled into a semblance of a feminine shape again. Lightning flickered along its outline.

It collapsed again, screeching, and Ariock sensed that every dust particle was imbued with life. They were almost like cells.

"Save us!" Garrett shouted over the roar.

The last eight mirrors exploded with a sound like heavy artillery. Glass sprayed the room. Ariock hardly noticed the shards slicing him, as frothing water sluiced through broken walls and mixed with ionized dust and blood and wind and whatever else.

Boulders slammed into Ariock's shielding while the energized Lady of Sorrow wove madly through the tempest, whipping, slicing, mixing, and conducting what seemed like an orchestra of moving parts.

She was writing a symphony.

Or maybe Thomas was writing the symphony, and she was conducting it.

Either way, Ariock sensed trillions of madly whirling particles and energy waves crashing together in the center of the room, again and again, building what was beginning to seem like a person.

"You need to help her, Ariock!" Thomas's weak voice was nearly lost in the storm. "Join with her! Add your power to hers!"

Ariock was confused at first. But as he crept his awareness into the supercondensed storm, he sensed creation. Particles outlined a vague form of a woman above the crystal throne.

She needed more power?

Ariock flung his arms wide, and lightning poured off him in continuous waves.

The particles flew apart, screaming toward Ariock as if drawn to his power. Dust, water, blood, electricity . . . it all smashed into Ariock.

The impact would have killed an ordinary person. But this time, Ariock was braced and ready. He was a conduit for a life-form he couldn't comprehend.

The life emerged from his back, carrying blood, and swirled madly toward the center of the chamber. The female form materialized again. This time, she almost had a face. Partially formed eyeballs bulged madly. Long hair rippled like cobwebs before blasting apart.

Particles slammed into Ariock, weaving through him, scraping his veins.

She coalesced near the throne again, carried on wind and electricity supplied by Ariock. Not quite a person. The dust ghoul screamed and blasted apart again, back to Ariock.

She crashed into him again and again, stronger, a little more substantial each time. Every crash was a little harder to take. Ariock gritted his teeth and stood his ground, even while he held the room together. He had to prevent it from collapsing and flooding his friends.

His mental focus became grim and battered. He was a pillar of lightning. Sand scoured him, and his innards felt like dust.

Fire bloomed in the center of the storm. Beads of molten gold illuminated the female shape that struggled to emerge from chaos.

Wildfire? Ariock didn't think that was a power he had. He wanted to check on Thomas, but he could hardly form coherent thoughts anymore. All he could do was hold tightly to the reins of everything he was controlling and brace himself for the next crash.

This time, the woman almost looked alive. Her hair was colorless, and her skin was a patchwork of gray, but she could almost pass for human.

She blasted apart, shrieking back into Ariock.

Wind whipped dust across him. Beads of his blood lifted into the chaotic air from a thousand stinging cuts. When she screamed away from him, he staggered.

Dust and water and electricity all collected into a female shape on the throne dais. Colors sharpened. Contours solidified.

The storm died all at once.

Ariock swayed from exhaustion. Blood dripped from multiple wounds, and black wraps hung off him in tattered shreds. He continued to hold up the ceiling and walls with his extended awareness.

A beautiful woman with flawless, ageless skin stood in front of the throne. Waves of metallic purple hair cascaded past her waist. Metallic wings arched off her shoulder blades, taller than her statuesque body. Her eyes were a brilliant violet color.

When she shifted her hips, the gossamer gown she was clothed in broke apart in puffs. It was dust.

Ariock swallowed the dust in his throat.

But it seemed he was not the most stunned or exhausted person in the room. Jinishta had crawled away from the dais, but she looked too ragged, too injured, to stand.

The winged woman peered around, blinking in confusion. She swayed. Then she began to collapse in a faint.

Ariock darted forward with his arms outstretched. He caught her before she hit the floor.

She was as lightweight as a sheet of paper, yet soft and warm in his arms.

She seemed to recover a little bit. She gazed up at Ariock's face with her violet eyes shining and said something that sounded grateful in a lyrical language that was utterly foreign to him.

CHAPTER 12

GLORY

Thomas didn't need to see the flashing digits on the tablet to tell him that the countdown was over. He had a timer in his head.

Which ached brutally.

He had sensed that the prisoner needed fire in the mix, and he had judged that his warning headache was gone, so he had given what he could. It was the barest fraction of a fraction of the power Ariock had donated. Still, Thomas felt drained and on the verge of collapse. He wanted to sleep for a week.

"Holy hell." Garrett let out his breath.

The corridor was groaning, as if strained.

Garrett floated the hovercart into the wreckage that used to be the throne chamber. The pillars and walls were churned into rubble. Water seeped through cracks in the upheaved mess of the ceiling, dribbling into growing puddles.

Jinishta was picking herself up off the floor. Her white hair was matted with grime, and bruises discolored one side of her face, but Thomas thought she was lucky to have survived in the magical equivalent of a nuclear reactor.

Ariock looked worse.

Cuts streaked his face and hands. Also? Someone had to be holding the remains of this chamber together, and judging by the strain evident in his body, that someone was Ariock. He must be shielding them all from a crushing disaster.

How long could he support the weight of the subterranean lake overhead?

The idea of Ariock depleted scared Thomas. They needed to get above water.

The winged, newly freed Lady of Sorrow buried her face against Ariock's mummy-wrapped torso. Her wavy purple hair screened most of her nude body.

"It's okay," Ariock murmured. "You're okay." He was ginger about touching her, probably finding every place inappropriate.

"We have to bring her up to speed," Garrett said. "So we can rescue Vy and the other hostages."

Kessa glanced at the tablet screen. Thomas felt her spike of alarm. Through her eyes, he saw that the hostages looked terrified. They were somewhere dark, but something was happening that caused Cherise and Vy to cling to each other as if facing death.

"The countdown is over," Garrett said. "We have to prove to the Torth that we've won. We need to bring her aboveground."

Ariock gently pried himself apart from the winged woman. She gazed up at him like a frightened child. When Ariock cautiously tried to set her on her feet, she clung to him, shameless. Her hiccuping sobs were muffled against him.

As a mind reader, the Lady of Sorrow ought to be able to learn a language fairly quickly. But she probably wasn't a supergenius, which meant she might need hours, perhaps days, to absorb the slave tongue.

Thomas figured he could shortcut that process. "Put me within range of her."

"Why?" Garrett shot him a distrustful look. "You going to brainwash her?"

Thomas was used to insults, but this one was a shock. What sort of monster did Garrett think he was?

"I would never do that." Thomas let the words fall cold and heavy, making sure his sincerity was unavoidable. "Anyway, I have a warning headache. No. I'm offering to serve as a translator for her." He was irked that he needed to explain. "I can learn her language in a few seconds."

Garrett seemed reassured enough to swing the hovercart close to Ariock and the Lady of Sorrow, putting Thomas within range of them.

Ariock was indeed holding the underground chamber rigid, keeping it intact. Thomas checked his mind for signs of faltering. Incredibly, Ariock remained strong. There was no hint of a warning headache. His injuries and loss of blood would have crippled anyone else, yet to Ariock, the injuries seemed insignificant.

As for the Lady of Sorrow . . .

Her mind was a black hole.

She struggled to remember who she was. Or what she was. She had no words to describe herself. It seemed she still considered herself defeated, powerless, and trapped. Her confusion was overwhelming.

Thomas figured he could remedy that.

Amid all the anguish in her mind, he detected her native language. It was the rich soil wherein concepts could be sowed and words grown.

He absorbed syntax, context, and pronunciation as fast as he could. Her lyrical language held a few tantalizing similarities to the Alashani language, which enabled him to build a working vocabulary within a few seconds.

"You are freed from your imprisonment," Thomas told her. He had to pause, calculating the correct words while her archaic language finished compiling in the background of his mind. "We are here to rescue you. Will you accept our help?"

She focused on Thomas with her wide-set purple eyes.

Although she understood his words, she didn't seem to understand much else. She remembered being trapped. Alone. She had called for help . . . for what she felt sure was an eternity . . . and no one had come.

Now she wondered: Were these strangers truly rescuers? Their foreign nature scared her.

"We will explain everything," Thomas assured her in her archaic language. "I promise. We are friends."

She emanated uncertainty . . . until Ariock brushed a wave of hair off her shoulder with one big hand.

"We can't stay here," Ariock said. "Will you come with us?"

The Lady of Sorrow relaxed into Ariock's embracing hand. She didn't understand the words spoken by this giant who had rescued her, but she liked his gentle eyes and his kind voice.

Who was he? She was intrigued for the first time in what felt like millennia. Why had he gone to the great lengths necessary to rescue her?

"His name is Ariock," Thomas said, making a quick introduction. "And I'm Thomas." Really, he shouldn't need to explain such basics to a mind reader. Why did her telepathy seem attenuated?

Thomas probed her mind as unobtrusively as possible. He needed the Lady of Sorrow to be a sharp-minded powerhouse, not a sobbing wreck. What could he do to ease her confusion and bring her up to speed?

The Lady of Sorrow turned her gaze on him. Something about Thomas's attentive probing bothered her.

She vaguely remembered someone else probing her mind like this.

A traitor.

A Yeresunsa who should have been on her side, but who had instead . . .

She began shaking with rage and terror as memories bubbled up from the depths of her confusion. Mind readers—more than one?—had sealed her inside a mimicry of her crystal throne room. They had imprisoned her with mirrors. Starved her. Hurt her. Murdered her loyalists.

They were ENEMIES.

"I am on your side," Thomas said quickly in her language. He forced a smile, heart pounding, because he sensed the deadly certainty of her power coiled within her mind. She was definitely powerful. "I'm here to help you. I promise." His mind raced, searching for reassurances. How would Kessa handle this situation?

"Your enemies are my enemies," he told her.

The Lady of Sorrow studied Thomas, troubled. She detected his sincerity, yet she found his extremely disabled body jarring, considering his poise. He couldn't be royalty. So why did he sound like a prince? Why was he the only spokesperson among her rescuers?

Even his name, Thomas, sounded alien to her ears.

She tried to guess which foreign embassy would have sent such a weird rescue team. What allies did she have left?

The effort of remembering made her feel sick. Thomas caught names whirling through her mind, but as soon as she remembered each person, she remembered that they'd been murdered.

Belvik? Dead. Iriade? Dead. Suro? Dead. Ah Jun? Dead.

It was too much. She cried, helpless to stop.

Thomas chewed his lip in frustration. He had expected the Lady of Sorrow to be a stoic, Alashani type of warrior. They needed a courageous ally, not this mournful mess.

"What can I call you?" Ariock asked the lady in his arms. "Do you have a name?"

Ariock's good intentions glowed to anyone who could read minds. The Lady of Sorrow did not understand his language, but she read his surface thoughts and figured out what he wanted to know.

She pondered the question.

She had trouble remembering her own name. The ruined chamber held no clues for her. Glass glinted. She felt glad that the mirrors were broken, but the enormous gaps in her memory made her afraid.

Thomas forced himself to remain patient, to resist the tantalizing gleams of buried memories in her mind. Kessa would be patient in this situation. Polite. That was how Cherise and Vy would handle it, too. They would be respectful.

The Lady of Sorrow saw her crystal throne. She remembered, in a vague way, that she used to rule the world.

Wasn't she someone regal? Someone whose power could not be challenged?

She had been an empress. A goddess-empress.

And yes, she did have a name, she was sure. Royalty, and ambassadors, and sycophants, and all the lesser lords and ladies . . . they all referred to her as . . .

"Glory," she remembered.

Ariock and the others heard her whisper, "Evenjos." They did not know that those syllables meant "glory" in her archaic tongue. Only Thomas soaked up that truth.

"Evenjos." Ariock tested the name. "Will you come with us, Evenjos? Will you trust me to keep you safe?"

She gave Ariock a considering look. At least she understood his good-will, if not his foreign words.

Thomas realized, with dismayed fascination, that Evenjos was slow on the uptake, telepathically. Her ability to read minds was . . . impaired. She was the telepath equivalent of someone who was legally blind or mostly deaf.

The Torth Empire killed "deficient" individuals like her, who had less-than-optimal mind-reading ability. Committees that oversaw baby farms screened out anyone born with intellectual disabilities, disruptive mood swings, or any behavior the Torth deemed unacceptable. This woman, despite her many positive attributes, would have been destroyed as a fetus, because she would forever be unable to join the Megacosm. She couldn't even probe memories.

She was a mind reader. But just barely.

Thomas tried to shove aside his frustration at her guilelessness and confusion. *So what?* he asked himself. *So she's handicapped.* It shouldn't be a big deal. He was handicapped. Everyone had problems.

But if Evenjos could not rapidly absorb new information, things were going to be difficult.

She did sense Ariock's expanded awareness. That was simple and easy for Evenjos to read, and she relaxed a little bit. Clearly, he was protecting everyone in this ruined chamber. She saw the strain he was under as he inhabited stone walls and the ceiling, as well as the river and boulders above.

Yes. She believed that she could trust this strong giant, despite his foreignness, despite his incomprehensible language.

But his strength was shocking. Was he a stormbringer? His power index should place him high up in the Yeresunsa Order.

Evenjos wondered, with fresh unease, why she had never encountered this outlandish giant. He had to be royalty. A king or a prince. Surely she would have met him at an imperial dance or banquet, or at least heard tales about him? Why was he so utterly unfamiliar?

"Um, let's get moving," Thomas said in English. "Let's go rescue our hostages." He didn't think they could afford to let Evenjos think too hard about her circumstances. There was no time for long explanations or post-traumatic stress disorder. Not while the Torth were ready to torture or kill Cherise and Vy.

Jinishta had already staggered onboard the hovercart. She showed no joy that she was still alive, although now that she was within range, Thomas sensed that she harbored a faint hope that the resurrected Lady of Sorrow might save the Alashani people.

"Do you think you can clear a path for us to go back through that lost city . . . ?" Garrett trailed off, because he must have sensed Ariock's awareness skyrocket.

Thomas sensed it as well. Ariock's mind was ablaze with focused intensity, drilling upward through miles of solid rock and sediment.

Garrett limped over to put his hand on one of Ariock's massive arms. "Ariock, let's go back the way we came. You're too injured to—"

"I'm fine." Ariock sounded unmoved. No headache, as far as Thomas could tell, but Ariock's cuts and scrapes throbbed. Ariock was wise enough to not complain. He had no room for discussion while tunneling through miles of rock. He was shifting multiple tons of earth. That was difficult to do without causing a major earthquake.

Thomas gazed longingly toward the corridor of prophecies.

All the broken walls and ceilings would collapse the instant Ariock let his focus wane here. Tons of water and sediment would destroy those murals. Their ancient secrets would be lost. Forever.

But living people, such as Cherise and Vy, needed help.

The living had to take priority. Their knowledge was more dynamic, and therefore more valuable, than the dead stuff.

Wasn't it?

"You really shouldn't overuse your powers." Garrett sounded concerned. "When you're injured, that's when you need to take things easy."

Ariock lifted one black-wrapped hand, which was streaked with bloodied glass cuts. "I'm fine."

The invisible extension of his arm churned water and boulders into a frothing whirlwind, opening up a tunnel that elongated into darkness. Thomas knew, from reading Ariock's mind, that the path would lead directly to Bloodbath Plaza.

Ariock was maintaining the temporary tunnel. Miles of solid rock, all whipped into a new configuration and held in place by the power of one person's mind.

Ariock tried to place Evenjos in the hovercart. She clung to him, hugging him with her wings, but Ariock was insistent. After a moment, Evenjos let go, apparently trusting him. She stood next to Garrett and eyed the other occupants with regal unease.

Garrett politely averted his gaze.

Evenjos gave him a puzzled look. Shame might be an unfamiliar emotion to a goddess-empress who had suffered for eons, Thomas thought.

"Hold on tight," Ariock said.

That was barely enough warning. The hovercart zoomed into the darkness of the tunnel at superhuman speed, propelled by Ariock.

Water crashed behind them.

Loss wrenched Thomas's insides. The instant he lost sight of the corridor of prophecies, he knew the pain of regret. It was worse than any physical ache. Knowledge ought to be treasured. Protected. It should never, ever be abused or mistreated or forgotten or destroyed.

He felt as if he'd witnessed something akin to a massacre.

The only solace he had was the fact that copies must exist. Garrett knew where. Evenjos might remember a few ancient secrets, as well.

Thomas decided to probe their minds as soon as he could. He needed to do it before their knowledge could dissipate or die. He absolutely could not live with himself if he allowed that to happen. He needed their secrets.

CHAPTER 13

REDUCTION OF ALL

Commander, the Majority sang.

Commander of most—

—but not of all living things.

The Commander of Most Living Things tried to accept her reduced title with grace. It was inescapable. Her influence was on the wane. She would have to prove herself all over again.

But she was almost eager for that challenge.

The Commander paced Bloodbath Plaza. *We have a baited trap*, she reminded her multitudes of listeners.

Raindrops sizzled and evaporated before they could ruin her pristine armor. She had spread her awareness to encase herself in cleansing heat. She needed every scrap of regal dignity she could manage.

At least she no longer needed to hide her powers.

She paced the other way, giving her orbiters a full view of the baited trap. She'd had a nuclear bomb constructed around the cage, in the form of a large cube. The hostages were trapped within the cube, surrounded by nozzles, plus layers of triggers for the bomb.

One twitchy move, one mouthed warning, and the hostages would be gassed to death.

They had been warned.

And even better: a nuclear arsenal floated in orbit. Every warhead was locked onto the nuclear cube.

The Giant and the Betrayer had both promised to submit to the Torth Empire. Where were they? Surely they had not abandoned the hostages? They could not be permitted to wiggle out of the bargain. If they tried?

Well. They would fail to see all the firepower aimed their way.

It was a magnificent trap. Her own idea. She did not need to rely on supergeniuses, and she would prove it.

You had better prove it, her many orbiters warned.

Destroy Our enemies.

Destroy the threat to Our innocent population in Stratower City.

Or We—

—will destroy you.

The Commander of Most reversed direction, not allowing hundreds of billions of critics to annoy her. The enemies would show up. The Betrayer was smart enough to abandon the hostages, but he was not actually in charge. The Commander felt sure of it.

The Giant was in charge.

Everyone knew that nontelepaths could not be entrusted with power. Their egos grew unchecked, unhampered by an inner audience. They dwindled into hedonism. They grew overconfident and reckless.

That was why alien sapients were so easy to conquer. A thousand generations ago, the tech-savvy ummins had been overconfident. The nussians used to be overconfident, as well. And the mer nerctans. The jodinak, especially.

All the major conquests had concluded long before the current Commander was conceived on a baby farm, but she knew basic history. Mnemonic replays of ancient battles were available in the Megacosm. Anyone with a modicum of curiosity could seek them out.

By now, the overpowered Giant probably believed he could triumph without breaking a sweat. His type was predictable.

You (Commander) did not see his hammer blow coming, her inner audience sang.

Okay. Well, that was a lucky strike. It would not be repeated. The Giant was mostly predictable.

Her orbiters debated that. Many sang that she herself was overconfident. They doubted that her baited trap would defeat the Betrayer.

He is too smart for you, they sang.

The Commander tightened her jaw. The Majority might be right. Perhaps the Betrayer had the resources to outwit her, although she doubted it.

But she was not going to beg for brilliant ideas from the Upward Governess or the Twins or any other supergeniuses.

Those children already had too much social influence. They did not need to be praised as galactic heroes.

How could so many decent citizens consider voting to promote the Upward Governess to the status of Commander of All Living Things? Such a promotion should be unthinkable! Supergeniuses were not trained to serve the Majority of the galactic population! They were mere scientists! They were not suitable as military leaders!

You (Commander) are not suitable as a military leader, many Torth accused.

Why command a citywide evacuation? the local governor complained. *I left behind most of My slaves and bodyguards. Not to mention My irreplaceable gym equipment.* He was currently lounging aboard his luxury streamship in a mood that was tangibly foul. *I am displeased.*

Local citizens chorused their solidarity. The Stratower elevators were forced to run at reduced capacity, thanks to the lobby wreckage caused by the Giant. People actually had to wait in line.

We are displeased, they silently complained.

   We feel unsafe.

     We feel harried.

      Our day was disrupted by your (possibly stupid plan) bargain with the Betrayer.

        We do not appreciate that.

The Commander of Most Living Things brushed away their complaints with a mental flick. Even if she had to unleash a firestorm of bombs upon the Giant, everyone indoors would remain safe. The city was fortified.

As for the Stratower itself? Nothing could wreck it.

According to very ancient memories, the Stratower had weathered violent nuclear firestorms as well as Yeresunsa stormbringer attacks. The most violent bombs in existence could not break it. Everyone knew that the Stratower was eternal. Its majestic strength and size were a physical representation of the spine of the galactic Torth Empire.

Everyone inside the Stratower would remain safely shielded from whatever bombs or havoc ensued in the aftermath of the Betrayer's bargain.

The Commander reversed direction, watching the nuclear cube. Where was the Giant already? The countdown had ended. Didn't he care about his one-legged female friend?

You (Commander) should have set up the trap outside the Border River. That criticism came from an unexpected direction. It was one of the more roguish Servants of All, the Swift Killer. She strutted aboard a luxury streamship, using her powers to tickle the chin of a frightened albino captive. *That way, you could rattle these Alashani savages.*

The Commander of Most Living Things disagreed. The dead city was crawling with wild zoved and other nasty creatures. Why should her troops have to deal with those threats on top of having to deal with the Giant?

How about if you (Commander) utilize Servants of All instead of common Red Ranks? the Swift Killer suggested. *We can easily fend off wild zoved by using Our powers. Let Us familiarize Ourselves with what We are capable of.*

A surprising number of military ranks chorused to back her up.

Yes.

Our enemies (Giant) (Betrayer) (Imposter) use their powers freely.
So We (Torth) ought to do the same.

The Majority debated that. No one wanted to encourage power usage. However, as long as the Giant remained at large, perhaps a onetime exception should be made?

Just until the Giant is eliminated, many Torth assured each other.

Yes.

And then We will (kill) (eliminate) get rid of the corruption
(the Servants of All)—

—and vote on Whom (so many choices!) to replace Them with.

The Commander stiffened as millions of Torth chorused a whirlwind of agreement. She used to secretly yearn for Yeresunsa acceptance, but not quite like this.

If only she could have converted the Betrayer into a loyal Servant of All.

Despite his physical disabilities and shortcomings, he would have been valuable. Who could challenge a Servant of All with a secret power to forcibly change other people's minds? So she had given the feral hybrid from Earth an opportunity. A chance to rise high. Wealth beyond anything a mere human could imagine. Power. Authority.

She had assumed that he would be as greedy as the Upward Governess, as greedy as most children and especially most supergeniuses.

Instead, he had rejected everything she'd offered. He had spit on the opportunity freely given to him.

That was his loss as well as hers.

She would make sure that he suffered.

The Betrayer has buried himself under the Stratower,
like a tumor in Our Homeworld.

He isn't going to show up!

Impatience dominated the Megacosm. The collective mood filled the oceans of discussion like fog, obscuring other matters. The countdown had ended several minutes ago.

The ground rumbled ominously.

That started a panic. Torth abandoned their luggage in Bloodbath Plaza, seeking any which way to get indoors and away from ground zero. Throngs of citizens jammed the narrow entrance to the Stratower. They ordered slaves to shove other citizens out of their way. Hoverchairs crashed into people.

The Commander readied herself. At the age of one hundred and eighty-six standard years, she would rather end her life in a blaze of glory than live in ignominy. She would render the Torth Empire safe and at peace again—even if it killed her.

Such a death was far superior to the torture her predecessor in office had suffered.

The Commander had been known as the Pragmatist when the infamous former Commander was justly stripped of his mantle of office and then tortured to death in the Isolatorium. She had witnessed that justice firsthand. Ten thousand years from now, historians would remember the Twisted One as a failed Commander, an idiot who had accidentally allowed a dangerous renegade—the Imposter—to escape death and survive long enough to breed.

Had the Twisted One done his job properly, the Dovanack family would never have been born.

Consequently, the Betrayer would never have existed, because his mother would not have been sent to kill the Dovanack family. The galaxy would have remained safe, peaceful, and complacent, led in secret by Yeresunsa known as the Servants of All.

The Commander of Most Living Things regretted how turbulent her reign had become. She had not intended this series of unfortunate mistakes.

But at least none of it was her fault.

!!!!!!

A section of Bloodbath Plaza screamed apart, so loud that her troops cringed. Rocks and dirt sprayed upward.

The Commander fixed her gaze on the ferocious eruption of earth. Her inner audience surged, peering through her eyes, but she forced herself to remain as still as ice.

There hadn't been enough time to make everything perfect. Her baited trap had to work. She would not allow her troops to panic the way the local citizens were doing. They had to destroy the Giant and do their best to capture the Betrayer and the Imposter. Above all, she could not fail.

Death was acceptable. Failure never was.

CHAPTER 14

BETWEEN COMMANDERS

Untold tons of bedrock had to be broken into such small chunks that they interacted like beads, liquid and loose. Ariock crushed rock into scree. Then he blasted that scree against more solid bedrock, embedding his makeshift tunnel with pebbled mica. He did all that with enough force to crush trucks. And he did it fast enough so that he could levitate upward at a speedy pace.

Ariock's own core body might as well be just another boulder to move. He propelled himself in front of the hovercart.

Light, when it came, was sudden.

Ariock levitated into the rain-soaked night, overshooting the ground by several yards due to his speed. His ears popped.

Searchlights illuminated Bloodbath Plaza. The place was still crowded, but now the horde surged toward the Stratower, fighting to get inside. Torth leaped off vehicles and hoverchairs. A nussian tried to barrel past Torth and got blasted to pieces. Abandoned slaves milled about, burdened with luggage.

Not far from that panicked exodus, a few thousand Red Ranks stood in a tidy square formation. They ignored their fearful civilian comrades just as much as they ignored the eternal downpour. Helmets masked whatever facial expressions they might have.

They turned to face Ariock. But not to attack. They seemed to be guarding a large cube structure.

Ariock maintained a protective shield of pressurized air around himself and the hovercart. He wanted to catch his breath and do a little reconnaissance before seeking Vy and his other hostage friends. He anticipated a battle. He just wanted to give himself a chance to size up the situation before getting bombarded.

The Commander strutted in front of the Red Ranks and Servants of All in her bleached armor. She assessed Ariock with empty white eyes. What did she see? A Giant? A monster?

She was no less monstrous to Ariock. Steam rose from her billowing shroud as she caused raindrops to evaporate.

"S s s s s s s s u r r e n d e r r r r—"

"—t o U s s s s s."

The Commander opened her stringy, skeletal arms in invitation. Her Servants of All imitated her, moving in sync.

Ariock sent the hovercart gently to the ground. But he did not soften his own landing.

He slammed down with enough force to crack the tarry surface of Bloodbath Plaza. Then he straightened to his full height and met the Commander's blank-eyed gaze. If the Torth thought they could claim an unearned victory . . . ? Well. Not this time.

"We won." He used power to amplify his deep voice so it rolled like thunder. "We have the Lady of Sorrow."

Garrett gestured to the winged woman with a flourish.

Evenjos did bear a resemblance to the various shrines and statues dedicated to the Lady of Sorrow. Although she was not weeping at the moment, her large violet eyes looked lost and frightened. She stared at the army. The searchlights. She turned in a circle, the wind wrapping her long hair around her nude body. Her wings were a textured metal, like lizard scales, and they added a quiet majesty to her appearance. By comparison, Ariock was a mess of tattered wraps, dust, and blood.

The Commander looked unimpressed. "Y y y o u s h o w w w w e d u p—"

Other Torth breathed along with her, so their creaky voices collected together.

"—l a a a t e."

Evenjos made a peeping noise of fear and confusion. She hugged herself. Maybe she wanted clothing.

Thomas sounded cold. "We rescued her within the allotted three hours. We stuck to the terms of the bargain. You're welcome to probe our minds if my word isn't enough."

"Y o u i i i n t e r f f f e e e e r e d w i t h h h h U u u s s s." The Commander shook her head in refusal.

"Y o o o u w r e c k k k e d O u r r r e l e v a a a a t o r l l l l o b b y."

Ariock stared in disbelief. That was the flimsiest technicality he had ever heard. He had put effort into saving Torth lives in that lobby. How many nasty Red Ranks had he levitated to safety? Dozens! He had left slaves to suffer and die in the Isolatorium, but Torth were free to go back to their rapacious lifestyles, thanks to him! Did that not even matter?

Thomas spoke to the Torth in a forbidding tone. "If you want to count that as interference, then you interfered with us, as well. So we're even." He beckoned. "Hand over the hostages."

The Commander stood proud in the rain. Perhaps she was holding a silent debate with her inner audience?

Or springing a trap.

Of course the Torth would break the bargain as soon as it went unfavorably for them. Not a surprise. But they had better reveal the hostages, or else Ariock was going to destroy their puny, pathetic little army, just like he'd churned up bedrock.

Evenjos sank to her knees, wings folded protectively over herself. She said something plaintively in her foreign language.

" . . . the crystal spire?" Garrett frowned at her, as if struggling to decipher her words. "What is she talking about?"

"The Stratower," Thomas translated. "She doesn't understand where we are." He went on in a soothing tone, offering a stream of melodic syllables to Evenjos in her archaic language.

Apparently Thomas was not comforting enough. Evenjos doubled over and began to cry like a scared and hopeless child.

"Don't worry about it." Thomas gave Ariock a humorless smile. "She's just suffering a little bit of PTSD."

If the Stratower had ever been crystal, well, now it was coated with thousands of years' worth of grime. Sludge fringed its countless eaves.

"We have a problem." Garrett spoke in a low, urgent voice, full of alarm.

Ariock bent closer, inviting an explanation.

"The Torth have a nuclear arsenal locked on us," Garrett said. "And you see that cube?" He pointed with his beard. "They've fitted it with a fifty-kilo nuclear bomb. Our hostage friends are trapped inside."

Ariock stood still, trying to process the dangers.

"Also," Garrett said, "the Torth can remotely gas the hostages to death if we make a threatening move. They're ready to bludgeon us."

Ariock figured he could shield everyone here from a nuclear arsenal. Probably. Maybe. He had never tried a shield on that scale, but he felt . . . well, maybe not in totally peak condition. He was weary and scraped up.

So what? Ariock inwardly shook off that irrelevant concern. Even if he couldn't fend off a nuclear Armageddon, he would certainly try.

The problem was, if he was busy shielding everyone in the vicinity, then he would not be able to protect the friends who were trapped inside that cube.

They were a target inside a target. He couldn't split his attention in refined ways while he was undergoing a hammering. If he focused too much on protecting himself, Vy and the others would die. The Torth knew his mental processing limits.

"C o m m m m m m m m m m m m e," hundreds of mind readers whispered. "T o U s s s s."

One of them held a shock collar sized for Ariock, and she waggled it as if to entice him.

"S s s s s s u r r r r r e n d e r r r r r r r."

Ariock extended his awareness into the cube, hoping to defuse it.

The five life sparks he sensed inside were likely his friends: Vy, Weptolyso, Yuey, Flen, and Cherise. Unbalanced elements suffused the cube in puzzling arrangements, which Ariock could not hope to pick apart. He would be blindly guessing. If he tried to defuse any part of it, or if he tried to dismantle the contraption, he was likely to trigger a deadly chain reaction.

No doubt the Torth had designed it especially to confound him.

"You cheated." Thomas sounded disappointed as he gazed at the bony Commander and her backup force.

At least he didn't sound surprised. He had known what to expect from the Torth Empire.

"You know we won," Thomas went on. "But you changed your minds about the details of our bargain. That's your slimiest trick. You lie to yourselves. You change little details to confuse your victims, plus any constituents who are paying attention to your minds."

"S s s s s i l e n c c c e."

"You lie to your inner audiences by lying to yourselves," Thomas said. "You feed the Majority every reassurance. You say that you live to serve. That you're on their side. But the smart ones who are listening right now? They see through your platitudes. They know that the instant you see an opportunity to rule the Majority again, instead of serving them, you will simply adapt to a new paradigm. You'll change your minds at the drop of a hat."

One of the Servants of All gestured, and a slave collar rocketed through the air.

"Let me fake defeat!" Thomas whispered.

Just in time.

Ariock let his shielding around the hovercart dissipate, so the collar slammed around Thomas's skinny neck instead of bouncing off pressurized air. Thomas rocked backward from the force of it.

"Use my glove," Garrett whispered. He surreptitiously slid his custom-tailored blaster glove toward Thomas, helped along by Kessa, so the Torth didn't see it.

Thomas used the glove briefly, switching it to some kind of nonlethal mode and tapping the collar around his neck. The collar remained locked in place, but its glow strip dimmed. Ariock assumed it had been deactivated.

Thomas pretended to check on the data tablet, so the Torth did not see his face, but Ariock heard his whisper, masked by the downpour.

"Shield your neck, Ariock."

Ariock tightened his invisible shield just as a giant-size collar slammed around his thick neck. It would have dug in, cruelly tight, but Ariock prevented it from making contact with his skin.

Needles inside the collar tried to puncture Ariock, to deliver microdarts of the inhibitor. He very nearly ripped it away.

"Fake defeat!" Thomas whispered. His yellow eyes seemed to glow in the nighttime darkness.

Ariock fell to one knee, head down, pretending he was in anguish. His shame and fear felt real enough. He didn't have to fake those. The proximity of so much inhibitor was terrifying. Ariock wasn't sure how long he could maintain this tight a shield around his own throat, protecting himself from needles. One little distraction . . . one little problem . . . and he might lose focus.

He couldn't do this while also protecting Vy and other people from a nuclear detonation.

Thomas had that glove hidden in his arms. It was too small for Ariock's hands, and he didn't know how to use it. He could lift Thomas. He just needed a reason to do so, something the Torth would not question.

The Torth must fear the Imposter, because they went for overkill and tossed a slave collar at Garrett, as well. They used their powers to snap the collar into place around the old man's neck. Now Garrett was doubly inhibited. He staggered.

Ariock seized the giant-size collar and pretended to try to yank it away, without success.

"Evenjos," Thomas said, his tone begging. "Please. Can you help us?"

Evenjos had curled into a ball of misery. Her whole body shimmered for an instant or two, almost as if she was not quite real, or losing bodily cohesion.

"Why . . ." She enunciated each word, as if feeling her way through a foreign language. She must be absorbing the common slave tongue, because Ariock understood every word. "Why am . . . I . . . here?"

"We'll explain everything." Garrett sounded desperate. "I promise. But only if you help us survive!"

Thomas and Garrett had intended for the Lady of Sorrow to be their weapon. They had overestimated her, Ariock thought. Even if she had substantial power . . . and he had sensed her blazing life spark, overwhelming all others in the vicinity . . . she seemed overcome by the threats and the nightmarish cityscape. Maybe this all seemed like an extension of her torturous imprisonment?

"S s s s s s s u r r r e n d e r r," many Torth breathed.

"O r y y y o u r f f f f r i e n n n d s s s s—"

"—d d d i i i e."

The Commander of All Living Things could trigger a nuclear Armageddon here and now with just a thought—a command to her loyalists.

But *would* she? Would a Torth really sacrifice herself? Was she truly that determined to win?

"They're not bluffing, Ariock," Garrett said through gritted teeth.

And deep down, Ariock knew that Garrett was right. The Torth Empire would sacrifice a few for the good of the many. The Majority had little care for individuals, even one at the highest rank. They had voted the Commander into office. They could vote for her to die.

Besides, Torth could not lie to each other. Only to themselves.

"What happened to the . . . the sky?" Evenjos wept.

"Boy?" Garrett spoke with quick desperation. "Now would be a good time to brainwash her."

Thomas looked at Garrett with disgusted incredulity.

"Can't you do it lightly?" Garrett made urgent motions.

Thomas's tone dripped with condescension. "I'm wearing an inhibitor collar."

Ariock had seen him deactivate that collar. Maybe he hadn't done it fast enough?

No. Thomas tended to be bluntly honest. If he was on the inhibitor, he would have said exactly that. He must want everyone to think his powers were disabled.

And he probably had reasons to avoid using his brainwashing power. Ariock remembered his tale about accidentally killing a pair of neglectful foster parents. If Thomas wanted to avoid using that power, who could blame him?

"All is lost." Evenjos spoke in a small, hurt voice. Waves of hair hid her face as she pressed her forehead to the floor of the hovercart. "Put me back."

Did she think this reality was even worse than her mirror prison?

Ariock had never felt like such a failure. The Lady of Sorrow must think herself surrounded by enemies. He had to wonder if he had done the right thing. Maybe he should have left her alone.

"Put me back where you found me." Evenjos turned to Ariock, beseeching.

"Ariock can help you to your grave," Kessa gently told Evenjos. "Or to wherever you wish to go. But not if he's a slave."

Evenjos gave the ummin a quizzical look. She didn't seem to understand what was at stake.

Ariock gritted his teeth as he maintained the shielding around his neck. If a microdrop of inhibitor touched one of his lacerations, everyone was doomed.

How long could he keep up this stressful act? Any second now, the Torth would force him to make a horrible choice. Could he bat away warheads before they exploded?

Not while literally shielding his own neck.

"L a a a s s s s s s t c h—" the Torth began.

"We're defeated." Thomas sounded as if he meant it.

Ariock eyed him sideways. He'd hoped that Thomas might have a back-up plan. Was he really going to just give up?

"I'll come to you willingly. I promise." Thomas paused. "How about if you send me one of those hoverchairs, so I can obey without needing someone to carry me?"

Bloodbath Plaza was littered with abandoned hoverchairs and other detritus. Nevertheless, that sounded like a delay. Thomas was stalling for time.

The Torth breathed, "T h h h e G i i i i i a n t—"

"—w w w w i l l c a a a a r r y y y y y o u."

Thomas's voice was barely audible over their moaning reply. "You've got to do it, Ariock."

Ariock leaned over the hovercart railing to retrieve Thomas, bundling him in such a way as to hide the blaster glove from sight. Here was a perfect excuse for Thomas to get close enough to deactivate his giant-size collar.

And this should make shielding easier. Ariock enfolded Thomas within his personal shield without sacrificing much extra focus.

But Garrett was on his own. So were Kessa and Jinishta.

If there was a plan, Garrett was apparently not in on it. He knelt and tried to grab Evenjos's attention, pleading in her face. "Those are enemies." He flung a pointing finger at the Torth. "They're the evil mind readers who imprisoned you."

Evenjos seemed to be beyond caring or listening. She wept.

"You have to fight them!" Garrett said urgently.

Jinishta prostrated herself in front of Evenjos. "Lady of Sorrow?" She gripped Evenjos's arms with her albino hands. Her cowl had fallen, exposing tightly curled white hair to the polluted rainfall. "Please. Save my people?"

Evenjos peered at the Alashani woman, her violet eyes brimming with tears. Maybe Jinishta's despair resonated with her own?

"My people are descended from your people." It seemed Jinishta was finally accepting the kinship between Alashani and mind readers. "We are yours. But we are dying. Please? We need your help."

Evenjos listened, rapt, as Jinishta switched languages. Her mushy Alashani tongue was similar to the lyrical ancient language Evenjos knew.

"I will do anything," Jinishta said.

Evenjos merely lowered her head to the ground, as if it weighed more than a world. "I am sorry," she whispered sadly. "I do not recognize you."

Jinishta must look alien, with her rounded features, her long neck, her albino lack of color, and her ink-black wraps. Perhaps Evenjos saw her as just another wrong feature in a wrong world.

The two women remained prostrate, unmoving. Rain poured down on them. Neither Jinishta nor Evenjos seemed to find any point in rising.

"C o m m m e." The Torth voices were creaky and sharp.

Coils of air wrapped around Ariock. He dared not fight them off.

"N n n n o m o r r r r e d e e e e l a a a a y s s s s s."

Servants of All used their telekinetic powers to reel Ariock toward them. He turned and stumble-walked backward, gazing at his friends on the hovercart. That way, he blocked Thomas from the Torth army.

The boy raised his gloved hand and . . . yes. He deactivated the horrid choker.

Ariock didn't dare to rip the slave collar off his neck. He reminded himself to act helpless, although the act was wearing thin. He turned and trudged toward the Torth army as if defeated.

Was he?

Red Ranks lifted their arms, aiming heavy-duty blaster gloves his way. They must suspect that he was faking his despair. Maybe they were holding a silent vote right now, choosing which unlucky Torth would get to dart forward and blast him at close range.

"Where are you going?" Evenjos pleaded.

For the first time, there was something in her tone other than grief. She sounded argumentative.

Ariock risked a glance over his shoulder.

Evenjos stood, fully clothed in a regal gown of satiny purple and brocade. Where had the dress come from?

Her wings shone metallic. Her eyes remained wet and full of uncertainty, but there was something determined there, as well.

"Where are you going?" she asked.

Thomas called a reply in her lyrical dead language.

It must be an explanation, because Evenjos said, "You made a bargain?"

"Yes," Thomas said.

Evenjos's tone rose, becoming brittle. "With the spawn of Unyat?" Her voice went flat with fury. "Only an idiot would make a bargain with them."

Thomas spoke apologetically in her dead language. Ariock could not afford to contribute to the conversation, since he had to maintain a full-body shield around himself and Thomas. But was that wild hope in Thomas's eyes? Or just wishful thinking?

"Do not leave me," Evenjos commanded.

And it was a command. Her voice was dark and final, as if she spoke an incontrovertible fact.

"We have to," Thomas said. "We have no choice."

"Sorry." Ariock turned to face her, but he was forced to walk backward, pulled by invisible telekinetic chains. He dared not provoke the Torth or Vy would be gassed to death.

For a second, Evenjos lost bodily cohesion. She loosened into dust particles that sparked with unnatural light.

"Come back."

Just as quickly, she took shape again. Her winged form was silhouetted by magenta-white electricity. Her eyes glowed like headlamps.

Ariock gave a helpless shrug. He was dangerously close to the Torth army. He had to pour all his focus into shielding himself and Thomas. If the collar around his neck were still activated, this would have been impossible.

A cold wind blew across the plaza.

Ariock's awareness wanted to leap into wind and rain, to become one with the impending storm. But he needed to be ready for any sort of attack. Torth were unpredictable. One might lunge at him and disable him with a pain seizure while their comrades shot him with the inhibitor.

He could not allow himself to get sucked into orchestrating a storm. Too many people in too many places needed his protection.

He turned to see how the Torth would confront this unexpected new threat.

Frost whitened the tar beneath the Commander's boots. Rain pattered around her in the form of hailstones. The twisted horns of her mantle grew icicles, fringing her bony shoulders.

The Commander tilted her skull-like head this way and that, as if to loosen it.

Then she strode forward.

Ariock turned to see Evenjos striding forth to meet the Commander. Evenjos looked as bold as a killer robot, her whole body rippling with blinding light.

CHAPTER 15

ILLUSION DEFUSION

Thomas opened his mouth to scream a warning about the inhibitor serum. Evenjos's damaged mind needed time to recuperate. Judging by what he had absorbed, she assumed the Torth were thuggish minions of a powerful political enemy. She had no concept what the Megacosm was.

Before he could shout, Evenjos raised one sculpted arm. A bar of brilliant light burned from her, like nuclear fission.

Everything in that beam got vaporized.

The remains of twenty-four Red Ranks fell, useless chunks of meat encased in sliced-off armor. Their upper bodies were gone. Only a few heads remained intact. They rained down, bouncing.

Thomas closed his mouth. Maybe he didn't need to worry about Evenjos so much.

A grim, powerful look settled on the ice-cold features of the Commander of All Living Things. Thomas did not need to read her mind to know that she had just signaled her remote troops. The nuclear arsenal must be rocketing toward Bloodbath Plaza.

The cube was triggered.

Within its dark walls, Cherise and Vy would be choking to death on deadly gas. Meanwhile, a chain reaction around them guaranteed detonation within five minutes. Everything at ground zero would get vaporized.

"Take me to the cube," Thomas urged Ariock. "I need your help to defuse it right now."

Ariock hurled himself in that direction. He rolled in muck from his momentum, then somersaulted to his feet, Alashani-style, with Thomas still cradled against his chest. He pressed close to the cube, using its bulk to shield himself from any Torth who might try to open fire on him.

"There's no time to save them!" Garrett shouted over the downpour. "Run!" He frantically waved for Ariock to rejoin him aboard the hovercart.

The Commander spread an ice shield in front of herself. Evenjos tried to vaporize it, but the ice regenerated as fast as she could destroy it.

Thomas saw a trap. Torth circled around behind Evenjos, blaster gloves ready. Evenjos would fail to detect the microdarts flying her way until it was too late.

Ariock saw it, too. He threw a shield between Evenjos and the Torth behind her, just in time.

"Get onboard!" Garrett sounded desperate.

"I'll talk you through disarming that cube," Thomas told Ariock. Factors fanned through his mind. He visualized the fissile material, rounded in a supercritical mass, melting into critical density. Without the blueprints or the exact parameters of the bomb, he would have to rely on guesswork. He forced himself to sound calm and measured. "I need you to send your awareness inside."

Ariock explored the cube with his awareness.

Thomas tried to guide him. "First of all, block the laser—no, not there. It's . . . down. To your left. You sense that solid piece? The vacuum beyond that. Block it."

Thomas kept the frustration out of his tone, but it was difficult. Ariock had no concept of what a krytron trigger was, let alone how a nuclear bomb was constructed.

The war zone and the deactivated collars around their necks did not help.

Thomas reached out with the glove Garrett had loaned to him. "Ariock," he said. "Let me remove your collar."

Ariock obligingly lifted Thomas. His giant-size collar dropped away. Next, Thomas freed his own neck.

"The Torth are running!" Garrett parked the hovercart nearby. "That means we absolutely need to run, too. We have less than five minutes until Armageddon! Forget saving anyone. We'll be lucky if we survive!"

Alone in the middle of Bloodbath Plaza, Evenjos snarled. Perhaps she'd detected something like an impending bomb drop, because she did not give chase to the enemies. Instead, she hesitated. She seemed to weigh a few inner options.

Then she grew.

Her lower body spread into an amorphous tangle of darkness. The rest of her shot upward. Her skin became stone, cracked and faceted. Her elongated mouth scissored open, like an impossibly huge construction crane. She no longer resembled anything remotely human.

Ariock stepped back, staring up at the monstrosity that Evenjos had become.

The clouds flickered. In that flicker, the misshapen silhouette of Evenjos slithered overhead, slow due to her titanic size. She raised one enormous claw and stabbed a building.

"Holy mother." Garrett gaped upward. "She's magnificent!"

He sounded like he meant it.

Thomas had to agree. Whether by accident or on purpose, the Evenjos monster was protecting them. She probably had no idea what a nuclear bomb was, yet detonations must be taking place above her, in the stratosphere, or in the mesosphere, or higher. She was positioned to shield her rescuers on the ground.

Torth panicked. The Commander and her Servants of All boosted their speed with powers, flying over the crowd and vanishing into the Stratower. Red Ranks skidded and struggled to follow them, to hide indoors.

A few Red Ranks whirled around, no doubt driven by commands from the Majority. They aimed their heavy-duty blaster gloves at the monster, but Evenjos no longer existed in a comprehensible form. Her clawlike legs supported a body that was cloaked above the storm clouds. Her wings stretched into the clouds, darker than a storm, wider than the sky.

When she screamed, distant bridges wrenched apart.

Many of the remaining Red Ranks scattered. The Megacosm offered endless vacation options, and if these Torth chose to spend their final seconds in bliss instead of in reality, well, Thomas understood. It was nice to be able to live vicariously through other people's minds.

A few staunch Red Ranks remained planted in reality. They turned their blaster gloves toward easier targets.

Kessa fired back. Jinishta wielded her scimitar, but that was futile, so she hid behind Kessa.

Ariock hugged Thomas close, shielding him from blasts. Determination glowed in him like a nuclear reactor. "Tell me how to save them."

"All right." Thomas tried to sound confident. "You blocked that laser, good, so search for anything that feels unnaturally dense. You're going to siphon off the energy by drilling a hole—"

Garrett made a growling noise, as if disgusted with himself. "I can help." He moved the hovercart close, then used his staff to haul himself even closer to Ariock and Thomas. "God, I hate being powerless."

As soon as Garrett was within Thomas's range of telepathy, knowledge, heretofore unknown, compiled in Thomas's mind.

Thomas gawked in stunned amazement. He would never have guessed that a holograph simulation power was possible.

It was all about manipulation of light waves. Vapor, light waves, and strong visualization skills. Garrett could blow smoke rings and make them morph into whatever shapes he imagined. Apparently, he suspected that Thomas was capable of doing the same.

Thomas did not waste time thanking the old man. Nor did he try to force him to stay nearby, although he yearned to pump Garrett for more information.

The rain gave the air a slight mist. Thomas tentatively spread his awareness into that vapor.

There was no time to coddle himself. Thomas was aware that his warning headache might return at any second, but he had to risk it. Cherise and Vy and Weptolyso were suffocating. Their time was limited.

Thomas visualized the krytron trigger in intimate detail, as well as its surrounding mechanisms. He mapped a mental blueprint of what Ariock needed to do.

Then he projected that blueprint in perfect detail.

His illusion—his holograph—hung in midair, its components drifting only slightly. No doubt this was a lot more advanced than the smoke shapes Garrett was capable of. Thomas was able to keep track of the way light waves bent.

"Like that." Thomas used his heat power to nudge water vapor this way and that, optimizing the illusion.

Ariock did not waste time gawking. Thomas sensed that Ariock was impressed, but he was too sensible to let it distract him from the task at hand. He set to work.

The technical parts of the process made Ariock emanate alarm. Thomas did what he could to soothe Ariock's nerves, complimenting him, talking him through each step. "That's right." He updated his projected illusion while Ariock worked, rotating it whenever he sensed that Ariock wanted a different view. "Okay, now seal off that . . . closer to the valve. Yep. You got it."

Working together like that, they defused the bomb within a minute.

Light wave manipulation seemed to cost Thomas very little effort, much to his relief. It was less draining than wildfire or glaciation.

This holograph power would be impossible for anyone with an ordinary imagination.

Normal people could not keep track of light waves with the ever-shifting variables of wind and rain and darkness while also holding a rich visualization in mind. Only a supergenius could subitize enough to reproduce an architectural rendering, or its equivalent design, all by himself.

Thomas let his projection dissipate in the rainy air. "It's just an inert cube now. Take it apart. Set them free."

Ariock tore the cube apart. He was hasty, yet careful to pull debris away from life sparks.

Soon the cage was exposed. Their hostage friends lay on its floor, unmoving.

Ariock ripped away tubes and nozzles and cracked open the plexiglass walls of the cage. Thomas sensed that his attention was partially in the sky. Ariock was wary of bombs, although the Evenjos monster seemed to be handling them.

Was she swallowing nukes? Batting them away? Disrupting launches?

The monster stalked farther away, wrecking buildings. To her, Thomas knew, this world resembled an obscenely wrong mirror of the land she used to love. Did she assume that all the people who lived in Stratower City were twisted enemies?

That would explain why she was lashing out indiscriminately. Slaves must be screaming in terror. She was killing people by the thousands.

"Ariock, we can heal our friends later." Garrett stood at the helm of the hovercart, plainly eager to get moving. "We're targets here."

But Ariock gently set Thomas down in the hovercart, then went to his friends. He knelt and healed them one by one. Vy. Weptolyso. Cherise. Yuey. Flen. They picked themselves up, gratitude shining in their eyes.

They must have been terrified, choking on gas. Thomas didn't want to absorb their recent memories.

"Healing is an intensive power." Garrett sounded frustrated. "You're draining yourself."

Ariock clearly didn't care. He looked proud of a job well done, although he was streaked with blood and grime from the rain. His wraps were in tatters.

Before he could rise to his feet and tower over everyone, Cherise flung her arms around him. Ariock was surprised into a smile.

Nobody looked at Thomas that way, of course. He was just the sidekick.

Vy approached Ariock, but she stopped short of hugging him. "You're hurt." Her tone was soft with worry.

Ariock looked momentarily surprised and confused, as if he'd forgotten the cuts. No doubt he had. But he gazed at Vy as if she was the solution to all his problems, and he offered a self-deprecating grin. "It's been a rough day," he said.

"The day's not over." Garrett motioned for everyone to join him. "Come on. Chop-chop!"

Vy hurried aboard the hovercart. As she gazed at the rescue crew, she winced at the bruise on Jinishta's face.

Garrett snatched his blaster glove away from Thomas. He used it to release the collar around his own neck, then tossed the collar away into the night.

The rain was worsening. In addition to the unnatural flickers of nuclear detonations in the stratosphere, lightning webbed the city in near-continuous sheets.

"Did you find the Lady of Sorrow?" Vy asked.

Garrett pointed at Evenjos in monster mode. "There she is. We can chit-chat later." Everyone was on board except for Ariock, and Garrett yelled at him. "Hurry up! The Torth know we're here."

The sky flickered blindingly, underscoring his words.

An enormous object hurtled out of the night sky. Thomas braced himself for an impact, but the thing was high above him, and it seemed to go on forever.

It was the serrated tail of the Evenjos monster.

That tail could have belonged to a titanosaur, knobbed with enormous bone spikes, except it was larger. It slammed against the Stratower.

Everyone except Thomas cringed. No doubt they expected a spray of heavy stones, but the impact only knocked loose a few sludge stalactites. The Stratower itself remained undamaged and unchanged. It was one of the most indestructible terrestrial buildings in the known universe.

The monster that was Evenjos screamed in apparent defiance. She lost bodily cohesion, and then she coalesced again.

Madder than ever.

A new sort of darkness began to spread above her. Lightning, and even nuclear flares, could not mitigate the thickening of clouds. The sky bunched up, churning. Rain became icy sleet and hail.

A massive hurricane was brewing.

CHAPTER 16

BEYOND MONSTROUS

Before Ariock stepped aboard the hovercart to join his friends, he took a moment to survey the apocalypse.

Parts of the city were flattened, or raging in white-hot flames that defied the rain. Countless thousands of transports streaked toward the Stratower. Some were knocked spinning from fierce winds. The docking bays must be full past capacity, and the Stratospheric Spaceport had to be a chaotic madhouse. The city was being evacuated in earnest now.

Good.

Ariock was glad to see the Torth fleeing instead of him, for a change. This was how justice ought to work.

He strode to the hovercart and got on board, although part of him yearned to join Evenjos and force even more Torth to run away. Let them suffer. Let them trip over their embroidered robes and cower under their fancy furniture. And let them die.

"Is that really the Lady of Sorrow?" Vy stared in disbelief at the titanic, amorphous form of Evenjos.

The titan stalked across storm-battered fortresses on stilt-like legs, screeching as she went. She knocked over towers. She battered walls with her dinosaur tail. With her crane-like beak, she caught transports and threw them so they crashed into smithereens.

"Yup," Garrett said. "And she is not in a forgiving mood."

Vy stared at the distant titan with a look that was so full of horror, she looked pained. She was seeing a monster.

Was this how she looked at Ariock when he was wrecking things by accident?

As much as Ariock hated the Torth, he inwardly acknowledged that they aimed at legitimate targets. The Torth did not go into mindless wrecking mode. But he did. He had. Because he was a monster, too, and this was what monsters did. They rampaged.

Lightning webbed outward from Evenjos, adding to the chaos. She was utterly indiscriminate in her destruction. Wanton.

"Nuts." Garrett shifted the hovercart into driving mode and circled toward the mob that clogged the Stratower entryway. "Well, the Torth are planning to bomb her into oblivion. I suggest we use this opportunity to bully our way into the Stratospheric Spaceport and skedaddle off this planet."

Thomas lay propped against the railing, in need of some dignity. He looked miserable. No doubt he was burdened by too many nearby minds.

No one had thanked him for his role in freeing the Lady of Sorrow, delaying the Torth, and saving the hostages. Without Thomas, Ariock was certain the Torth would have won today.

Discarded hoverchairs and other items littered the plaza.

Ariock used his powers to seize an upright hoverchair and whisk it on board. Crimson might not be the most suitable color for Thomas—this chair had ridiculous red glitter on its armrests and crown—but it was the only one sized for an underdeveloped boy.

Ariock used his powers to clear off the tarry muck. Gently, he placed a grateful-looking Thomas upon the leathery seat.

"Thank you." Thomas immediately began to look more confident. He settled in, calibrating the red hoverchair. Soon he floated at eye level with the rest of the crew.

"Hey, Ariock!" Garrett yelled to be heard over the sound of rushing wind. "Any chance I can get you to steal a functioning transport? We'd be better off if we can skip the line."

Ariock had no words. Garrett wanted to abandon their friends who were trapped in the Alashani underground, enduring a flood and a Torth invasion and who knew what else? The refugees from Duin did not deserve that.

The Alashani did not deserve that.

Ariock thought of the albino family who were his cousins. Jinishta's sisters and brothers, nephews and nieces. Not to mention Orla and all the other warriors with whom he had sparred. And the nussians he had feasted with. And the councilors, such as Chaniyelem, who had hosted him in her palace. Pung, the smuggler. Varktezo. And so many other people.

"I set her loose," Ariock said numbly. "I gave her power."

Garrett glared at him. "You did the right thing."

Vy gave Ariock a look of fresh concern and scrutiny. "You gave her power? What do you mean?"

Ariock only shrugged, allowing her to see his guilt. If he apologized for every wrong thing he had done today, they would never get anywhere.

Bloodbath Plaza heaved and rolled like a monstrous shrug. Metal cracked apart.

Ariock sensed the earthquake a second before it slammed through his location. He plunged his awareness into the ground beneath their hovercart, just in time to keep them from sliding into an abyss.

"My people." Jinishta curled up in a ball of devastation.

Garrett drove their hovercart, skirting dangerous fissures and debris from wrecked transports. "We have got to get off this planet before the Torth turn it into pavement. They're evacuating all cities now. Not just this one." His tone had a warning edge to it. "I'm sorry, Ariock, but it's too late for the Alashani. They're goners."

Vy looked aghast.

"The Torth abducted a few dozen of them," Garrett said, as if that was any kind of comfort. "How about if we focus on rescuing those guys later? Like, when we aren't running for our lives?"

Hailstones the size of baseballs began to rain down.

They shattered against Ariock's shield and broke harmlessly beyond the hovercart. Anyone who happened to be caught outside in this hailstorm— anyone without Ariock for protection—would be maimed and probably killed.

It's Duin all over again, Ariock thought. Except this time, it was infinitely worse. Instead of abandoning a slave village full of desperate ummins, he was supposed to abandon an entire civilization to annihilation. How could he do it?

The distant monster of Evenjos tore through a building, leaving a trail of wreckage and countless bodies in her wake. She had made herself into a brute force of nature with no more intelligence than a natural hurricane or earthquake.

Should Ariock flee in a luxury spaceship while Evenjos destroyed this city's population of innocent slaves?

And what were the Torth going to do to her? Once she ran out of energy, she would be helpless. Was Ariock supposed to abandon her as well?

"I'll be right back," Ariock said.

Garrett screamed for him to stay, to not be an idiot, but Ariock had already vaulted over the hovercart railing. He didn't care about the breakneck velocity of the vehicle. He injected his body with extra strength, Alashani-style, and flipped in midair to bleed off excess speed. He landed on his feet.

He wasn't sure if he could grab the attention of the titanic Lady of Sorrow, and he certainly didn't know how to handle her if she turned her violence against him. All he knew was that he had to try.

"Evenjos can take care of herself!" Garrett braked the hovercart, making it skid. "We can't delay!" He reversed, trying to catch up with Ariock. "The

Torth are evacuating this planet. Don't you understand? They have a limited number of space shuttles. We need to grab one before it's too late!"

Ariock centered his awareness and steeled himself. He would stick to his word, no matter what. He would save the Alashani, and the slaves of this planet, even if it killed him.

He didn't know if he could transform his body the way Evenjos had. But he knew how to make himself monstrous in his own way.

He hammered his fists down and connected to the metal and stone of the Plaza.

He sent his awareness branching outward like a web of lightning, through fissures, then throughout the passageways of the city. Life sparks danced through his veins.

Ariock twisted into the city for miles, seeking airy spaces that were devoid of life sparks. He was so vast, he barely felt the tornadoes that raged against his various parts. The pummeling hailstones were nothing to him.

He gathered areas with which to form a gigantic voice.

"EVENJOS."

His rumble shook the city. Destabilized pillars collapsed. Stonework cracked. Debris slid off broken balconies in mini-avalanches.

Evenjos ignored him, as mindless as a beast. Her immense tail smashed through a forum and destroyed multiple stories full of screaming people.

Ariock heard tiny, distant voices, insignificant in size. But they were distinctly the voices of friends.

"Ariock is right," Thomas was saying. "We shouldn't abandon Evenjos. She's one of us."

"Well," Garrett replied, "who knows if he can stop her? A timid little hallo isn't going to cut it."

Grim, Ariock added to his stature. He inhabited buildings, making them his muscles, tendons, and bones. Water flowed through pipes, irrigating different ecosystems inside his vast body. His awareness filled struts and frameworks.

He continued to stretch, fitting himself into buildings that had withstood eons of constant rainfall. Metal twisted and cracked. Stone crumbled as buildings realigned themselves slightly to fit the contours of his body. Thick coats of toxic tar comprised his skin.

"She doesn't understand what the inhibitor is," Thomas's distant voice said. "Ariock needs to intervene, or else they'll figure out a way to harpoon her with it."

Transports circled the titanic version of Evenjos like gnats. Indeed, she seemed unaware of the danger they posed.

"EVENJOS." Ariock slowly held out his arms, trying to be inviting. Each hand was larger than a cliff. Steel struts screamed and broke, and walls crashed. Canals and plazas cracked from his weight.

He had to focus on all the tiny life sparks within him. He sheltered people hiding out in parts of his immense body, memorizing their locations. He wanted to treat them gently.

Evenjos swung her enormous, elongated head to confront him. She was eyeless and earless. Her jaws could have swallowed a thousand people.

Ariock unfurled plumes of smoke. He connected with the wind and swatted away all the Torth transports, uncaring if they crashed and died. He didn't think Torth military pilots would bring slaves aboard those tiny transports.

Lightning strobed from the friction of Ariock's movements. He must be visible for miles, a titan every bit as horrific as Evenjos. He was craggy and unnatural, an immensity who trailed debris. His height would dizzy any human.

What did Vy think?

She would probably never come near him again.

Even Weptolyso must be unnerved. And Kessa. They must think he was reveling in his freakishness.

Ariock didn't want his friends to see him like this.

Ashamed of his own stature, he prepared to downsize. He gently rested each part of himself, ensuring that his amalgam of steel and stone would not crash into the city or crush people once he ceased to inhabit it.

The titan Evenjos went still. She appeared to study him, even without any eyes or any apparent face.

Ariock could only hope she would follow his example and downsize. He rested, mile by mile. Granite and steel settled across the city.

Finally, Ariock dared to withdraw his awareness from miles of matter.

His ordinary stature felt fragile and horrifically constraining. The change was disconcerting. Ariock the person stood, swayed, adjusted his stance, and shifted. He tried to feel comfortable in his own skin.

The Lady of Sorrow barreled into him.

She was back to human size, yet she still did not quite look human. Light throbbed around her. She had those metallic wings, and her satiny gown was molded to a body that now appeared lusciously feminine.

Ariock was off-balance from his own change in stature. He had to firm up his stance in order to hold her, even though she barely had weight. She hardly seemed real.

Evenjos buried her face against his tattered armor and wept. She was so much smaller than him, she could not reach his shoulders, yet her grip was tight enough to injure a normal person.

"It's okay." Ariock made himself sound reassuring.

If only someone else could tell him the same thing.

Feeling quite a bit older than his twenty-three years, he put his arms around the Lady of Sorrow. Each of his hands was thicker than her midsection. How could she feel so fragile? So light?

Yet her life spark blazed in a way that washed out everyone else's.

"It's okay." Ariock couldn't figure out an appropriate way to hold Evenjos, or really, whether a muck-covered human like himself should touch her at all. Wasn't the Lady of Sorrow supposed to be holy? Wasn't she a goddess of some sort?

"Lady of Sorrow?" Jinishta prostrated herself, facing them both. "Please. I beg you. Save my people?"

"The Torth are discussing worldwide annihilation," Garrett reported. "The smart move is to get off this planet ASAP. We cannot save everyone! It's impossible! I'm sorry, Jinishta."

Ariock tried to let go of Evenjos. He was such an oaf, he would probably touch her in an unwanted way without meaning to, by accident.

But Evenjos melted against him when he tried to back away. He could not take a step without letting her slide down.

She seemed pitiable. Although Ariock could not read minds, he sympathized a little bit with what Evenjos was going through. She was new to this era. Like anyone, she must fear the unknown.

Foreboding filled him.

Ariock could not guess what small signal told him a catastrophe was unavoidable. Perhaps it was a tendril of his own awareness that remained connected to the atmosphere above, tasting air currents and temperature fluctuations.

In any case, dreadful certainty overwhelmed Ariock and drove all other concerns from his mind.

He threw his arms up, iron spikes outward, and unraveled his awareness along those trajectories. Shields were second nature to him. He threw all his focus and strength into a monster of a shield. Never mind Evenjos. Never mind his friends in the hovercart.

He counterblasted the vaporizing furnace that scoured Bloodbath Plaza.

Evenjos stumbled back, pushed by the excess energy rippling off Ariock.

The cloud-covered sky glowed brighter than a noonday sun. The clouds were on fire. The bombing tore fortress walls apart.

Ariock collapsed to his knees. The air beyond his superdense domeshield was a death oven.

Evenjos's voice was amplified. "Monsters have this world."

Ariock struggled to pull fresh air from miles away, to render the air breathable. He needed a few moments to recover his equilibrium, although he knew, from bitter experience, that he had to refresh the air immediately. If he failed to diminish the superheat and radiation, then the next bomb would destroy his airtight shield and open him to death.

Evenjos strode away. Light and smoke trailed her, rapidly growing in size. "I shall cleanse it."

Ariock took a deep breath. Someone was helping him clean the air, leaving him with extra focus so that he could scan for more bombs. It had to be Evenjos.

"They shall suffer as I suffered." As Evenjos spoke, her feet and gown disintegrated in a swirl of dust. "Tenfold."

"Stop her!" Thomas shouted.

But Evenjos disintegrated before Ariock could figure out how to hold on to her. She became dust. Her wings, hair, and head fell apart into particles, which then shot away in flashes of light.

"Intense." Garrett shivered. He actually sounded admiring.

The ground heaved. Smoke coalesced over flattened buildings, so dense it looked liquid. The sky churned, dropping hailstones as large as basketballs. Those ice balls were probably radioactive.

"I don't think we can reason with her." Thomas sounded grim. "And she's going to destroy this world if the Torth don't. She's traumatized from millennia of imprisonment, and she wants retribution."

"My people." Tears made tracks on Jinishta's bruised and dirty face. She knelt toward Ariock, facing him like a worshipper. But there was no hope in her gaze. Jinishta had learned that Ariock was nothing but a failure.

Ariock tried to see through the storm, to figure out how he might soothe Evenjos. He wondered if even the Torth would be able to stop her. The inhibitor was designed to penetrate biological flesh. Evenjos had become a billion particles of dust. She was a storm.

"I'm sorry." Garrett sounded more sincere than usual. "Believe me, I wish we could save everyone. But we have limits."

Jinishta watched Ariock with quiet, nearly extinct hope. "If you ever had any will to be the savior," she said, "I beg you. Please. Please? Save my people?"

Alashani must be dying by the thousands. Drowning. Collared as slaves. Attacked by panicked hordes of wild zoved. Dying in hailstorms, earthquakes, and radioactive shock waves. Soon they would be flattened by a nuclear bombardment, plus whatever apocalypse Evenjos felt like bringing.

Ariock was responsible for all those calamities.

How could he even contemplate the idea of escaping in a luxury stream-ship while his Alashani cousins screamed and died? While their cities crumbled and flooded? While innocent people died by the millions?

A voice of hope came from an unexpected source.

"There might be a way to save the Alashani," Thomas said.

CHAPTER 17

KNOWLEDGE TO THE RESCUE

Ariock hardly dared to breathe for fear of distracting Thomas.

Everyone else looked disbelieving, and that was fair. It did seem unlikely that Thomas would want to save the people who had imprisoned him and nearly let him die from neglect.

Thomas did not like the Alashani. And they liked him even less.

But Jinishta seemed to overcome her last vestiges of revulsion. She threw herself to the floor at the foot of Thomas's crimson hoverchair and begged. "Can you save my people?"

Thomas nodded.

"This is insanity!" Garrett sputtered. "Whatever you're thinking, get it out of your head. We can't protect an entire world! Even if we could, the Alashani would just get enslaved the instant we leave!"

"Unless we take them off planet," Thomas said.

Jinishta looked like she was rediscovering hope.

Garrett's mouth worked. No doubt he had a dozen counterarguments, but Thomas went on.

"The Alashani can't stay underground. And they can't stay aboveground right now, either. They need an ark. It's the only way to save them."

"Please." Jinishta gazed at Thomas with determination and fresh hope, as if she had found a new messiah. "What can I do to help?"

"We need a colony ship." Thomas's yellow eyes had a calculating look. "That's the only type of vehicle large enough to hold the entire population."

Ariock did not like the idea of stealing a starship and slaughtering every Torth aboard. The Torth would likely use nussians as kamikaze troops and slaves as living shields. It would be a bloodbath. He would almost certainly end up killing slaves by accident.

Was that much death worth it to save the Alashani?

Vy seemed to have similar misgivings. "Is there—?" she began, but Thomas must have detected her question, because he answered before she could finish.

"There are no colony starships within an attainable distance. I'm not talking about stealing one from the Torth. We have plenty of raw material to work with—a whole planet's worth. And we have blueprints." Thomas indicated the destroyed skyline, where a few intact buildings teetered. "The real challenge will be constructing such a gigantic ship in a short amount of time."

"Oh my God." Garrett gawked at Thomas as if he was a freak.

"There's an astronautical engineering office in that building over there," Thomas said. "Every hub city contains repositories for diagrams. That office will include starship assembly blueprints."

"Are you kidding?" Garrett said. "We don't have time for you to absorb a zillion manuals on how to construct a starship!"

"I'll just need twenty minutes at the terminus," Thomas said, completely ignoring Garrett. "I can absorb data fast."

Cherise regarded Thomas with a strange, speculative expression.

"Why do you even want to save the Alashani?" Garrett demanded.

Most of the crew must be wondering the same thing, because they exchanged glances. Kessa studied Thomas with an alert, probing gaze.

"I don't care about the Alashani themselves," Thomas admitted, unapologetic. "But I'd rather not let their knowledge disappear. If that means saving the people, then it's worth doing."

"Please." Jinishta clutched at Thomas's feet, then seemed to remember how fragile he was and clutched the air instead. "Tell me what I can do?"

Thomas looked embarrassed by the wild hope aimed his way. "We need Ariock's cooperation."

"You have it," Ariock assured them. The framework of the plan seemed obvious. Thomas had that marvelous power to project holographic visualizations. He had guided Ariock through defusing that nuclear cube. Constructing a massive starship would be the same process, only more complicated—and a lot more ambitious and exciting.

"This is incredible!" Vy's eyes sparkled.

Ariock inwardly agreed. Thomas's gambles had a way of paying off.

"It's madness!" Garrett sounded like he was choking on his own disbelief. "You're talking about evacuating an entire planet! Who's going to shepherd all those people? We don't have time!"

Thomas turned his yellow gaze to Jinishta. "Would you command a few Alashani warriors to protect me while I absorb the blueprints?"

Jinishta stood. Despite her bruises and scrapes, she looked more determined than Ariock had ever seen her. "You will have as many warriors as you need."

"Ten should be sufficient," Thomas said. "They'll need to be vigilant and shield me from damage."

Ariock figured that he could shield Thomas better than any number of warriors. "I can—" he began to say, but Thomas cut him off.

"You're going to be flying from city to city, rounding up the Alashani into departure zones. They need to be ready to board the starship as soon as it's spaceworthy." He turned back to Jinishta. "You'll need to choose your warriors wisely. While I'm soaking up the blueprints, I can't be distracted by worries that your people might stab me in the back or chop my head off."

Jinishta took no offense. She even looked ashamed of her people. "I will make sure they understand."

Garrett stared defiantly at everyone. "Look at Ariock. He's exhausted! And he's injured! He can't construct a giant-ass colony starship right at this moment!"

Ariock tried to look energetic. Any risk was worth it for a chance to save millions of people.

"Healing him should be a top priority," Thomas said, acknowledging the concern. He turned to Jinishta, but before he could ask, she was already nodding agreement.

"When we return to my people," Jinishta said, "I will make sure he gets healed."

"You can't replenish raw power!" Garrett sounded apoplectic. "Healing will help, but it's not like starting him fresh. He hasn't had any sleep. He got scoured by hydrogen bombs. He needs some time to recover!"

"Let's do this." Ariock wasn't going to listen to negativity. He would save the Alashani even if it killed him.

Thomas gave him a nod. They were on the same page. "Take us to Hufti."

Radioactive storm clouds roiled overhead, spewing hailstones. The liquefied air formed a tornado that must be miles wide—easy enough to avoid.

Ariock pushed his awareness into their hovercart. He had a long way to fly and a lot of people to save.

Flying a platform felt almost familiar by now. It was like wearing a comfortable suit of armor. Ariock maintained his bubble shield over their hovercart, protecting them while they soared over a scorched and radioactive city.

Bombs lit the clouds. None hit the ground, thanks to the hurricane of Evenjos. Hailstones the size of basketballs crashed and shattered everywhere. A black downpour hid anything that was not on fire, so Ariock had to navigate by his Yeresunsa awareness.

It seemed Evenjos was amping up her rage. Ariock wondered if anything could stop her.

Had he tried hard enough?

The problem was, deep down, Ariock was afraid to be more forceful in gaining her disembodied attention. He always seemed to exceed whatever limit people said he was supposed to have. He didn't want to become ever more titanic, scrambling to grab her.

And he suspected that Thomas was right about her mind-set. Evenjos had been mistreated for unfathomable eons. Now that she was uncaged . . . ?

At least her wrath was aimed mainly at the Torth.

She would likely never return to her ineffectual, weeping ghost state.

"Hufti is that way." Thomas pointed, floating next to Ariock in his newly appropriated hoverchair.

Ariock banked in that direction. He didn't want to imagine the lamplit cities wrecked and ruined, and he feared what he would find. Flooded cave-ins? Millions of corpses?

"I think there's likely to be a lot of survivors," Thomas said. "There's plenty of high ground people can get to, and they would have had some warning. They'd have heard the distant rumble of the flood as it approached."

"Right," Garrett put in. "Plus, some warriors have a mild precognitive power."

That was cold comfort. Alashani warriors could not barricade endless tons of whitewater, Ariock knew. Nor could they fly. They could not do half of what he was capable of.

"Mushroom corkwood is buoyant," Thomas said, reassuring. "So their wagons and rickshaws could serve as boats. And the messianic army will do everything possible to help people survive. Most of those warriors are powerful enough to lift people to safety."

They were probably cursing the name of the messiah who'd abandoned them.

"They're probably all gathering in Hufti," Thomas said.

The last lights vanished as Ariock flew their platform over the border wall and into the dead city. He skimmed past heaps of wreckage. The twisted remains of transports mingled with armored corpses from his battle against the Torth, the whole mess battered by large hailstones.

"Listen." Garrett spoke in an unusually gentle tone. He put his hand on Ariock's arm, peering up at him with concern. "I understand why you feel like you need to save everyone. I can even respect you for it."

Ariock pulled his arm away. What would Garrett know about heroism?

Garrett withdrew his hand. "I know what it's like to be powerful," he said stubbornly. "And I'll tell you this: no one else is going to look out for your safety. Not Vy. Not Evenjos. Not the boy. They all depend on you to be mighty and one-of-a-kind. The whole world is crying out for your help. But take it from me: even people like us can reach an end to our strength."

Ariock moved farther away. He wasn't interested in Garrett's thinly veiled attempts to stop him. The old man was definitely an expert on weakness and defeat.

"I just want to remind you that it's vital to take care of yourself." Garrett inched away, unbalanced as the platform sped through the hailstorm, insulated by Ariock's power. "No one else will do that. They assume people like us are invincible."

Ariock decided that even if Garrett had a point, it was irrelevant. The strong were supposed to protect the weak. Therefore, saving people was his duty. It was his moral obligation. Should he ask for help? That would be laughable. And pathetic. Anyone with common sense could see that.

"We are over Hufti," Jinishta said.

Ancient skyscrapers slumped in the downpour, burdened by the shrieking hailstorm and the weight of untold eons.

Ariock caused their platform to hover, resisting the forces of tornado-driven winds. At least he didn't need to waste time hiking around, searching for the hidden entry boulder. Underground crowds glowed to his extended awareness. He sensed life sparks moving in chaotic channels less than a mile below the surface.

A day ago, Ariock would have struggled to shield his vehicle while also holding it aloft during a violent storm, simultaneously protecting a faraway cavern as he drilled through its ceiling. It was a lot to focus on. Combined actions like these were more intensive than operating an aqueduct factory. And drilling through solid bedrock required a lot more brute strength.

Today, however, Ariock had already tunneled through a mile of bedrock. He had shattered the floor of the Stratower. He had resurrected a goddess. He had discovered a lost city, and become a titan, and comforted a monster, and hammered the leaders of the known universe, and absorbed the shock waves of hydrogen bombs, and really, this was just more of the same.

Ariock levitated thousands of tons of rock out of his way.

He tore enormous chunks out of the storm-ravaged ground. He had to spread his awareness far and wide, which felt oddly like a strain. Maybe he could use a short breather before he started to construct a colony starship?

Fortunately, it was all rock and air. Those were his favorite elements to inhabit. Water was the one that gave him trouble, and there was not much of that here.

The ground swirled upward, flying past him while he caused the platform to descend, amid freezing rain and lightning.

CHAPTER 18

SUNBEAM

Chaos reigned. Nussians shoved overladen wagons through the lamplit streets. Door lintels were knocked askew, and some were collapsed. People ran helter-skelter, yelling news or acting as porters. Some people looked shell-shocked. Others looked pissed off.

Ariock knew that he was directly responsible for some fraction of this mayhem. He couldn't help his dramatic entrance, descending through a hole he'd wrenched in the ceiling. People gawped and pointed. They recoiled from the fine mist of toxic rain that drifted down along with his floating platform.

The mist was cold and polluted, but not life-threatening. Just rain. Black drops pattered onto terrified albino people.

There was no point in trying to escape attention. Jinishta would need as much attention as Ariock could give her. So he aimed for the big marble outcrop, the highest platform that overlooked the grand plaza.

A lot of frazzled, angry albinos already stood at the center of attention. High Councilor Chaniyelem gawked at Ariock and his crew.

Ariock reached out with his awareness and very gently moved the councilors out of the way. It was rude to manhandle people, but he figured he would apologize to the councilors later, once everyone was safe. He had a long list of apologies to make.

Once he had cleared enough space, he set the platform down on the marble stage. Finally, at long last, he felt safe enough to withdraw his focus entirely.

As soon as he was back to being solely human, he nearly collapsed. He had to lean on the railing until he regained his equilibrium. The shock of returning to his weak human body seemed far greater than usual.

"Ariock?" Vy touched his hand with concern.

He forced himself to straighten, towering over everyone on the stage. "I'm fine." He must be a particularly freakish sight, dripping with rain and muck and sliced by cuts. People were definitely staring.

"Ariock needs a healer!" Jinishta shouted to the vast crowd below.

Ariock tried to protest, but an argument broke out.

"You took all the healers with you!" one of the councilors snapped. He glared at Jinishta in an accusing way. "Not everyone in your messianic army has made it back home!"

Jinishta turned her stare on him, and the councilor shut up. Perhaps he saw how bruised, scraped, and filthy Jinishta looked. Maybe he saw a threat in her eyes that had never been there before.

Jinishta hopped off the hovercart and strode to the lip of the outcrop. Ariock remembered, from bitter experience, that anyone who shouted from here was likely to be heard throughout the grand plaza as well as the richest bazaars. The acoustics were excellent.

"Warriors!" Jinishta shouted. "Rally to me!"

Her voice was powerfully loud. It rippled across the seething, lamplit streets.

"All the warriors are busy." That disdainful voice came from Chaniyelem. "I don't know where you've been. Or what you've been doing." She approached Jinishta, looking mildly sympathetic about her injuries. "But . . ." Her gaze slid past the premier and focused on the boy in the floating crimson hoverchair. "We've had unprecedented disasters."

The blame in her gaze was unavoidable.

The councilors had no idea that Garrett was a mind reader—they didn't know who he was—so he did not attract all the glares. But Thomas was obvious, and his flashy red hoverchair symbolized exactly what he was and where he came from—the Torth realm.

The councilors, elegantly dressed and disheveled, muttered with outrage. One tried to lecture Jinishta about not bringing a *rekveh* into the city during such trying times.

"Just listen and let me speak," Jinishta said.

Chaniyelem interrupted, steamrolling over her. "Half our warriors are drained because they've rescued people from invading Torth! And more than a dozen of them were captured by Torth! They were collared and taken away."

Jinishta blanched. "Who did they take?"

Chaniyelem was taller than Jinishta, and she drew herself up, imperious. "I will give you a list, but first you should know, the warriors who remain active among us are overburdened. They are healing unbelievable amounts of injuries. They've saved people trapped in rubble from earthquakes. They have to repair vital equipment, smashed by a terrible flood. And you left us, Jinishta." She included Ariock in her furious glare. "You both abandoned us. And now you have the temerity to . . ." Her voice trembled with outrage. "You want to rob us of our remaining warriors? For what?"

Jinishta showed her empty palms. "I'm sorry. But things will get worse."

Chaniyelem looked disbelieving.

"It's true," Ariock put in guiltily.

His deep voice drew attention. The albinos looked at him with varying degrees of dismay.

". . . what?" one of the councilors whispered. She looked shocked by the idea of even more disasters.

"Our world is in terrible danger." Jinishta's face reflected the guilt Ariock felt. Nevertheless, she faced the councilors, stoic. "The Torth are engaged in a battle that may wreck our world, and when they are done, if any of us survive, they will come to collar us. There is no way to stop them. It will happen. We are no longer hidden."

Her grim words were those of a doctor telling a patient of a terminal illness. The councilors looked for a cure.

"Ariock can save us," Jinishta said. "With help from the *rekveh* Thomas. But we need ten warriors to aid our endeavor."

The councilors exchanged appalled frowns. No doubt they felt that a *rekveh* did not deserve the dignity of having a name.

And perhaps they had noticed that Jinishta had referred to Ariock by name, instead of using the reverential title *Aonswa*.

"I would not ask this if it were not vital." Jinishta paced the outcrop. "I need ten strong warriors. They have an important task. If they fail? Then all the Alashani will perish."

Her statement fell on the crowd, shocking, like the sleet that pattered through the hole in the ceiling. She had their attention.

Or maybe it was Ariock who had their attention. He loomed in the background, wreathed in mist from the confluence of outside air mixing with the cave's atmosphere.

Not that he could help looming. Ever since he'd drilled his way into the city, people had stopped their frantic activities and rushed to the plaza, faces turned toward him. Maybe they expected him to announce something?

Warriors began to push through the dense crowd. Black outfits and spears made the warriors obvious, but apart from their outfits, they looked more exhausted than everyone else. Their wraps were in tatters or splashed with blood. Dark bags underlined their eyes.

Ariock tightened his jaw. The warriors were in rough shape from battling Torth and fighting disasters, but they would have to ignore their exhaustion and step up.

A geriatric warrior climbed the stone steps toward the outcrop, wheezing with every breath. "I can heal the messiah." A mantle draped his bony shoulders over wraps that were tattered, soaked, and bloodied.

Ariock figured this old warrior was in far worse shape than himself. "It's all right," he said. "I feel fine."

Jinishta threw Ariock a sharp look. "Don't be foolish. You need healing, and you will take it from Baritch."

"I have a fair bit of energy left," the geriatric man, Baritch, assured everyone.

Ariock backed away, unwilling to leech energy from someone who clearly could not afford to lose much. "I feel strong. I'm sure other people need healing more than—"

A wave of refreshing strength washed through him.

Baritch withdrew his gnarled hands, leaving Ariock feeling incongruously strong, as if he hadn't spent all day battling Torth and freeing the Lady of Sorrow. When he took a deep breath, his healed skin whispered against his wraps. Nothing hurt.

"I am honored to heal the messiah," Baritch said.

"Thank you." Ariock stood straighter. He was aware of being ravenous, and he tried not to think about hot mushroom stew or cave-fish steak.

"Here." Garrett tapped Ariock on the arm and handed him something that looked like a pack of protein bars, wrapped in the clingy fabric the Torth preferred over cellophane.

Garrett shrugged when he saw Ariock's surprise. "I like to be prepared for a variety of situations." He made shooing motions. "Go on, eat up. They're for you."

Ariock figured that a petty argument wouldn't be worthwhile. He peeled off the wrappers and ate each bar in a single bite. It wasn't enough to satisfy someone of his size. The taste, however, was as decadent as what he would expect Torth to enjoy. It was manna from heaven.

"I would have collapsed by now if I'd done as much as you." Garrett gave Ariock a critical look of assessment. "All that healing did was replenish your physical health, *not* your powers. Do you understand?"

Ariock tried not to roll his eyes as he turned away. Garrett was a worrywart, just like Jinishta.

"Please don't push yourself more than absolutely necessary," Garrett said, his tone begging. "Will you promise me that?"

"I'm fine," Ariock said, tolerant.

Jinishta was thanking Baritch for his generous healing. She stopped when he grasped her cheeks in his gnarled hands. The bruise on her face faded to yellow, then cleared away. Her cuts and scrapes knitted and vanished.

Baritch let go, looking self-satisfied, albeit more grizzled and exhausted than ever.

Jinishta drew back her hand and slapped him.

The old warrior placed a gnarled hand against his hurt cheek. He stared at the now healthy-looking Jinishta with pained confusion.

"That is for healing me without any order to do so." Jinishta's tone seethed with rage. "You wasted precious energy on a defunct warrior"—she gestured to herself—"who can no longer join in battle."

Shame entered the old warrior's eyes.

"My powers are disabled!" Jinishta ranted. "*Your* powers are needed!"

Ariock thought the slap was a little harsh, but otherwise, Jinishta's re-action was magnificent. The Alashani could not afford the added chaos of a leadership crisis. Jinishta was stepping up, acting as the premier Yeresunsa, even without her powers.

Because Thomas had asked her to. Because she was desperate to save her people.

Jinishta strode to the edge of the outcrop. "Shevrael," she said, address-ing another filthy and exhausted warrior who had joined them. "Will you amplify my voice, please?"

Ariock sensed the airflow change, optimized for carrying sound.

"Warriors!" Jinishta's voice saturated the cavern. "Do not heal civilians, or any warrior whose powers are depleted or nonfunctional. You must pre-serve your strength. We are in deadly times. This is doomsday." Her voice cracked. "Much worse is to come."

People looked uncomprehending.

Then a panic began.

Well-dressed people dashed about, screeching orders at their servants. Lower-class people ran roughshod over each other, scrambling to gather supplies, to secure family heirlooms, to find loved ones, and to spread warn-ings. The majority of people cupped their hands around their mouths and demanded answers.

Ariock was heartbroken to see people he recognized amid the desperate crowds. There was Pung. There was Varktezo, along with several other ad-olescents from Duin. There was Garrett's erstwhile slave. And over there—Orla. She looked so defeated, so drained, with her powers gone.

An earthquake caused the whole city to shudder.

Off-kilter buildings collapsed. People screamed in the streets.

The violence was over before Ariock could spread his awareness to stabilize every corner of every neighborhood, but it underscored Jinishta's point. The premier Yeresunsa was not spreading needless panic. People needed to accept the reality of what was happening. They had to prepare for the worst—right now.

"I need ten strong warriors!" Jinishta called. She repeated it, her voice amplified by Shevrael's power. "I need ten strong warriors. If you have power, then come join me here. I need you to secure a future for our people."

Grim, exhausted warriors made their way toward the outcrop stage, coming from various directions. They had to push through crowds.

One of the councilors spoke to Jinishta in a cold tone. "What would you have these warriors do?"

"Yes," another councilor said in an even icier tone. "Instead of bracing our city against further damage and healing people who are injured, what would you have them do that is so important?"

Several warriors joined them onstage, looking grim and ready. Jinishta waited until they numbered ten.

"What would you have us do, Premier?" Shevrael asked respectfully.

Jinishta dropped the verbal bomb on them. "Thomas is going to prepare a shelter for all of us." She pointed to the boy, floating in his hoverchair. "You must protect him, with your lives, while he works."

Their reactions were what Ariock expected. Outrage. Disbelief. Shevrael seemed sure that Jinishta was joking. Many people glanced toward Ariock to see if he supported such nonsense.

Chaniyelem went so white, she almost looked blue. "What does the messiah say about this?" she demanded.

"Jinishta is right," Ariock said simply.

"The *rekveh* Thomas is on our side," Jinishta said, her loud voice daring anyone to fight her. "He has proven it to my satisfaction. He is going to save our people, and I trust him to do so."

People exchanged looks of anger and confusion, checking with their neighbors to see if they were just as confused.

"What about the messiah?" a councilor demanded. "Isn't he the one who is supposed to save us?"

"Ariock will do his part," Jinishta said.

This time, no one could mistake her lack of respect for the messiah. Ariock did his best to look supportive and willing, but people grumbled. Very few Alashani would discard their respect for the Chosen One named by their prophet. Fewer would trust a *rekveh*.

Distrust swept through the warriors and councilors.

"We don't have time for arguments." Jinishta pointed to the warriors and named ten of them. "You will go with Thomas."

"This is preposterous!" a councilor said.

"Beyond preposterous!" another shouted.

The warriors sized up Thomas in his hoverchair, no doubt wondering what witchcraft he had worked to gain the trust of their premier and the messiah.

Chaniyelem's tone was uncharacteristically hard. "What do you expect us to do while you take away our best warriors and go off with the *rekveh*? Are we supposed to cower here and wait? While the world falls apart?"

Jinishta met her steely gaze. "You will gather your loved ones. Gather supplies. Get ready to go to another place."

If the people had been outraged before, this was the last straw. The masses shouted, demanding explanations.

"Where do you expect us to go?" Chaniyelem appeared to be struggling with a new reality. She might be asking just for herself, but her question echoed that of the crowds. That was the topmost question amid angry shouts.

Uncertainty entered Jinishta's face, and Ariock realized that she could not answer. She did not understand what a starship was. Alashani had no concept of stars or ships, oceans or space. They never left their caves.

So Jinishta faltered. "Uh, a place of safety," she said, backing away from the thousands of people with despair and anger burning in their gazes. "You'll see."

Common laborers, mothers holding babies, fathers with small children, ummins and nussians, upper-class merchants, artisans, maidservants, warriors, councilors . . . all were desperate for an answer. Something not vague. Something they could believe in. Something to give them hope.

"Where?" someone shouted.

"Where?"

Others took up the cry, angered by the lack of clarity, while floods and earthquakes ruined their homes. Many focused on Ariock instead of Jinishta. It was plain that they wanted reassurance from someone they could believe in.

"Where can we go?"

Hurricane winds ripped through the ruined ceiling, shaking rocks loose. Beyond the rough opening above, enormous clouds churned with unnatural speed.

"Where will you take us?"

The force of the wind tore the clouds asunder. A beam of sunlight caressed the plaza.

Not lamplight, not lightning, not artificial searchlights, but actual sunshine. The violence of Evenjos's storm had given the true sky of this world a chance to peek through.

Sunlight touched white hair and sparkled on diamond jewelry. The sunbeam shone through rain and mist, down through the funnel Ariock had drilled, shedding a never-before-seen light into the Alashani underworld.

How many millennia had passed since this world had last experienced natural light? The sight stirred wonder in everyone. Albinos stared in dumbstruck awe. Their cries of "Where?" fell silent.

The light played across the stage and illuminated Ariock.

That gave him an idea of how to assuage their fears, how to get them onboard.

"To light." He raised a hand toward the heavens and extended his awareness along that trajectory. "And glory."

He widened the hole in the ceiling so the masses could see the ruinous remains of skyscrapers far above, lit by that sliver of blue sky. They blinked and stared. Most were seeing the outside world for the very first time.

Rushing clouds blotted out the sky and covered the dead city. The ray of sunlight vanished.

But the Alashani people no longer looked afraid. They knew their ancient prophecy by heart. The messiah was supposed to lead them to light and glory.

They looked determined.

Ariock felt confident enough to forget his own desperation for a little while. He was ready to forge a new future.

PART FOUR

"You will kneel before destruction. Your cities will blacken with rot. Rain will poison you, and your children will grow ignorant and feeble and hide in burrows like animals. Weep for your future. I see a shadow that blights a thousand generations."

—fragment from the Prophecies of Ah Jun

CHAPTER 1

MORE OF A SUPERGENIUS

Thomas relished having a hoverchair again. It meant equality with the rest of the crew, at least in terms of individual mobility.

He sped through a spacious, airy office, the Torth equivalent of a co-working space. Icy wind tore through the partially wrecked building. Citywide power was out, and dead workstations lined the enormous transparent wall, with its spectacular view of the Stratower.

And the apocalyptic storm. Tornadoes raged across the city skyline. Fiery geysers erupted out of cracked plazas, spraying red fans against the doomsday darkness. Bombs made the sky flicker. Perhaps the Torth were trying to shoot inhibitor darts into the storm, but nothing seemed capable of stopping Evenjos.

Vy clung to the back of his red hoverchair. Hitching a ride might not look dignified, but he knew it was more pleasant for her than walking on her peg leg.

As he glided to a stop at one of the workstations, he sensed Vy's curiosity. Why this workstation and none of the others?

"Garrett gleaned the info from the Megacosm," Thomas admitted. "He let me know which workstation has the astroengineering blueprints we need."

It was galling to Thomas that he needed to rely on someone else for trivial matters of guidance. He put aside his shame, reminding himself that the old man's ability to peek into the Megacosm without being detected was an enormous advantage. If anyone dared to go to war against the Torth Empire, they would want Garrett on their side.

Vy hopped off his appropriated hoverchair. She glanced at the storm outside, and Thomas could overhear her worries.

"Ariock will be fine." Thomas floated around the pedestal of the workstation, searching for a tiny power switch. Most Torth devices harvested ambient electromagnetism as a backup energy source. "If you want to worry, keep an eye out for Torth or other problems. We're not exactly secure here."

"The city looks empty." Vy went to a cushy chair and plopped down. "I saw a few slaves, but they hid."

Thomas had also glimpsed a few unsupervised and stunned-looking slaves, who had darted behind furniture or into slave zones as soon as they saw him in his hoverchair with the retinue Ariock had assigned to him.

Besides the ten grim Alashani warriors, there was Varktezo, armed with a blaster glove and his usual exuberance for learning about technology. Weptolyso had elected to stay with Yuey and help her family. Pung had also stayed behind. But several other ummins from Duin accompanied Varktezo, and they all knew how to shoot.

Garrett limped after the rest of them. He leaned against a doorway, looking like a grizzled guard. "I could teach you how to use blaster gloves," he offered the shani warriors.

The albinos eyed Garrett with deep mistrust. They had suspicions that the old man might be a *rekveh*. Jinishta had done her best to explain the situation, but even so, the warriors remained twitchy and nervous.

Which made Thomas nervous.

If only he could have asked Jinishta to stick around and supervise her warriors. But that was impractical. Ariock needed the premier Yeresunsa of Hufti or else he would struggle to coax various Alashani leaders to get their whole populace packed up and moving. Jinishta's authority and skills would be wasted if she'd stayed with Thomas.

"I don't understand why the Lady of Sorrow is so destructive," Vy said. "The Torth are all gone, right? They evacuated? Doesn't she realize that?"

"The Torth are in the process of evacuating the planet." Thomas located the backup switch for the terminus. He flicked it on, and holographic menus flickered into existence. "But plenty are still around. Hiding. Waiting out the storm, so to speak."

"Okay," Vy said. "But there are slaves here, too. She's killing innocent people." Her disapproving tone made it clear that she trusted Ariock to never do such a thing.

Well, Ariock had killed a few innocent people by accident. But he would never do it on such a huge scale. Or so Vy thought.

Perhaps Vy was right. Perhaps Evenjos was evil and Ariock was good, yet Thomas had doubts, and he found himself wanting to defend the freed prisoner. He understood how it felt to be abandoned and unsure of whom to trust.

"The Torth are attacking her from orbit," Thomas pointed out. "And she's been hurting for a very long time. It's a lot to ask to get her to tell friend from foe. She doesn't know what millennium it is. She doesn't know who we are."

Vy propped her peg leg up and leaned back in the recliner, arms crossed. "So her natural response to confusion is to destroy a city?"

Thomas thought that a lot of people reacted negatively when they operated on incomplete information or ignorance. It was human nature to jump to bad conclusions. When he had failed to rescue his friends from slavery right away, Delia and Cherise certainly had not given him much leeway.

"Is she immortal?" Vy asked.

"I don't know," Thomas said. It was one of many things he was determined to learn.

He parked his hoverchair in the center of the terminus, giving himself the best view of the wraparound holographs. He began to flick through multiple pages. It was his good fortune that starship schematics were too complex to store solely in the Megacosm. If Thomas had needed to ascend in order to learn what he needed . . . ? Well, the Majority would have detected his massive mind and kicked him out.

Starship blueprints and other specialized topics had to be physically stored, usually in data marbles or termini. Few individual Torth—only supergeniuses—could store this much knowledge in their minds.

"Is Ariock . . ." Vy's tone grew hushed and serious. "Is he like her?"

Thomas dipped into Vy's mind, analyzing her anxieties. He wanted to offer truthful reassurance, but he also wanted to make it quick. He had a staggering number of diagrams to absorb.

"I have a theory about superpowerful Yeresunsa." Thomas paged through several dozen blueprints. "Ariock is of 'three bloods.' That's what the Alashani prophecies say about the messiah, and it fits him. He has human blood, Alashani blood, and Torth blood."

"So?" Vy leaned forward, interested. "What does that mean?"

"Let's presuppose that all three races, or species, are distantly related," Thomas said. "When they fractured into different bloodlines, each bloodline inherited a different suite of powers. Like, the Torth have telepathy and wildfire. The Alashani got prophecy and telekinesis."

"What do humans have?" Vy asked, more interested than ever.

"My best guess is that humans are an augmentation factor," Thomas said. "Humans equal raw power. Or perhaps they have some dormant powers."

Vy looked taken aback.

Thomas went on quickly, not wanting her to get sidetracked with concerns about what the Torth Empire might do with humankind should his augmentation hypothesis prove correct. "So," he said, "Ariock did not inherit just one suite of powers. He inherited the full deck. He has everything from all three bloodlines."

"Hybrid strength," Vy mused.

"Right." Thomas skimmed a menu, selecting the most essential blueprints and deprioritizing the luxurious frills.

"Is the Lady of Sorrow a full-deck hybrid like that?" Vy asked. "Is she part human?"

"Who knows what weird genetics she has?" Thomas absorbed several manuals. "But she comes from before the genetic split between Torth and Alashani, so it's safe to say she didn't inherit a divided deck. She probably has qualities that both the Alashani and the Torth have, and maybe some they've lost, as well."

Vy looked apprehensive.

"And my theory fits Garrett, as well," Thomas went on. "He inherited the ideal suite from each parent, with a fast-tracked Servant of All for a father and a premier Yeresunsa Alashani warrior for a mother. He got the best of their powers, combined. And he passed that on to Ariock."

Vy studied Thomas. "You're a hybrid."

Her unspoken question hung between them. *Are you superpowerful?*

Thomas supposed it was possible that spinal muscular atrophy was holding him back, cutting off whatever untapped potential he had. Or maybe his theory had a hole in it. Or . . .

"Maybe I inherited a limited combination," he said. "I could be a tigon instead of a liger."

"What?" Vy gave him a dubious look.

"Ligers grow to be giants," Thomas said, "because they never inherit growth-suppressant hormones. The suppressor genes are on the X chromosome of a lion and the Y in a tiger, so a hybrid born from a female tiger ends up with unchecked growth. But if you swap the parentage—make it a male tiger and a lioness—the offspring is normal size. They're called tigons rather than ligers."

That should be enough to occupy Vy's thoughts for a while.

Thomas shifted his full attention to the holographs, familiarizing himself with the complex wraparound interface. He understood Torth glyphs and coding syntax, but this file hierarchy alone was daunting.

Or it would have been, for most minds.

Wind roared through the office and tremors shook the floor, but Thomas tuned out the chaos and dug in. His task might look casual when compared to everything Ariock had to do, but it was still insanely difficult. He had a very limited amount of time to absorb an amount of data that would stagger even the Upward Governess. He must become an expert in astronautical engineering, antimatter engine infrastructure, quantum mechanics, nuclear fusion, interstellar navigation, advanced life support systems, gravitational emulation, cosmic radiation, solar wind, temporal vectors, and a thousand other topics.

He sped up the display process until the holographic schematics flickered like strobe lights. Every detail stuck in his flawless memory.

"What is it doing?" That was one of the warriors.

Thomas struggled to ignore the albinos, but nevertheless, his scanning slowed by a microsecond. He had specifically asked the warriors to stay at a distance while he worked.

"No one can absorb information that fast," another warrior said.

"It's impossible."

The warriors were within spear-throwing distance, and Thomas didn't like that. They were not supposed to come so close. What if one of them decided to reap his head as a trophy?

"Don't worry, Thomas," Vy said, seeing his distraction. She adjusted her blaster glove. "I've got your back."

"Thanks." Thomas tried to focus. Vy made him feel secure in a way the others did not. It had nothing to do with her combat skills or the blaster glove she wore. Her true value was her status. Most Alashani would think twice before crossing a woman who was considered beloved of the messiah.

His breath came fast. Absorbing this much data, this rapidly, put him at risk for making errors. And astronautical engineering was outside his comfort zone. His preferred expertise centered around neurobiology and neurochemistry, although he had, at least, built up a substantial foundation in all branches of science.

"Is this how Torth learn things?" a warrior said with disgusted fascination.

"It's insane," another breathed.

"Leave him alone," Vy said, answering on his behalf. "Get back, guys. Let him work."

Thomas heard the Alashani shuffle back, albeit not quite as far he would like. These warriors would never obey Thomas, but they respected the "angel from paradise" enough to take orders from her. On a purely pragmatic level, they knew—as Thomas knew—that Ariock might abandon other people to their deaths, but he would never abandon Vy. Ariock was conscientious, and more human, when in her presence.

Thomas refined his own streamlined reference library with each new data point he absorbed. He downgraded nonstructural information, such as materials and strategies, to a secondary hierarchy in a lower level of his mind. Structure had to take priority. He could use his baseline knowledge to substitute or postulate any missing data.

"How can it remember those drawings?" one of the warriors asked, disbelieving. "It is impossible to remember things that quickly."

"What sort of freakish mind does it have?" another said.

Thomas struggled to stay hyperfocused on the task at hand, but unbidden memories occluded his attention. *Freak. What is wrong with him?*

How many times had he overheard thoughts and remarks like that from people who were supposed to be his protectors?

Foster parents. Social workers. Physicians. Psychologists. And now warriors.

They accused him of cheating. Even the ones full of sympathy for a handicapped kid would not accept his mental acuity. Whether he grew someone's investment portfolio, or made a medical breakthrough, or saved a planet . . . people always assumed that someone else was the hero. There was always someone bigger—even if just a vague, shadowy "adult" figure—to take credit for his accomplishments.

Cherise had always made that feel all right. Because she had seen the truth.

Thomas forced himself to dive deeper into schematics and numbers. He was gaining an affinity for astronautical engineering, and he welcomed the mental exercise. After months of deprivation, it was like manna from heaven.

He didn't need gratitude.

Were accolades important, in the grand scheme of things? No. Surely not. The Alashani were a unique and interesting people, and Thomas did not require outside validation in order to save them. He wasn't that pathetic.

Nor did he need a friend to silently honor him and boost his confidence. Cherise had better things to do than cling to the disappointments of her past. She was helping Flen with search and rescue.

Lava geysers exploded beyond the window, and warriors stood behind him with their spears, but that was okay. Reality had to take a back seat for now.

Thomas pushed his speed up several notches, and fireworks of knowledge bloomed inside his mind.

CHAPTER 2

AROUND THE WORLD

Ariock lost track of the cities he visited.

He flew over dead skyscrapers, their skeletons battered by toxic hailstones, with Jinishta tucked under one arm and Kessa nestled in the other. He crossed the shoreline of a sea as black as ink. At one point, he flew over a mountain range, its stony peaks slick with polluted ice.

Whenever he sensed thousands of life sparks moving deep beneath bedrock, he would drill a hole and descend into a lamplit central square.

"I am here to save you," he would announce in the slave tongue.

Then, mostly, he loomed in the shadows, trying not to let his tiredness show as he fortified cavern walls to better withstand rolling earthquakes. He was buying time for the Alashani.

Jinishta and Kessa were the ones with enough mental bandwidth for speeches. They answered questions posed by city leaders, or they gave it a good try.

"You must gather your loved ones." Jinishta's voice boomed unnaturally, amplified by Ariock's power.

She always seemed wobbly right after Ariock landed. Her hair was wild. Either she had a problem with flying, or she didn't like the lack of control.

It didn't matter. The bedraggled mobs no longer cared about perfect coifs or clean tunics. Their cavern palaces and apartments were broken or collapsing. Their aqueducts were flooded, their crops ruined, their livestock drowned. Opportunistic thieves were stealing whatever goods the overburdened survivors failed to guard.

"Fill every keg and canteen with water," Kessa suggested, her voice likewise amplified by Ariock. "Bring whatever you need for survival."

"We have nothing left!" a merchant protested.

"The lower city is completely flooded," someone else shouted. "Our cave sheep are dead!"

Each Alashani city presented its own challenges. Some were hard for Ariock to find, even with his awareness extended. But mostly? It was the people themselves who proved obstinate.

"We just fought off a horde of Torth." A premier Yeresunsa glared at Jinishta, perhaps seeing her as a foreign rival who challenged his authority. "A third of our city population is gone, collared or dead. Now you want us to fight more Torth? And cannibals?"

The crowd muttered angrily.

"No danger can be greater than the danger aboveground!" another premier protested, in the city of Lemlashar. "Our warriors are overwhelmed. I will not ask them to fight mind readers while we await a 'big palace that floats to other worlds.' Whatever that means!"

"We have no choice!" Jinishta snapped.

How Ariock wished he could offer more than uncertain promises.

"The surface?" a councilor sputtered, losing his politician's mask. "It's madness. You cannot seriously ask families to go up there?"

Ariock understood their resistance. The surface was a nightmarish wasteland where even trained warriors had trouble surviving. No one wanted to drag their children or their elders into that deadly realm. And for what? Stars and foreign planets were whimsical myths to an Alashani.

"We can rebuild," one white-haired councilor insisted. "I am sure the danger is exaggerated."

Another councilor folded his arms and glared at Ariock with skepticism. "If this truly is the messiah, then he should be able to reach underground to save us. We do not need to sacrifice ourselves to cannibals, and sludge serpents, and Torth."

Ariock tried to explain that he already was reaching underground to save them. He was doing all that he could. "I need the Alashani in one place."

"Ariock cannot be expected to track down and protect each and every person," Jinishta put in. "We must help him."

But no matter how persuasive Jinishta and Kessa were, some Alashani leaders were simply too rattled by recent disasters to take additional risks. They would not go aboveground, into the unknown. They refused to have blind faith in the messiah.

Were they right?

Ariock shook his head, thinking in circles. He didn't trust himself. But what else could he do other than trust Thomas?

Even if he managed to persuade Evenjos to quit ravaging this world, the Torth would return with vengeance on their collective minds. Ariock could not watch over every individual on the planet. His Yeresunsa awareness might stretch over an as-yet untested scope, but his attention to detail was merely human. He could not stop the Torth from collaring any Alashani he wasn't watching like a hawk.

The only way he could possibly save everyone on this planet was to gather them up in one place.

Thomas had already thought this through.

A major tremor rattled the subterranean plaza where he currently stood. A cracked pillar shattered, its granite pieces crashing to the floor. Bridges collapsed. Alashani whirled into action, running to grab their children and possessions.

"Calm!" a councilor yelled.

"If you have a free hand," Kessa called, "offer to help others."

"This is not a time to show how rich you are," Jinishta shouted at a wealthy family who were abandoning their overburdened maidservants. "We have many more cities to visit. Run. Grab your children, your families, and run to the surface. Ariock will save you. I promise. But if you stay underground? You die."

Ariock used his powers to churn the bedrock where he pointed into a craggy ramp. The angle would be steep for out-of-shape people, such as elders, but it was manageable for rickshaws and wagons. He added a suggestion of crude stairs to each side.

"You have a path to the surface," Ariock said.

The Alashani crowd quieted. People stared at the ramp with dumbstruck fear and awe.

"I am protecting the area." Ariock extended his awareness far upward, into the dead city. He disassembled ancient skyscrapers and rearranged their parts to create a protective barrier aboveground. The interlocked walls of rust should be enough to keep wild zoved from attacking the Alashani population.

"Cannibals will not reach you," Ariock assured the populace. "Hail and sleet will not touch you."

He built the barriers higher and higher, since he knew how well the cannibalistic apes could climb. His barriers met in a point. They formed a massive pyramid.

"I will know where to pick you up," Ariock said to the anxious crowd. "I will look for pyramids like the one above."

That should remind this crowd that they were not the only people who needed saving.

"And now," Ariock said, holding out his arms for Jinishta and Kessa. "If you will excuse me, I have other cities to visit."

"The messiah will return," Kessa said. She had a knack for polite, unassuming reassurances, and people seemed more at ease as she spoke. "He will come back."

"I promise." Ariock made himself sound confident, like he could save everyone, although he had his own doubts. There were dozens of underground cities. He wasn't sure how much his imperfect—ordinary—human memory could handle. What if he forgot a city? What if he forgot a neighborhood or a hamlet?

Not to mention slave zones.

Subterranean outposts would inevitably get left behind. Flooded tunnels made it impossible for survivors to send messages or get help.

How many people were dead already?

Ariock flew to the next city. He raised another pyramid.

And another.

He faced desperate, terrified crowds and defensive leaders.

"How are we supposed to reclaim our lost cities?" one premier Yeresunsa dared to ask, in the city of Entchaggo. He was a lively old man with bushy eyebrows, not unlike Garrett, albeit thinner and albino. "It's nothing but garbage up there."

Ariock inwardly admitted that it was a valid point. The prophecy didn't really make sense.

Jinishta had no answer. She searched for a reply, probably struggling with her own doubts about the messiah and her faith.

Kessa stepped forward. "Your lost cities are not the ruins up there." She gestured all around. "They are here."

Her confidence grabbed people's attention. Everyone in the Alashani underworld believed that slaves were timid and weak willed, and they saw the scar around Kessa's neck. Confidence seemed incongruous for a slave, even a runaway.

"If you are to have a future," Kessa said, her voice amplified, "then you must reclaim what you have lost—what you are losing right now." She pointed up the ramp, at the stormy world above. "Remember. Follow him or perish."

She quoted the ancient prophecy as if she was a prophet herself.

The lively old premier lost his doubts. He nearly bowed to Kessa, then turned slightly to aim his bow at Ariock. "We will rebuild," he said fervently. "With light and glory."

"Light and glory!" his warrior underlings shouted, punching the air with enthusiasm.

Ariock flew to the next city.

Eventually, after half a dozen more lamplit cities in chaos, the crowds of Nyaddish informed Ariock that there were no more major hubs of civilization along the River of Tears. And Ariock figured it was time to pick up Thomas. The boy had had at least thirty minutes to soak up whatever he needed to learn. That had to be enough time.

Once Ariock drilled a ramp for the population of Nyaddish and protected them with a pyramid structure, he sped back the way he'd come.

The planetwide storm was worsening. Evenjos seemed to have thrown herself into a black ocean, causing it to boil. Radiation and lava rained down. Even the wild zoved were driven into a panic, rampaging through the dead city in search of a stable shelter that would not collapse.

A shameful corner of Ariock's mind was envious of Evenjos. Destruction was simple. Hedonistic. Evenjos didn't need to worry about protecting anyone.

It was far more difficult to create, to innovate, to build, and to offer shelter and salvation to untold millions of people.

Ariock was still learning self-restraint. He forced himself to prioritize it. Berserker rages did not require care or focus, and anyway, he refused to put his friends in danger. He was not going to accidentally kill or maim any more people. He cared about people.

What did Evenjos care about?

Ariock remembered how sorrowful she was. Did Evenjos assume that she was alone? That she had no friends? Did she even care about protecting herself?

Someone ought to help her rediscover reasons for hope.

Ariock landed next to the pyramid he had built for the city of Hufti. There, he used his powers to part the barrier long enough to drop off Jinishta and Kessa. He figured they could offer hope and leadership to the evacuees. Kessa was an elder and Jinishta was a premier; both had plenty of experience with taking charge and organizing people.

"Watch over your people," Ariock said, trying to sound reassuring. "I'll be back soon."

"Take care," Kessa told him.

The sympathetic look she gave him . . . it was as if Ariock was one of the millions of now-homeless refugees. He nearly reminded her that he could weather any storm. He was fine. It was the grieving, displaced populace who needed sympathy and support, not him.

But he wasn't going to insult Kessa's good intentions. He managed a nod and then took off, flying toward the data building in Stratower City.

With his awareness plugged into the vast storm, he was able to swerve around lava geysers and tornadoes. He inhabited miles of volatile, irradiated air. That way, he was ready for anything, whether it be a nuclear detonation, or . . .

Or something disturbing.

For a confused moment, Ariock assumed that he was detecting an earthquake at the center of Stratower City. It had the grinding enormity of a tectonic plate.

But it was not underground. It seemed to be in the sky.

Only one structure on this planet was big enough to feel like a mountain. A broken, teetering mountain, off-kilter from the rolling ground.

Ariock flew faster, swerving toward the Stratower.

CHAPTER 3

SHATTERED PRIDE

The Megacosm frothed like a storm-tossed sea. The masses wanted to kill the Shapeshifter formerly known as the Lady of Sorrow, along with the Giant, the Imposter, the Betrayer, the Servants of All, the Commander of Most Living Things, and even those weird albino people.

Kill, the sentiment ran. *Kill all Yeresunsa. Kill. Kill. Kill!*

Inhibitor serum factories worked in overdrive. Skepticism and suspicion were rampant. Trillions of Torth would not be satisfied—would not go back to sleep—until a lot of blood was spilled.

The Commander of Most Living Things glared down at the roiling surface of the planet known as the Torth Homeworld. That apocalyptic storm matched the mood of so many Torth. She had the illusion of being distanced from the chaos. Here she was, standing inside her own tightly controlled environment. She had escaped aboard her private luxury streamship.

Yet she was far from safe. Because she had fled.

Torth should never be forced to flee.

A revolt was brewing. If she failed to regain voter confidence, she would be executed and replaced.

She touched the floor-to-ceiling view screen with one ungloved, skeletal hand. She caressed the famous contours of the Stratower. It shone against its own velvet-black shadow, starkly lit, as if it stood independent from the marbled planet.

Jumper shuttles swarmed out of its tapered pinnacle. Torth still crowded the Stratower, waiting in turns to be ferried to one of the five large battleships in orbit.

Do not panic, the Majority tried to soothe residents of the Torth Homeworld. *There is no need to evacuate the entire planet.*

That was probably true.

A more salient truth was that the battleships in orbit could not absorb a population of two billion Torth.

Low ranks crammed into cargo holds as if they were slaves. They'd ceded the good seats to the higher Crimson and Blue Ranks, most of whom owned the luxury streamships. For their part, the high ranks—and the former elite ranks, such as the Commander of Most Living Things—felt peer pressure to welcome low ranks aboard. The Majority wanted to mitigate this disaster as much as possible.

Local Torth had had to abandon their own slaves, even the most prized ones.

No one wanted to be in the same city as the monstrous Shapeshifter. No one wanted to endure her unnatural storms and earthquakes.

You should have shot the Shapeshifter. The Torth Majority chastised the military ranks, whether they hid inside buildings, waited for a ferry, or sat securely aboard a vessel in space.

The military Reds and Servants of All were defensive. *We were given no warning.*

How could We have guessed—

—that the Lady of Sorrow (or whatever she is)—

—has Yeresunsa powers?

And so much raw strength?

In normal times, the Commander would have ordered the highest-profile military leaders to kill themselves, as punishment for the failure. Now she dared not even berate anyone. The common troops had failed, indeed . . . but the same was true of her.

And everyone.

Hadn't they all made the same wrong assumptions?

Slave-like emotions made people weak and stupid, so it should have been easy to destroy the Giant. They had shot and disabled the Imposter with ease. A second's distraction was all that was needed.

But the Torth Empire had miscalculated with the Giant and the Betrayer. They had underestimated those enemies again.

And again. And again.

For the first time in her long life, the Commander questioned her own fitness for the job of ruling the galaxy. She had welcomed Yellow Thomas into civilization as much as anyone. She had even granted him the honor of sentencing the Giant to death. It had seemed a clever way to test his loyalty. Millions of Torth had helped her form that idea, and the Majority had approved of it.

Then the Betrayer had flipped the whole situation in a way no one quite predicted. And now the enemies were—

!!!!!!!!!!!!!!

The Stratower was falling.

The Commander leaned closer to her view screen, ignoring the faint pixelation that composed the visual data feed. It should be impossible. Lesser buildings might fall, but the Stratower was eternal.

Alarm spiked in the Megacosm from those trapped inside the Stratower.
*!!! * ( ) * !!!*

Screams punctuated multiple news feeds, dominating the landscape of conversations like the Stratower itself. The building was toppling sideways. People slid into each other, smashing against furniture and ornaments or slaves. They tumbled, helpless, into airlocks, or into transport docking bays. A few people got sucked outside, to die a horrible death in the upper atmosphere, or in the vacuum of space.

The Commander stared as the Stratower collapsed into the pillowy cloud covering that part of the planet. Its passage tore a hole through the storm, scraping clouds downward to follow its descent.
!!!!!!!!

The largest structure in the known universe—the iconic backbone of Torth civilization—vanished from sight.

Perhaps it had grown unstable? Perhaps its internal structure should have been better maintained? The Majority only preserved a few scraps of ancient knowledge about the predecessors. Not even the best historians could clarify the hazy degradation of ancient memories. The Stratower was full of mysteries.

Or it had been full of mysteries.

The Torth Homeworld looked strangely naked without its huge spike, like it was just another planet.

One of the monsters *(the Shapeshifter) (the Giant)* must have fractured its enormous base.

The Commander of Most Living Things realized that she ought to make a political remark. She should offer a profound insight, or at least throw out a few empty reassurances to appease the masses.

Nothing occurred to her.

She wasn't sure if the Torth Empire had ever experienced this much upheaval all in one day. A planetwide evacuation? Torth were usually the cause of such terror, never the recipients.

They had faced tough enemies in the past. But all the major battles were ancient history, more than twenty thousand years ago. The nascent Torth Empire had been much fiercer and hungrier, with most of the galaxy left to conquer.

Our enemies are powerful, the Commander acknowledged to her galactic audience. That offered a subtle reassurance that she understood the scope of the problem. She was aware, yet calm. And she was calm because *they are mere brutes.*

The falling Stratower would undoubtedly crush millions of left-behind slaves, as well as millions of slave-like albinos. Torth were not the only victims here. Whichever monstrous enemy had felled the tower, she or he was mindless. The Shapeshifter might as well be a natural disaster.

They lack the advantages of civilization, the Commander of Most assured her listeners. *The Shapeshifter and the Giant have freakish raw strength, but they are like berserk bodyguards. They will eventually grow weary.*

Commentators backed her up.

All We have to do is wait—

—until they are exhausted.

The Commander tapped her skeletal fingers against the glass, her version of excitement. If a nuclear bombardment was not enough to destroy these enemies, then the Torth Majority must realize that they needed her and her kind, the Servants of All. They alone could—

!!!!!!!!!!!!!!!!!!!!!!!!!?

Shock reverberated through the Megacosm, disrupting her musings. The broken Stratower rose out of the clouds, erect.

It balanced there, wavering yet resurrected.

Torth who hid in Stratower City served the Majority as firsthand witnesses. They saw the Giant fly out of the dead city to catch the Stratower before it fully hit the ground. The mass of it had scraped lesser buildings, knocking off spires. Yet the Giant supported its weight.

He stood immovable, sandwiched between the broken wall and the tower's enormous foundation. He looked like a pebble between boulders.

He should not have that much raw strength.

As eyewitnesses watched, the Giant used his immense powers to launch the broken Stratower straight upward.

Never mind that it was larger than anything ever launched from a planet. The Giant propelled it through miles of resistant atmosphere. The structure burned red-hot from atmospheric friction. The web of lightning around it was as brilliant as nuclear detonations, tempered only by extreme distance.

The Commander was lucky to be far away.

The trajectory of the Giant's throw seemed unimportant, until the enormous skyscraper broke free from the mesosphere and hurtled through suborbital space, faster than any shuttle. Then the Giant's aim became shockingly obvious.

The broken Stratower was going to smash into one of the five large battleships.

!!!!!!!!!!!

Panic suffused the Megacosm. Its epicenter was that battleship. Soldiers hurled themselves into emergency escape pods—as if that would save them. Pilots in nearby streamships or jumper shuttles put on illegal bursts of speed, desperate to escape the probable debris field. Everyone else braced for impact.

The Commander of Most Living Things gaped, openmouthed, like a common slave, as the formerly eternal Stratower slammed into the near-indestructible hull of the battleship.

On the scale of planets and stars, they were mere slivers of rock. They were the size of asteroids. But on the scale that sapient life was accustomed to . . . ?

This might as well be a continental collision at high speed, without the friction of air or the weight of gravity to slow things down.

There was no gradual rise of mountains. The Stratower splintered into billions of pieces. Some glinted like crystal. The rocks ricocheted off each other, and off the dented battleship hull, and off smaller vessels in the vicinity, flying in crazy directions and wreaking havoc. The impact knocked the battleship off its orbit. Unexpected torque caused it to shed pieces, losing one of its engines. Its tumbling mass wiped out any smaller shuttles in the vicinity.

*!!!!! * ( ) * !!!!!*

The command crew of the spinning battleship struggled to calculate the best way to stabilize its rotation. Its engines were crippled. Many people and slaves were injured, and they feared that their ship was on a dangerous course unless they could regain control of their trajectory.

Help? They tentatively begged the Servants of All aboard their vessel.

The Commander of Most gave a mental nod to those Servants, encouraging them to do their duty and serve the Torth Empire. Perhaps telekinetics or thermokinetics could save that spinning battleship? It was worth trying.

The death tally was instantaneous in the Megacosm. There was no real need to witness the destruction firsthand, so she turned away from the mayhem on her view screen. At least her luxury streamship was beyond the collision zone.

Today would be preserved in the Megacosm as the worst loss the Torth Empire had ever suffered.

And she was inextricably linked with it, immortalized not for her clever triumphs, but for her epic mistakes.

The Torth Empire would prevail, of course. Civilization always won over nontelepathic savages. But the Commander knew, now, that defeating these freakishly powerful enemies would require more than a space armada.

Servants of All would be needed. All of them.

And more than that—the Torth Empire would need to call upon its greatest strengths, the qualities that had enabled them to defeat alien civilizations. Cooperation. Logic. And most of all: knowledge.

The Commander flattened her mind, smoothing away her various reasons for shame. Ironing out her emotions came naturally to her. She had never needed tranquility meshes.

In that emotionless frame of mind, she cruised the Megacosm in search of supergeniuses. The Upward Governess. The Twins. The Death Architect. And, she supposed, even the younger, lesser supergeniuses.

Just as the stricken battleship crew was begging for help from *(Servants of All)* people they disdained, she would need to do the same.

So would all Torth.

CHAPTER 4

EPIC CONSTRUCTION

Ariock straightened, coated with tarry grime. His hands felt raw. His bones felt like sacks of grinding pebbles.

For a short while, he had become the broken Stratower: billions of tons of rock.

Catching the Stratower before it could slam down and blast tidal waves of force throughout the planet had been almost more than he could handle. He had felt his bones compressing. The weight had seemed enough to crush him.

Then he had figured out where he could throw it.

Ariock dusted off his hands, glad to have gotten rid of at least a few thousand Torth, along with that ludicrously massive tower.

He didn't want to think about the innocent slaves who had died along with those Torth. Dozens? Hundreds? All he could be sure of was that their casualties were not nearly as many as the dead Torth.

Today was disastrous on many levels. Ariock figured he would mourn the casualties later. Perhaps he should have hurled the Stratower into empty space instead? But he was worn-out from making heart-wrenching decisions. Everything he did was a trade-off between something awful or something worse. The tension in his shoulders was not only from catching the largest building in the galaxy, but also, at least somewhat, from stress.

Ariock landed atop the wrecked office building. It was a cinch to detect where life sparks were congregated and then to wrench apart the nearly indestructible roof. Ionic steel, or whatever it was, felt almost as flimsy as tissue paper after the workout he'd just had.

He jumped down and landed amid his friends.

The albino warriors and ummins regarded him with wariness, awe, and fear. That was to be expected, but this time, even Vy looked a little bit frightened.

It must be because of the toxic slime dripping off Ariock. He brushed off excess tar and resisted his urge to slouch or hunch down, the way he used to. Vy accepted him despite his freakish traits. She couldn't be afraid of him.

"Ready to go?" he asked Thomas.

Holographs flickered in Thomas's field of view, each one a hellishly complicated blueprint that appeared and vanished faster than a microsecond. The tandem blueprints were accompanied by a fast-scrolling periphery of Torth glyphs. It was hard to believe that anyone, even Thomas, could absorb information that fast.

"Boy." Garrett limped closer. "You almost done?"

"Done." Thomas spoke without moving or blinking. The holographs continued to flicker in their ultraquick fashion.

Ariock looked to Vy for a clue, and she shrugged. "I guess we might have to tear him away?" she said uncertainly.

"I'm maximizing my time here." Thomas spoke in a cold, distracted tone. "The more the better, but what I've learned is sufficient for structural integrity and baseline functionality."

An earthquake rocked the building. Furniture slid around, wall screens quivered, loose items crashed to the floor, and warriors caught themselves before they could fall.

Evenjos was out there, beyond the horizon. Ariock sensed her power chewing through the tectonic plates of this world, pushing atmospheric pressures to insane highs and lows.

Thomas's hoverchair slid around, but his focus on the wraparound holographs remained steady.

"I just want you to note that this plan is insane." Garrett leaned on his staff for balance. "You're attempting something that has never been done before. And we have an armada of pissed-off Torth who want to murder us. These are less-than-ideal conditions for you to experiment with your powers."

"Noted." Ariock considered polite ways to tell his great-grandfather to make himself useful elsewhere.

"No one has ever attempted anything this crazy," Garrett said.

"Thomas?" Ariock wondered what he needed to do to get the boy's attention. Smash the console?

"Okay, okay." Thomas drew a shuddery breath, like someone emerging from warm water into frigid air. He made a gesture, and the colorful holographs paused, then disintegrated.

That left only dimmed, yellowy orb lamps for illumination. That, and sheets of lightning, as well as lava spouts, all of which glowed against the black clouds.

Thomas rotated his hoverchair to face everyone. "Let's start with this."

A dazzling projection assembled itself in the air where he focused. It was more complex, more tightly packed with details, than any holograph Ariock had ever seen. One of the warriors gasped in awe.

"This is the spinal cord of the ship," Thomas said. "It's an artificial gravity rod wrapped in superionic ice."

Ariock examined the bundle of four segmented, puffy pipes floating in midair. He struggled to envision what materials Thomas wanted him to build with. And at what scale?

"Anything stronger than steel, and noncorrosive, should do for containment," Thomas said. "Incorporate tungsten boride at the junctures. Like here, and here." As Thomas spoke, multiple parts of his holograph glowed, illuminating where he was talking about. "It's a super hard and dense metal." Thomas made a secondary holograph appear. "You can find it in Torth buildings that look like this. And you'll need water for the ice. You can get it from the flooded River of Tears, but make sure it doesn't get contaminated by sludge."

Ariock nodded his understanding.

"The starship will be roughly the size of the Stratower," Thomas said. "Although it will be shorter and wider. Keep in mind that you'll need to support its entire weight. You cannot let it rest on the ground. A colony starship would normally be constructed in space, but we'll have to wait until it's finished and everyone is aboard, or else we'll risk damage from Torth comet-class warheads."

Ariock tightened his jaw. The Stratower had been a difficult mass to support, and Thomas was telling him to do it again, and for a longer duration?

Oh, well. He would manage.

"Also," Thomas said, his holographic projection wavering as he spoke, "the Alashani need a way to get onboard. That's going to be a mess no matter how we approach it. My suggestion is to lower the ship toward the tops of the pyramids you built and extend ramps upward from them."

Of course Thomas knew about the pyramids. Ariock had instinctively stepped within his friend's range of telepathy.

Garrett folded his arms and muttered, "Crazy."

Thomas turned a yellow stare toward the old man. "I can think of an alternative way to get them aboard." His voice had a challenging edge.

"Absolutely not," Garrett said. "That would wear Ariock out quicker than anything."

Neither of them explained what they were hinting about, and they dropped the subject without so much as a glance at Ariock.

"All right then." Thomas refocused on his holographic projection. "We'll construct the ship in stages, but here's a ghost of what it should look like."

Semitransparent overlays appeared. First a framework, like jacks strung together across the bundle of ice cores. Then an exoskeleton. Then unfinished compartments. A patchwork of flooring, on multiple levels. Mysterious engines, more complex than any aqueduct factory. Insulation layers. And finally, a series of interlocked hoods, protecting the rest. That must be the hull.

"That should give you an idea of the scale and scope," Thomas said.

Ariock forced himself to nod in a determined way. He didn't want to invite Garrett's criticisms, but inwardly, he admitted to himself that this task might be beyond his skill level. This starship was more complex and larger than anything he had ever built or managed, by multiple orders of magnitude.

But Thomas did not express doubts. Thomas merely watched him.

Ariock stood straighter. "I'm ready." This construction would strain his ability to multitask, but Thomas had a knack for being right—which meant it had a solid chance of working. It didn't matter what doubts Ariock, or Garrett, or anyone else had.

"Let's start with the sky ramps." Thomas let his ghostly projections fade away. "It doesn't matter what they're made of as long as they can withstand earthquakes and tornadoes. You may need to do some background maintenance on those while you work. Let's get the Alashani moving upward."

Ariock closed his eyes and flooded his awareness outward.

He started with the closest pyramid, but there were dozens of others. Ariock swirled his awareness inside each Alashani zone, one by one, and extruded ramps and crude staircases, with reversals of wall blocks to expose the way upward. The Alashani would have to fend off wild zoved on their own.

Maybe they wouldn't be hassled? A lack of life sparks swarming in the wilds of the dead city told Ariock that the cannibalistic apes had been driven elsewhere. Either they had invaded the underground, which was exposed through massive holes, or they were hidden and scared.

Or maybe the apes were dead from earthquakes and tornadoes and lava geysers.

"We have a lot more to do," Thomas said. "Let's build the core."

His projection of bundled pipes reappeared in all its dazzling detail.

"To make superionic ice," Thomas said, "you'll need to compress the water and treat it with intense pressurization. Insulation is vital. You need to rip ceramic boride out of reservoir wells and use it to coat the containment system." Thomas created a holographic map, showing where to find each thing. "Add packed sediment for a layer of insulation. Sandwich it in, like this."

The holographs animated, detailing each stage of construction for the starship's core.

Ariock allowed himself a deep breath in preparation. He tried to anchor his awareness, so he wouldn't forget who he was. He relished one final moment of being small.

Then he crammed his awareness into everything in sight.

He spun a web across the continent, shrugging into every ruined tower, filling out bedrock, sloughing through grime.

When he lifted his arms, thousands of megatons of debris lifted with him.

He assembled the first of the massive pipe segments, displaying it in the sky beyond the window for Thomas's approval.

"A little smaller," Thomas coached him. "Nope, bigger. That's perfect. Now fill it with water. We'll work on crystallizing it once you have the whole core built."

As the pipe structure took shape, Ariock wanted to admire his handiwork. He caressed every insulating block, every rivet, trying to achieve perfection.

"We're going to have to skip perfection," Thomas said. "Just give it a stress test. Like that, right. Test the joinder."

It went on. Ariock did not always understand what he was building, but when each part was complete, he felt as if he'd just solved a clever jigsaw puzzle.

Sometimes he had to reshape parts in midair, forcing them into alignment. Sometimes he had to refer to Thomas's projection multiple times, double-checking details. A few times, he needed to disassemble something in order to shove a forgotten part inside.

"Let's start the framework," Thomas said. A fresh holographic overlay took shape, its details sharpening. "This will be the gravitational shield. It's crucial to get its magnetic alloy composition just right. I'm afraid you'll have to steal the knowledge of how to build the composite material from ships in orbital space. Can you do that?"

"Uh . . . wait." Ariock inhabited megatons of ice and tungsten boride. He was still stress testing parts of it while smoothing other parts. On top of that, fragments of his awareness remained with the pyramids. Countless life sparks tingled on his skin.

And he had to remain planted in his own core self so he could receive instructions. Thomas seemed distant and insignificant to him, so he forced himself to be present, to study the holographs.

"Let it be imperfect." Thomas sounded impatient. "As long as it's functional, it's good enough. We still have ninety-nine percent of the ship left to build."

Ariock swallowed his doubts. He redoubled his efforts to subdivide himself. "I'm ready."

"Excellent." Thomas went on to describe how Ariock should spread his awareness into orbital space and wrap his mind around how the gravitational shields of battleships were composed. "You can duplicate the material," Thomas said, "with a lot of energy and meticulous attention."

Ariock steeled himself.

"Or," Thomas said, "you could destroy a couple of battleships and repurpose their materials."

The easy way was tempting. But when Ariock thought of the battleship he had pounded with the Stratower, guilt twisted inside him. Slaves died every time he took an action like that. Their lives should matter. They needed to matter, or else why was he fighting the Torth Empire?

So Ariock merely breezed through the battleships in orbital space. He inhabited one for a minute, just enough to study the composite materials he needed to duplicate.

Then his construction went on.

Each additional component of the starship in progress stretched Ariock's focus beyond what he thought he could handle. Distant parts of himself sifted through megatons of debris, ignoring organic matter—corpses—encountered along the way. All that mattered was the construction.

Another holographic overlay appeared. And another. And another.

Garrett watched with skepticism, as if expecting Ariock to fall flat on his face.

"Ariock? Pay attention."

Thomas was relentless with his instructions, restating things until Ariock figured it out.

Even so, Ariock's work was getting sloppy. Sweat trickled down his face, despite the ice storm raging outside. Part of Ariock marveled at what he and Thomas were accomplishing together. But mostly, he felt strained.

He began to feel desperate to get the whole thing done.

CHAPTER 5

SPACEWORTHY

Vy stood with her arms folded, watching Ariock. He was the most dependable person in existence. When he set his willpower toward making something happen, it happened. Obstacles moved aside. When Vy had lain dying in that nuclear cube, choking to death on toxic gas . . . well, she'd had doubts, but she had known that Ariock would show up in time. And he had.

So why did she feel apprehensive?

Ariock had the distant, intense, glowing-eyed look he got when using his powers on a massive scale. Throughout the ruined office space, small items floated, caught in extra eddies of his power.

"Say that again?" Ariock said tiredly.

"Magnetic plasma generator," Thomas repeated. "For the tertiary reactors. You really need to shift more focus into this."

Ariock looked grim. The instructions he was dealing with sounded overwhelming. The blueprints were insanely complex, and Thomas kept jumping ahead, layering more additions to his mental holographic projection, as if he expected Ariock to process information as fast as a supergenius.

The starship in progress filled the sky. Its immense size gave Vy a queasy impression that outdoors was indoors. It blocked the hailstorm completely, although the ground continued to quake and ooze lava, and fires burned here and there.

She had seen Ariock catch the Stratower just before it flattened the city. He had saved them all. He must be able to hold up this new structure.

"Round out that fulcrum point." Thomas looked as tired as Ariock, and Vy remembered that he was still dependent on his NAI-12 medicine. It was a good thing Garrett had magically refilled his supply.

"This represents a thruster." Thomas wove another holograph in thin air, beautiful in its complexity. "We're going to need twenty-two of them."

Vy could only watch in silence, witnessing magic take shape in the sky. Even the most chatty of the warriors allowed Thomas and Ariock to work uninterrupted. They seemed aware that this job could, or would, save their people.

Garrett, too, was respectfully silent.

"A gyro looks like this. They're going inside this. You can repurpose scrap metal for the gyros, and also for this piping and these vents." Parts of the holograph glowed to illustrate. "This part here needs to be ultratough . . . right, like the rubber we used for the antivortex siphon."

The holograph loosened into a fog, then tightened again.

Thomas kept talking. " . . . we'll build an oxygenator here. Use that leftover nitric alloy . . ."

A few seconds later, his holograph went blurry again.

Thomas faltered in his instructions. He quickly regained his equilibrium and kept talking, determined, but Vy switched her scrutiny to him. And she saw a tightness around his eyes.

She recognized that look from her years taking care of Thomas on Earth. Pain.

If she'd had access to a medicine cabinet, she would have offered him some ibuprofen. But all she could do was watch helplessly.

"Good enough," Thomas said, impatient and tense with pain. "Let's finalize the aft fuselages. Scrap metal is fine. Even rock. We'll insulate it in a bit."

He winced. His holograph went blurry.

Garrett watched with sharp concern. "Lela." He snapped at one of the Alashani warriors and pointed at Thomas. "Heal him."

Lela had the milky eyes of blindness. She could not focus on anyone, but she apparently guessed that a *rekveh* was ordering her to heal another *rekveh*, and she hesitated.

"Please?" Vy asked the blind warrior.

Lela began to move toward Thomas, but another warrior spoke in a laconic tone. "It won't help. The warning headache cannot be healed."

"You won't replenish his power, that's true," Garrett snapped. "But an extra burst of energy could give him another few seconds or something."

Thomas was sweating and shaking. He went on as if his holograph was still sharp. "That wall needs to be canted at a forty-five-degree angle. More. That's good. You can fit it against the next one, like . . . right. Make sure they're vacuum sealed together."

Lela approached Thomas with caution. Vy wanted to prod the warrior or outright give her a command.

Thomas gasped when Lela healed him. His holographic projection vanished, but as soon as she stepped back, it returned, crisp and sharp. Thomas's determination returned as well.

"Drill a hole in the subduction zone." The holograph lit up with illustrative points. "That will connect to the ventilation system. You'll . . ." Thomas paused for a wince of pain. " . . . follow this diagram." His holograph lit up in new places. "Vent shafts." More areas lit up. "Gravity wells." Another overlay. "Finish the temporal rudder, like this. Photocells and receptors go here."

Ariock eyed Thomas with unease. Sweat beaded on the sides of his head. Judging by the tension in his shoulders and the uncomfortable way he held himself, he was levitating quite a lot of matter.

Garrett dug into his robe and pulled out a tiny bottle. "Torth painkillers." He handed the unlabeled bottle to Vy. "Give one to the boy."

Colorful designs swirled on the soft glass. Torth products always looked artfully engineered, even when they were commonplace.

"It won't heal anything," Garrett said, "but it might take the edge off his pain."

Grateful for a way to help, Vy shook out one pill and gave it to Thomas, who chewed it eagerly.

"Skip that for now," Thomas told Ariock. "Let's hook up photocells to the steering system. You're going to need to coat them on the thrusters and the sensory equipment outside the hull. You can steal them from any un-damaged spire in the city. Paint them on, like this." His projection animated with instructions. "Then fuse the backing to a twinned magnetic plate. You already did something like this . . ."

Vy had a few swallows of water left in her canteen. She uncorked the lid and held it for Thomas to drink. He was shaking so violently, she steadied him with one hand, helping him to take a feeble sip.

"I'm . . . not sure . . . I can." Every word Ariock spoke was strained and distant.

Disaster scenarios whirled through Vy's imagination. She looked at the tiny pill bottle and wondered if it could help Ariock.

"Does the messiah have a warning headache?" One of the warriors stepped forward, hands in the healing pose.

"No." Garrett assessed his great-grandson with disbelief and speculation. "His focus is just stretched." He whipped out his staff, blocking the warriors to keep them away from Ariock. "Don't interrupt him."

Thomas wheezed with painful breaths. His holographic projections wavered and blurred even as he explained how to build sensor fins and anchor couplings and how to finish the undersides of hull plates. Tears of pain leaked from his eyes.

Ariock's breathing was slow and heavy. Judging by the stone-stillness of his posture, his awareness was far away and spread across a vast area. Vy knew that the giant standing in this office was only a tiny part of what he was currently experiencing.

It was easy to think of Ariock as human. They had watched the same TV shows. They had strolled lamplit Alashani streets together.

But Vy had seen him turn into a titan. He'd caught the mountain-size Stratower and launched it into orbital space like it was no heavier than a baseball.

She could no longer quite minimize his brute strength to an endearing level. Not anymore. He was not performing parlor tricks.

He had power on a cosmic scale. It was scary.

He's learned a lot of restraint since Delia died, Vy tried to reassure herself. *And since I lost my leg. He's a lot more self-controlled.*

Every muscle in Ariock's huge body stood out. His gaze focused on a distance that no one else could see, no doubt rearranging and sculpting huge structures hidden by bulk and clouds.

The holograph vaporized.

Thomas whimpered. "I'm sorry." He doubled over, crying from pain. " . . . sorry."

The warriors exchanged concerned looks. Perhaps they understood the consequences for their people.

"Lower the ship." Thomas sounded rushed. "Connect ramps. Get . . ." His voice hitched from pain. " . . . Alashani. Aboard."

"Is it functional?" Garrett assessed Thomas with incredulity and sharp consideration.

Thomas emitted a squeak that might have been a yes.

Vy realized that they'd all been watching Ariock, worrying what might happen if he ran out of strength. None of them had considered the same problem for Thomas. His airy projections seemed so lightweight in comparison.

"I mean," Garrett said, "does it have working life support? Is it spaceworthy?"

"Most . . . everything." Thomas's answer seemed to require great effort. "Good. Enough. Sorry." He remained doubled over, seeming unable to lift his head. "Thought I could. Last. Longer."

CHAPTER 6

INSIDE THE TITAN

Vy went to Ariock. Sweat rolled down his huge face. His gaze remained distant, but anyone could see that he was struggling. If only she could help him.

"You've got to get the Alashani aboard." Garrett stepped toward his great-grandson, hands out like he wanted to help. "Just get them onboard, and we're done."

A tear leaked from Ariock's eye. Was that from effort? Or was it sorrow for people he could not save?

"He can't hold the ship up forever." Garrett's expression was a study of frustration. No doubt he wished his own powers were not defunct. He had been shot with inhibitor only a few hours ago, although to Vy, it felt like days had passed.

One of the Alashani warriors pointed to the huge window. He made a rasping sound, as if he was too scared to scream.

With good reason.

A tower of black rain whirled toward them, as solid and relentless as a tidal wave. It churned everything in its path to muddy debris. Skyscrapers collapsed and vanished in the miles-wide deluge.

Ariock grunted with herculean effort.

The storm stopped short of their window, shrieking outside, its shape vaguely feminine. Immense arms of wind-driven black rain reached to embrace their building.

And then the tornado broke apart.

It became smaller whirlwinds that spun away, howling. Debris hung outside, suspended by eddies of excess power. Vy did not need to see Ariock's grim face to know he was their protector, the one who had blocked the storm.

Ariock went to one knee. He looked on the verge of collapse.

"He's losing track of it all." Garrett had a faraway gaze, as if witnessing something awful. He was close enough to Ariock to see through his eyes and experience whatever he was experiencing. "They're falling off ramps."

The Alashani warriors watched Ariock with an outsized concern that had little to do with him and everything to do with their beleaguered world. Vy wished she could do something, anything, to help stop the far-away deaths.

Garrett's tone changed, suddenly brusque. "Lift it into space, Ariock."

Ariock looked like someone nearing the end of a death march.

"I'd hoped we could avoid the teleportation option, but . . ." Garrett aimed a questioning look toward Thomas. "Do you think he can learn really quickly?"

Thomas grunted in pain. Maybe that had been a yes. Garrett seemed to take it that way.

"Raise the ship into orbital space, Ariock," Garrett said. "I'm sorry. But your focus is completely maxed out. You're strained past your limit."

Ariock made a sound that might have been dissent.

"If you keep trying," Garrett said, "the ship will crash down and kill everyone." He sounded sympathetic.

Thomas croaked agreement. "Lift. It."

Ariock stood, straining, lifting the unseen immensity. Veins stood out. He trembled from the effort.

Garrett leaned toward Thomas and lowered his voice. "I don't know if it's possible to bring passengers when teleporting, though. I've never been able to."

Thomas's eyes were slitted from pain.

"The biggest thing I can drag through is a suitcase," Garrett muttered, as if defensive against something Thomas had not said aloud. "But fine. You're right. It's worth a try."

The strain Ariock was under seemed to be easing. He straightened. His gaze remained distant and focused, but he blinked. The subtle glow of power cleared from his eyes.

"All right, Ariock," Garrett said. "Now pay attention. You're going to pour all your awareness inside the starship." He held out a fist, illustrating the point. "The trick is to leave your body. I mean, you'll exit your core self."

Ariock looked alarmed.

"Just for a second," Garrett said. "Once you're there—this is important—you'll feel a tug to return to your body. Resist it. Do what you can to force your body to snap to you, instead. Your body plus whatever else—and whoever else—you can take. You might want to prethink this and mentally cordon off the area that includes us." He gestured.

Ariock looked baffled.

"Go ahead." Garrett gave him a friendly, ineffectual shove. "Try it."

Ariock closed his eyes. His brows furrowed with frustration. He was clearly trying. And failing.

"Reassign . . . your core," Thomas wheezed.

Ariock looked considering.

"Close." Garrett watched with academic interest, as if his great-grand-son had become an engrossing movie. "You'll want to stop being so spread out. Withdraw yourself from the pyramids. I know the Alashani are in a predicament, but if you can mass-teleport them, you can save them all."

Ariock looked pained by his own limits and his hope.

"Okay, good," Garrett said. "Right. Pinpoint a specific location inside the starship, on one of the decks. Teleportation requires one hundred percent of your attention. It's like healing, except even more intense."

Both Thomas and Garrett watched him with keen anxiety, one on either side.

"Almost," Garrett said.

"No nexus," Thomas said hoarsely. "Be. Disembodied."

"In the target location," Garrett added.

A moment later, both mind readers spoke at the same time.

"Good!" Thomas said.

"Bingo," Garrett said. "Now do it again. This time, stay disembodied—"

Reality shifted for Vy.

One moment, she was standing in the ruined office building while an apocalypse raged outside. And then, all of a sudden, she stood in a dry, pitch-black, antiseptically clean environment. The sounds of the storm were gone.

The air smelled of ozone.

Garrett continued his sentence, the different air quality flattening his pitch. "—and pull yourself . . . oh!" He sounded pleasantly surprised.

Vy felt light on her feet. Gravity had less of a hold on her. She realized that she was no longer on the Torth Homeworld.

Light strips glowed in the distance, outlining cavernous walls.

The vast chamber seemed carved from sheets of rock. Its uncomplicated hugeness, and the way every angle fitted together, made her think of Ariock. There was a formidable neatness to the way doorways and lights were arranged. She could tell that this was a place he had built.

Ariock was on his hands and knees beside her.

"Are you all right?" Vy asked. But she knew, even as she spoke, that it was pointless to ask Ariock anything when he had that distant gaze. He was elsewhere. Exploring their surroundings?

He pushed himself up off the floor with a determined look.

"Don't overdo it." Garrett stood nearby, leaning on his staff.

Everyone was with them. The ten warriors. The former slaves. Thomas, floating in his hoverchair and looking miserable from pain. In this gigantic chamber, even Ariock looked tiny and insignificant.

"Ariock!" Garrett yelled—but Ariock vanished in a sudden whooshing crackle of air.

Vy stared at the space where he had been.

"Crap." Garrett looked like he wanted to attack something.

Thomas spoke with wincing effort. "It'll get . . . crowded."

Garrett whirled to face everyone, his face bristly with determination. "You five." He pointed to half the warriors. "You need to guard the boy while he gets to work on crewing this behemoth of a starship. Make sure no one attacks him."

A warrior interrupted. "Who are you to command us?"

"We do not take orders from a powerless old man," another warrior said.

"Especially not a *rekveh*." That came from a third warrior, and the rest looked stony with defiance.

No doubt Garrett was simmering with angry retorts. Vy could think of a few on his behalf, but hurling insults would accomplish nothing.

"Your premier isn't here," Vy said. "But if she was, she would command you to take orders from Garrett and Thomas. We need—"

Screams of panic and pain interrupted her.

Not from the warriors, or anyone nearby. The huge room suddenly held thousands of dirty, frightened people. Most were albinos. Many wore packs, and there were a few wagons laden with supplies. The people were so filthy and noisy, Vy assumed at first they were all common laborers.

Then she glimpsed jewelry and brocaded cloth, streaked with muck. Some of these people were upper class—or they had been. But they had lost their palaces and wealth. They had been out in the storm.

Ariock towered over the crowd.

Before Vy could call out to him, he vanished like an apparition. He might as well have been a holograph.

"He's dropping refugees off on every deck." Garrett sounded mortified, but Vy could only think that saving people was a good thing.

"Uh . . ." Garrett turned to Thomas. "Any chance you have a plan for the chaos?"

"Life support is incomplete." Thomas winced, as if speech hurt him. His yellow eyes were reddened and watery. "I'll be in the control center. Got to adjust things."

"Right." Garrett sounded dismayed. "I guess that means I need to, uh, man the defense system? Or something?"

Thomas gave a faint, painful nod.

Vy dug out two pills from the painkiller bottle and placed them in the treat compartment of the hoverchair's sparkly armrest, within Thomas's reach. The chair's previous owner had apparently used it to store a packet of sucking candies.

"In case you need them," she told Thomas. She supposed she could trust him not to overdose on purpose. "Should I go with you?"

"No, Vy. You're needed here." Garrett blocked her with his arm. "But the boy needs guards."

"I need a crew." Thomas peered at the seven adolescent ummins from Duin. The ummins were oblivious, gawking at the crowd of Alashani refugees.

"Varktezo!" Garrett snapped, grabbing the adolescent's attention. "And the rest of you. Go with Thomas and help him!"

The ummins exchanged glances.

Vy stepped in. "Please?"

That seemed to work. With a few final glances of skepticism, the ummins hurried to follow Thomas as he glided away in his hoverchair.

Vy watched them head bravely into a sea of angry, frightened albinos. She remembered how contemptuous the Alashani were toward former slaves and the yellow-eyed *rekveh*. A lot of Alashani probably still blamed Thomas for the death of their holy prophet.

"We can't just let them go off alone," she realized. "They need protectors."

"Indeed." Garrett turned a frustrated gaze toward the ten warriors.

"Weptolyso would do it," Vy told them. "Maybe I need to go find him." She adjusted her glove weapon, feeling all too inadequate. She was no soldier, no warrior. The last thing she wanted to do was to threaten scared refugees from the lamplit cities. They simply didn't understand that Thomas was on their side.

The swaggering warrior in charge seemed to change his mind. "Nulshta." He nodded toward one warrior. "Stay here. The rest of us will protect that *rekveh* in the red chair."

They got moving.

Vy considered joining the nine warriors, but Garrett stepped in front of her. "Okay, Vy, I need you to—"

Fresh screams filled the air. The room became twice as crowded, all at once, as people and debris fell out of thin air and hit the floor.

"Ariock!" Garrett interrupted himself.

Ariock rose out of the crowd quite a distance away. Although he towered over the terrified refugees, he looked just as battered and filthy as any of them.

Garrett's voice boomed across the vast room. "Do you have a warning headache? You should . . ."

Ariock vanished.

Air rushed into the place where he'd stood with a popping suction sound. People screamed in surprise. The crowd surged, trying to find their savior.

"Agh!" Garrett whirled to face Vy. "I would like to stay." He spoke loudly to be heard over the terrified babble. "But I have to go find our armament system and defend us against the Torth armada. I'm the only one who can figure out the missile launchers and predict when and how the Torth will strike."

Why did he sound apologetic?

Garrett did not give Vy a chance to ask questions. "Sorry. But you need to keep an eye out for Ariock. If he looks like he's wincing or in pain, then you need to make him stop. Make him lie down and rest."

Vy met Garrett's intense stare, exasperated. Stop Ariock? How was she supposed to do that, exactly?

"You may be the only one who can." Garrett leaned close, in her face, so they could hear each other. "This is important. This is life or death. All right? Do whatever you can." He squeezed her arms gently. "Whatever it takes."

He seemed to have forgotten that Vy was just a nurse. A nurse from New Hampshire who had lost half her leg.

Vy rubbed her arms, staring at Garrett's back as he limped away. She put her hands on her hips. "How do you know Ariock has limits?" she called.

Garrett turned and gave Vy a level look. "Everyone has limits."

She could not hide her disdain. Everyone could see that normal rules and limits did not apply to Ariock.

Garrett limped back to her, frustrated. "You've seen the power of the Lady of Sorrow, right? Well, someone was able to imprison her." He tapped his leg with his staff, drawing attention to the places where it was crooked. "This healed wrong. When I was at the mercy of Torth brutes, all my power couldn't save me. Ariock may be strength personified. But even he has weaknesses."

Vy tried to remain defiant, but doubts crept in. She knew Garrett was right. Ariock had fallen in battle once before, and it had been devastating.

"We can't afford to let Ariock learn his limits the hard way," Garrett said. "Not anymore. There's too much at stake." He gestured at the pressing crowds. "When Ariock wins, millions of people win. When he makes a mistake? People die." He gave Vy a look heavy with meaning. "We cannot afford to let him fall."

Vy supposed she knew that, on some level.

"Just keep your nurse's eye on him," Garrett said, begging. "Please."

With that, he limped into the crowd.

The last warrior stayed with Vy. Perhaps she meant to help grab Ariock's attention. An impossible task, Vy knew.

Yet Vy scanned the crowd and steeled herself to try.

CHAPTER 7

REFUGEES

Kessa visually traced the line of refugees as they zigzagged up the interior of the pyramid, balanced on ramps that protruded from slanted walls. Everyone was burdened with extra cloaks and packs slung over their shoulders. Many carried lanterns. A few struggled with extra burdens: chests full of wares, or handcarts piled high with bundles, or squirming children, or elders. They streamed upward, out of the ground, like a geyser of despair.

Beyond the open top of the pyramid, the ramp extended even farther, like the interlocked vertebrae of some great skeleton. Slime dripped from its segments.

People trudged up that flimsy ramp, trusting in the power of Ariock to protect them.

And why not? The Bringer of Hope had manifested a starship in progress so large that it replaced the sky. It was occluded by airy gloom, but it had ended the eternal rainfall. It blocked the hailstorm.

Kessa could only imagine the other pyramids, beyond sight. Each pyramid must have a similar ramp feeding into the incomprehensibly large ship.

How long could Ariock hold all these things steady?

It seemed like it would be a lot to concentrate on, even for an ummin. Kessa knew the limitations of human minds, and Ariock had a human mind. One little distraction would result in a catastrophic number of deaths.

Yet no one else worried about Ariock's limits.

They hunched their shoulders and complained about the arduous climb. They yelled for children to stay close, or they asked people to pick up items that got accidentally dropped.

"I don't see Ranhashi," Jinishta fretted. "She has three young children."

Most of Jinishta's family were on the ramps. They had survived the flood, the short-lived Torth invasion, and the earthquakes, which made their family among the luckiest of survivors. All the same, Jinishta kept searching for her missing cousins.

It seemed fruitless. If Ranhashi and her children were alive, then they would show up eventually. Or not. Either way, there was nothing Jinishta could do about it. She was as powerless as a commoner right now. As powerless as a former slave.

Maybe she still believed she had power?

People kept running up to her, begging hopefully for a healer. Each time, Jinishta had to send them away, disillusioned. No one looked as frustrated as the premier. Kessa imagined that if Jinishta had one dominant thought running through her mind, it must be *Never lose my powers again.*

All the Yeresunsa warriors who survived would be on guard against the inhibitor serum. Flen in particular.

Kessa was glad that Cherise had guided Flen away, up the ramp. They were probably inside the starship by now. When they had heard the devastating news about Flen's parents and sister . . . ? Well, Flen might have gone on a rampage had he had his powers.

Hopefully Flen had found a quiet place where he could glare impotently into space and mourn.

Haz had reported the tragedy. Flen's mother and sister had survived the flood. Their father was smashed to death on rocks, and their maidservants were killed, their wagons wiped out, but the two women had flung themselves into an alcove shielded by Haz and other warriors. When the waters smoothed out, the bedraggled group had chosen to float downriver on buoyant debris.

But parts of the river cavern had collapsed. The rough waters split into dead-end channels, and many of Haz's companions were stranded on the dreaded surface of the world.

"They got surrounded by Torth," Haz had told Flen with grave sorrow. "One person from that group, a child, survived. He sneaked away and ran back underground and told us what happened. The warriors were slain or taken. Everyone with them, including your sister and mother, was taken. By Torth."

Flen had looked stunned.

"I am sorry," Haz had said, slump-shouldered and avoiding his friend's eyes. He had known, as anyone would, that apologies in the face of such tragedy were too feeble to matter. Mere words could not bring loved ones back.

Enslavement and death were nearly the same thing. Kessa agreed with the Alashani on that point. She remembered when the Torth had visited her slave village and prodded her into a transport while her family wept silently. Her parents. Her sisters and brothers. Her entire tribe in that farmland, with its sweet fruits and crops. None of them could say a word or save her.

Even now, after a lifetime of not seeing them, she continued to miss them.

Kessa had touched Flen's arm. That was all. His loss was like an open wound, too fresh for any words.

Cherise had looked uncertain until Kessa went over to her and whispered, "Be gentle with him. He is hurting. It may be a long time before he is himself again. Even if he does not respond to you, he will notice kindness. It matters."

Cherise had nodded as if she understood that on a deep level. And she had gently urged Flen to trek up the ramp with her.

At least they were walking toward a future.

Flen was not the only newly orphaned refugee. Hollow-eyed children trailed after adults, begging them to find someone—a parent, or a sibling— who no longer lived. There were adults who looked lost. Friends leaned against each other, sobbing. Almost everyone had lost someone they loved.

Kessa did what she could. She adjusted packs that were hanging askew. She filled or refilled water skins, tapping huge urns that were too unwieldy to be pushed up the ramps. She handed out extra canteens. She offered reassurance to those who were afraid of heights or of the unknown. "The messiah will not let you fall," she said. Or "There are no monsters up there in that ship."

Deep down, she had doubts.

Could she really say there were no monsters on that starship? Ariock was a monster. Thomas and Garrett were monsters to the average Alashani.

And Kessa kept wondering what the Lady of Sorrow was doing to the slaves of this world. While Alashani refugees zigzagged upward, ascending to their salvation, millions of slaves must be hugging each other in the dark bowels of dying cities. They had no messiah. No prophecy. They were just abandoned, like unwanted luggage.

Other than Kessa, would anyone even mourn them?

Screams of terror came from above.

Kessa could guess what was happening, but she forced herself to look.

The ramp swayed alarmingly, and people clung to it, shrieking. The starship was lifting away. Ariock, wherever he was, must be distracted. Maybe the Lady of Sorrow was growing more savage? Maybe Torth were attacking? Whatever the reason, he was abandoning the Alashani.

Hailstones began to fall.

Sleet and hail pummeled the Alashani. Wind howled across the ramp, and Kessa watched, sick with helpless horror, as one person fell. Then another.

"Ariock." Jinishta straightened, fury igniting in her gaze. "What is wrong with him?"

"He is protecting thirteen cities." Kessa recalled the number of pyra- mids. She guessed Ariock was also protecting the starship, as well as his own human body and possibly other friends.

It was a lot. It was unfair to expect him to rescue the slaves of this world on top of all the rescues he was already doing.

The screams abruptly cut off.

Everyone inside the pyramid gawked upward, perplexed. Kessa was no less astonished than the others.

Where was the sky ramp? Where were those desperate people?

No one fell. No one slammed to the ground. There were no falling items, no debris. Even the hailstones seemed to stop for a second.

Thunder rolled, angry and deafening. A wall of radioactive debris rattled the pyramid, tearing at its walls—

—and suddenly, Kessa sprawled on her hands and knees in a much different place.

The overwhelming humidity was gone. The air had a frosty tang, but it was not toxic. It tasted like indoor air.

Kessa picked herself up. Despite the chaos of confused, frightened people, she noted that the storm was gone. The floor and ceiling looked solid. Light strips glowed on distant walls, somewhat like the slave Tunnels.

There was comfort in that unwavering glow.

"Where are we?" Jinishta sat on her knees. She searched Kessa's face with pleading, frightened eyes. This shift in reality must be strange beyond anything in her experience.

Shifted reality was beyond Kessa's experience, as well. But she recognized the atmosphere of a slave zone, with metal walls and white light strips. This looked like a cavernous slave zone.

And clearly, there were no enemies here. No threats, no monsters, only scared refugees.

"We are safe." Kessa put a comforting hand on Jinishta's shoulder. "Ariock must have brought us into the ship."

"The ship?" Jinishta looked around with wide eyes.

"Yes."

Nearby Alashani overheard, and they turned to Kessa with fervent hope. They looked at her as if she could provide answers.

"That's the ummin chieftain who came with the messiah," someone said.

"Yes! They call her Kessa the Wise."

"Where is the messiah?" someone shouted at her. "Can you tell us, Kessa?"

"Yes, tell us!"

People began to reach for Kessa, clutching her wraps, touching her feet.

"Where should we go?"

"What happened to my brother?"

"Where is my daughter?"

"Are we safe?"

"Where is the messiah?"

"What is he doing?"

Kessa tried to back away. She bumped into the crowd. Alashani were all around her, towering over her, demanding answers.

Jinishta stood, shouting for everyone to calm down, to have patience. But the stress was too great. People wanted answers. They wanted instructions. Jinishta looked frustrated, and no doubt she was struggling to think of what to do next herself.

Kessa glimpsed a wagon not too far away. That would give her some high ground to stand on. She struggled toward it, hopping over debris, avoiding robes and grabby hands.

"Can you tell the messiah to help us?"

"Where is he?"

"We need a healer!"

"Did anyone bring a chamber pot?"

"We need—!"

"We need—!"

Fresh screams inundated the room as more Alashani fell into their midst.

There were cries of pain and shock. The smells of ozone and rain. New arrivals had to shove others out of their way, and vice versa. Parents clutched children to protect them. The room seemed twice as crowded.

Kessa wondered if Ariock had considered the consequences of over-crowding. Fights often broke out in the slave Tunnels whenever a bunk room got overassigned. That was why gangs dominated certain neighbor-hoods. They stole bunks from anyone who lacked friends.

Kessa felt sure that Ariock would not want homeless Alashani to mur-der each other.

Nor would he want to deal with petty fights.

"Spread out!" Kessa yelled.

Few people could hear her over the hubbub. They were too busy yelling at each other or begging for a healer, or the messiah.

Kessa climbed the spokes of the wagon, pulling herself onto its wheel rim and then higher.

"I speak for Ariock!" she shouted.

A bunch of albinos sat on the supplies. They stared at the ummin who wore black wraps, like a battle-ready warrior. Then they whispered to each other—"It's Kessa the Wise!"—and they graciously moved aside, offering her the platform.

"I speak for the messiah!" Kessa balanced on the highest stack of bundled wares. "He wants you to spread out. Make room for your neighbors."

A few albinos tried to shuffle away. Most gaped up at her.

"Please seek an exit." Kessa had noted doorways cut through the thick walls, exposing other crowded rooms. "If you can walk, then find a place to lie down."

They shuffled with reluctance, a churning mass of despair and hope.

"Where are the councilors?" Kessa muttered. She searched the crowd for anyone who might provide authority. Someone ought to set up a messenger network, to facilitate newsworthy updates and to help separated family members locate each other.

Also, there should be a hospital area for grave injuries.

And really, the limited survival gear they had brought ought to be under guard. Maybe someone—whichever unfortunate councilor or warrior wound up in charge—should ask nussians to put together a peacekeeping force? That might mitigate the theft of food and blankets.

"There's Jinishta!" someone shouted.

The grim premier made her way toward Kessa amid desperate pleas and shouts. Kessa was relieved when Jinishta climbed the wagon, apparently ready to take control of her people.

Kessa prepared to hop down. She needed to make sure Pung was all right. And Weptolyso. Also, what about the refugees from Duin? And Cherise? And so many others.

"Kessa." Jinishta stopped partway up the wagon. "Will you act as leader for a while?"

Kessa gawked at the premier, wondering if this was a tasteless joke. "I cannot." That should be obvious. The job of leadership surely belonged to a full-blooded Alashani, not someone with a visible collar scar on her neck.

"Just for a little while?" Jinishta gave her a begging look. "I must find my warriors and make sure they don't drop dead from exhaustion. We have already lost two that way."

Kessa closed her beak. She was sorry for the deaths. She sympathized with Jinishta's concerns. Yet . . .

"How long will Alashani listen to a runaway slave?" Kessa pointed out.

"You're doing a better job than Chaniyelem would." Jinishta plucked at her wraps, as if to show poverty. "Please. I must go." She began to climb down.

"Wait!" Kessa called.

Jinishta hesitated.

"If you encounter any herbalists," Kessa said, "please ask them to ration painkillers to people with the gravest injuries. That should take some of the pressure off your Yeresunsa and give them time to recover their powers."

Jinishta looked grateful. "That is a very good idea. Thank you."

She departed, shouldering her way through the crowd. Kessa felt stranded. Albino hands grabbed at her feet, pleading.

A fresh flood of Alashani appeared, adding to the chaos. People screamed and jostled each other. They begged and whined and demanded.

Kessa clicked her beak, imagining how she might organize this unruly mess of a crowd. There was so much that ought to be done. A survey of rooms, for instance, would empower people to organize themselves by healthy versus injured and by city neighborhood. She would need to deputize people.

"You." Kessa pointed to a steady-eyed woman who looked capable of getting things done. "And you." She chose a man who retained some quiet dignity. "The messiah requests your help."

And she began to assign tasks.

A runaway slave could not lead a nation, of course, but for now, Kessa figured that she could ease some of Ariock's workload. He would not have the time or the inclination to patrol this ship like a hall guard patrolling the slave Tunnels. The "messiah" was doing more than anyone here seemed to realize. He should not need to deal with petty squabbles or whining supplicants.

Before long, her task force branched out, seeking their own subsquads of helpers.

CHAPTER 8

FASTER

Life sparks crawled over Ariock.

Millions of lives, each one as lightweight as a particle, barely dusted his skin. He was hardly aware of his human body anymore. It was just an overused machine, a tired heart beating at the center of a vast world.

He searched the chaotic surface of the planet. As always, he found yet another huddled, desperate population. They would die unless he acted fast.

Lava spewed from rents underground, melting tunnels and ramps. The survivors hid in the remains of a wrecked pyramid, struggling to ward off cannibals while protecting their supplies.

Ariock leaped to them.

That was, he threw all his awareness in their direction—a monstrous feat. His awareness spanned the entire planet, plus orbital space, as well as the colony starship. Ariock had to withdraw from all that. He had to lose it all—and become nothing.

It felt like self-mutilation. A myriad of sensations vanished. He lost his sense of stature, the map of space and substances, the distant babble of voices, and the thunder of blood in his ears. He even lost the subconscious signals of being alive.

For one horrible moment in time, Ariock was a ghost. He had no heartbeat. He lacked a mind.

His sight jerked around, no longer constricted to eyes. He floated, disembodied, among the desperate survivors. His surroundings were desaturated and murky. There was no sound. No odors. No sensations upon skin.

Travel without a body was as simple as thought, but it felt like trying not to breathe while drowning. The urge to snap back to his core self was overpowering.

Save them, Ariock remembered.

He forced himself to resist the urge to return to his body in the starship. Instead, he centered himself in a spot he had chosen, and he forced that area to become his core.

Ariock—the ordinary, human version—appeared in that space.

It was as traumatic as being born, in some ways. His heart fluttered as if he'd received a megadose of adrenaline. It had just restarted. He caught himself on his hands and knees, gasping, skin prickling from the sudden climate and pressure change.

People were screaming. If anyone noticed that the messiah had suddenly appeared nearby, their reactions were drowned out by a savage fight against cannibals.

Ariock picked himself up, fighting off the nausea and disorientation that came every time he teleported.

He wished he could take a moment to savor the fact that he had learned to do something impossible. His newfound mass-teleportation power would make him very hard to catch. Or to kill.

"*Aonswa!*" People were shouting and pointing. Certainly none of these people would ever guess that Ariock used to be an agoraphobe hidden in a mansion in the woods. They would never imagine that he used to be as powerless as they were.

Wild zoved chomped at spears and supply packs. There was no time to waste.

Ariock spread his awareness, just enough to form a tight perimeter around this population of survivors. He didn't want to include any of the cannibalistic apes or any large chunks of muck-slick debris.

As soon as he'd figured out what to include and exclude, he hurled all his awareness back to the starship.

Disembodied, he sought out the first relatively empty room he could find. There weren't many of those left.

No time for second-guessing. Ariock relocated himself to this new location, and this time, he brought more than just his ordinary core self. He included everything, and everyone, within the perimeter of awareness he had just defined.

Hundreds of people appeared with him in the starship.

Ariock was ready for the violent disorientation, the different-tasting air, the screwy changes in direction and barometric pressure. He caught himself on his hands and knees. No one else did. They sprawled, shouting, frail bodies falling against each other and him.

Ariock lurched to his feet. That was easier here, where gravity was lighter. It made him feel flimsy, even insubstantial.

"He saved us!"

"*Aonswa!*"

If only Ariock had to time to heal their injuries. Some of the people he'd rescued had been bitten by wild zoved, or they had broken bones from falling, or being shoved, or from the flood or earthquakes.

But even as he thought about it, he knew more people were suffering and dying. Had he rescued the city of Lemlashar yet? What about Nyaddish?

"We need a healer!"

"*Aonswa?* Heal us?"

Their gratitude curdled as they became aware that they were not in their familiar city cavern, but in an alien place full of other terrified strangers.

Ariock didn't have time to apologize or explain. He would do that later—once he'd saved everyone.

He stretched his awareness wide. Back to the planet, back to searching for life sparks huddled within the apocalypse.

He was proud of his newly constructed starship, despite the fact that it was not his own design. It was something grand.

He had believed he could carry it indefinitely. But holding up thirteen boarding ramps while also protecting millions of people . . . and while also holding the starship steady against the raging storm . . . all that had proved too much. His attention had broken in several critical places.

Ariock hoped that he had caught most of the falling people before they could smash to their deaths. Each mass-teleportation was a desperate juggling act.

The first few were the worst. Ariock had sent himself to each location in midair, heedless of the lack of solid ground, his own body falling along with the Alashani. Each time, he'd whipped coils of air around the flailing people. He'd caught them. Brought them to the rest of the group, not caring if their supplies continued to fall.

Unfortunately, he had failed to catch three or four people in time. They were dead, for certain.

As for the rest? When Ariock had teleported them into the ship, he'd tried to cushion their landings. He'd done his best. Even so, he knew there were survivors with broken bones. They were hurting.

He would heal them as soon as he got a chance.

First, he had to save another survivor group huddled inside a pile of rubble that used to be an underground hamlet. And another. And another.

The starship grew overcrowded. Nothing Ariock could do about that. He began to drop people off above other people, solidifying the air enough to slow their falls.

What else could he do? No time to think. No time to figure out a better way.

On the planet's surface, clouds roiled and plumed, caught in fierce updrafts. Roving bands of telepathic cannibals invaded anything that looked like shelter. Unnatural storms knocked down ancient skyscrapers. Radioactive hailstones the size of beach balls flattened wreckage.

Ariock was with a survivor group, protecting hundreds of people from hailstones and tornado-force winds while engulfing them within a perimeter when a new problem slammed into him.

The ground rolled and fell away. At the same time, the dead city humped into a towering black mass of wreckage, roaring toward him.

Not a normal earthquake.

Ariock threw his awareness back to the starship. He teleported the survivor group in a messy way, taking debris rather than risking people left behind. They escaped the rolling mountain of ruination just in time.

As Ariock regained his balance, he remembered Evenjos's promise to make her enemies suffer. He remembered the shrieking phantom trapped in mirrors for untold millennia. How far would her vengeance go? When would she consider it a job well done?

He was plastered with sweat and muck, and he felt as if he'd been doing heavy lifting for weeks without enough food or sleep. What if he failed to wrap everyone within his awareness the next time he mass-teleported? He might accidentally leave someone behind. Or worse, if he got too hasty with his perimeters, he might teleport only half of someone's body.

He had to risk it. This was the worst time to stop.

Ariock threw his awareness back to the heaving, tortured surface of the planet. There were still so many millions of life sparks.

Torth?

Vehicles streaked the tumultuous sky. Telepaths must be mobbing the few remaining spaceports on the planet.

What about their slaves?

Ariock gasped. He had all but forgotten the slaves, but they must also have desperate survivors among them. He could picture slave zones packed full of desperate people. His mother and Vy had told him all about the slave Tunnels.

Ariock didn't think he could ever repay Kessa, or Weptolyso, or Pung, for their roles in keeping him or his friends alive. But he wasn't going to let their downtrodden people get slaughtered along with their cruel masters. Not as long as he could draw breath.

Besides, Thomas had said it was possible to rescue the slaves. Hadn't he?

Ariock flung himself into a densely crowded underground tunnel beneath a Torth city. Thousands of slaves clung to each other, showered by debris from crumbling walls.

Back to the starship.

Ariock gulped air and hurled himself to another slave zone on the planet. He didn't even make sure the rescued slaves landed safely amid the Alashani. There were too many people to rescue.

"Heal us!"

He scooped people out of shelters where they waited for the world to end. He snatched them away from lava eruptions. He swiped them away from cannibals who were devouring them. Sometimes he was too late, but he brought them to the starship even if they were critically injured or dead. Then he went back for more.

"Save us!"

Soon he couldn't even take the time to recover from the disorientation. He didn't try to regain his balance or stand up. He was juggling anvils and dodging ninja attacks.

Whenever he stretched his awareness, he included an incomprehensible number of miles. That was like constructing the starship in terms of complexity. He gained a macro view of life sparks. He knew where the densest clusters were. If he hadn't been so single-mindedly determined to save people, he would have liked to cradle the planet within his awareness, just to admire its fractal-like beauty. Maybe this was akin to how a supergenius saw things all the time.

But it was wearying.

He plunged one way, then the other, across thousands of miles of space, heedless of pain, rolling through muck, ignoring his own worries about making a mistake. Once, he somersaulted through what felt like a geyser of lava. That was agony. He dared not stop, though.

"Heal us, *Aonswa*!"

Once or twice, he thought he heard Vy yelling at him. Begging him to take a rest. As if that was feasible. Every time he spread his awareness, he always found more people in need of rescue.

He tumbled across a metal floor, again and again. Then he plunged back to the planet and scooped up survivors within his awareness. Then back into one of the stuffy, overcrowded rooms.

The babble of confused voices roared in his ears. He fell, and thousands of people sprawled with him. His heart fluttered after each teleportation, yet the adrenaline no longer seemed adequate to fuel him. It didn't matter. He had to save them all.

He mass-teleported again and again. Each time, he brought a fresh wave of screaming apocalypse survivors aboard the ship.

Later, he figured he would reward himself with a nice long rest.

But first he had to visit several thousand more crumbling shelters. And then he had to heal everyone. And shield them against the Torth armada. Would he need to propel the starship to a safe quadrant of the galaxy?

He plunged back to the apocalypse. One crisis at a time.

CHAPTER 9

A NEW MYTH

Praw had never seen Torth behave so strangely. One moment, the slave auction block was dotted with Torth shopping for a fresh slave. The next moment, Torth dived beneath sturdy marble tables as if expecting the nussian sentries to go berserk and attack them.

A few Torth fled the forum altogether. They left their personal slaves behind, blinking in confusion, while they glided away on hoverchairs. A couple of Torth actually hiked up their robes and ran.

Praw had never seen a Torth run. They were very clumsy at it. Comical, really.

All throughout this wake cycle, he had seen Torth act more preoccupied than usual. They stood staring at walls. They forgot to punish slaves. Some forgot to eat or get out of bed, according to the gossip in slave zone water closets. More than a few Torth, including Praw's owner, had hurried away and failed to return.

Praw wondered where his Red Rank owner was right now. Still jogging through indoor streets? Gaping, openmouthed, at nothing?

Mind readers were truly incomprehensible.

But a good slave carried on with work, no matter how bizarrely the masters acted. Praw gathered up empty slop buckets. He trundled past shackled slaves who were on display. The genderfluid slaves all postured as males, just like Praw. That was prudent. Males had a slight survival advantage.

He passed a bug-eyed Torth hiding beneath an ornamental table. Weird. Surely Torth could not feel fear?

Speculation was not worth the risk of punishment. Praw had never seen Torth play games before, but then, he had never seen them run or hide until today, either. Perhaps this was all some sort of citywide game.

He deposited the buckets in a janitorial bin, then turned to collect more. With his hands free, he dared to drop to a quadrupedal stance.

The Torth wouldn't like it. They preferred their govki slaves to waddle on just two of their six limbs, freeing up four hands to clean and carry. Govki were perfect for toting supplies, preparing food, giving massages, and wiping butts. Praw figured that was why his species was among the most popular and common type of slave.

However, two legs made him top heavy and unbalanced. He could move at a faster, more natural gait on four legs.

The Torth did not seem to be in a punishing mood right now, so he gathered slop buckets in his uppermost pair of hands only, which was easier. He kept an eye out for messes. Sometimes newly collared slaves got sick.

Chained and shackled slaves watched him with dull envy, as if he had more freedom than they did.

Praw inwardly chuckled at their youthful naïveté. Yes, he served a high rank. Anyone could see the red hue of the glowing collar around his furry neck. But he had been torn from a factory clan at a young age, the same as anyone else.

He had once stood in this very auction forum in chains. And he had learned, as all slaves must learn, that slavery had nothing to do with the chains, or even the collar.

Freedom was a fable. It didn't exist. Not for slave species.

The only way to survive, Praw knew, was to make the most of a meager life. Serve and obey. Grab as much food as possible during mealtimes. Join the most powerful gang. Win wagers. Identify as male. Survive and kick down anyone who got in the way of that. Strive to be an elder who had all his wits. Life would never offer anything better, and any fool who dreamed of gaining more freedom or power than they were born with was doomed to die young.

Praw figured he was halfway to becoming an elder.

He was also halfway through his second work shift. Midmeal was a long way off. He inspected a mostly empty slop bucket and considered sneaking a gulp or two. If he slurped quietly, maybe no one would notice?

The few Torth who remained in this forum seemed preoccupied with their hiding game. They were oblivious to him.

Nussians patrolled this big forum, as usual, but their stalklike eyes looked twitchy and distracted. No doubt they were trying to figure out how to prioritize their duties with so few Torth about.

Praw took a cautious slurp.

He nearly dropped the bucket when he saw a Torth-like figure staring at him.

Then he observed the shackles and slave collar on the small figure, and he regained his composure. It was only the new exotic. This newly imported species was called *Alashani* or something like that.

Praw could not imagine why the Torth were breeding slaves that looked like pale, ghostly mockeries of themselves. But why not? Some exotics required special apparatuses just to breathe. Some exotics were too tiny to serve their owners. They lived as pampered fashion accessories . . . at least, until their owners grew bored with caring for them.

Some Torth had peculiar tastes. That was a fact.

"Help?" The exotic slave spoke in a child's voice, with a mushy foreign accent.

Didn't the stupid child know it was illegal to speak out loud? It must be quite pampered, to come from a place of such ignorance.

Praw trundled away before any Torth could overhear. He risked one glance over his shoulder, marveling at how closely the creature resembled the slave masters. Of course, it—well, a he, Praw assumed—was too emotive. And the fabrics he wore were not opulent or rich enough for Torth garments. His childlike proportions signified that he was not full grown. He must be freshly plucked from a factory clan or slave farm.

His pigmentation was striking. Curly hair, alabaster white. Praw felt some pity. White fur was commonplace among govki, and it made self-grooming a daily ordeal. Most Torth valued clean slaves, and there was no way to hide stains on white fur, so Praw had to use up a lot of his free time in the bath zone. He often wished he'd been born with a darker pigment, or at least some freckles to offset his whiteness.

Also, that young Alashani slave would endure unwanted gang attention in the slave Tunnels. One could not sneak around with pigmentation like his. Praw knew all about that. The only way to survive was to join a gang and make oneself useful to them.

The polished floor groaned and shuddered in a thunderous, rolling way.

Praw kept his footing—it took a lot to knock a govki off his feet—but he lost hold of a couple of empty buckets.

Chained-up auction slaves skidded and banged into pillars. Nussians bellowed in surprise. Vocalizations were illegal here, yet none of the Torth punished them.

A pillar cracked. Part of the ornate ceiling buckled, and everyone beneath it scrambled to get away. Big, dewy chandeliers hung askew.

All the Torth in sight collectively seemed to decide that the slave auction block was not the safest place to hide. They ran to hoverbikes or hovercarts. Praw glimpsed slave-like fear on their faces, even though they wore circlets of the sort Torth usually wore when relaxing.

Were they unnerved by the debris spilling from the broken ceiling? What was happening?

Lights flickered and died.

Emergency lights glowed to life, but the dim orbs were hardly enough for such a vast space. It was as if the eternal nighttime had invaded indoors. Even the nussians looked alarmed. Slaves stared at each other with frightened eyes, seeking answers. Their worries were plain. What was happening? Were they in danger?

The ground shuddered.

Praw dropped the empty slop buckets and fell to all six of his hand-feet. Never mind his duty. Never mind hunger. If the Torth knew a better place for survival, then that was where he would go.

Other slaves might avoid Torth whenever possible, but Praw took pride in being useful to the masters. Torth were the most powerful gang in existence. Anyone with eyes and ears could see that. Torth were worth serving.

On all six, Praw could run as fast as the fastest ummin. He could probably beat a kemkorcan in a race. Naive young ummins and mer nerctans tended to dismiss govki as plodding, due to their stout figures and stubby legs. Now those types gawked as Praw breezed past them.

He put on a burst of six-legged speed. Surely he could catch up with the last departing hovercart.

He dodged around luggage that was stranded in the middle of the boulevard. And hoverbikes. There was even a discarded data tablet or two, and that was scary. Torth never let those tablets out of their control. What was going on?

Gashes in walls let in shrieking wind and a patter of ice balls. The view outside was so different from what Praw was used to, he feared it was a hallucination. Muck and rain obscured the skyline. Violent gusts of wind lifted the veils of chaos long enough to reveal buildings that were smashed and pounded, as if by heavy fists.

Where was the Stratower? It appeared to be gone.

Praw spotted Torth cowering in lounges or gardens, but those places were wrecked. Even the street looked torn asunder. And . . .

Praw skidded to a six-legged halt.

A torrential mob of slaves thundered up the corridor, straight toward him. Grimy nussians, govki, ummins, and all manner of other alien species ran toward the relative safety of the slave auction forum. At least the forum had sturdy walls. It was intact, buried in the interior depths of the indoor city.

Praw did not want to get trampled.

He whirled around, no longer sure where to find safety, or even if it existed. On six legs, he stayed ahead of the mob.

A fountain split the entrance intersection of the slave auction forum. It ran dry, but it was still an imposing structure, supported by pillars and carved stonework. Praw scurried up a carved pillar. With all six hands and feet, he could climb fast.

He perched atop the dry fountain and prepared to defend his chosen spot. No one was going to knock him down.

The mob of slaves erupted around the pillars.

Praw gripped the stone ledge and wondered how this chaos would end. Terrified slaves clogged the forum. They tripped over chains; they kicked aside slop buckets. Laws were forgotten. Slaves shouted at each other, demanding news, asking whether the gods were angry.

"Have you seen how many Torth ran into the Stratower?"

"Is that where they went?"

"Not all of them."

"My owner is hiding in her bathroom."

"Right? Mine is hiding in his marble spa."

"At least they aren't punishing us."

"Do you truly think Torth are our biggest concern? Have you seen what it looks like outside?"

"I wonder if any of the Torth in the Stratower survived."

"What happened to it?"

"I saw it topple. But it stopped, like this. Horizontal." The speaker was a govki, and she flattened all four of her hands, to illustrate. "It blocked the storm. It blocked the whole sky."

Praw figured her for a tale teller. She must be one of those nervous, ingratiating types who tried to impress gangs by making themselves sound like news sources with special insights.

"I saw that, too," an ummin said, excited. "And then the whole tower flew upward!"

"Like this." The govki threw four hands in the air in a sudden burst.

Praw snorted with disbelief. Maybe the Stratower had collapsed from earthquakes. That seemed more likely.

It was possible that the Stratower had never existed at all. What was it, really, but an image glimpsed through windows? Few slaves ever claimed to have gone inside the immense tower.

So maybe it had just been an illusion, like the views of alien paradises that no one ever visited. Plains of wildflowers? Tropical beaches? Torth lounges were full of simulated paradises, but everyone knew that those views were just pretty falsehoods. Like the legend of Jonathan Stead. That was a fun story.

If anyone told a story about today, Praw figured it would be a cautionary tale. He clung to the ledge and peered at the traffic jam, which extended as far as he could see.

"Make way!"

"Get out of the way!"

"A Torth is coming!"

The crowd rippled, trying to clear an aisle. Two surly-looking nussians loped forward, shoving lesser slaves out of their way. Behind them, Praw could just see the head of a beefy-looking female Torth with stringy hair, red eyes glaring. He recognized this one as a frequent associate of his owner.

She glided, very slowly, on a hoverbike, nose wrinkled as if offended by the stench of so many slaves.

"Return to your duties!" the Red Rank screeched. "Get out of My way!"

Praw had never heard a Torth yell. Sometimes they whispered commands to go with their hand signals, but shouting? That was what slaves did, and only in slave quarters.

This Torth had a weak, stringy voice, and overall, it made her seem much less imposing than if she'd remained silent.

But a Red Rank was a Red Rank. Their kind was quick to give punishments, and besides, any Torth could summon more Torth. They alone knew how to operate weapons and machines. They commanded nussians. And they knew everything. They could anticipate anything a slave might intend to do.

It was best not to take chances with a Red Rank.

Slaves jostled aside. They pushed their neighbors, trying to get out of the Torth's way. Perhaps she sought shelter in the auction forum?

Thunder crashed and echoed as something huge collapsed somewhere in the city. The crowd surged, and Praw considered offering his perch to the Red Rank, just to impress her with how well he could anticipate her desires. From the top of this dry fountain, she would be able to signal commands to the mob. A Torth might impose some law and order on all these pushy slaves.

He reared to two legs. But as he waved his four furry white arms, something immense barreled into him from behind.

Not even a govki like Praw could keep his balance after such an impact. He tumbled in the air. He went spread-eagled, hoping the dense crowd below would catch him.

Something cushioned Praw's landing. He had no time to figure out who or what had caught him, because he was too busy trying to figure out what sort of strange, gigantic alien had displaced him atop the fountain.

The giant was so outlandish, Praw struggled to figure out whether it was an exotic slave or an abnormally large Torth, dressed in filthy black wraps that dripped muck.

It surveyed the crowd with deep-set purple eyes. A quiver full of spears bristled on its back. How tribal! Praw had heard stories of hunters on the most primitive of slave farms, who used handcrafted weapons as a means of slaying and butchering animals.

Reality shifted before he could make any further guesses.

Praw flailed and fell amid slaves, some of whom were passingly familiar, and some of whom were strangers he had never seen before. He landed on shoulders. He got dumped to a steely metal ground.

Since he was a govki, it was a simple matter to flip upright. He reared on two legs—then swayed, because he felt too lightweight.

Why did so many of the people in this crowd resemble pale, ghostly Torth?

They were Alashani. Praw recognized them as such right away, because the exotics were emotive, and they spoke aloud. They all had the mushy accent of that shackled child.

In fact, Praw glimpsed the exotic child among them. Adults with the same tightly curled white hair enfolded the child in their arms, exclaiming like relieved parents. They tugged at his slave collar—they did not wear collars—and they remarked upon it with dismay.

Beyond them, the black-wrapped giant stood, taller than anyone in sight, even taller than most nussians. Who wasn't going to stare at that with horror—or wonder?

The giant had bold, prominent Torth features, yet a mind reader would never look so battered and exhausted. They owned slaves. They were immaculate.

Also, a Torth could not vanish into nothingness with a faint popping sound.

Praw blinked hard. Was reality unraveling? Or was the tired giant some kind of haunting apparition, like the Weeping Lady or the Lady of Sorrow or whatever people called that myth? She only appeared to slaves who were alone and dying. Maybe this giant appeared to slaves who were annoyed and overcrowded together.

One of the nearby Alashani shouted in a language that sounded utterly alien.

Others took up the cry, waving their hands above the crowd, seeking attention from the giant who was no longer there. Some of them used the slave tongue, albeit with strange accents. "It's the messiah!"

"I just saw him!"

"He vanished again?"

"Heal us!"

"Ariock!"

Praw turned in a circle, ignoring the fervent mob in favor of assessing his new environment. He felt protected by the immense, dark, unadorned walls. This looked like a slave zone. And it was exceptionally clean, and sturdy enough to withstand tornadoes and even earthquakes.

Myths didn't matter. This was real.

Slaves cried for the giant—Ariock?—to reappear, to perform more miracles. It seemed Ariock could materialize at will and transform reality. Or transform the world. That made him more formidable than any hero of legend. Even Jonathan Stead.

And he was real.

Shouts of dismay. Someone screamed in pain. Praw heard a wet exploding sound, and unfortunately, he knew what that was. A blaster glove had gone off.

People shoved each other, screaming.

Praw caught glimpses of the heavyset Torth woman, protected by her Red Rank armor. "Get away from me!" she hissed. "Filthy slaves!"

Spiky nussians loped toward the Red Rank, each with grim determination. They had little trouble cutting through the crowd.

"*Rekveh,*" one of them said with disgust. Praw had never heard that word before, but it sounded like a curse.

"We'll take care of it," another nussian assured the crowd.

The Red Rank seemed overwhelmed, perhaps overloaded by so many minds nearby. "Clear Me some room!" she demanded. She held her gloved hand high above the crowd, beyond the reach of shorter slaves. Ummins could not reach her glove, and Alashani would have to jump.

A determined-looking mer nerctan made a grab for it. He swung his triple-jointed neck, enormous beak open, ready to sever the Torth's arm.

His head exploded in a spray of gore.

The Red Rank triggered her glove again. And again. She kept blasting into the crowd, turning in circles, her red eyes fearful. "Slaves!" she commanded. "Defend Me!"

As a Red Rank, she had every right to expect obedience. Praw shuffled forward.

He worked extra hard to please Torth. He was reliable. He was the best slave, which was what empowered him to serve a high rank. His owner gave him little rewards whenever he unexpectedly pleased her. A pat on his furry head, or a sugary candy to suck on while he worked.

A nussian dropped, felled by multiple blasts. He collapsed, his armored skin broken and bleeding, but instead of deterring the other nussians . . .

More of the behemoths surged toward the ruckus. They looked enraged.

The blasts suddenly stopped. The Red Rank kept thumbing her trigger, but her glove needed to recharge.

A speckled govki reached for the weapon.

The Red Rank frantically scanned the crowd, and her gaze settled on Praw's glowing collar. Did she recognize him? Or perhaps she was simply glad to see a high-class slave who explicitly served a Red Rank, and who was on duty.

"Defend Me!" she commanded.

Praw considered it.

The govki who was trying to grab her weapon collapsed, writhing on the ground from a pain seizure. "Bad!" the Red Rank shouted, as shrill as a parent scolding a mischievous child. She thumbed her glove, wild-eyed, and Praw realized, *There are no other Torth here.*

This was a slave zone.

And Praw suspected it might be a special, magical sort of slave zone.

If this Red Rank had her way, there would be a bloody pile of corpses. That was her prerogative as a Torth, of course. Maybe she had some high-minded motive that mere slaves could never hope to comprehend.

But Praw thought she looked like a cornered animal.

This was not her opulent world. Her gang was not in charge here.

Praw knew that her blaster glove would be fully recharged at any second. No doubt she would keep fighting, but her glove would die again, and Torth could only give pain seizures to one slave at a time. Everyone knew that. They needed time to recuperate in between.

Soon this Torth would run out of energy. It was inevitable. The only question was how many lives she would devastate before she fell.

"Defend Me, you filthy slave!" the lone Red Rank demanded of Praw.

Praw reared onto two legs. On two, he matched the Red Rank in height, and he had four arms free. He tackled her.

Hauling buckets every day made him strong, and he enveloped her, pinning her two arms to her sides.

The Red Rank struggled, but she was unable to break free. She could not defend herself when an ummin snatched her glove away.

Pain sizzled through Praw's mind. The Red Rank was fighting him the only way she had available, but it was hardly the worst punishment he had ever endured. The weakness of her attack made him grin.

That, and her shortsightedness.

Praw let her go, amazed that she had wasted the last of her mental energy on him, a mere govki. How could a Torth be so . . . well . . . stupid?

Her blaster glove was already gone. An ummin had absconded with it, vanishing into the crowd.

One of the furious nussians seized the Red Rank by her arm, flinging her in the air. Another nussian seized her legs.

It seemed Torth could bleed like slaves, after all.

Praw backed away, wanting to shield his white fur from spurts of blood and gore. Then he remembered that there were no masters here. He did not need to please anyone with his spotless appearance.

So he inserted himself among the nussians and joined their savage frenzy.

CHAPTER 10

An impossible starship floated above the seething planet.

Torth witnesses in local space could not stop staring at the behemoth. Their inner audiences gazed through many perceptions, transfixed. They marveled at an enormous colony-class carrier that could not—should not—be there.

The thing was so impossible, some Torth insisted it must be a massive illusion. *Perhaps it is constructed from clouds?* That was more plausible than . . .

Well.

Yet any Torth pilots who attempted to dock at its crude bay got attacked by laser cannons. They had to back off before their hulls melted. That meant someone was aboard the mystery starship. Its defense system must be manned, and not by ignorant slaves or cave-dwelling savages.

A renegade Torth was at the helm.

BETRAYER, trillions of minds seethed.

The Commander of Most Living Things considered the likelihood that it was him. Might there be other renegades? What if it was the Imposter, or some other unknown, emotionally unstable problem?

No. She needed to own up to her biggest mistake.

She pictured the sickly child, hunched in a stolen hoverchair, the glow of holographic workstations reflected in his yellow eyes. He had stolen skills from the collective knowledge of the Torth Empire, like some sort of evil goblin from a prehistoric tale.

The Giant was a tank. The Shapeshifter was an uncontrolled force of nature. The Imposter was a subtle knife twisting in one's back. But the Betrayer was, undoubtedly, their mastermind. He was orchestrating all the enemies. He was a tactician, an engineer, and a commander, all rolled into one person.

Now everyone understood that she should have executed him.

Supergeniuses. The Torth Majority flooded toward the biggest and brightest minds in the Megacosm. They swung into orbit around each towering pillar of knowledge, like stars orbiting galactic nuclei. *Help.*

Save Us.

Save civilization.

Stop the Betrayer.

At any cost.

The Commander tried to sneak past political opponents. Whenever she was confronted by a challenger, all she could do was offer meekness. *I live to serve and obey.*

At least the Upward Governess was impossible to miss. She gloated at the center of countless fools and admirers, her mind smug, indigo, and larger than the combined weight of a planetary population. Judging by her perceptions, she floated on a lounge in her indoor lake, massaged by slaves. She was so weak that she required medical aid just to keep breathing.

What is your plan? the Commander demanded.

The fat girl barely peeled a fraction of her enormous mental attention away from her admirers. It was the equivalent of a dismissive glance. *I don't have time for you (Former Commander). Somebody (Me) has to fix your mistakes.*

The Former Commander paced across the carpeted floor of her luxury streamship. Attendant slaves followed her movements, cringing at each step. They'd never seen her move so briskly.

If the Upward Governess wanted her dead, she would be dead. She knew that. Normally, the Majority would debate such a drastic action as having the Former Commander assassinated. But with all the uncertainty . . .

The fat girl had only to desire something. Her eager admirers would make it happen.

I did warn everyone that the Betrayer was likely to be the biggest problem We (the Torth Empire) have ever faced. The Upward Governess sent that callous reminder to her billions of listeners.

The idiot masses chorused with admiration.

The impossible starship had to be the Betrayer's handiwork. It was painfully obvious. Only a supergenius could mock up monstrous machinery in any sort of functional way. Only a renegade supergenius would figure out how to construct it from ether, or whatever materials he could coax the Giant into picking up and smashing together.

And what was he going to do with a huge starship?

No doubt the Betrayer would crew his ship with runaways. He would twist former slaves to dark purposes. It seemed the slave revolt he had masterminded in Duin was just a preliminary test. He was gearing up to do much, much worse.

Stop the Betrayer, the masses chorused. *Find him. Kill him.*

The Former Commander thought it would have been nice if the Upward Governess, in her immense wisdom, had sent out a more effective early warning. Had she anticipated the hidden barb in the Betrayer's bargain? Had she not guessed his trickery?

The Former Commander stopped herself from pacing. Too many minds were watching hers, tallying her failures and her flaws.

Some of you doubt My wisdom. The Upward Governess heaved a mental sigh, milking the anticipation. *I could have been more effective in warning the foolish leaders of the Torth Empire, it is true. But . . .* She forced everyone to wait, eating a cube of gelatin. *It is difficult to think while My health is in such a terrible state of deterioration.*

The Majority exchanged mental glances. Soon they came to their own conclusions.

The Upward Governess needs medicine.

That stuff the Betrayer invented?

Someone ought to go to the primitive wildlife planet.

Fetch it for Her.

Mental voices tripped over each other, forming a great tidal wave of promises. Of course the Upward Governess should have any boon that might extend her life.

The Former Commander found herself pacing briskly again. No one seemed to care about the irony of who had invented that medicine.

We need the medicine—

—also.

The Twins wove through the thunderous Majority, reminding everyone that they were also supergeniuses.

And Me. That came from the Rind Topographer.

I request NAI-12 as well. That was the Spin Overture.

More of the greedy children showed up, apparently emboldened into making demands.

Defeating the enemies should not prove too much of a challenge, the Death Architect thought with her usual sublime rationality. *The Betrayer contains far less knowledge than any one of Us. He spent barely three moon cycles in the Megacosm.*

The Upward Governess threw caution on that thought. *The Betrayer has utter freedom to do (to invent) whatever he desires. He is not constrained by laws. As We are.*

Just so, the Death Architect agreed. A chamber of torturous experiments passed through her mind. *We will need the freedom to invent new weapons. That is a given.*

The Former Commander nearly dropped out of the Megacosm, struggling to mask her disapproval. *Let Us not be blinded by haste*, she thought to her own smaller audience, desperate to reach the Majority. Didn't they understand why supergeniuses were never permitted certain freedoms? *The Empire needs fail-safes against tyrants. Otherwise, We are no better than savages.*

She was gratified to gain a substantial audience. She had not entirely lost her loyalists.

These supergeniuses want to overturn laws that are cornerstones of civilization, some among the Majority whispered.

Their promises are (so far) empty.

That medicine should be granted as a reward.

Let Them prove Their usefulness.

The Twins exchanged a set of private mental glances. Complaints tumbled from them in an alternating pattern.

The law against Yeresunsa—

—was also a fail-safe against tyranny.

We (supergeniuses) have adult responsibilities.

Yet We are not granted the (same) rights and privileges as adults.

We must work an estimated five hundred and thirty-six times harder than any ordinary citizen—

—in order to get promoted.

We have (far) more knowledge than the average Torth—

—yet in important matters, We are (still) treated like children on baby farms.

Their thoughts melded into a single mental voice. *We deserve equality.*

The Former Commander wondered if the Twins pictured themselves as oppressed. They'd been born with a mutation that gave them far more influence than an average child on a baby farm. They wallowed in their own private, luxurious palace, served by a veritable army of slaves.

I cannot be effective in countering the Betrayer, the Upward Governess thought, *if I am dying.*

Why were all supergeniuses such greedy, entitled brats?

The Former Commander imagined them with enough NAI-12 to grow to adulthood. That idea was far more disturbing than anything the enemies might do. Supergeniuses were free to earn a high status, but longevity . . . ?

Given their mutant brains, they would be empowered to take over the galaxy.

The Majority would be reduced to slaves underneath a handful of ruthless, self-serving individuals. Their tyranny would make everything the Betrayer was doing look like a petty glitch. Civilization would fall apart.

Anyone with a shred of common sense could see that. Couldn't they?

!!!!!!!!!!!!!!!!!!!!!!!!!

Death screams filled the local corner of the Megacosm.

Ghostly echoes of dead Torth—minds who had been active and engaged just moments ago—plowed through everyone's thoughts.

Perceptual replays from the Torth Homeworld showed what had happened. Fortresses didn't matter. Shelters were useless. Concentric waves of devastation rolled through the entire planet, unnatural, swallowing millions of lives. No one could survive where buildings collapsed, folded into the very ground.

Ninety-nine million lives winked out.

That many citizens. Gone. Murdered by the Betrayer and his cadre of rebels and runaways.

They should have evacuated the planet earlier, distant Torth murmured to each other in the silence left in the wake of shock.

As soon as the Giant and the Betrayer showed up.

As soon as the Lady of Sorrow (the Shapeshifter) proved to be real.

But realistically? There were not enough ships. The dreadnoughts and the streamships were overcrowded beyond capacity. Even the jumper shuttles were overcrowded.

Who expected a planetary evacuation to be necessary? Especially a planet as well fortified and well armed as the Torth Homeworld.

Chaotic storms raged across the planet. Survivors navigated their aerial transports through the thunderheads, or else they were trapped in rubble.

A few fools cringed with filthy slaves, deep underground in slave Tunnels. That seemed stupid. A lone Red Rank might dominate thousands of slaves for a while, but . . .

One of those survivors reported a strange shift in reality.

I am transported to a new place. She found herself disoriented and sick with nausea, surrounded by ragged masses of slaves and albinos.

Another Red Rank reported, *Me, too.*

A Brown Rank chimed in. *I think . . . is this possible?*

Their audiences pasted clues together and spat out a stunning conclusion.

!!!!!!!

We have agents inside the Betrayer's starship!

The Former Commander put aside her dark musings about tyranny. She turned to the big view screen and gazed at the improbable colony starship. The Torth Empire now had eyes inside that enemy vessel.

The three Torth trapped inside were military ranks. Each was brave enough to hide in a slave zone, yet now they seemed to be soaking up emotions from the mob of disgusting slaves around them. They stank of fear.

Each Torth ordered slaves to get back, to give them space. When that didn't work, they attacked with pain seizures. And they began shooting.

Slaves exploded in gory chunks. But there were more and more, and blaster gloves needed time to recharge. Mobs of stinking aliens tore the gloves off their hands. Tore their clothing. Wrenched their limbs.

Fight! the Former Commander urged, fists clenched. *Probe their minds! Find out where the Betrayer is! Kill him!*

It was already too late for the Red Ranks. One died when a nussian stomped on her spine. The other died from a twisted neck, wrenched violently by a brawny nussian.

The Brown Rank, however, remembered her duty to the Empire.

She focused on nearby minds, soaking up everything she could learn from the nasty savages while broadcasting her stream of consciousness in the Megacosm. She fought, but she also learned.

Her attackers had no clue where the Betrayer was. Few of them even seemed aware that he existed.

The savages believed that they owed their survival to the Giant, whom they worshipped as some sort of demigod known as "the messiah." They did not know where he was. Many of the albinos felt unsettled and frightened, and they were eager to blame their messiah for the loss of their homes.

The Brown Rank was known as the Chat Tangent. Now the Majority redubbed her the Glorious Chat Tangent, with millions tuned into her mind.

Billions. Hundreds of billions.

She died inundated with praise, even as slaves and savages wrenched her limbs out of their sockets and literally tore her apart.

Analysts studied every aspect of her personality. Experts commented on the lens through which she had soaked up information, and discussions eddied throughout the Megacosm. Now the Torth Empire knew what the Betrayer was working with. Primitives. Savages . . . but savages bolstered by a terrible power.

The Giant, it seemed, had a fearsome new ability. He could teleport.

With passengers.

And no one knew where the Betrayer was. He might be stashed anywhere. He might pop up on any planet, in anyone's suite. He might operate from a fortified lair anywhere in the galaxy. Who could possibly find him? Who could predict his next move?

The Former Commander wanted to clench her fists, suffering an almost slave-like degree of frustration. *We need to be smarter than the Betrayer.* She was just not used to relying on anyone for military tactics, especially not on mentally unstable children.

Perhaps the Torth armada could still destroy that starship?

This battle wasn't over. The enemies must be exhausted. They were outnumbered and outgunned. Soon, perhaps even now, the Giant would be vulnerable to attack.

!!!!!!!!!!!!!!!!!!!!!!!!!!!

!!!!!!!!!!

!!!

Reports crashed through the Megacosm with fresh shock.

The Former Commander blinked tightly, needing to be certain that her vision was working properly. Unfortunately, her view screen was functioning as it should. She could confirm the reports with her own eyes.

The Betrayer's starship was on the move.

Its engines burned white, reactors flaring at maximum capacity. Apparently, the Betrayer did not care that his ship was in a crowded orbital zone. Laws meant nothing to him.

Lesser vehicles melted from the radiant heat and energy. A few streamships went to illegal speed themselves, trying to get away.

DESTROY THEM! The Majority thundered an unequivocal command.

This battle could not be allowed to end with the Torth Empire reeling and coping with major casualties and the Betrayer victorious. If the enemies escaped without punishment . . . that was unthinkable. Ridiculous. Inconceivable.

! DESTROY ! DESTROY ! DESTROY ! DESTROY !

The Former Commander reached into the Megacosm and urged the armada to throw all its firepower at the Betrayer's starship. Never mind the scheming supergeniuses for now. There must be time to turn this tragic day into a victory.

Dreadnoughts fired up their deep space engines. The Torth armada maneuvered toward the behemoth of a starship and prepared to launch its comet-class warheads.

CHAPTER 11

LASTING STANCE

A fresh heap of arrivals crowded the air. They dropped, and the previous wave couldn't move fast enough to get out of their way. For one shining moment, Ariock was in sight, plastered with muck and rolling at high velocity.

Vy leaped toward him.

But he vanished within a second. The hundreds of people he'd brought with him remained, and they looked even more injured and bedraggled than previous waves. They were battered, injured, possibly sick from radiation or terror, and screaming. They jostled and shoved. A lot of them were nussians with dangerous spikes.

Vy got shoved against a sallow albino teenager. She lost her balance and steadied herself on a nearby shoulder.

"Torth!" a nussian bellowed, pointing straight at her.

"I'm not!" Vy screamed so hard, her voice cracked. Couldn't people see her tears? Her torn black wraps?

"She's with the messiah," someone shouted on her behalf.

"She's from paradise!"

"Where is the messiah?" A muck-streaked albino woman threw herself down onto her knees, begging Vy. "Can you heal my daughter?" She presented an injured toddler.

Vy recalled her training as a triage nurse.

"I can help." Maybe she couldn't stop Ariock from wearing himself out, but she could certainly do a few minor things. She could treat dislocated joints. She could advise people who were confused about hygiene and bandages. Perhaps that would ease some of the workload Ariock faced.

And, Vy remembered, she'd tucked away the bottle of Torth painkillers that Garrett had handed to her. She had given a few pills to Thomas, but there must be fifty or more left. She could offer them to anyone in severe pain.

And couldn't she do something benign with the blaster glove?

"Let me remove your slave collars!" Vy yelled, remembering the "unlock" mode that she'd learned from Thomas and various Duin refugees. "Let me treat your injuries! Are you in pain?"

Skeptical people turned her way.

As Vy set to work, the cries of joy were contagious. People seeking the messiah began to move toward her instead. At least she was present. The messiah must be in another room, vanishing and appearing elsewhere, helping distant people.

"Lady of Paradise!" an albino man called her.

That title stuck. Every time someone guessed that Vy was a Torth, the surrounding people shouted corrections. "No! She is the Lady of Paradise!"

"Beloved of the messiah!"

"She comes from the realm where there are no Torth, and where everything is perfect and happy!"

"She will set you free!"

"She will fix your child's hand!"

"She has the touch of paradise!"

Vy gave up on searching for Ariock. She was needed.

She washed bite wounds with trickles of pure water from canteens. When she asked for cloth, someone brought folded linens. Two adolescents perched nearby, and at her direction, they used knives to cut the linens into bandage strips. The babble of voices told Vy what an apocalypse these people had survived.

She gave her glove to a motherly govki with striped fur. Former slaves lined up, and soon their collars were falling to the floor. That was a relief. These people had enough to worry about without collar shocks and spikes prodding them to wake up or take meals.

"Worst injuries here!" That deep-throated bellow came from a nussian.

"Life-threatening injuries?" another nussian bellowed. "Move them up here!"

Nussians patrolled the mob, cutting through the frenzy like boats on a frothing sea. Orange, bronze, or red, the huge aliens paused here and there, inspecting injuries.

" . . . did you say?"

It was a whisper. A distant whisper. But Vy heard.

"The messiah has fallen?"

Vy stood, bandages still clutched in one hand. She was taller than any Alashani, taller than ummins, and if she stretched, she could see past the furry shoulders of upright govki. But there were always nussians. She couldn't find Ariock.

"I don't know. It's just what I heard."

Vy figured the gossip had to be wrong. Ariock was too strong to fall. He could uproot the Stratower and throw it. He could do anything.

"Look at her."

People were staring at Vy, seeing her concern.

"The Lady of Paradise knows."

"Maybe she can help him?"

As that message bounced from person to person—"They say he's this way!"—the mob surged in one direction, like a high tide in a narrow chasm.

Vy thrust the rolled-up bandages at one of her adolescent helpers. She didn't know what she could do for Ariock, if anything. And he was probably fine. But she had to at least check on him. She let the crowd shove and sweep her along, step by teetering step.

When people saw Vy's awkward gait, they pushed their friends aside, clearing an aisle for her. A couple of brawny nussians caught sight of Vy. They exchanged looks, then veered toward her.

"Are you the Lady of Paradise?" one called.

"Violet Hollander?" the other said, pronouncing her full name, the way nussians did.

"We seek your skills as an herbalist," the first nussian said. "For someone important."

People were rarely circumspect about Ariock, so Vy figured these nussians were worried about someone else. Weptolyso, perhaps. Maybe Jinishta? Or Thomas.

"You may ride upon my shoulder." One of the nussians extended his thick, pebbly arms.

Vy made sure that her adolescent helpers were confident and well supplied. Once they'd given nods, she accepted the nussian's help.

She sailed through the crowd, perched high up, clinging to nussian spinal spikes. People shuffled aside even faster than they'd done for Vy alone. It was a good thing, because the starship seemed endless. The nussians trekked through one immense room after another.

Each room was the size of a convention center floor. Conversations echoed. Every place was overcrowded. Vy saw, through crude square-cut doorways, that there were more rooms beyond. More and more and more.

"He healed me!" an albino woman bragged loudly to anyone within earshot. "I was almost dead. My ribs were broken. And the messiah healed me!"

"He heals everyone!" another person was shouting. "He healed me, too! See?" That person showed off an albino limb that looked unharmed.

Their destination was yet another overcrowded room, but the entrance to this one was a knot of congestion. Nussians blocked the way.

"Come back later," one of the nussians kept saying.

Another held out his thorny arms, stopping ummins and other small people from sneaking past. "The messiah is busy."

Vy's escorts were allowed past the blockade.

From there, they edged through a sea of people, their voices echoey in the steel chamber. Light strips offered a dull, desultory white illumination. A few Alashani carried lanterns or big candelabras on poles. Vy hoped the open flames were not a fire hazard.

Nussians clustered at one end of the room. They formed a barrier, all facing outward, as if protecting something. Or someone.

Vy recognized one of the nussians. "Weptolyso!"

The former hall guard blocked a group of albinos, aided by his nussian sweetheart, Yuey. When he heard Vy call his name, he looked pleased. "I am so glad they found you."

"My mother needs healing!" one of the albinos screamed.

"I need to be healed!" another albino said, her arm in a makeshift sling. "Let me through. I am the daughter of a councilor, you big oafs! Let me see the messiah!"

The nussians were obstinate.

Meanwhile, Vy's escort gently set her down. She was usually the tallest person in any given group, but next to so many nussians, she felt like a mouse. She hoped no one would accidentally step on her. She had to crane her head up to meet their shifting reddish eyes.

Weptolyso curled down so he could rumble softly, "Ariock needs your healing skills."

Was he making a tasteless joke? Vy studied the nussian, but he looked as serious as she had ever seen him.

"Please." Weptolyso moved aside, allowing her enough room to slip past him. "See if there's anything you can do."

Vy took two limping steps, encouraged by a gentle nudge from Weptolyso. The thorny wall of living bodies closed up behind her, sealing her in.

Ariock lay face up on spread blankets.

He looked peacefully asleep. Except his skin was the wrong color, chalky gray. Someone had removed his quiver of spears. His scarf-veil was tucked under his head as a makeshift pillow. He smelled like mud, rain, and ozone.

Vy threw herself next to him. She wanted to fling her arms around him, but he might have injuries hidden beneath his wraps and leather armor.

Vy held a hand above his nose, watching his chest for the motions of breathing. He had to be alive. Ariock, of all people, was too strong to be a victim.

A despondent voice spoke nearby. "The messiah cannot be helped."

Ariock was breathing. Of course he was. Vy shook him gently. Then she poked him. "Ariock?" she said in his ear.

He had no reaction whatsoever.

Very gently, Vy raised one of his eyelids. His pupil contracted slightly. That was a promising sign.

But his skin was cool, and too ashen. Shock. And he wouldn't wake up. Something was very wrong.

"I am sorry," the despondent girl nearby said. "There is nothing you can do. There is nothing anyone can do."

Vy looked up, angered by the defeated tone.

Orla sat cross-legged on the other side of Ariock. Judging by the clean white tracks on her grimy cheeks, she had been weeping.

Over Ariock?

How long had this teenage healer sat alone with him—apparently writing him off as dead?

"He's alive," Vy snapped. "Have you tried healing him?"

Orla shrugged as if nothing mattered. "They sent for me, of course. But I am useless." She plucked at her shoulder, where her Yeresunsa mantle would be if she wasn't swathed in battle blacks. "I cannot heal anyone right now. My powers are depleted. But others have tried. They cannot heal him, either."

Vy struggled to hide her rage. Of course depleted healers could not help. Orla should not have even been granted the privilege of being here.

"The messiah overused his powers," Orla said. "No one can heal that."

Vy vaguely remembered Alashani lectures, aimed at Ariock, about power overuse. The consequences of depletion were supposed to be severe.

"He ignored the warning headache." Orla tapped her own temple, as if to illustrate. "There is no way to recover from that. Everyone knows what happens. Ignore the warning headache and you die."

Vy glared at the teenaged healer. It was crazy to write off Ariock as dead. And wrong. He was breathing!

She loosened Ariock's armor, recalling her first aid training. She checked for constricted airways. She observed his breathing and checked for irregularities. She would elevate his legs. Test his reflexes.

"Has anyone sent for Thomas?" Vy asked. "Or Garrett?"

"The *rekvehs*?" Orla's lip curled in disbelief.

That made the answer obvious. No one had bothered to send for the only people aboard this starship who could make educated medical guesses.

"Weptolyso!"

Weptolyso lumbered around to look at Vy.

"I need either Thomas or Garrett," Vy said. "Can you please send someone to bring them here? Whichever one is available."

Since Weptolyso was not an Alashani, he did not sneer or balk. "It will be done," he assured her and turned back around.

Vy went back to loosening Ariock's clothes and checking for injuries, all the while knowing the problem was more serious than the superficial cuts and burns on his skin. The signs of shock weren't going away.

"How do you know he ignored the warning headache?" Vy asked Orla. "What did you see?"

"It is what I heard," Orla said. "The last few people he healed said he was wincing and blinking a lot." She gestured. "Those are definite signs of a warning headache. Besides." She gave Vy a level look. "You know him."

There was no denying that.

Vy blinked back tears, unlacing the gauntlets from Ariock's forearms. He would have thrown all his energy into saving people. He would have kept going, despite pain, no matter what. Nothing would stop him when he was determined.

"Idiot," she whispered through clenched teeth.

The floor quaked. Nussians bumped into each other, grunting and muttering apologies. Beyond them, people screamed.

The lights flickered.

For one terrifying instant, everything went pitch-black. Body odors and fear surrounded Vy.

Torth must be shooting missiles at their ark of a ship. This place was all any of them had. If the Torth destroyed it . . .

Ambient lights glowed back to life.

Someone is defending us, Vy realized. Someone was keeping the lights on. Was it Garrett? Thomas? The Lady of Sorrow? Vy shuddered and figured the monster woman would not do much more than wreck buildings.

Only Thomas could navigate their starship through a temporal stream.

Vy regretted sending for him, because escaping danger needed to be a top priority. She had almost forgotten that.

"Messiah?" the mob roared.

"We need the messiah!"

"Where is he?"

The enclosure of nussians drew tighter, pressured by the insistence all around them.

Vy wished she could protect Ariock the way he so often shielded people. But she wasn't even big enough to hug him all the way. How could she defend him against the demands of random strangers? The mob did not care about him. They only knew him as a distant, godlike figure who was supposed to provide for their needs.

"Orla," Vy said. "Will you go and discreetly fetch some Yeresunsa? I mean Yeresunsa who actually have some power left?"

Orla gave her a pitying look, as if she had been asked to bring Ariock back from the dead. "No one can—"

When she began to protest in her whiny voice, Vy felt something inside her snap.

"Get out of here and do it." Vy straightened. "Yes, I realize that no one can revive Ariock, as far as you know. But they can help me keep him hydrated. They can help him breathe. There's a few things we can do to prolong his life."

"But . . ." Orla sounded anguished. "He's dead."

Vy jumped up, driven by a blaze of fury. How dare Orla sit there and tell such a cruelly blatant lie? Why did she feel so entitled to sit with Ariock? Had she earned the privilege? No. Of course not.

"I am sorry." Orla shrank back. "He died a hero. I mourn him, like you. I worshipped him. But—"

"GET. OUT." Vy reached over to throw Orla. "Do what I told you!"

The albino girl scampered before Vy could shove her. She darted through a gap between nussians and was gone.

That left Vy alone with an unresponsive Ariock.

She felt like a monster. A giant who towered over albinos, who terrified warriors, and who could not control her own rage. Was this how Ariock felt at times? She wanted to ask him. She wanted him to wake up.

Sobbing, Vy folded up against his chest.

Although she shook with sobs, it was more rage than anything else. Orla wasn't her real target. She wanted to yell at Ariock for being such a noble fool. What sort of overconfident idiot went past his own limits? Hadn't he remembered any of the dozens of warnings that Jinishta and Garrett had given him?

He had not bothered to give Vy, or anyone, a chance to stop him. He had made it impossible. Teleporting. Appearing in places where no one who cared could reach him.

She could picture him kneeling in this overcrowded room, tiredly offering to heal an endless mob of people. Millions. Literally. He would have held his hands up and invited them, one by one. Concussions. Broken limbs. Lava burns. Dislocated shoulders. No injury was too small for Ariock to turn them away.

He would have kept at it, healing an endless line of injuries, until his vision blurred and his head pounded with sharp pain. Even then, he would have kept at it.

The fool.

Now he was sick, maybe dying, while their ship trembled from blasts. All his heroic efforts and sacrifices would be for nothing if they got blown up here in Torth orbital space.

What an idiot.

Vy gritted her teeth and repressed a whimpered scream. This time, it was aimed at herself. How many times was she going to have to watch Ariock fail? Every great thing he did seemed greater than the last, but if he died . . . this would be the biggest failure ever.

She should have grabbed him after he tossed the Stratower into space. She should have clung to him, relentless, whispering directly in his ear, until he remembered that he had mortal flaws and a knack for putting himself in danger.

She should have acted sooner.

LIVING CONDITIONS

The flood of refugees seemed unending, more people than Kessa had ever seen in her life. Few recognized her face, yet everyone seemed to know her name. They'd been told about an ummin elder who slew Torth and dressed in Alashani battle garb.

Rumors claimed that Kessa the Wise came from paradise. They said she had saved the messiah from death. She had the answers. She knew what to do.

"You'll find spigots of water on the lowest deck." Kessa pointed for the benefit of a shivering old councilor and her hangers-on. "It's a hike, but there are volunteers at every doorway. Go straight for three doorways, then descend the series of ramps to your left. The spigots are between ten rooms with humming machinery."

"Thank you, but . . ." The councilor hesitated. "My people have visited the spigots. They don't work."

One of her crew leaned around her, teeth chattering. "It is true. They are blocked with ice."

Kessa did not let her dismay show. A long line of people watched her, eager for someone who might suggest solutions to their immediate problems. They wanted a leader who could be trusted not to show favoritism toward any particular group. That was why they were coming to Kessa. Many of these people had gotten into arguments over basic necessities: water, clothes and blankets, food.

"The messiah is busy," Kessa said. "But I promise, he will be apprised of the situation. I will also report the situation to our steward."

She meant Thomas, but there was no reason to explain that their pilot was a *rekveh*. Let these people imagine a cheery head-of-household-staff albino. Most of them believed they were in a cave, anyway, despite the big screens embedded into walls.

Those blank screens had transformed into windows, all at the same time. They displayed a view of stars, battleships, and space debris . . . and in the distance, an angry-looking planet. That was the Torth Homeworld.

Of course, very few people aboard this starship understood what planets were. To most of them, the windows displayed meaningless, abstract imagery. It was just part of the grim decor.

"In the meantime," Kessa said, "please find a way to make your water last. It is important to ration our supplies until the messiah can attend to our needs."

She did not like making promises on Ariock's behalf. Where was he? Probably still rescuing people, or perhaps shielding their vehicle from nuclear detonations. No doubt he was busy. Everyone was getting thirstier, colder, and more miserable, but Kessa figured that no one would die from those complaints. They could wait.

"Are there any extra blankets?" the councilor asked sullenly. "Or anything we can use to keep warm?"

"I assume you know where to find your nearest hospice center?" Kessa replied, impatient to hear the next complainer in line.

She had set up multiple hospice centers on every deck, thirty-six in all. That was where emergencies got taken care of. And anyone with surplus supplies was encouraged to set up camp near a hospice center, where they could sell or donate their supplies.

"We received a few rags there," the councilor said, dismissive. "But the valuable supplies, like the mushroom ale, are under guard by dozens of nussians. And not the friendly type."

By "friendly type," she meant Alashani nussians. Many albinos were distrustful of—and downright fearful of—the formerly enslaved nussians who had served Torth masters. That type had harsh accents and brusque attitudes.

"Do you think that's fair?" the councilor demanded.

"I am sorry." Kessa tried to sound sympathetic. "But I have entrusted Weptolyso to keep the peace. Remember, nussians do not require water or blankets the same way you do. They have no interest in hoarding supplies. They are protecting what little we have so it doesn't all get used up right away. The messiah is busy protecting all of us from Torth and disasters. We must be independent for a little while."

Kessa was extremely grateful to Weptolyso. He had become a unifying force for the nussians, a bridge between the free, friendly types of nussians and the enslaved, unfriendly types, some of whom still felt loyalty toward their absent Torth owners. Under his leadership, all the nussians were becoming cooperative. They were unified in what Cherise called a police force. They patrolled each deck, intervening in fights and protecting miserable people from hurting each other too badly.

"I am sure the spigots will be working soon," Kessa told the councilor. "Next." She pointedly looked toward the next person in line, a careworn govki who wore a slave collar.

The albino and her crew sauntered away. Most seemed dejected. A few gave Kessa distrustful looks over their shoulders, as if she might be concealing a secret stash of water and blankets.

Any fool should be able to see that the handcart Kessa sat upon was empty. The rough woolen shawl she wore wrapped around her small body was barely enough to stop her from shivering. Her joints ached, and her beak felt half-numb from cold.

I need to find out what Ariock and Thomas are doing, Kessa thought, not for the first time.

But she had already sent informants to find out.

She had deputized a web of informants, trusty ummins from Duin. Each ummin had an assigned direction, plus a mission to learn what they could, then report back. By now, Kessa had a rough map in her head. She knew the layout of all four decks, which enclosed each other like concentric prisms. The top decks had ten sections; the bottom ones were octagonal. She understood where the control center was, buried in the cordoned-off aft of deck two, and she had a vague impression of hundreds of utility rooms and offices on decks four and one.

She had learned that Garrett Dovanack was in one of those rooms, limping from workstation to workstation, frantic. He claimed to be operating a defense system. Nussians and warriors guarded him, keeping out any *rekveh* haters who might try to assassinate him.

Cherise and Flen were in a large office-like room on the top deck, where depleted warriors lay, trying to sleep and recover their powers.

Perhaps Jinishta should be in that room, as well, but according to reports, she was roving the starship with a group of active warriors, acting as their de facto premier. Warriors who still had some power were apparently trying to help or heal wherever they were needed.

Kessa wanted to visit the suite of offices known as the control center. There, Thomas was reportedly hard at work, aided by seven ummins from Duin. They were safeguarded by nussians, but Thomas seemed to be depleted and in severe pain. Kessa wanted to check on him. And she was curious to learn what he might be accomplishing.

As for Ariock? Reports were scattered. No one knew where he was.

Kessa used her blaster glove to unlock a slave collar, removing it from the grateful govki. She unlocked another. She had already unlocked hundreds of slave collars, and lately, she'd heard some of the refugees refer to her as Kessa the Liberator.

It was a title Cozu would have been proud of.

Kessa smiled as she removed yet another slave collar. Every time she did this, she honored her mate, proving that his idealistic yet doomed effort to lead a mass escape had had some viability, after all.

And she was not the only liberator. Vy was probably liberating slaves as well. Cherise and Varktezo had each loaned their gloves to a friend, so they were in use, freeing slaves. Councilor Deschuba was using an extra glove Kessa had loaned to him.

Many thousands of slave collars would be broken today. There were so many former slaves, Kessa figured it might take a full wake cycle before they were all collarless.

She scrunched her bare toes, trying to keep warm. Was it her imagination, or was the air even colder?

Her own mild discomforts were nothing. She had endured worse.

She listened to fretful questions from parents who could not find their children, and farmers who had lost their mushroom crops, and merchants without wealth or wares, and former slaves who wondered what their future held. There were many people who were suddenly bereft of homes or purposes in life. They all craved assurances that life was not over.

"Light and glory," Kessa said without any trace of doubt. "We are all rescued for a purpose. I used to be a slave. When I ran away, I faced the unknown, and it was terrifying. But freedom was worth it, many times over."

Her reassurances could have been dismissed as empty. Yet people walked away from Kessa with a lightness in their steps and fresh determination in their eyes. They must hear her sincerity. Unlike most people, Kessa knew Ariock personally, and everyone seemed aware of that.

"Wait your turn," an albino snapped as an ummin ducked and darted through the crowd.

People muttered their resentment, but Kessa recognized the off-kilter head cover and long beak of Pung. "Please let him through," she called.

Pung had a strange look on his face. Somber. She didn't like that, because he was usually insolent. This looked like bad news.

"Can you please tell the nussian patrol to pay more attention to theft?" A sad-looking albino stood before her, having complained about his family heirlooms getting stolen. "I understand that water is important. But my beaded coin purse was extremely valuable, and it was all I—"

Kessa cut in. "What is your name?"

"Uh . . ." The albino wrapped his arms around himself, shivering. He looked confused. "Gechel."

"Gechel," Kessa said. "I want you to spread word that thieves should be identified, and their identities should be reported to you, whenever possible. You will compile a list."

Gechel gawked at her. "I don't think I'm qualified to—"

"I'm not qualified to organize people, either." Kessa clicked her beak. "I know you're exhausted, Gechel. We all are. If you are unwilling to list thieves, do you think you can find someone who is willing? Ariock will want to punish anyone who steals. We'll sort it out later. For now, just a list will suffice."

The albino gave an uncertain nod.

"Recruit people with good memories," Kessa suggested. "And I hope you, or whoever takes charge, is judicious. Ariock will not deal well with false reports."

Gechel dipped his knees in a gesture of respect, as if she was a councilor. "Thank you. I will get it done, Kessa the Wise. Should I report back to you?"

"That isn't necessary," she said. "Tell Weptolyso, the leader of nussians, what you are doing. We will seek you out when the time comes."

Gechel thanked her and hurried away with new purpose.

The next person in line looked impatient as Pung cut in front.

"Can I report in private?" Pung asked in a low, urgent voice.

The whole ship had been quaking from time to time, and lights had flickered. Kessa expected an update on their defense situation. She beckoned to the rear of the handcart. It was the closest thing to privacy, if they turned their backs to the crowd.

"Ariock fell," Pung whispered. "Orla and other warriors say he is very ill—that he is dying."

Kessa stared at her old friend. This had to be a false report.

"Couriers have been sent to Thomas and Garrett," Pung went on, oblivious to her shock. "But I figured maybe we can go and judge for ourselves?"

Kessa could not imagine Ariock dying from a random illness. This was not part of the prophecy. And this was not how hero stories were supposed to go.

Pung curled his hand around hers. "Can you get someone else to take your glove for a time?"

Kessa removed the glove, thinking. Perhaps the Torth had injured Ariock? At least he'd had the presence of mind to make it back to the starship on his own, teleporting. That meant he should recover.

Thomas would know.

"I need to go visit Thomas." She slid off the handcart.

"What?" Pung gawked at her with disbelief.

Kessa leaned close to Pung, to whisper. "I cannot help Ariock. Even if the worst is true, the most good we can do is to help our pilot. Somebody needs to make sure this huge ship stays afloat."

Someone needed to operate their defenses. And figure out how to warm the chill in the air. And how to make the water spigots work. Kessa figured that if Ariock could not tend to the living conditions, then Thomas was likely their key to survival.

"Besides," Kessa said, "I can bring him new trainees." She nodded toward three adolescent ummins who waited in a corner. They had helped to map the ship, and they had expressed interest in learning how to use Torth technology.

Pung whispered fiercely, "Let the *rekveh*—I mean, Thomas—come to us! He needs to check on Ariock, too."

"It is dangerous for him to float around in crowds." Kessa should not have to explain that Thomas, floating in that red hoverchair, with its splashes of glitter, was an obvious target for anyone who wanted to kill a Torth.

"What if . . . ?" Pung licked his beak with uncertainty.

The worst-case scenario was too horrific to speak out loud. What if Ariock really was dying? Or dead?

"Go to Ariock," Kessa urged her friend. "We can meet back here. Let me know what you see. I am going to Thomas."

CHAPTER 13

FINAL DESTRUCTION

Vy cuddled next to Ariock. That way, she could feel his breathing. Shallow breaths, and his body gave off less warmth than usual, and she tried to ignore those symptoms.

Weptolyso and his nussian crew had moved Ariock to a secluded corner. They no longer ringed him, but more than a hundred nussians squatted around the room, ever watchful. They questioned anyone who approached the inert messiah. If the visitor lacked an explicit errand, they were asked to leave or they were expelled.

Vy lost track of the visitors. Without Weptolyso's guardianship, she supposed that she would have had to fight off a mob of needy people all by herself. How? With her peg leg? Or with the blaster glove she had given away, uncaring? Either way, it would have been a disaster.

Instead, Ariock lay in peace. He was covered in donated blankets, as undisturbed as someone in a coma could be.

There were other donations.

Vy could not begin to count the worshippers who brought oils and seeds, fine woolens and golden coins, mushroom wine and wafers. Gifts piled up. A couple of worshippers had organized the donations into a multileveled shrine, neat and pretty.

When the starship quaked, jars had toppled and pottery had shattered. Ariock might find that amusing. If he ever woke up.

Newly freed slaves had no tokens to offer, so they were not allowed to approach, yet they seemed more curious and worshipful than the Alashani. Vy saw aliens rubbernecking from a distance. Such a variety of sapient species. They wanted to glimpse the powerful being who had snatched them from slavery and set them down into freedom.

Vy kept an eye out for help.

She noticed right away when two Yeresunsa women approached. One was Jinishta. But the other, an elderly woman dressed in dirty clothes and a purple mantle . . . might she have some active power?

The nussians allowed the two warrior women to pass.

"Are you a healer?" Vy stood, trying to show respect to the elderly one.

The elderly woman gazed at Ariock with a troubled expression. She gave Jinishta a nod, as if to confirm something they both suspected. Her voice was tough and creaky. "His life spark is weaker than the ashes around the last ember of a dying hearth."

"So he is depleted?" Jinishta sounded pained.

"Without a doubt," the elder Yeresunsa said.

Vy did not like their tough, sorrowful expressions. Shouldn't Yeresunsa be flocking to Ariock's aid?

"Do what you can," Jinishta said.

The elder sighed. "I will." She stretched her hands in the healing pose. "For whatever it's worth."

Vy balled her hands into fists. Was apathy the best the Yeresunsa warriors could offer to the hero who had saved their lives? Couldn't they see how many people Ariock had rescued from certain death?

"I am sorry." Jinishta squeezed Vy's shoulder. "Depletion usually means an instant death, but in rare cases, it takes hours. It depends on how quickly the Yeresunsa drained himself."

Vy nearly screamed that Ariock could recover. He was breathing!

"I have never heard of anyone recovering from it," Jinishta went on. "There is no cure."

Vy wanted to hurt the useless warriors. Instead, she sneered, "Let's see what Thomas has to say. He's a lot smarter than your people."

The elderly woman scoffed, but Jinishta only looked sympathetic. "Ancient tales say that it used to be possible to revive Yeresunsa who were depleted," she said. "But no one knows how it was done. That knowledge is lost."

"Thomas will figure it out." Vy felt sure that Thomas would have an answer, or at least a solid theory or two.

"But according to those ancient legends," Jinishta said, "only weak warriors ever recovered from depletion. The strong always died." Her gaze shifted toward Ariock, as if to imply that he was not a candidate for recovery. "The greater the Yeresunsa, the greater the fall."

Vy began to argue.

"That is common wisdom," the elder said. "It hearkens back to ancient times."

Vy did not care how rude she sounded. "What about your messiah prophecy? What about all the things Migyatel predicted he would do?"

The elder shrugged. "He has fulfilled the prophecy."

Jinishta looked less certain. She gazed at Ariock with a troubled expression. "Heal him again, Dishra," she commanded.

"I already—"

"Heal him again," Jinishta urged. "Put everything you have into it."

The elder Yeresunsa, Dishra, assessed Jinishta's determination. This time, her neck muscles strained as she healed Ariock. The air writhed like translucent snakes.

Afterward, Ariock continued his shallow breathing. He made no response when Vy touched his face. Nor did he stir when she lifted his eyelids, one after the other, searching for signs of consciousness.

"I am sorry." Dishra sounded gruff, even as she swayed with exhaustion.

"Keep him alive." Vy looked from one Yeresunsa to the other. "Please?"

Dishra winced. She looked like she might be suffering from a warning headache herself.

"We will do what we can." Jinishta looked earnest. "Most of the warriors are drained or else hit with the inhibitor." She indicated herself. "But I have spread the message. Any healers who are fit will join you here."

Vy wanted to be gracious and thank Jinishta. All she could muster was a nod. Drained healers with paltry power were not good enough. Ariock needed a healer of Garrett's caliber.

"Depletion cannot be healed." The exhausted elder begged them both to understand. "The messiah knew this. He sacrificed himself to save us." She gave Ariock a look of admiration.

As if Ariock had put himself into a coma on purpose.

"Must we tarnish his memory by preserving him?" Dishra sounded like she was pleading. "Let him die with dignity."

Vy considered picking up small items and hurling them at Dishra. Anyone who believed Ariock was on his deathbed was wrong, moronic, or insane.

"Come on." Jinishta tugged on the older woman, giving Vy a nervous look. "Let's get you to the recovery room."

They hobbled away.

Vy clenched her fists, watching them go. Jinishta had better make good on her promise to send more healers.

Her comment about the prophecy must have hit home. It seemed Jinishta had some renewed faith in the messiah prophecy, at least enough to suspect that Ariock might do more than lead the Alashani into the "light" of nuclear explosions. He was supposed to bring them to glory. He was supposed to lead them to triumph over the Torth Empire.

Vy sank down next to Ariock again.

If he were conscious at all, he would have snuggled closer to her. He would have enfolded her in his huge arms. But he did not move.

Floor-to-ceiling windows broke up the nearest wall. Vy gazed at blocky battleships, each one shooting beams of liquid fire or spraying burning missiles. Each attack slammed into a counterforce. Missiles exploded in a tumbling, white-hot froth.

It seemed their colony starship was defending itself.

In the background, beyond the collisions and debris, the planet slowly tilted in its orbit. Storms whorled its surface into knotted patterns. Its predominant color was angry purple, splashed with bursts of faraway lightning.

"What are we looking at?" Weptolyso asked.

He had sidled up near Vy and Ariock, and now he squatted in a nussian crouch, his version of a comfortable sitting position.

"That's a space battle." Vy wasn't interested enough to ask for clarification of what he meant.

"Is it really happening?" Weptolyso asked.

"I assume so." Vy huddled closer to Ariock, trying to keep him warm. "You feel the ship quake when we get hit, right?"

The windows were actually high-definition monitors, although they looked indistinguishable from clear panes of glass. They conveyed a real-time view.

Weptolyso studied the explosions outside, fascinated and curious. Vy realized that he had no one else he could ask. Neither slaves nor Alashani understood much about technology or the universe. The way Torth hoarded knowledge, everyone else tended to crave it.

"Who is winning?" Weptolyso asked.

Vy sat up, still pressed against Ariock. She gazed sideways at her immense nussian friend. "Uh, I don't know. I think we are."

Judging by all the motion outside, their colony starship must be flying away from orbital space at a fast clip. And they were being bombarded. With so many missiles aimed their way, it seemed miraculous that they hadn't been hammered to death.

"Who is protecting us?" Weptolyso eyed Ariock with concern.

"I don't know." Vy gently caressed Ariock's cheek. "Garrett, I guess. It looks like he's using some kind of missile defense system."

Weptolyso looked impressed. "You mean he is using Torth weapons?"

"Yes." Vy felt irritable, still seething with leftover anger. "I'm sorry, Weptolyso. I'm not the best person to answer your questions."

"A missile defense system." Weptolyso lumbered upright. "Perhaps I will seek out Garrett. I would like to help."

He loped away. Vy was marginally aware of him asking other nussians to take over certain tasks. She wondered if Weptolyso would be at all suited to operating holographs or computers, with his stubby fingers and huge hands.

Then again, she had met nussian architects and sculptors in the Alashani underground. The species happened to have tough, pebbly skin, like rhinoceroses, but it was a mistake to associate them with animals. Nussians were just as highly evolved as ummins or humans. They had probably pioneered their own advanced technology in the ancient era before Torth subjugated them and forced them to serve as guards.

The crowd thinned as gawkers grew bored. Vy overheard people mention that lamps and candelabras would provide heat. They just had to make the oil last.

She heard them speculate about the magical windows. No one could comprehend the mysterious view.

People whispered about a murderous Red Rank who had appeared, apparently rescued by accident. Former slaves had torn the dangerous intruder to pieces.

Cherise visited briefly. She sat with Vy and did not say much. "Garrett is defending the ship," she said, offering an update. "Thomas is piloting us, last I heard."

But she could offer nothing more. After a while, she left.

Pung visited as well. And there were other people Vy recognized. Chaniyelem. Deschuba. Irarjeg. Haz and other Yeresunsa, including Shevrael and Nulshta. They all looked exhausted to the point of collapse.

None of them stayed long. None had anything useful to offer.

Ariock breathed.

His breaths made ghostly puffs. Vy tucked the blankets around him, trying to warm him up. She rested her head on his chest. If Ariock was going to die lonely and cold, after all he'd accomplished, then maybe she wouldn't mind freezing to death right beside him.

The room seemed too silent.

Perhaps that was what caused Vy to raise her head and look around.

A statuesque woman with a tangle of purple hair and metallic wings as sharp as blades stood by the nearest window.

The Lady of Sorrow gazed outside at the view. She must be untroubled by the cold, since her opalescent gown barely clung to her curves. A lot of flawless skin was exposed.

Vy's skin raised in goose bumps. She hardly dared breathe. This woman— or whatever she was—could morph into a titanic monster. No doubt she could destroy this entire colony starship if she felt like it. Why was she here?

Ariock had tried to thwart her rage.

Perhaps the Lady wanted to finalize her murderous frenzy by destroying the powerhouse who had rescued so many slaves. Vy could not shield Ariock, but she would try. She climbed on top of him.

The Lady of Sorrow continued to gaze out the window, as if curious about the space battle. She placed one slender hand against the faux glass.

A delicate touch. Not monstrous at all. Graceful and human.

The Torth Homeworld exploded in a brilliant ring.

The shock wave vaporized streamships and shuttles like tissue paper in a furnace.

An immense dreadnought blew apart into a billion pieces, each one careening at high speed in the shock wave. Space debris tumbled outward.

The shock wave passed well below the window view. Even so, the violent burst of debris made the metal world of the starship quake and shudder. Ariock was thrown like a heavy rag doll.

He landed hard, his head lolling to one side. Vy braced herself and landed atop him.

Outside, rocks flew past their ship. Some of those enormous rocks featured the melted remnants of skyscrapers and cave cities.

The Torth planet of origin was simply . . . gone. A disintegrating cloud of debris floated in the dark space where it used to be.

The Lady of Sorrow slowly turned and looked at Ariock and Vy.

Waves of hair shadowed her face, but she had fine features. She looked very composed and delicate for someone who had just destroyed a planet.

Vy did not want to meet her gaze or challenge her. So she watched the destruction outside. Now the Alashani would never return home. They had no home. Jinishta, Flen, Yuey, Orla . . . their lamplit cities were gone forever.

The winged woman stood directly in front of Vy.

But she had not taken a step. One moment, the Lady of Sorrow was standing by the window, and then she disintegrated to dust and reemerged whole. She had done it all within a second.

Vy craned her head to meet the purple gaze of the goddess.

A lacy diadem glittered in her hair. The Lady of Sorrow looked tired, but her gaze toward Ariock was unexpectedly tender. Almost kind.

As she leaned down to caress Ariock's face, her body lost cohesion, becoming a cloud of glittering dust. The cloud poured downward into a winged figure again. The Lady of Sorrow was in a graceful kneeling pose, with one hand outstretched to caress Ariock. Altogether, her disintegration and reintegration were faster than muscle movement.

Her tired gaze shifted to Vy.

Now there was no tenderness. That icy stare promised a brutal death.

Vy did not flinch. She expected the Lady of Sorrow to murder her, yet she returned the stare with her own defiance, be it mortal and pathetic. She could not shield Ariock. She could not revive him from his coma. But she would do her best, regardless, no matter what evil this world-destroying poltergeist intended.

The Lady of Sorrow held her gaze, as if expecting Vy to cringe, or look away, or blink in fear.

Vy did not.

After a few moments, the winged woman melted into a cloud of dust.

Instead of reforming with a noose around Vy's neck, or a blade stabbed into her back, the dust flitted away. It swirled into the dark recesses of the room, heading toward the air vent.

Vy let out a shaky breath and lay on Ariock's chest. She did not know if he had protected her or if she had protected him.

CHAPTER 14

IN FRAGILE COMMAND

The jolt knocked over burning oil lamps in the thoroughfare. It spilled mugs of ale, and it scattered dice games and supplies.

Peopled grumbled all around Kessa. They were annoyed, whereas she . . .

"Kessa?" one of the ummin adolescents asked. "What's wrong?"

Kessa walked closer to the huge window, horror-struck.

She walked until her beak touched the cold surface of the window and she could see the faint outlines of the cells that composed the imagery.

The artifice did not negate what she saw. The marbled planetary sphere had exploded like the biggest nuclear bomb in existence, and all that was left was disintegrating matter and tumbling rocks bearing the remains of sky-scrapers. And probably the remains of Alashani, and slaves, and also Torth and wild zoved.

She rested her forehead against the glass and closed her eyes. How was she, or anyone, supposed to inform faithful messiah worshippers that they would never return to their cities?

Her three ummin trainees crowded near her.

"That was something bad," one guessed. "Wasn't it?"

"A world just died." Another ummin elbowed that one. "Don't you remember what the Teacher taught us, when we were on the streamship from Umdalkdul? When we saw our world from the window?"

The first ummin looked considering. Kessa did not know how anyone could forget the sight of Umdalkdul, swirled with clouds and deserts and forests and oceans. Her home planet had looked majestic from afar. But so had the Torth Homeworld, in its own troubled way. Perhaps all worlds looked like that.

"Well." The second ummin pointed toward the rock fragments that careened through space. "That was the Alashani world."

"Ohhh." Now the other two trainees looked as dismayed as Kessa felt.

A family of Alashani camped nearby, huddled in blankets. They looked from the window to the ummins and back again. The mother shrugged with a lack of comprehension. The father looked troubled, but he resumed holding a bowl of mushroom paste for each of his young children, coaxing them to eat.

Kessa backed away from the view. There was no reason to linger and watch the remains of the dead world, unless one had a morbid curiosity. Some slaves would gawk at a gory corpse after the victim was torn apart by a blaster glove shot.

"Come," Kessa urged the three trainees. "It is more important than ever that we meet with Thomas."

She led the young ummins past encamped families, past rowdy gov-ki or nussians, past groups of albinos getting drunk on mushroom ale or quiet groups huddled around meager oil lamps. Some groups were mixed, Alashani and former slaves getting to know each other.

She overheard snatches of conversation.

"The messiah will recover." More than a few said that.

"He has to. He needs to fulfill the prophecy and lead us to light and glory."

Whenever someone expressed sourness about the messiah, others replied with optimism.

"The Lady of Sorrow will watch over us," they said. "Let us pray."

These crowds had no comprehension that their world was gone, even though they had seen it explode. Blame might come later. Would they blame the Lady of Sorrow? Or would they blame Ariock? Or the machinations of *rekvehs*? Or all three?

For now, former slaves celebrated freedom from Torth and slave collars. Alashani celebrated survival and the fact that they weren't enslaved. There was talk of rebuilding family homes and reestablishing mushroom farms.

Kessa confirmed her mental map of the starship as she hurried through overcrowded decks. Plain rectangular pillars subdivided each massive section of each deck. The whole place must be the size of a Torth metropolis, yet it looked more like an industrial complex than any sort of plush habitat. Ariock and Thomas had not had enough time to add furniture or luxuries.

Dozens of nussians guarded the hallway leading to the control center. They blocked the passage and stared suspiciously at Kessa and the trainees.

"I am no threat." Kessa showed her bare hands, which lacked a blaster glove. "I am Kessa."

Before she could say more, the nussian in charge relaxed, looking impressed. "Kessa the Wise?" His spikes flattened and retracted, and the other nussians also loosened up. They shuffled aside as if Kessa was a fearsome warrior.

"Weptolyso gave us a list of who we should let in," the leader explained. He studied Kessa with curiosity. "He was adamant that we not allow any Alashani past this point. Do you know why?"

Kessa noted that some of the guards had the soft, fleshy look of nussians who had spent their lives in the underground cave cities. They wore accoutrements, such as spinal ridge liners made of silver. No doubt they considered themselves Alashani—which meant they would be tempted to kill Thomas because he was a *rekveh*.

Weptolyso must have offered some sketchy pretext as to why the control center needed to be under guard. He would not have mentioned Thomas. And he had wisely appointed a battle-scarred former slave guard to be in charge of the whole group, so that the softer nussians would not be tempted to allow their Alashani brethren to sneak past.

"Alashani can be overly curious," Kessa said, trying to turn the forbiddance into a compliment. "I agree with Weptolyso. The control center is vital to our survival, and the former slaves operating those workstations cannot afford interruptions from well-meaning people." She trotted through the opened aisle, beckoning for the trainees to follow. "I expect these three to be of service in there. The slightest mistake, and our new home will fall apart and we will all die."

That gave the nussians enough to chew on. They muttered to each other, but they allowed Kessa and her adolescent followers to enter the narrow hallway.

The control center looked as unfinished as the rest of the ship. It was a hive of small, empty rooms interconnected by crude doorways. The passageway ended in a large, bustling chamber, filled with holographic displays, work pedestals, and harried ummins. They wore tunics and crisp head covers. Kessa recognized them all as adolescents from Duin.

Windows lined the curved far wall, each with a slightly different view, which formed a panorama of space. Debris and jagged asteroids floated in the void. Farther away, Kessa recognized the formidable Torth armada. Every battle cruiser seemed locked on their location.

Thomas hovered behind a jungle of holographic schematics and displays. His hoverchair, his yellow eyes, his aloof demeanor . . . everything implied that he was a sinister Torth.

Beside him, Varktezo listened with rapt fascination while Thomas rattled off a list of esoteric instructions. They were both scrolling through holographic menus and selecting glyphs.

Kessa blinked. The way Varktezo operated the workstation, with such assurance, one could be forgiven for assuming that he was a mind reader magically stuffed into the body of an ummin.

Neither one of them seemed aware of Kessa until she cleared her throat.

"Kessa!" Varktezo exclaimed.

Thomas looked sick, with dark bags under his eyes. Kessa doubted that anyone else had checked on him. Now she was glad that she had thought to pick up a water skin from a hospice center. She'd tucked it in her wraps, so that her body warmth kept it from freezing into ice. That also prevented feverish people from trying to steal it.

"Do you need water?" Kessa uncapped the container.

"Please." Thomas looked grateful.

Kessa held it for him to drink. Once he'd taken a few hearty sips, he stopped himself, possibly aware that the water supply was being rationed.

"Thank you," he said.

Kessa tightened the lid and placed it next to him, on the seat of the hoverchair. Now she had to think of a polite way to tell him about Ariock and to ask him what needed to be done.

"Kessa, guess what?" Varktezo looked like he was bursting with pride. "Guess what? I can read Torth glyphs!"

She gave him a warm look.

"It's easy!" Varktezo said. "I'm learning a lot!"

"That is very good," Kessa said, trying to give Varktezo attention while her mind worked on serious matters. "Thomas . . ."

"I heard about Ariock," Thomas said tersely. His focus was already back on the holographs, and he entered data even as he talked. "I'm sorry, but I can't help. I suggest you seek Evenjos and ask her advice. We have less than ten minutes to get this ship navigated through a temporal stream. The maneuver requires unfailing precision, and we barely have the equipment. Or the hands." He gestured at the small crew of ummins. "I'm calculating our vectors, but if anyone in this room makes the slightest mistake, we'll be vaporized."

Kessa closed her beak. Perhaps it had been a mistake to come here. Thomas didn't need nagging questions or interruptions while he worked.

"I don't have much leftover processing capability," Thomas said. "I can't hold an extensive conversation right now, but I'm glad you checked in. Would you please send a message to Garrett? Tell him that our life support is deteriorating. Everyone on this ship will freeze to death if the subfusion reactor interface isn't brought online and addressed within the next few hours. But obviously our defense situation is top priority until we get through the wormhole. There's no point to any of this if the Torth smash us with a comet-class warhead."

It must be awkward to operate a major starship without the Megacosm. "Of course," Kessa said. "I will make sure the message is delivered."

The three trainees gawked at everything. They were clearly afraid to go near Thomas, having grown up with horror stories about mind readers.

Kessa clicked her beak, signaling the trainees that they ought to leave along with her. They would probably just be a needless burden right now.

"The trainees are welcome to stay and learn," Thomas said, "if they can be helpful and not harmful. It was a nice thought."

Kessa looked at him with surprise. Thomas had a knack for speaking without emotion, like a Torth, yet his words were kind.

Thomas glanced at her for a split second. Anyone else might have read such a brief look as rudely dismissive, but Kessa recognized the honor. Thomas needed all his mental processing power in order to move their ship to somewhere safe. Even so, he was sparing her a sliver of attention.

"We need to train former slaves to use technology," Thomas said. "As soon and as much as possible."

Kessa tried to envision ummins using data tablets, piloting fleets of jumper shuttles and substituting amputated limbs with cybernetic enhancements. Perhaps Thomas wanted to sound generous, as a way of thanking her for bringing water, but he must know that slave species were not suited for technological prowess. Everyone knew that.

"It's a top priority." Thomas sounded serious. "As much as life support and defense. Ummins with some basic understanding of how the universe works, such as my crew here"—he swept a gesture—"should train others. And not just ummins."

She stared at him, trying to guess what he had in mind, and why.

"I'd like you to set the groundwork for a school," Thomas said.

Kessa cocked her head. She never would have expected Thomas to recommend such a quaint practice.

Cherise and Vy had informed her about schools. They were places where human children went to learn facts, daily, most of which held no immediate relevance in their lives, and much of which they forgot by the time they were adults. Kessa didn't understand it. No one understood it, not even her friends, and not the Alashani, either. Why learn how to engineer a pendulum clock if you were going to be a mushroom farmer?

No other species attempted to inundate their children with math and reading and science and philosophy. Only humans. Some Alashani apprenticed themselves to learn a valuable niche craft, such as deciphering runes or painting urns. And of course, all nontelepathic species passed ancient proverbs, legends, and hymns from one generation to the next. But schools?

Kessa had always figured it was a factor of the leisure time they had in paradise. With endless freedom, humans probably fell into strange habits, such as learning esoteric things simply for the sake of learning. It was like how some Alashani browsed their local bazaars in search of strange but useless trinkets or traveled to other cities along the River of Tears simply to say they'd been there.

"Varktezo," Thomas said. "Open the third engine interface and throttle it to sixty percent. And let's engage our vector chutes. Remember where that is . . . ? Good. Tack up the burn routines. Yeah, it's on the lowest menu bar . . ."

He went on. The two of them seemed engrossed in their work, although it was apparent that Thomas was making all the important decisions and probably handling a lot of unseen variables while he did so. His thin hands moved rapidly, creating new glyphs in the air.

He looked exhausted and unwell. No doubt he would rather rest while someone else piloted the ship.

The notion of a training program began to make some sense. It was unfair for just Thomas and Garrett to be burdened with operating all the technology critical for supporting a population equivalent to several cities.

A nearby ummin beckoned to a trainee. "Would you like to learn? I am monitoring a fueling cycle."

Others did the same, and soon the three trainees each had a mentor. Young ummins gazed at holographs, their gray skin and head covers awash in colorful reflections.

Kessa guessed the Torth military would keep pursuing the rebel starship. If only two people aboard the starship were experts in navigating interstellar space, life support, defenses, and utilities, such as how to make the water spigots run, and a million other things . . . that was a strained point of vulnerability.

Especially with Ariock incapacitated.

Former slaves needed to step up and shoulder some of the responsibility for their own continued freedom, whether they were suited to it or not.

"I will set the groundwork for a training program," Kessa agreed.

Her mind always felt full after a visit with Thomas. She hurried out, determined to get Thomas's message delivered to Garrett and to spread word that the Lady of Sorrow was to be sought. She also needed to continue her organizational efforts.

And she wanted to make sure that Thomas stayed well and got time to sleep. Who else was concerned about his fragile health? Almost everyone in command was too busy worrying about Ariock.

Perhaps Cherise would be willing to take charge of the technology training program?

After all, Cherise used to attend an actual school on Earth. She knew all sorts of terminology for mysterious things, such as "batteries" for devices that stored energy and "writing" and "icons" for Torth glyphs.

CHAPTER 15

WAR

The Torth Homeworld shrank with distance. Chaotic storms knotted and whorled its surface, but the Former Commander was too focused on the enemy starship to pay much attention to the rear view.

Until the planet vanished in a white-hot flash much too big for a thermonuclear explosion.

!!!
!!
!!!

The Megacosm quaked and buckled with death screams and their echoing impacts. Millions of eyewitnesses on the Torth Homeworld had been cowering under furniture, or curled up in spas, or even hiding in filthy underground slave quarters. They should have been safe.

Instead, they were obliterated.

Millions. Dead.

Things had gone horribly wrong. Throughout the Empire, Torth called for narcotic drinks or tranquility meshes. As for those within the orbital shock-wave zone . . .

The jolt knocked the Former Commander off her feet. She floated in zero G, her shroud billowing around her.

A battleship was shattered. Thousands of Torth aboard that vessel screamed and died in the Megacosm, along with half the armada. The Former Commander only survived by sheer luck. She happened to be outside the path of greatest damage.

Dreadnoughts, gone. Military streamships, gone. Jumper shuttles, gone. Half the arsenal was gone.

And the enemy starship was speeding away, carried by the shock wave.

The Megacosm ignited like wildfire. Towering waves of extreme, slavelike emotions ripped through everyone who was tuned in, throwing them this way and that. The masses—the entire Majority—felt afraid.

KILL. Impulses in the Megacosm raked her mind.

KILL THE ENEMIES.

KILL THEM.

The three remaining battleships were in pursuit, but they had failed to warm up their thrusters for an interstellar turbocharge. Speed like that was dangerous and pointless within solar orbital zones for multiple reasons. For one thing, macroscopic dust and larger space debris were common near planets or space stations. At turbocharged speeds, a rock might cause serious damage or even punch through a ship's nearly indestructible hull. For another thing, the ambient warmth and lower density of space medium within a solar system led to unpredictable boosts in speed. A ship's navigation system needed time to calculate trajectories with volatile influences taken into account. All of which made the fuel burn wasteful.

Gravity returned to the Former Commander's streamship. She landed on her feet, still watching the window, as missiles arrowed toward the Betrayer's starship.

On faraway planets, Torth forgot to punish slaves. They paused in the middle of meals or baths and closed their eyes in order to fully immerse themselves in the Megacosm.

Kill, they urged. *Kill. Kill. KILL.*

Colors flared in the black void, distorted by ionic wind and radiation. The missile strikes were falling short or exploding prematurely.

No enemy had ever damaged the empire like this. Never. Their history was a series of conquests, victories, and progress.

The Former Commander was shaken to her core. Like most Torth, she had never questioned the invulnerability of Torth galactic civilization. They were born superior to all other life forms. That made them unassailable. A few Torth might die when conquering inferior beings, but the collective always thrived and grew stronger.

Now she was forced to reexamine everything she'd believed. *Are We weak?* she wondered.

Are We safe? the Majority wondered.

That should have been a joke of a question. Yet it was not an idle musing, or a theoretical concern, but quite literal. To build a colony starship, to explode a planet . . . those were displays of astronomical cosmic power.

And the Giant had the ability to teleport.

He might pop up anywhere and throw another skyscraper. Or lay waste to a city. Or steal a hundred thousand slaves.

Fresh terror spread throughout the Megacosm as many Torth considered the possibilities. Evidence suggested that the Imposter might be able to teleport, as well. And what if the Shapeshifter had that power? She might destroy another planet. Just for fun.

This is a weapons race. The Swift Killer flaunted herself in her own luxury streamship, well out of harm's way. *This is why the Torth Empire needs Servants of All (like Me!) to learn how to teleport, so that We can inflict real damage upon Our enemies!*

Low ranks began to mutter that anarchy might be a better alternative to any of their current choices. The Megacosm fractured like an eggshell, barely holding together.

Kill the enemies of civilization! military leaders urged. *Do not let them get away with murder and planetary annihilation.*

The enemy starship looked like a meteoric streak, outpacing the shock wave. It appeared to be heading toward interstellar space. But there was nothing out there.

Nothing except the temporal stream—one of those space-time anomalies that made interstellar travel possible.

No, the Former Commander thought.

The Betrayer was a developmentally disabled supergenius, mentally stunted from his childhood among primitives. Surely he could not navigate a temporal stream at that insane speed? Vectorization for interstellar leaps required precise and astronomical computations. It was dangerous even at slow speeds. Everyone knew that.

The sort of computations that a supergenius can work through extra fast? distant Torth sang in dismay.

Others tried to reassure each other. *The Betrayer is probably just escaping the debris field.*

Or he's trying to fool Us.

To lead Us on a wild chase—

—to waste Our firepower and fuel.

Solar orbital zones meant slow travel. That was the way it was always done. The Majority tried to take comfort in that fact, although many wondered what was possible. Could the Betrayer calculate a vector field at the last second and jump into the temporal stream unscathed?

He might. A supergenius, the Geodesic Flux, weighed in. *If he trains a crew of slaves to perform the minutiae, and if he works uninterrupted . . . he is not reliant on the Megacosm. We cannot guess what constraints he is working within.*

The worst nemesis the Torth Empire had ever faced was on his way to a clean escape.

PURSUE THEM.

The enraged Majority glowed like lava. Even the Former Commander bared her teeth. If the enemies made it to the temporal stream . . . and if their navigation system was functional . . . with a competent helmsman . . .

Servants of All! she commanded. *Throw all your power into destroying that enemy starship. Propel yourselves into striking range. Do whatever it takes.*

Most Torth harbored uncertainties about her leadership, but right now, they all had a common nemesis. *Kill. Kill. Kill. Kill.*

Hundreds of military streamships and battle cruisers hurtled after the Betrayer's starship. They risked hitting deadly debris, and a few smashed into rocks and were annihilated, but they accepted the risks. Whoever destroyed the enemies would be gloriously immortalized in the Megacosm for eternity.

Nuclear explosions and plasma spread across the night.

Whoever was defending the starship was using conventional weapons. That implied that the enemies must be depleted in power, or close to it. Not a surprise, after their orgy of wreckage and starship building and teleportation.

They are depleted! the Former Commander realized. *Stretch your powers to the limit. Launch a comet-class warhead. Do whatever it takes to kill the enemies!*

For once, she was in harmony with the Swift Killer, who urged the same. Even the Upward Governess and other supergeniuses encouraged the armada. Failure was unacceptable. Now was the time to kill.

Kill. Kill. KILL.

The Former Commander tried to stretch her awareness toward the enemies. It was futile. The distance was too vast.

She sensed her brethren, other Servants of All, stretching their awareness farther than they had ever dared. Thrusters gained energy, boosted by wildfire, catalyzing reactions. Military vessels sped ever faster toward their target.

The dreadnought closest to the Betrayer's starship was finally able to launch its comet-class warhead.

The Former Commander tracked its glowing flare with her eyes. Even with an expert defense tactician and an expert helmsman, that five-hundred-thousand megaton comet-class warhead would cripple the enemy starship and knock it off course, away from the temporal stream.

One more second.

This was it.

The Torth Empire exhaled in collective anticipated relief. Soon they would be able to go back to their normal, comfortable lives and forget about major threats and emotional tidal waves in the Megacosm.

Dead.

The enemies are—

(No)

(Wait)

The enemy starship vanished, yanked out of sight by the temporal stream.

The comet-class warhead streaked onward, pointless now. Its path was futile.

And the Betrayer's chosen destination was anyone's guess.

He might be on the other side of the galactic disk.

Missiles and plasma balls sparked in the wake of the comet, most of them automatically detonating now that their target was gone. Pursuing vessels burned fuel to slow down or reverse direction.

One streamship jogged the wrong way, trying to avoid a burned-out missile shell. Its pilot failed to account for the temporal stream. It was speeding too fast to avoid the warped space, too fast for its pilot to request and receive safe vectors.

Most Torth who were tuned into the Megacosm winced, collectively, when the streamship spun into the invisible temporal stream, where it visibly crumpled into an ultradense rock. The pilot and four passengers began to suffer stretched-out deaths, trapped in slow time, otherwise known as wrong time. Listeners had to ignore them—tune them out—in order to escape their glacial agonies.

The other vessels managed to miss the zone of greatest danger. Some of them had to burn all their fuel in a blaze of effort, but at least they managed to slow or turn around.

The Torth Empire sat in stunned silence.

War.

It began as a whisper among the low ranks in the Megacosm.

We are at war.

The Torth Empire had conquered all known major alien civilizations, but it had never waged a war. Not unless one counted its early beginnings.

Memories of the war against Yeresunsa were eroded by eons. No one knew the details anymore. All they knew was that logical, coolheaded Torth had invented the inhibitor serum and used it to overthrow Yeresunsa tyrants.

If they had done it before, they could do it again.

Until now, the Torth Empire, in all its great and mighty history, had never lost a single conquest.

This challenge must be answered.

WE ARE AT WAR!!!!! trillions of Torth roared.

EPILOGUE

The bleat of Thomas's wristwatch woke him from a dream about that suffering little girl in the Isolatorium.

Her identity had shifted, in the manner of dreams. She had looked like his mother at one point. But one truth remained steady. She was not a slave, not a refugee, and not a captive human, yet she suffered. She was a nameless Torth, which meant no one, not even Ariock, would deign to rescue her.

Beep beep . . . beep beep . . . beep bee—

Thomas silenced his timer with a practiced touch.

A million tasks needed to be done in order to maintain a starship of this size, but Thomas had been in too much pain to work indefinitely. Varktezo had insisted that he sleep. And so, after guiding them through the temporal stream, Thomas had only done a few more things. He had reset the magnetofluid superconductor, purged the proton-exchange membrane, and optimized the primary tokamak.

Then he had succumbed to fatigue. He'd taken a painkiller alongside his dose of NAI-12, set his wristwatch to his regular injection schedule, and fallen asleep.

Which meant that this was six hours later. Time for another dose.

Thomas blinked, trying to rid his eyes of bleariness. His neck ached from napping, unmoving, in the hoverchair.

At least his warning headache was reduced to a migraine level. His Yeresunsa powers, unlike Ariock's, were on a path to recovery. Thomas figured he would regain full use within a couple more days.

He suppressed his urge to ascend into the Megacosm. He yearned to glimpse whatever mayhem the Torth Empire was experiencing.

But he dared not allow himself into that paradise of knowledge just now. It was too risky. Any of the elder supergeniuses would be able to dip into his thoughts and absorb his chosen destination, and he wanted that to be a secret from the Torth Empire.

They would find out eventually. No doubt the Torth were sending probes to every possible solar system, searching for his renegade starship.

Thomas smiled grimly. He had bought a week of freedom, or more. Possibly even a month.

He hoped Garrett would update him on whatever bitter arguments the Torth were embroiled in. No doubt they were throwing blame around and cobbling together a fresh leadership committee. The Majority had probably voted to upgrade their Betrayer from a minor threat to a major nemesis.

Good. A fearful Majority was more likely to make cognitive mistakes.

Thomas wanted to damage the Torth Empire before it even had a chance to retaliate. He wanted the Torth Majority on their knees. The Upward Governess, the Swift Killer, and the Commander, whether or not any of them retained power after today . . . they should fear him. Let them regret every bad decision they'd ever made.

He just needed Ariock to get better and wake up.

Ummins worked amid a forest of glowing holographs and space-view windows. Thomas began to float out of his alcove, but he couldn't quite bring himself to interrupt these industrious former slaves for something so demeaning, so mundane, as physical aid.

He wanted a drink from his water skin. He would need to use a latrine urn at some point. And he needed another painkiller in addition to his regular dose of NAI-12.

But these tidily dressed ummins were recovering from slavery, just like he was recovering from being a Torth. They should not feel obligated to perform tasks that they considered slave labor.

In fact, Thomas thought the whole population of the starship—upward of ten million people—should throw a party to honor these ten adolescent ummins. If not for their quick hands and minds, and their capacity for remembering instructions, the starship would have smashed against the temporal stream instead of riding it.

Obliteration had been a very near thing.

No one else seemed to realize it, but Thomas had nearly failed to get the master hydrogen line dippers functional. If he had been one second slower . . .

Well. Garrett would probably pick up on the near disaster, even if no one else did.

Embarrassed and reluctant, Thomas hovered toward the nearest ummin, Varktezo. He loathed his own neediness . . . but, well, he needed to get his day started. Half the holographs blinked with warning symbols. The subfusion reactor thresholds were corrected—otherwise everyone would be frozen to death—but the life support system still needed a lot of adjustments. So did the navigation system and the superconductors.

Thomas figured he needed to teach his crew some rudimentary astronautics, as well as—

Dust sparkled in the air in front of him.

The dust coalesced, solidifying into wings and a white gown, bathed in colorful lights from the holographs. Evenjos took shape.

She was regal, her hair a silvery-purple cascade, pinned on top by a delicate crown. The mood she emanated was curiosity.

Not despair. Not rage.

Thomas struggled to avoid delving into her mind. Curiosity was a major improvement in her mood, but even so, she had blown up a planet. This woman, or whatever she was, probably contained more power in her pinkie fingernail than all the reactors of this starship.

Unless she was depleted?

She ought to be drained after her frenzy of destruction. Thomas did detect a certain exhaustion in her mind.

Evenjos backed out of his range of telepathy.

Thomas followed her with his gaze. How much raw strength did shape-shifting require? Perhaps it was as effortless as telepathy, or prophecy?

He craved her secrets. He yearned to lap up her memories.

But he didn't dare offend her, especially since she might be the only person in the universe capable of reviving Ariock.

They studied each other in the dim light of stars and holographs for a full minute.

Evenjos was the one to break the silence. "What are you?" she asked in her dead, archaic language.

"I'm just a . . ." Thomas swallowed. Just a boy? A mind reader? A renegade Torth? He was many things, and probably none of those were an answer that Evenjos wanted to hear.

"A friend." He settled for that.

He almost added, *my friend Ariock needs your help*, but he canceled that phrasing in his mind. It seemed whiny. That wasn't how Kessa would make the request.

"Are you a god?" Evenjos asked, her tone curious and innocent.

Thomas snorted laughter. His neuromuscular degeneration would kill him in a few months or less, he was too weak to lift his NAI-12 briefcase, and he had to pee. He didn't believe in gods.

Then he saw Evenjos's open curiosity turn to suspicion.

"Uh, no." He stopped grinning, not wanting Evenjos to think he was mocking her. He made himself sound serious. "I am not immortal."

She began to walk a casual circle around him, just beyond the perimeter of his range. "You contain worlds of knowledge."

Now Thomas understood how she had mistaken him for a god. To anyone who could read minds, he was a towering presence.

"Like me," Evenjos said.

The way she was pacing around Thomas . . . it was like she was a fighter, sizing up a potential opponent.

"Yeah," Thomas admitted. "But I'm not a god." He rotated his hoverchair to keep Evenjos in view. "I'm actually pretty weak." *Not a threat.* That was his subtext, and he hoped she understood. "Knowledge is one thing, but power is another."

Evenjos disintegrated and condensed. Her dust solidified, shrinking, until a barefoot Alashani girl stood there. She wore her white hair in pigtails. She stared at Thomas with ancient, knowing eyes.

"I can pretend, too," she said in a girlish voice.

The child version of Evenjos looked vulnerable, helpless, and innocent. But they both knew that was a pretense. She was a world destroyer.

Thomas tried not to shudder. He didn't like her morphing power. It seemed to defy a few fundamental laws of physics.

"I have known other lives," Evenjos said. "Just as you have."

She grew. This time, her body gained the thorns and spikes of a nussian, majestic in size. Instead of red or bronze, her version of a nussian was obsidian. Her pebbly skin sparkled like black granite embedded with mica, and she had telltale purple eyes.

Thomas fought his urge to back away. The black nussian version of Evenjos could surely morph her head into a monstrous mouth and swallow him whole, if she wanted to. There was no escape.

"We are neither of us what we seem." Her voice was incongruously human and feminine, coming from that enormous tank of a body.

"I am." Thomas curled his weak hands into fists. Unlike Evenjos, he was not pretending. He was not a faker.

And even if he was a monster—so what? He had better things to do than measure himself against a fellow monster.

"Do you remember Ariock?" Thomas asked. "The big guy who rescued you?"

Evenjos morphed back to her beautiful form. Each wing arced high over her head, and they touched the floor, composed of interlocked, blade-like plates. The metal looked like it had been dipped in opalescent honey. Starlight silvered her gown, which was far too sheer for the frigid climate. Her face and nose were long, but that only added to her imperious, regal bearing.

"Ariock needs help." Thomas hesitated, torn between diffident respect or warm friendliness. How would Kessa handle this?

Evenjos regarded him with cool apathy. "I will consider it."

That wasn't good enough.

"He rescued you," Thomas reminded her, frustrated. He needed to make Evenjos understand their precarious situation. Without Ariock, there would be riots aboard the starship. Maybe worse. Their food supply was dwindling. They were not equipped for anything.

"As I recall," Evenjos said in her archaic language, "he was not the only one. You were there, too."

Thomas tried to read her face, unsure what she was driving at.

"I do not forget my debts," Evenjos said. "That is why I am speaking with you. And it is plain that you speak my language." She circled him. "You are of my people."

Thomas considered correcting her.

"I have discovered that you planned my rescue," Evenjos said. "You made it happen."

That was true enough. Thomas did not deny it.

"I have read your mind," Evenjos said. "So I know that you are unlike anyone else aboard this vehicle. That body"—she indicated Thomas's withered self with disgust—"cannot be your true form."

Thomas glanced down at his underdeveloped limbs and his sunken rib cage.

Evenjos's tone was polite. "Will you do me the courtesy of revealing who you truly are?"

"Uh . . ." Thomas stalled, unsure how Evenjos would react to the truth. "I'm sorry." It felt awkward and wrong to apologize for his body. "But this is who I truly am. I was born with a neuromuscular disease."

She frowned at him, uncomprehending.

"I'm thirteen years old." Thomas gripped the armrests of his hoverchair, embarrassed for some reason. "I'm a kid. But I contain many thousands of lifetimes of knowledge because . . ." He hesitated, wishing he could gauge her mood, her thoughts, from this distance. "I'm a mind reader with an infallible memory. I never forget anything, or any mind, I encounter."

Evenjos stepped back. Her eyes went wide with fright.

"Are you okay?" Thomas asked.

She stepped back again, trembling. She looked terrified.

Thomas checked behind him, just to make sure she wasn't scared of something else. No bogeyman lurked in the workstation alcove.

"Monster!" Her voice was choked with terror.

Thomas was at a loss for words. Most people thought he was a monster, but coming from Evenjos, it seemed hypocritical.

"*I'm* the monster?" he said, so she could hear the irony out loud. "Me?"

"Stay away from me." Evenjos lost cohesion and began to crumple.

Thomas hadn't moved at all. He couldn't figure out if her fear was sincere or if this was her idea of a joke. "I'm harmless," he said. "I can't walk."

Her dust particles gathered into a long, ropy structure. She rippled away, sinuous and dragon-like.

Thomas was left staring at the darkness where she had stood.

He had always known he was a monster, he supposed. But was he so terrible that a world-destroying goddess-empress had reasons to flee from him? Was he really that bad?

Beyond the nearest workstations, ummins peered at him with wide eyes. They had seen the whole exchange. At least they had not understood the foreign, archaic language.

Cold sweat coated Thomas. A strange emotion seethed inside him. It took him a few moments to identify the feeling, because it was alien.

Fear.

He had not felt so helplessly vulnerable since he was a little kid caught in bad foster care situations. A woman who could destroy worlds considered Thomas Hill to be a threat.

Maybe he had a few superficial similarities with whoever had imprisoned her?

On the other hand . . . Evenjos remembered that Thomas had freed her. She owed him a debt. That was why she was allowing him to live, rather than smiting him with a bolt of lightning.

Maybe she would get over her fear? Maybe they could be friends?

The ummins were still staring.

Thomas braced himself for unwanted questions and reactions to his embarrassing requests. Never mind his fear. He would figure out how to persuade Evenjos to do the right thing and revive Ariock.

He raised his voice. "Let's get to work!"

AFTERWORD

Thank you so much for reading *World of Wreckage.* Your support is more monumental to me than the Stratower!

In the next book, *Megacosmic Rift,* the heroes and refugees are primed for war, and the rulers of the galaxy no longer feel sure of victory. With Thomas at the helm of a nascent rebel nation, even the mightiest Torth quake in fear.

If you liked what you read, please leave a review wherever you bought this book. Your feedback will ripple across the internet and make me feel as if I have an inner audience, and I will love it.

If you'd like to hang out in the Megacosm, join the Torth Discord server at: https://discord.gg/gDYVXdS2qz, or subscribe to Abby Updates at: https://abbygoldsmith.com/subscribe/

The Torth series:
Torth Book 1: *Majority*
Torth Book 2: *Colossus Rising*
Torth Book 3: *World of Wreckage*
Torth Book 4: *Megacosmic Rift*
Torth Book 5: *Greater Than All*
Torth Book 6: *Empire Ender*

ACKNOWLEDGMENTS

Special thanks to my readers on Royal Road and Wattpad. You know who you are! I only know you by your usernames, but I've learned to recognize those names. I appreciate you very much!

I particularly want to thank readers who supported me on Patreon. That means a lot, and it's hugely helpful to my crazy writer lifestyle. You help me feel legit!

I'm also grateful for Rebecca Roland, a physical therapist who helped me to get a handle on caretaking for Thomas, and Kayla Whaley, who answered my questions about spinal muscular atrophy. Additionally, I learned a lot about living with SMA from Shane Burcaw's videos and books.

Working on this series has given me a lot more respect for epic series writers. These beta readers offered constructive advice on the first draft: Brian Rappatta, Sarah Kelderman, Rebecca Shelley, Susan Shell Winston, Marc Geddes, Jose Gustavo Costa Jr., Ethan Reid, Michael Ceranko, Mike McCauley, Marissa Engel, Colleen Robbins, and my mom. Thank you! And the Bat City Novelocracy group: Ellen Van Hensbergen, Leigh Berggren, Katy Stauber, and Marshall Ryan Maresca. Thank you!

Especially, as always, thanks to Adam Robert Thompson, my wonderful alpha reader and husband. You really are Thomas and Ariock combined! (Minus their flaws, of course!)

ABOUT THE AUTHOR

Abby Goldsmith is the author of the Torth series, originally released on Wattpad and Royal Road. She continues to write novels and has sold short works to Escape Pod and Writer's Digest Books, having attended the Odyssey Fantasy Writing Workshop. Goldsmith is a 2-D and 3-D game animator, has lived on all three coasts of the United States, and is married to her alpha reader.

Website: AbbyGoldsmith.com
Twitter: @Abbyland
Facebook: facebook.com/TheTorth

Podium
DISCOVER
STORIES UNBOUND
PodiumAudio.com

www.ingramcontent.com/pod-product-compliance
Lightning Source LLC
Chambersburg PA
CBHW030922120726
47906CB00002B/452